ERROR OF JUDGMENT

ERROR OF JUDGMENT

DEXTER DIAS

THE MYSTERIOUS PRESS

Published by Warner Books

A Time Warner Company

First published in 1996 in Great Britain by Hodder and Stoughton, a division of Hodder Headline PLC.

Copyright © 1996 by Dexter Dias
All rights reserved.

Mysterious Press books are published by Warner Books, Inc., 1271 Avenue of the Americas, New York, NY 10020.

A Time Warner Company

The Mysterious Press name and logo are registered trademarks of Warner Books, Inc.

Printed in the United States of America

First U.S. printing: November 1996

10 9 8 7 6 5 4 3 2 1

Library of Congress Cataloging-in-Publication Data
Dias, Dexter.
   Error of judgment / Dexter Dias.
      p. cm.
   ISBN 0-89296-651-3
   I. Title.
PR6054.I24E77   1996
823'.914—dc20
                                                          96-22485
                                                             CIP

For Katie

My first editor and my last critic
With all my love

ACKNOWLEDGMENTS

Firstly, I would like to thank the professionals. My agents, Mark Lucas in London and David Black in New York. My editors, Carolyn Caughey at Hodder & Stoughton and Sara Ann Freed at Mysterious Press. Secondly, a big thank you to friends and family. My brother Mike for his drive (and the occasional slice). Valerie for her research into rats, rodents, and other things creepy. My father for his sound advice and continual support. Antoinette, Shane, Phyllis. And finally, Katie for—well, almost everything else.

PART I
JANUARY

I am—yet what I am, none cares or knows;
My friends forsake me like a memory lost

John Clare

Chapter One

"Why *do* men commit adultery? I mean, is it always *just* the sex? Or is there something else? Take this case, M'Lord.

"The defendant went to a Bayswater brothel on Christmas Eve. But he did not go there just for sex. He went there to talk. To confess. To a murder."

From his position in counsel's row, Nick Downes looked at the woman addressing the court. She was a captivating advocate, she was his opponent and his prosecutor for the day, and she was his girlfriend, his partner, the only woman he had ever really loved. But Nick knew that their life together was about to fall apart.

He watched Sally Fielding, her cotton gown hanging elegantly from her shoulders, as she opened the case. Sally had been with him for twelve years, for as long as the two of them had been barristers. And in that time they had both become experts in two things: defending the indefensible and hurting each other.

They had been together for twelve years—was he *really* going to end it in less than twelve hours?

"The facts of the matter are bizarre," Sally continued, glancing at the empty public gallery high above Court 8 in the Old

5

Bailey. "We know next to nothing about this man—except that he keeps calling out the name of a woman. Elizabeth or Liz, over and over again. And when the accused was at the brothel, he had a *claw hammer* with him."

"What is so significant about that particular item of ironmongery?" the judge asked.

"Well, it's obvious, M'Lord."

"Not to me," the judge said.

Nick looked at Sally and tried to decide what to do. Should he help her out? The judge, Mr. Justice Cromwell, bully-in-chief at the Bailey, was in fearsome fettle. But should Nick keep quiet for the sake of his client?

The issue was decided the moment he studied Sally's face. She looked exhausted, with the faint darkening beneath her eyes. He knew that he was responsible. The two of them had been up all night, not making love into the early hours as they used to, but arguing. Arguing bitterly about marriage and children.

He rose to his feet. "Perhaps Miss Fielding's point is that a claw hammer is not just a hammer. It is a symbol, a weapon. The claw hammer was the weapon of choice of Sutcliffe."

"Sutcliffe?" the judge asked.

"Peter Sutcliffe, the Yorkshire Ripper. Used claw hammers to shatter the skulls of several prostitutes. Many people say it was the trial of the century—*perhaps* Your Lordship has heard of him?"

The judge was silenced.

Sally shuffled along counsel's row and whispered, "Thanks, Nick."

"It's all right," he replied. "It's only a bail application—my client isn't even in court. And besides . . ."

He paused, for at that instant Sally smiled. She had that rarest kind of beauty, fresh and poised, the kind that didn't require makeup, that was set off by a single string of pearls. And then her eyes; it was her eyes that Nick had first fallen in love with. They were predominantly grayish, but when she smiled, as she did now, they darkened and became shot through with a color that Nick would boast to other people could only be described as cornflower blue.

"And besides what?" Sally asked.

If Nick had had the guts to speak truthfully, he would have said: And besides, I love you, Sals, and I can't imagine loving anyone else.

But, being a barrister involved in a difficult case in court, and being a man involved in a difficult relationship out of it, he said nothing.

"When the two of you have *quite* finished," the judge boomed, "may we proceed with the application for bail?"

"Yes, M'Lord," Sally replied. "Mr. Downes's client admitted to the prostitute in the brothel that he had buried a body. It was in a chalk quarry in Kent. But he didn't know who the corpse belonged to."

"How did he come to be arrested?" the judge asked.

"Pure chance," Sally said. "There was a search warrant executed by the Vice Squad at Notting Hill Gate police station and he was arrested along with all the other . . . visitors and staff."

"And did the police find the body where he said it would be?"

"That's only the start. The defendant admitted that he buried the body—but not *immediately* after the death. The timing is critical. You see, the flies provided the first clue as to how long the corpse had been buried."

"Flies, you say?"

"Yes, M'Lord. Blowflies, in fact. They're attracted to human flesh shortly after death. While it's still warm. The human body provides the perfect nursery for the blowfly's young."

"Fascinated as I'm sure we all are by entomology, Miss Fielding, what relevance has all this to an application for *bail*?" the judge asked.

Sally ignored him and continued. "It means that there was long enough for the corpse to be exposed to a fly before burial."

"So what?" the judge queried.

"So it provides corroboration for the confession—"

"The *alleged* confession," Nick said, getting to his feet. He knew that it was time to make things difficult for the woman he lived with. "I mean to say, M'Lord, what has all this to do with my client? It's the end of January. My client has been in custody for four weeks now. Where is the concrete evidence? Perhaps I'm being just a little obtuse—"

"I wouldn't say just a little," hissed Sally so that the judge could not hear. Then she continued more loudly, "My point, M'Lord, is a simple one."

"Well, I wish you'd make it, Miss Fielding," the judge said.

Nick sat down. He was pretty sure that he had got the judge on his side. He noted how Sally licked both her lips—they were always chafed—and looked at her feet. After years of what she called cohabitation and he called shacking up, he knew that this was how she tried to compose herself.

"Let me be quite frank," Sally said. "The evidence against the defendant at this stage is entirely circumstantial. But there is a match between his own admissions and the flies on the corpse. You see, there *must* have been a delay between death and burial for the flies to have had time to lay their eggs. The question then is, how did he know? Or to put it another way, how could he possibly have known unless, of course, he was the murderer."

"Is that your best point, Miss Fielding?"

"It is," Sally said. "That and the fact that the partially scavenged bones of a small animal were found in the bowels of the corpse."

"Well, what animal are we talking about?" the judge asked.

"I don't know."

"Then why mention it?"

"It has all the hallmarks of a particularly brutal torture."

"What torture?"

"I—I don't know, M'Lord," Sally admitted. "But in any event, the Crown invites the court to refuse bail in this case."

"Mr. Downes? What do you say about all this?"

At the moment Nick got to his feet, he was pretty sure that the judge was leaning in his favor. Cromwell had certainly given Sally a hard time. There was only one problem. He did not know who on earth it was he was defending.

"Miss Fielding has told you about the flies," Nick began, "but not about the maggots."

"*Maggots?* Is microbiology compulsory at Bar School these days?" asked the judge.

"No, M'Lord."

"They do still teach law there, do they?"

"After a fashion," said Nick. He could see that the purplish veins were beginning to stand out on the judge's head. He always found it off-putting having to apply for bail to a judge in chambers, without the comforting familiarity of a pile of horsehair on his head. With his wig off, he felt professionally naked. But time was short. He knew that he had to make his point and shut up.

"Well, can we deal with the legal principles involved?" the judge said, sucking on a Biro. The color appeared to drain from his scalp.

"It is of great importance to the defense," Nick said, "that the maggots have consumed most of the decaying flesh on the head. Thousands of eggs are laid on the moister parts of the face: the eyes, the lips, the mouth—I understand it looks as though the face is covered with rice grains—"

"So?" the judge interrupted.

"So our forensic scientists are trying their best to reconstruct the face, M'Lord," Sally said, jumping up excitedly.

"Sit *down*, Miss Fielding." Cromwell was furious. "Please continue, Mr. Downes."

"So the prosecution," Nick said, "consequently have no idea who the dead man is and what, if any, his connection is to my client. They don't know exactly how he was killed, where, or why. They don't even know if he was buried dead or alive."

"But your client claims to have buried the body, Mr. Downes."

"That does not make him the murderer."

"And it doesn't put him above suspicion either."

"Suspicion is nowhere near enough for a conviction, M'Lord."

"But reasonable suspicion is enough for me to refuse bail. Unless, that is, you have any other riveting biological details to put before the court?"

"No, M'Lord," Nick said. "Except that there are no witnesses."

Again Sally sprang to her feet. It was, Nick thought, advocacy beyond the call of duty; it was unnecessary, it was personal.

"Mr. Downes is quite wrong," she began. "The insects are the best witnesses it is possible to have. They are perfect detectives. They cannot lie. They tell us facts. Fact: The eggs were laid last summer. Fact: Blowflies are attracted to human flesh before it putrefies. So, fact: This body was not buried immediately. All these details corroborate the confession of the defendant, the confession of Mr. Downes's client."

The judge glanced at Nick. "I suppose Miss Fielding's point is, with flies like that, who needs evidence?" The veins on his scalp surged with blood as he enjoyed his bon mot.

Nick looked at Sally beside him. He had given up biology when he was thirteen years old. But in his limited experience, there was a law of biology that went something like this: The rate of intercourse is inversely proportional to the period spent living together.

"Is there anything else you want to add, Mr. Downes?" the judge asked.

Only that I'm sorry, thought Nick. But he said nothing as he took his seat next to the counsel for the prosecution. He imagined that somehow the flies must have eaten away at the affection they had once felt for each other. He had loved Sally and he respected her, which was about as much as a guilt-ridden Catholic boy from a lower-middle-class family could safely feel toward a woman.

As the judge was about to make his ruling, Nick got to his feet once more. "People end up in brothels for all sorts of reasons," he said. "Not all of them sinister."

"Bail is refused," snapped Cromwell. "Are either of you in

the buggery on next?" Neither of them answered. "Very well. Please don't let me detain you."

Sally's gown brushed against Nick's as she headed out of court. He vaguely discerned the perfume to which he had introduced her. It smelled lightly of lemon trees and was a hundred miles away from the gaudy fragrances that reminded him of church incense.

Picking up the bundle of photographs of the exhumed corpse, he looked again at Sally. She seemed tired. He really wanted to hold her hand, but that would have made matters worse. Wouldn't it be kinder to end it? To put both of them out of their misery? But he wondered if he really had the guts to do it. Or was it, perhaps, that he had doubts?

"I want to speak to you tonight," he said, surprising himself, not entirely sure where the words had come from.

"Why not now?" Sally replied.

"I've got a conference."

"When?"

"Fifteen minutes ago."

She left without saying another word.

Nick studied the police photos of the corpse, pausing when he reached an extreme close-up of the head. The skull was caved in, as if someone had smashed in the top of an eggshell rather than cutting it off.

"In which prison is the unknown man being held, Mr. Downes?" asked the judge.

"In the Heath," said Nick. "Actually, I'm going there now."

"Well, you'd better find your client a name as well as a defense."

Nick wondered whether the case would be another example of the only other biological law he knew: Boy plus Girl equals Trouble.

Chapter Two

"I've never seen a patient like him."

"Really?" said Nick.

"Actually, I'm lying," the psychiatrist, Dr. Ann Barnes, said. "What I mean is that I've never seen anyone like him in prison. Most of my patients hear different voices at one time or another. But your man just hears one voice. Over and over again. Sometimes it almost takes over."

"What do you mean?"

"It's as if there were two people in there."

"So who is Liz—the person he keeps talking about?" Nick asked.

"Liz is the woman *both* sides of him seem obsessed with."

Nick looked at Ann Barnes and wondered how she managed to put up with the fantasies of hundreds of incarcerated men. It must have been the last psychiatric posting any modest, self-respecting woman would have wanted. But Ann Barnes loved it.

In the ten or so years Nick had known her, Ann had always been cheerful, despite the nine hundred prisoners, nine hundred sets of genitalia, and one thousand egos—when you took into account the split personalities that were Ann's specialty.

Later that Thursday, barrister and psychiatrist walked along the empty corridors of the hospital wing of Her Majesty's Prison Wormwood Heath. It was a new prison, being built beside the old one on the Scrubs in West London. But Wormwood Heath was a high-security prison, a designer detention center. Once finished, it was to be the respectable residence of the cream of the convict classes.

The stone floors resounded under the doctor's one-inch heels, her short steps accelerating as they went past one glass door after another. Nick was finding it hard to keep up with her and was slightly behind when she suddenly glanced round. He blushed when she caught him looking at the back of her legs. They were long, with the firm flesh of someone who worked out. But one of her stockings was not quite straight.

"You briefs are all the same. You always wonder about that," she said.

"What?"

"What you're thinking about now."

"Which is?"

"Whether it's a little tarty to wear heels and twelve-denier stockings in a place like this."

"How did you know I—"

"I'm a psychiatrist, remember? Men's wet dreams are my bread and butter, if you'll excuse the imagery. Lawyers are no different to the cons in that."

"Come on."

Ann laughed. "Do you know what barristers are, Nick? People who think they have the God-given right to earn pots of money, drive sporty cars, and make passes at pretty young boys. And that's just the women barristers."

They reached the final door, which was made of reinforced blue glass. On the other side was a square room in which a man was sitting. He had his back to Nick.

"But isn't it a bit cruel?" Nick asked. "I mean, don't the stockings and heels provoke them, or whatever the word is?"

"Of course, they don't provoke a man of your sensibilities, do they?"

Nick did not answer but continued to look into the cell. He

tried to fight back the blush rising to his face and the involuntary surge of blood to another, lower part of his anatomy where, as Ann always put it, men usually lost the battle of the bulge.

Ann Barnes used a dirty key to open the door. "It turns you on a bit, right? To know that I'm wearing stockings in here. But that doesn't mean you'll want to shove my stockings in my mouth and rape me in the car park. That's about all that separates your normal man from the average sexual psychopath."

"That can't be all."

"You're right, Nick. There's something else. Your average psychopath is more reliable."

"Reliable?"

"Predictable. When he's in love or lust—he knows what he wants and is not afraid to get it."

By now the two of them were in the room.

"You know," Ann said, "I've often thought it must all have been easier in the old days."

"How do you mean?"

"Well, Mr. Caveman swings down with a stiffy the size of a brontosaurus's tail—"

"Pardon?"

"He swings down and clubs Neolithic Nina over the head, has his wicked way with her, then moves on to the next semidetached cave. There's a lot to be said for the simplicity of it all."

"So what about love?" Nick asked.

"Oh, love is a purely modern invention." She paused. "It sort of replaces the head-clubbing stage. That's all."

Nick sat down on the soft foam seat next to Ann Barnes and opposite the incarcerated man. He tried to move the chair, but it was screwed to the floor.

"And how are we today?" Ann asked.

The man was silent.

Sinking a little into the soft chair, he sat very still.

"You can hear me, can't you?" Ann said.

Nick saw how she leaned forward a little to catch the patient's attention. Her white coat opened half an inch, and Nick tried not to look at the gentle swell of her left breast under her polo-neck jumper.

"Will you speak to me today? I know you can. It's what you really want, isn't it?"

Again, there was no response.

"Go on, Nick. Try to make contact. He won't bite, you know."

"All right, then. My name is Nick Downes. I'm your lawyer. Well, your barrister in fact. Do you know what a barrister is? . . . It's no good, Ann. He makes a Trappist monk seem talkative."

"You've just got to be patient. Listen, there's something I've got to tell you, Nick."

She reached across the table and laid a manicured hand on the silent man's prison fatigues.

"You see?" she said. "He's as meek as a lamb."

The man did not move; he showed no reaction to the soft touch of a woman. But Nick could only think of the photographs of the corpse: the empty sockets where the eyes had been eaten, the rest of the face badly decayed. This was the man who admitted burying the body.

Nick felt better the minute he was out of the cell. He sensed that the back of his shirt was sodden. And tiny droplets of sweat gathered on his palms and dribbled down his fingers.

"You said you'd seen another case like this one?" he said to Ann.

"A few years ago. When I was studying psychotherapy in America."

"I've never understood, Ann. Are you a psychiatrist or a psychologist?"

"Both. I've got a medical qualification as a psychiatrist, a psychotherapy qualification as a psychologist, and the best pair of legs this side of Broadmoor. All men find me irresistible. Well, except you."

"That's because of—"

"Sally," Ann said. "You don't need to be a shrink to work that one out."

"Tell me about the other case," Nick said, trying to change the subject.

"The guy had been to Vietnam. His entire unit was ambushed. All of them cut to ribbons while he was behind a tree somewhere."

"So?"

"So he was masturbating. While his comrades in arms were being pumped with lead, he was bashing his bishop with a copy of *Playboy*."

"Do you know what our man is suffering from?"

"Chronic post-traumatic arousal."

"What on earth is that?"

"Nightmares."

"We all suffer from nightmares, don't we?"

"Not like these. This dream has taken over his waking life."

"Sounds a bit far-fetched. Are you quite sure?"

"I'm not sure. I'm certain." For the first time there was a harsher tone in her voice. "Just look at his eyes."

Nick saw that the man had barely moved since they had left the room. He sat with his bandaged wrists on his knees and stared at the high window fifteen feet up the wall. When Nick looked very closely, he could see that the man's pupils oscillated quickly from one bar to the next.

"REM," said Ann. Then, when Nick made no response, she added, "Rapid Eye Movement. One of the five stages of sleep. Only—"

"Only he isn't asleep," Nick said.

"Exactly. But he is dreaming. What he's dreaming about, we don't know."

"The police said he did speak to the prostitute in the brothel he was arrested in."

"I don't doubt it. Most men find it easy to talk to a hooker. In fact, easier than talking to their wives." She inspected the nail polish on the smaller fingers of her left hand. There were no rings. "Maybe that's an exaggeration. You know, about the wives."

"Just a small one," said Nick.

"How's Sally, by the way?"

"She's not my wife."

"Perhaps that's the problem," said Ann.

"Look, who are we meant to be diagnosing? Him or me?"

"Don't worry, Nick. I understand. First rule of marital combat: Don't get married in the first place."

Marriage and children were sore points between Nick and Sally. Sally wanted to get married. Nick wanted children. Sally wanted marriage but no children. Nick didn't want to agree to marriage unless Sally agreed to have children. Sally, on the brink of a brilliant career as a senior barrister, believed children would jeopardize that. Nick no longer cared about the Bar—he wanted to be happy, with Sally, and a family. But it was not working out like that.

Nick tapped on the glass window in the way a mischievous child rattles the bars of a bird's cage.

"Don't *do* that." Ann put on her most scathing professional tone. "It could be very dangerous. Like waking a sleepwalker balancing on a ledge."

Then the two of them were silent. Nick had suspected for a while that there was some kind of chemistry between himself and Ann Barnes. Sally, with whom Ann had worked on a number of cases, often accused him of flirting with her, which he did not think was true. Sally and Ann had almost started their careers together, and they had become good friends.

As he stood outside the cell of the dreaming man, he tried to work out what it was about the prison psychiatrist he found so alluring. She did not have a particularly pretty face. Her nose was too big and her pewter-colored eyes were too close together. But she always dressed enticingly, and she had a vocabulary like the open sewer that ran through the uncompleted prison. Perhaps that was the problem with Sally. She was too nice, too perfect. Just too good for him. That was it. Sally deserved better, Nick decided. Sally made him feel guilty.

"The poor sod is in a world of his own," said Ann finally.

"What do you mean?"

"Well, most of us only spend about a quarter of our sleep actually dreaming. This poor bugger is at the movies for eighty percent of the time. That's more than a newborn baby. It's almost as if he's been born again. Like the slate has been wiped clean."

"But how can someone forget who he is?" Nick asked.

"We've all wanted to forget who we are at some stage in our lives."

"Such as?"

"Such as when we wake up in a strange bedroom after the one-night stand from hell," Ann said. "Chummy here has succeeded, that's all. But you don't necessarily lose your memory. You change it."

"Change it?"

"Like changing buses. You get on another one and it takes you to a completely different place. The memory isn't a single organ like the heart or kidneys, Nick. We have several memories, and he's got lost in one of them."

"Can he return?"

"Is there a last bus back from Nutville? It's hard to say. Depends on the patient's response to drugs, his predisposition to mental illness, and above all to—"

"Yes?"

"Luck. You see, the mind is notoriously unpredictable. Although it's somewhat more reliable than the buses in London. If you want my professional opinion—"

"Shut up," Nick whispered. He grabbed Ann's wrist.

"What are you—"

"I think he's saying something."

Ann fumbled with the bunch of keys and tried two wrong ones before the door opened.

The man still did not move. But his mouth was open. And from his lips came a single word. At first, Nick could not make out what he had said. He moved closer to the table. He was now within touching distance.

Suddenly the man grasped Nick's hand. Then he said the word again, only this time he squeezed Nick's hand so hard that Nick could feel the pulse of the man's thumb.

"Wormwood," the man said faintly. *"Wormwood."*

Chapter Three

"The first person I murdered was a girl. She was ten years old and it was a summer's day, I remember. When I first saw her—are you listening?"

It was later that evening, and Nick tried to fight back a yawn. He had heard it all so many times before. He looked at the black man in front of him. "I'm sorry. Please continue. I'm afraid it's been a long day."

"Look, do you want to do this or what?" The man sipped a little of the dark liquid in the glass on the table they were sharing.

"Go on," Nick said.

"Well, I usually experience orgasm when I throttle someone, especially if they have tried to resist me. After coming, I am the goddamn picture of courtesy. It's then that I usually explain to the corpse that my actions are 'what love is really about.' But you, you soft pussy"—the man looked defiantly at Nick—"you haven't a clue who I really am."

"Peter Kurten," said Nick a little wearily, looking around the wine bar. "Now give me the bottle of Armagnac."

"Not so quick. Peter Kurten, also known as?"

"I've already won," Nick insisted.

"The full name or you get nothing."

"Also known as the Dusseldorf Vampire. About a dozen victims. Preferred modus operandi, scissors to the genitals."

"Shit," said the man, handing over the fifty-pound bottle of
spirits.

Nick poured himself a large glass and pointedly avoided his
companion's. "You know, Max, I'm sick of playing Monsters.
Can't we think of another game?"

"You invented it."

"I know. But it's become a bit of an albatross around my
neck. No one wants to speak to me about ordinary things anymore. Just look at them." He gestured expansively around the
wine bar. "Supposedly full of the best legal brains in the country. But none of them talks to me about anything other than
mass murderers, serial killers, and perverts."

"That's Devlin's for you. Is there anything left in the bottle?"

Nick did not answer but handed Max Baptiste the Armagnac. Devlin's was the favorite drinking den of the criminal
Bar. It was five minutes from the Old Bailey, spitting distance
from the High Court, and a short stagger from the Temple.

It was open to the general public, but the public generally
avoided it. The prospect of two hundred intoxicated lawyers
deterred even the bravest and thirstiest of London's drinking
classes. Occasionally, a pair of law students would dare to enter
and would be devoured alive. Sometimes, pupil barristers
would be initiated, but always under the watchful eye of their
pupil masters. The odd Chancery lawyer would come in after a
dangerous day behind the computer screen and would be
roundly ignored.

For Devlin's was the province of criminal barristers: the
trenchmen, the stormtroopers, the Legal Aid footsloggers of the
law. There they played, partied, and pontificated until they fell
over, fell out, or until the staff received an irate phone call from
a deserted spouse. At this point, an intricate series of tried and
tested alibis would be activated and cabs would scream off to
Hampstead and Highgate.

Without Devlin's the criminal Bar would have more money, more liver, but, almost certainly, less character.

As Max poured himself a large glass, Nick thought about the books beside his bed. It was from these that he had got the idea for Monsters. It made him feel a little ashamed.

So many of the legendary advocates from the golden age of the Bar had kept up fulfilling hobbies. Marshall Hall was a connoisseur of jewelry, and Lord Birkett loved the Lake District. And what about Nick? He was preoccupied. He told himself that he had a Gothic disposition and was academically preoccupied by the macabre and the morbid. But Sally merely said that he had a dirty little mind and was surprised that he didn't own a plastic mac.

On Nick's small bedside table, next to an alarm clock that never went off and the night-lamp that emitted a beam the coast guard would have been proud of, were three volumes: *The A to Z of Sex Fiends, 10 Murders You May Have Missed,* and *The Holy Bible.*

"So your guy knows where he is, at least?"

"Pardon?" Nick said.

"Mr. Nobody in prison. Knows he is in Wormwood Heath."

"Well, he said 'Wormwood' a couple of times, Max."

"That's a start, ain't it?"

"I just don't know. He seemed so far away when he said it. His eyes were open but there didn't seem to be much in them. It was as if he was trying to tell us something else. Apparently, he keeps calling out a woman's name. Elizabeth or Liz or something. Over and over again."

"That's the power of a beautiful woman for you," Max said.

"But we don't know who or what Elizabeth is. I mean, it could be his great-aunt."

"Sure, you're in the slammer and you call out for Aunt Betsy? I don't think so. Was it the name of the prostitute?"

"No, she was called Jackie, I think."

"Jackie?"

"*Cherchez la femme,*" Nick said. "Look for—"

"I *know* what it means. It's all pretty weird stuff, Star. The whole case sounds like the Christmas special from *The Twilight Zone,* if you ask me. Should be perfect for a screwed-up bloke like you."

"Thanks."

"The brothel was in Bayswater?"

"In Queensway," Nick replied.

"But that's where—"

"Yes, Max. It's where I live." And then he added, "With Sally."

"Unless she leaves you." There was a pause before Max continued. "Judge Cromwell refused him bail?" he asked. "You could always try Room 101."

"Room 101? In the High Court?"

"It's where High Court judges refuse you bail after you've been refused in the Crown Court."

Nick sipped his Armagnac, the alcohol biting the back of his throat. "Wasn't Room 101 where Big Brother tortured people in *1984?*"

"Sure. Orwell wrote that a cage of rats would be put on your face," Max said. "I always thought that was a doddle compared to the High Court in London."

Nick gazed at his drinking partner. Max's eyes caught a reflection from one of the brass wall fittings and shone brilliantly for a moment. There was no denying that Max was good looking. He had very short Afro hair. His skin was an even mahogany, and his cheekbones were high. He claimed to be nobility. The prince of somewhere in West Africa. They had anglicized their surname to Baptiste. Although he had only been practicing at the Bar for half the time Nick had, Max already had the reputation of a rising star. He was liked by judges, including those in the High Court, he was liked by juries, and he was loved by women. It was only the battalions of mediocre male barristers who loathed him.

Except, that is, for Nick. It was not that Nick was above such categories, it was just that he felt he was on the outside. The only thing, he had noticed, was that Max had a lazy left eye. It was often half shut, as though he were winking at people. The laziness seemed to deepen in the presence of women.

"Where is it in Africa your parents rule?" he asked.

"Well, they don't exactly rule."

"Who does?"

"Some jumped-up flight lieutenant. Ma and Pa are like the spiritual leaders."

"You mean they've nicked all the money and are living it up in exile, then?" Nick said. "What's the place called?"

"You won't have heard of it. It's a kingdom within a province within a state that's had a coup. But tell me, how was the factory?"

"What factory?"

"You know, the prison. That's what they call it."

"Why's that?"

"Because of what it produces."

"Which is?" asked Nick.

"Jesus," said Max. He poured the dregs of the bottle into his small glass. "What do you think men do when they are locked up in a cell for twenty-three hours a day?"

"Read?"

"*Jesus,*" Max said again. "The place has more seed than a garden center, Star. Haven't you noticed? It reeks of it."

"I rather thought that was the disinfectant they used," Nick said. "Anyway, can you blame them?"

"I don't blame them, but I ain't going to join them, either."

"What do you mean, Max?"

The West African glanced around furtively. He waited for a couple of Oxbridge types to finish their champagne and leave, heading for the mobile burger van parked outside.

"Come on, Max. Don't be a tease."

"I don't want you to repeat this."

"Promise."

"All right. But haven't you ever wondered what it would be like to commit a crime yourself?"

"No."

"Bullshit. I know you read all that twisted stuff and get a secret kick from it."

"So?"

"So here is the point. With what we know, I mean as
lawyers, don't you think we could do better?"

"Better?"

"How long have you been at the Bar, Nick?"

It seemed to Nick like it had been forever, since the slime
had first crawled out of the primordial detritus, had grown
legs, and suddenly got the bright idea to make money out of
other people's grief by slapping on a horsehair wig. It seemed
like eons, ages, millennia. "About twelve years," he said.

"And haven't you learned anything?"

"Yes. Don't shack up with another barrister."

"Listen, Star. Leave that sweet woman out of it. I ain't talking about Sally." By now Max was excited and was breathing
rapidly. "What I mean is, don't you think we could get away
with it?"

"Perhaps."

"That's what I think. Then here's the deal. What stops us
from doing it?"

"Fear, I suppose. Fear of the consequences."

"But consequences for who? For the victim?"

"For ourselves. Cowardice is what really controls crime. Always has."

After that, the two of them were silent. Devlin's was as bois-
terous as usual. Occasionally, a tipsy barrister with his tie loos-
ened would approach the two men, but would back off when he
saw the looks on their faces. Nick looked at the table mat,
which, like the others in Devlin's, sported a legal quotation.

It matters not how a man dies, but how he lives.
The act of dying is of no importance, it lasts so short a time.

For a while, he thought about the corpse. No face, no name,
an anonymous grave by the motorway, and the forensic scientists still didn't know the cause of death. As he stared at a cou-

ple of Silks buzzing around a female law student, he was reminded of a comment in the entomologist's report.

It was said that as early as the eighteenth century a Swedish biologist had noted that flies—and their maggots—could consume a corpse more quickly than a lion. In this case, the maggots had consumed most of the head, and Nick wondered whether sufficient remained for the scientists to reconstruct the face with any degree of accuracy.

"Nick," Max insisted, "we were talking about crime. Do you think we could get away with it?"

"You know, Max," Nick said, "I've always been obsessed with women's hair. In fact, even before I'd made love to a woman, I was obsessed with their hair. With the smell, the shine. With everything."

As he spoke, Max stared at the Art Deco mirrors on the wall opposite, saying nothing and only occasionally sipping from his glass.

"I met this girl once," Nick continued. "She was hitching. Must have been on the road for a couple of days. You know, caked in grime. So I invited her to my place. She was grateful for some shelter. It began raining, you see."

Max nodded twice but did not look at him.

"She went to have a bath. Left the door open as bold as you like. I made some excuse to walk by and she says, Get a good eyeful?—or something like that. So I went in. And then I couldn't control myself, Max. I just couldn't . . ."

"Go on, Star."

"I can't."

"Have you ever told anyone?"

"No."

"Well, tell me. You'll feel—you might feel better."

He turned his head to Nick, who continued.

"The truth is—"

"Yes?"

"Well, the truth is I asked her if I could shampoo her hair."

"You did what?"

"She let me, too. And then I had this urge to do it again.

Only by now I had run out of shampoo. I nearly went out of my mind. What could I use? So I went to the kitchen and got some honey. And then she started to protest. But I was, well, a bit out of control. I just had to do it."

"Nick," Max said, taking his arm. He very rarely called him by his first name.

"And do you know what I felt like doing, Max?"

"I don't want to know."

"I felt like slipping a noose around—"

"Jesus."

"Only I figured that she would start screaming or something and then the people downstairs would hear."

Max looked around again but there was no one in their corner of the bar. "When was all this?"

"In 1981."

"So that makes you—"

"That makes me Luigi Longhi, Max."

"What?"

"Luigi Longhi, the shampoo-and-strangle murderer of Denmark."

"Why, you son of a—"

Nick burst out laughing for the first time that evening. "Fancy another round of Monsters, Max?"

"Not with you. You are one sick mother."

Nick raised himself gingerly to his feet. The bar was practically empty. There were partly drunk bottles of claret on some of the tables. The piped Vivaldi had at last been switched off.

As they emerged into the night air, Nick tried to hail a cab. The first one drove right by.

"What time it is?" asked Max.

"Time I told Sally," Nick replied.

"Told her what?"

"That it's over."

"That woman, I swear, is a saint. How she puts up with you, I shall never—"

"Hang on. You're supposed to be on my side, remember?"

"What is wrong between you and Sally?" Max asked.

"She wants to get married."

"So?"

"You know marriage, Max? It's that dreary place our friends return to after their honeymoons, where they're placed under house arrest and strict curfew."

"It's a commitment."

"If you love someone, why can't that be commitment enough?" Nick didn't tell Max the other problem: Sally putting her career ahead of children. He calculated that if he said he wanted to end things, that would force the issue. Sally would see sense and would eventually agree to kids. Marriage without children made no sense to Nick.

Max was sullen and tried to hail the next cab, which also drove past.

"Don't be upset about that Monsters thing, Max. It should be me who's insulted. I mean, for a moment there you really thought I was some kind of sex beast or something."

"It wasn't just for a moment."

"What does that mean?"

"You're so goddamn clever, Nick. Work that one out for yourself."

As they parted, the two men did not shake hands, not only because by convention one barrister never shook the hand of another, lest clients thought they were doing a private deal, but also because Nick discerned a frostiness between them, a distance, a sense of bad feeling that he had never encountered before.

The spotlights that imbued the front arch of the High Court with a golden glow at night were switched off. Nick and Max Baptiste took separate cabs home.

Chapter Four

By the time the cab dropped Nick off in Queensway, the alcohol in his bloodstream had really started to take effect.

The piles of black plastic bin-liners that were stacked head high on street corners were torn open and spewed out streams of refuse. The rats that darted in and out of the fast-food doorways seemed to Nick to be as big as dogs. He thought he saw the moon sinking into the mansion blocks on the other side of the road, which had been taken over by squatters and pimps. He was very drunk. Sally would be furious.

The apartment block in which they lived was the oldest along Queensway. They had been there ever since that distant day when Sally finally decided that she had more of her possessions at Nick's flat than in her cubbyhole in West Kensington. She moved in for good.

It wasn't the most salubrious address for a couple of busy barristers, but it was central, it was convenient for most of the London courts, and—above all, as far as Nick was concerned—it was home.

After he had navigated his way through an assault course of refuse sacks, he finally arrived at the glass entrance door. For a minute he fumbled with the key, having no success. At his feet was the small stray tabby that had made the service areas of the block its home. The cat rubbed its fluffy body against his ankles.

He could have buzzed up to Sally, but that would merely have aggravated his offense. So he tapped on the glass and tried to summon the night porter, Kenny.

Nick knew that the sixty-year-old Hong Kong Chinese had a foul temper and regarded any disturbance of his night's repose as the height of rudeness.

When he knocked for a second time, the man looked up angrily. "What you want?"

"I live here, remember?" he called through the glass.

"I know that. You think I'm stupid or something?"

"No, Kenny. Of course I don't."

"Right, then." With that the tiny man resumed his seat at reception.

Nick banged on the glass again, this time harder. The cat was startled by the noise and scampered toward the nearest alley.

"Can you let me in, Kenny?" he asked.

"Why?"

"I've forgotten my key."

"Liar. I saw you trying to get your key in the lock. You drunk or what?"

"Just let me in, Kenny. Please."

With a tirade of Cantonese, the door was opened.

"Is she in?" Nick pointed upstairs.

"She been in for hours. You should be home long time ago. You in big shit."

Nick opened the door to the lift. "Thanks, Kenny. But I'm a big boy now. I can go where I like, you know."

The porter just raised his eyebrows a little and returned to the reception desk. He opened a contact newspaper from the back page and smiled. Nick knew it would be full of desperate girls looking for a husband.

"I think I'll get a new model," Kenny said.

As the lift started to rise, Nick faintly heard the tabby crying at the door, trying to find shelter.

"One day I kill that cat," Kenny shouted, throwing something at the glass door.

While the lift grumbled slowly to the seventh floor, Nick
tried to invent an appropriate excuse to give Sally. But as usual
where she was concerned, he was lost for words.

They had met on the first day of Bar School. Nick knew no
one and was wandering around feeling thoroughly miserable.
He didn't know where to go or what to do when he bumped
into Sally and laddered her tights. He was so embarrassed that
he said nothing. She told him in later years that he looked like
a frightened puppy out for its first walk, and she felt sorry for
him. They had lunch and had been together ever since.

When the lift stopped, Nick took a deep breath. In the wine
bar, he had convinced himself that this was the night he was
going to end it. For the last couple of years they had just hurt
each other more and more. He wanted to end the misery, and
yet he could no longer really imagine life without her.

All this thinking must have caused him to sober up slightly,
for when he got to the door of the flat the key went straight in.
He could see no lights on in the hall, but he knew that Sally
was there. The flat was warm and it smelled good, all down
to the woman who, if he were honest, he still loved. No, he
couldn't end it with Sally. He must have been mad even to
think it.

He switched on a light in the kitchen and quietly called out.

"Sally? Are you awake . . . darling?" He didn't usually call
her darling. But he had slurred the S in her name and wanted
to avoid further use of the letter if possible.

There was no reply.

When he reached the lounge and opened the door, he saw
Sally amid a pile of books on the floor. For the first time in
many months, he felt genuinely glad to see her.

"Hi, darling," he said, still remembering to avoid opportunities for slurring. "Really good to—"

"Is it?"

"Yep. Look, I know we've had a problem or two. But I really—"

"Nick, I'm leaving you," was all she said.

Initially, Nick did not reply. The announcement was like a blunt axe that scythed him somewhere below the knees. He sat stupefied for two minutes, watching Sally busily sorting through the books on the floor.

"I've made three piles," she said. "Those that are definitely yours, those that are definitely mine, and those we're going to have to squabble about."

"You can have them all," he said.

"But I don't want them all, Nick. What am I going to do with all your encyclopedias of sex crimes? I can hardly give them to Oxfam, can I?"

He was silent.

"I've devised a foolproof system," she said. "All the books about murder are yours. All those about art are mine. And all the novels are up for grabs. Sound fair?"

"Sounds unnecessary."

"Why?"

"Because you really don't want to leave me. You might think you do, but deep down you know it's wrong." The sentence contained many *s*'s and many slurs, but Nick was past caring.

"No, Nick. Deep down I know you're a selfish bastard who has taken me for granted for years."

"You don't really respect me, do you, Sals?"

"How can I when you don't even respect yourself?"

"So there's no hope?"

"Oh, there's hope all right. Hope for me. Hope that I'll never be as stupid again for as long as I live. Look, Nick, I don't want to apportion blame."

"Good."

"But it was *entirely* your fault, wasn't it?" She hesitated in order to get Nick's full attention. "I mean, the closest you ever got to mentioning marriage was on Waterloo Bridge. You *know*, Nick." She paused while he caught up. "When you recited that Shakespeare."

Nick knew only too well. Shakespeare's sonnet, "Let me not to the marriage of true minds admit impediments." He had learned the poem for Sally, who said that he had lost his sense of romance.

"It was a poem, Sals, not a proposal."

"Quite," she replied.

He got up and kicked over a neat pile of true crime anthologies. "I'm going to bed."

Sally looked up with a Piero della Francesca catalogue in her hand. "That's right. Off you go. When the going gets tough, the tough go to bed and start snoring."

"Good night," he replied.

From the bedroom, he heard her tip another bookcase onto the ground. He started to undress, taking more care than was usual, neatly folding the tie Sally had bought him in Paris and hanging his court shirt on a wooden hanger they had pinched from a hotel in Milan.

He got into bed and curled up in his baggy white T-shirt. He tried to go to sleep but could not. He wished he could cry but he had forgotten how to do it. He didn't know what to do, so he lay very still in bed and listened to Sally systematically dismantling what little remained of their lives together.

She came in an hour later. Nick made his breathing louder.

"I know you're awake," she said.

He did not answer.

"Look, I said some nasty things, Nick." She was sitting at the foot of the bed. "But what are we meant to do? If I don't do something like this, things will never change. You must know that."

Nick pulled the duvet further up until it reached the tip of his nose. He peered at her. He felt his eyes moistening a little.

"We've been strangling each other for years, Nick."

"No we haven't."

"All right, then. You've been strangling me. You've been strangling me so long, Nick, I can no longer breathe. All this talk about children."

"It's not just talk. I want children."

"No, Nick. You want *me* to have children. You contribute one-half of the ingredients, that's all. I just don't understand. Why do you want them so much?"

"I'm a Catholic, Sally. Children is what we do."

"It's all right for you. You don't actually have to give birth. What about my career? How many women at the Bar have the chance to make it to the extent I can? But you don't want me to become more successful than you, do you?"

"That's a lie," Nick said. "You're already more successful than me. Any other complaints? While you're on your soapbox, you might as well finish the job."

"We never go out during the week."

"Well, where would you want to go?"

"To the theater, to the opera, to an expensive restaurant like . . . Le Gavroche."

"But why?"

"Because it's boring as shit sitting on the sofa every evening mugging up our respective briefs in front of *Brookside* or having you cry into your cocoa every time Queens Park Rangers lose. There's no fun, no surprises."

"Is that it?"

"I'm sick of living in a pigsty. I'm sick of your socks. I'm tired of cleaning up after you."

"So I have faults."

"I'm tired of being your mother."

"Anything else?"

"You *know* why I don't want children. I'm not going through all that again."

"But, Sally—"

"And I'm not sure that I'm in love with you anymore, Nick."

That was the end of the conversation. Nick rolled over and switched on the light. He picked up the first book he could. It wasn't one of those about crime.

He opened it from the back as he had seen Kenny do with his newspaper. It seemed right to start from the back. That night everything seemed to be back to front. He had gone home with the intention of ending things with Sally, and she had been the one to give him the boot.

He read the minute type with the Bible up close to his eyes. "And there fell a great star from heaven, burning as it were a lamp, and it fell upon the third part of the rivers, and upon the fountains of waters. And the name of the star is—"

"Nick," said Sally. "You won't try to stop me, will you?"

But he was thinking of an answer to her real question: Are you going to make me spell it all out? Do you really want me to *pity* you?

Her voice faltered as she continued, "The only way you can keep me, Nick, is to let me go."

He finished reading the verse before he put out the light. "And the name of the star is Wormwood. And the third part of the waters became Wormwood and many men died of the waters, because they were made bitter."

Thinking about Sally's words, Nick was reminded yet again of the fact that killing people was easy. Living with them—that was the difficult part. Outside, Queensway was unusually silent. But every now and then he heard the stray cat crying out, and he was unable to sleep.

Chapter Five

"I didn't know there was a difference," Nick said.

"Between what?" Ann Barnes asked.

"Between nightmares and night terrors. Aren't they the same thing?"

She surveyed his face closely. "You look tired."

"We're meant to be discussing the patient. Not me." He moved nearer to the reinforced glass of the observation cell at Wormwood Heath. It was the next day, a Friday. Did it show already? he wondered. Only a day and people could tell already?

After Sally had broken the news, he hadn't really slept. But it wasn't the night which held terrors for Nick. It was the fear of loneliness, of life without Sally.

"What has he done to his hair?" he said, pointing at his client.

"He burned it off. One of the orderlies—he's been suspended—left a cigarette butt in a corridor. Laughing Boy here must have spotted it on the way back from the psychotherapy room. Then he set fire to his hair."

The man had a faintly ridiculous turban of white bandages upon his head. He continued to sit on the soft foam seat without moving. The room was specially designed with rounded edges and soft surfaces so that the inmates could not harm themselves.

"Ann, can I ask you a question?"

"What sort of question?"

"A rather basic sort of one."

"God, Nick, hasn't anyone ever told you about the birds and the bees?"

"Actually, I just wanted to know what a night terror is," he said.

"So you know about sex?"

"Well, my mother told me about the beast with two backs, original sin, and the rhythm method. It's the closest we ever got to discussing bonking in Beckenham."

"I've never really understood," Ann said, inspecting her nails, "how this brilliant rhythm method worked."

"You use a thermometer."

"A *what*? Why don't you just use a condom? Jesus, haven't you Catholics heard that the planet is a little on the overpopulated side?"

"Yes."

"So why are you playing Russian roulette with your reproductive organs?" When he did not answer, she added, "Of course, Sally and you never had kids."

"Sally isn't a Catholic," Nick replied. "Contraception seems to come with your confirmation in the Church of England."

"It's not infallible. Not even the pill's one hundred percent."

"I know."

But, in truth, Nick did not want to talk about Sally or sex or children. Suddenly the darker recesses of a disturbed human mind seemed infinitely more attractive. "I think we were talking about his night terrors," he said.

Ann Barnes bent over, took off her shoe, tapped it against her right hand, and sighed. "Wretched heel's buggered," she said. "The scientific term is 'incubus.' I think it's from the late Latin or something. I never went to the lecture. In the Middle

Ages it was thought to be an evil spirit that descends on a sleeping person."

The man slowly turned his head toward the glass and faced the two observers.

"Don't worry," said Ann. "He can't hear through two inches of industrial glass."

"I hope you're right," Nick said. He had made his second trip to the prison reluctantly. He knew that Sally, who was due to defend a child molester, was also scheduled to have a conference in the Heath.

"I am right, Nick. See his eyes? They're no longer oscillating rapidly."

When Nick looked, the man's eyes were open. He was staring but in an unseeing way.

"Night terror is an arousal from slow-wave sleep. Usually stage three or four, early in the night. The subject is awakened with a piercing scream. His heartbeat races. He sweats profusely. His breath is shallow. He cannot be consoled." Ann rubbed the back of her heel. "Damn shoes. The attack is often accompanied by somnambulation."

"By what?" Nick asked.

"By sleepwalking. And that's where you come in."

"Me?" He was incredulous.

"The prostitute reported him saying that he'd been walking for as long as he could remember. I want to find out where he'd been. And I need you."

"Why?"

"Sometimes we hear him talk when he's alone in the cell. You know, calling out to his beloved Liz. But when we enter, he's silent. The only time he's spoken in other people's presence was when you were present, Nick. That's why I called you this morning. I hope you didn't mind."

When he had first received the call from Ann, his immediate thought was that she was going to invite him out for a drink or something. "No, I didn't mind," he said.

"You see, Nick, I think you've made a friend."

Ann Barnes was now unlocking the security door. Nick

could sense his pulse increasing as he brushed against the back of her white coat, hoping she would not notice.

She smiled when the door swung fully open, the gap between her eyes appearing to Nick to narrow further.

"Ready for some psychodrama?" she said.

"Psychodrama?"

"Bit like amateur dramatics, but the people are more pleasant."

"What does he say?" Nick asked. "In the cell on his own. Apart from calling out to Liz."

"He doesn't *just* say things."

"Then what?"

"He has a conversation," Ann replied. "There are always *two* voices."

Chapter Six

Nick and Ann took a break from the session. It had not been going well. They stood outside the cell with their backs to the patient and tried to work out what they had been doing wrong. Ann had cut some fresh bandages and wrapped them around the man's head. After she had put her scissors back in the long coat pocket, she lit a cigarette in the corridor.

"Do you think you really ought to?" Nick said.

"They're my lungs."

"No, I meant—"

"I know what you meant, Nick." She exhaled for what seemed like ages, directing a small cloud of gray smoke up toward the ceiling. "How's Sally?"

"Well."

"Good."

"She's left me."

Ann looked at him, betraying no surprise, and Nick wondered whether she had already been told. She took another long drag from her cigarette and blew smoke a little closer to Nick.

"It's only temporary, though," he said.

"Sure." She tapped the ash on the floor and ground it into

the stone with her heel. "And I'm the Florence Nightingale of the night terrors ward."

Nick turned and looked at the bandaged figure in the cell. "I'll miss her, I suppose."

"Where's she staying?"

"Oh, apparently Max has agreed to put her up for a bit in Dulwich. Max's a good friend and has really helped out in this difficult time. I don't know what I'd have done without him."

"Well, you'd still have your girlfriend, for starters."

"I trust him."

"That doesn't count. You trust everyone." She paused. "Is Sally going to prosecute this case to trial, Nick?"

"Yes."

"Well, isn't that cozy?"

"It's a bit incestuous, I suppose," he said.

"A bit? It's more incestuous than Oedipus's dirty weekend with Mum in downtown Thebes."

"The Bar is a very small world. Take the famous case of Edwardian gambler Robert Siever. Defended successfully at the Old Bailey on a blackmail charge by Rufus Isacs, Siever sued his accusers for libel. By the time the libel action came to court, his former barrister, Isacs, was the trial judge. And Siever still lost."

"Can we return to the end of the twentieth century?" Ann said. "Look, Nick, you've got to face facts."

"Such as?"

"Such as you've been shafted by Sally and Max."

Nick did not answer but paced impatiently outside the door to the cell. "Let's do it," he said.

When they reached the foam seats, he did not sit down. He approached the man and laid a hand on his shoulder.

"It's Revelations, isn't it?" he said.

"Yes," the man replied.

Ann's face was frozen in amazement.

"And you want to tell us about the dream that's been troubling you. Am I right?"

The man nodded.

Ann leaned across the table and whispered to Nick, "Remember how I told you to do it."

"You must start at the beginning," Nick said.

The man put a hand to the side of his head. His wrists, too, were covered in bandages. When he placed his palms back on the table, he began to speak.

"He was standing in a big field—"

"Not he," Nick said. It was what Ann had insisted on. "You must say I. This is about you."

"I had been walking in the field for what seemed like hours."

"Use the present tense," Nick said. "This is happening to you now."

"I fight my way through the long grass. It comes up to my waist."

"Where are you headed?" Nick asked.

"Toward the noise."

"What noise?"

"The noise of the road. And on the road there is—"

"What is there?" Ann asked.

The man did not answer.

"Don't be frightened," Nick said. "Tell us what is there."

"There's a body near the road. But I just walk past." The man looked down at his lap.

"Don't be ashamed," Nick said.

"I just walk by. I know there's something else. I hear the odd bird singing but it's not like any song I've ever heard.

"The bones are crushed and the mouth is open but the body does not scream. But I do. Because then . . . then I see the woman."

Ann, who had given up trying to write the narrative down, jabbed Nick in the ribs. "You'd better make him stop, Nick. I think he's had enough."

"Don't you know who the woman is?" Nick asked, ignoring Ann's advice.

The man shook his head.

"Shall I tell you?" Nick said.

"Nick, leave it there," Ann hissed.

"She doesn't exist," Nick said.

The man put his hands over his ears.

Nick grabbed one wrist and spoke quietly. "And there appeared a woman clothed with the sun. And she being with child cried, and pained to be delivered."

"Nick," Ann said, "he's had enough."

"And he stood before the woman ready to devour her child and hated the whore and shall eat her flesh and shall burn her with fire." He took the man's other hand. "It's just a story. From the Book of Revelations. The story of the whore and the child. Just a story. Like the story about the star."

"Wormwood?" the man asked.

"Wormwood," Nick said. "The last book of the Bible. Revelations."

Of course, what Nick did not understand was why the man had become obsessed with the story of the whore and the child. What was its significance, its hidden meaning?

There was a sharp rap on the glass. When Nick looked around, there was Sally. He left Ann with the man in the cell.

Nick and Sally stood next to each other for a while and watched Ann Barnes speaking to the patient. There was so much Nick wanted to say, but he didn't know where to begin. That did not surprise him. He could speak to psychopaths, he could speak to psychiatrists, but he could not speak to the woman he was supposed to love. So after a couple of abortive starts, it was Sally who was the first to talk.

"You seem to be very cozy with Ann Barnes."

"I can see Ann if I like. It's none of your—"

"Ann Barnes would eat you for breakfast, Nick. But I don't even think old Annie gets that hungry." She stared into the cell.

Ann Barnes made some notes and then looked up at the patient. She smiled at him reassuringly, and there was a glimmer of recognition in his face.

"She's an impossible woman," Sally continued. "And I say that as a close friend."

"She's very good at her job," Nick said. "But it's more than just that. She jokes around and pretends to be heartless, but I don't think she is. She cares about people. You know, most people are the opposite." He half turned toward Sally. "Most people pretend to love you until it suits them not to. Then they go. I think I prefer Ann's way of doing things. Now what did you want to speak to me about, Sally?"

"We've received the results of the facial mapping."

"Pardon?"

"They've reconstructed the skull of the corpse."

"So?"

"We now know what the dead man looked like." She peered into the cell intensely.

"And what does he look like?"

"If I didn't know better," Sally said, "I would say that your man had killed . . . well, himself."

"Meaning?"

"Meaning that the face of the victim is his face, Nick." She turned to look at him. "It's *his* face."

Chapter Seven

Although it was a Friday night, Nick did not go out.

The explanation was straightforward. Middle age had been descending upon him like a bad mood. He had seen it coming, he had felt its effects, but he had not been able to do anything to shake it off.

He began to look forward to the weekend so that he could stay in. He found himself irresistibly drawn to country-and-western music. He decided that Tammy Wynette was a creative genius. He suddenly found slippers stylish. And worst of all, and to his great horror, he no longer found babies utterly revolting. And this, of course, had caused problems with Sally.

That particular Friday night, Nick could not sleep. It was the first Friday night without Sally. He paced around the seventh-floor flat trying not to think about Max and Sally and what Max might be doing with her on a Friday night in Dulwich.

Eventually, he decided that he could no longer stay in the flat. So, grabbing an old jumper and pulling it over his cotton T-shirt, he took the lift to the street door.

He pretended to himself that he was going out on official business: he was a lawyer, he was going to inspect the *locus in quo*, the scene of the crime; he was going to examine objectively the brothel in which his client was found. But in reality, he was sad and alone and hurting.

Outside, Queensway was alive. Cars were bumper to bumper along the street at 3 A.M. The tacky dive bars were open, peep shows were doing a roaring trade, and young girls loitered in the shop doorways putting on red lipstick and arguing with their pimps. It was Friday night, and, as Max had once said, all the creatures were coming out to play.

He held open the street door. He thought he had heard the tabby again. Before he ventured out, he looked at Kenny, who was sitting at the reception desk. "You haven't seen that little cat, have you?"

The porter did not lift his eyes from the latest contact sheet. "Perhaps the rats eat it," he said, chuckling.

Nick liked Kenny less and less.

Outside, it might have been rush hour in the city. Many of the cars were expensive coupés, drive by businessmen in designer suits. Mainly they rode alone.

When he crossed the junction that ultimately led to Notting Hill Gate, a voice came from a dark doorway to his right. "Are you looking for someone, baby?"

He did not reply.

"Hey. Do you like water sports?"

"Can't even swim," Nick replied, reaching the next alcove.

When he entered the all-night drugstore, he asked the man inside whether he could put an advert in the window offering a reward for the return of the cat. The man told him that there was a two-week delay, and he would have to wait in the queue along with the massage parlors and escort agencies. Nick bought himself a packet of cheese and onion crisps and departed.

Since Sally had left, he had been in a type of daze. It was like being drunk all the time, without having consumed any alcohol, and without the initial high.

The rules of the housing association strictly forbade the keeping of "any living creatures" in the block. Of course, they turned a blind eye to the cockroaches in the kitchens and the rats in the basement. And, in truth, Nick couldn't really claim the cat as his. But he had heard it crying out the previous night when Sally had ended their relationship, and he was beginning to understand what it felt like to be alone. He wanted some company, and if he found the stray he was determined to smuggle it past Kenny.

"Hey, mister. You need a friend?"

That night, it was a question Nick could not answer truthfully. The girl could not have been much over sixteen. She had beautiful Chinese features, delicate and slight. Her hair was straight and parted down the middle and tied in two ponytails. She must have attracted all the real crazies, Nick thought. In fact, she looked younger than sixteen.

"I'm a nice clean girl. I'll give you the time of your life."

He was curious. What was it that drove these young girls onto the street? He knew from his work that many of them were single mothers and had children to support. Others were on drugs. Still others came from broken homes. From a distance, this girl looked as if she had just taken to the street. Perhaps it wasn't too late for her?

That sounded too sanctimonious, he thought. He had to admit it. Sally had only just left him, but he was already lonely. If he were honest, he knew what drove men to these girls. Perhaps, like him, they had been knocked off balance, disoriented, deserted, abandoned.

"How old are you?" he asked.

"Eighteen."

"Really?"

"Why? How old do you want me to be? I've got a younger sister, you know. Well, she's sort of my sister."

"You're too young to be doing this. Where do you . . ." He wasn't sure what the correct term was. "Where are you staying? I mean, at the moment."

The girl pointed to an alleyway across the street. Nick was about to leave when he noticed a set of cards pinned to the door. They merely said JACKIE. It was the name of the prostitute Nick's client had seen.

In the yellow street lighting, the young girl's skin had an almost translucent quality. She tried to pull the sleeves of her tank top over her skinny biceps. The marks were strange. A mixture of bruises and lacerations, with the odd vein at the surface, black and somehow dead. Nick suspected that she had been injecting.

"I'm not into rough stuff. So don't get the wrong idea."

"No," he said. "I just wondered—"

"Well, don't. No one looks out for me except our Jackie."

"Jackie?"

"I used to have this pimp. He saw me trying to work the street on my own. Said I had to be part of his . . . family. Used to hit me with coat hangers if I didn't come back with two hundred pounds a night. That was rough."

"I'm sorry," Nick said.

"I don't want your sympathy."

"What do you want?"

"Your money. But I won't roll you or anything."

"Roll?"

"You know, rip you off. We have a menu at Jackie's. The prices are fixed. It's all aboveboard. That's all thanks to our Jack."

"She sounds quite a—"

"You want to meet her?"

"Well, I was really looking for—"

"You'd have to pay. Have you got any money?"

In the fog that had clouded his reason since Sally had left, this seemed the type of question that demanded an answer. He rummaged in his trouser pocket and felt his wallet. He took it out.

"Not here," said the girl. "You trying to get me arrested or what? Not here. In *there*."

"You speak better English than you want to let on," he said as they began to walk.

"I call it my Little Chop Suey act. It turns the punters on."

Pretty much before Nick had realized what he was doing, he was being led into the doorway of the salon opposite. He was not going to return to his empty flat—not just yet. He had found the *locus in quo.*

Once the young Chinese girl had ushered him inside the hallway, she disappeared. At the bottom of the stairs was a desk. Sitting behind it, in a beige tracksuit made of a heavy toweling material, was a woman of about fifty-five years. Her hair was mousy in color and frizzy. She was one of the maids.

"The young lady will be with you in just a tick, dear," she said.

It proved to be a very long tick; Nick was waiting for nearly ten minutes. On the low table in front of him were several magazines of a type he had not seen since his days in a Catholic prep school. The only real difference was that the literature that had circulated at St. Barnaby's was considerably more graphic than the magazines on the table in front of him. He experienced that mixture of fear and anticipation that he had only felt at court and in the dentist's waiting room.

A television set was in the corner of the room. It was propped up on two large boxes of elasticated nappies. It had been tuned to the satellite cartoon channel, which put Nick a little more at ease.

Above the television was a certificate from the London School of Reflex Massage. Next to that was a crucifix which someone had obviously forgotten to take down.

The sight of the cross brought Nick to his senses. He took a step toward the door.

"Hold on, honey. Where are you going?"

He looked at the woman who was coming down the stairs. She had straight blond hair that Nick suspected to be a wig. She wore a Lycra miniskirt and heels only marginally more precipitous than those of Ann Barnes.

"I'm ready for you now," she said.

The room upstairs was not large. For some reason Nick had always imagined that there would be a red light. But the only source of illumination was a table lamp with some kind of shawl thrown across it.

"What would you like, then, honey?"

Nick said nothing.

"The strong, silent type, eh? Well, just take a look at this." She handed him a plastic card.

"I don't really know what I'm here for," Nick said.

"Nor do most men. But they normally think of something." She laughed.

"I just sort of want to talk," he said. He was thinking about how he could tactfully broach the subject of his client.

"Not another one," the woman said. "Must be something in the air. You want to talk? Fine. But money talks, too." She indicated the prices on the card.

"I was just wondering about that young girl I met outside," Nick said. "It's just that she seemed so young to —"

"To what? To do what I do? Listen, honey. There's only one thing worse than being out on the street. And that's being out on the street with no money."

Nick looked at the mass of chains and handcuffs. "I see," he said.

"Do you? A girl's got to fight to survive. And then what do they call us? Hookers, whores? Tarts and tramps? But look at those respectable men with their fancy cars." She tapped the window and looked outside. "What percentage of the respectable male population has passed through the legs of the girls on this street?"

Nick had by now taken his wallet out.

The woman continued to survey the scene in the street and ignored him. "What do people know? Men and women. What do they call it? The battle of the sexes? Give me a break. It ain't no battle, honey. It's a massacre. There was this john who came in here—"

"I'm sorry," he said. "I don't think I can do this." He started to move toward the door. He took out some notes. He didn't know how many.

"He just wanted to talk like you."

"I'm sorry I've wasted your time," Nick said.

"And this sick son of a . . . only has a claw hammer in his . . . Hey, honey, where are you going?"

Nick had left the small bundle of notes on the bed. "There's the money. I've really got to go. I'm really very . . ."

The woman was looking at the notes. "You've given me too much. Not that I'm complaining. For that much you could have got—"

"Do you charge by the hour?" Nick said, taking a deep breath and deciding he might as well find out about his client.

"Sometimes—most men can't last an hour. I think three minutes is the national average." She looked him up and down. "You look about average, honey."

"Well, it's your meter that's ticking. So let's get down to business."

"You a cabby?"

"A lawyer."

"Oh, a professional," she said. "Like me." She approached Nick and pushed him onto the bed. She smiled. "Now you're talking, honey."

"No," Nick said. "I'm afraid it's you who's going to do the talking."

Nick was in the brothel for ten times the current average and in that time his zipper was never once lowered.

In those thirty minutes, Jackie described the prisoner as basically no different from others, a little sad, a little lonely—but occasionally she saw something inside him, a darker mood, a deeper tone, a different voice. Something not right.

When Nick returned to his flat, there was a light flashing on his answerphone. The message was from the solicitor.

"Mr. Downes, sorry to disturb you at this hour. But we've found Liz. And she insisted that I call you. Her name is Elizabeth Turner. I'll arrange a conference next week in your chambers. I think that's it. Oh yes . . . she claims to be our client's wife."

Chapter Eight

On the Wednesday of the next week, Nick waited in his third-floor room for his conference with Elizabeth Turner to begin.

His clerks had buzzed through from reception and told him that she was downstairs. But she wanted to make a quick call before coming up.

Nick felt nervous. He had heard the name of this mysterious woman so often; there was so much speculation as to why an accused murderer would constantly cry out her name in his prison cell. What could he expect from her?

The phone rang again.

He grasped the receiver and listened.

"Nick? Are you there? Nick?"

It was Sally.

"Look, Nick. Are you going to talk to me or just breathe heavily down the phone?"

"I can't speak," he said.

"Why not?"

"I'm about to go into con."

"With whom?" But before he could reply, she continued, "I hear she's quite a looker."

"She's my client's wife."

"So she says."

"What do you mean?"

"Where is she?"

"Downstairs."

"Bet you fancy her. All the detectives do."

Nick had imagined Liz Turner's face in a hundred different ways, and it was true, all of them were beautiful. "Was there some *purpose* to this call?"

"I'm going to keep the car for a while. Just wanted to check that was all right."

"Fine."

"Nick," she said, and then paused. There was a softer tone in her voice. "Truth is, I just really wanted to say how sorry—"

"Got to go."

"But Nick—"

The door had opened.

"Mrs. Turner has just arrived," he said, putting down the receiver.

After ten minutes, Liz Turner began again. "I said his name is Will Turner, and he is a painter and a poet—"

"Yes, I heard," said Nick. "He's a painter—"

"And a poet."

"A kind of Renaissance man," Nick said. "I suppose in a sense he *has* been born again."

"Or come back from the dead. I'd given him up as gone for good."

She was silent for a moment, and Nick took the opportunity to examine her more closely. She was stunning—but it wasn't the classical beauty that Sally possessed. This beauty was dangerous, magnetic—literally. She attracted all his attention; his gaze was drawn involuntarily to her, to the hips, the hair, to the swell of her breasts and back to the hips.

It was as though his mind had been wiped clean of reasoned, logical thought and his brain had been replaced with guacamole.

I *shouldn't* be thinking these things, he thought.

But he caught himself breathing more quickly, more deeply, not for air but to smell her perfume, to draw it to him.

Hair cascaded down her shoulders and shone in many colors, hints of auburn and reds setting the deeper black alight. Her opal eyes burned into Nick intensely. She was breathtaking and sensuous and bright.

He offered her another digestive biscuit. It was all he could think of. He looked out of the window. His chambers were south of Fleet Street and north of the river, in the privileged cloisters that were the exclusive province of lawyers and down-and-outs.

He had another conference scheduled for twenty minutes later, so he could not afford to prevaricate. "I will have to ask you this again. How would you describe your relationship with . . . Mr. Turner?" It seemed odd to him to have a name at last for the forlorn face with the bandages.

"I'm . . . his wife. Well, officially I am. I mean, in the sense that we had been married for five years and never got divorced. But for some time before Will—"

"Disappeared?"

"Left me." The woman seemed hurt. "Well, we simply had not been living together as man and wife. Funny to think that the first time he proposed, I turned him down." And then she added with irritation, "I've told all this to the solicitors and to the police."

"Actually," Nick said, "I wonder where the solicitor has got to. He should have been here. You and I really shouldn't be talking without him."

"Why not?"

"Bar ethics."

"Ethics are just rules, aren't they?"

"Yes, but—"

"There are always exceptions to the rules," Liz Turner said. "Don't you agree, Mr. Downes?" She tossed her hair, and the air around Nick was suddenly suffused with rich perfumes. "Rules are made to be broken."

"Some of them, I suppose," he agreed.

She smiled slightly and stared directly at him. "Which ones, Mr. Downes? Which rules are supposed to be broken?"

Nick, who had merely been playing along with his client's wife, was stumped. His mind raced, charged with the delicious smell of Liz Turner.

"I canceled the solicitor," she said evenly. "I knew you wouldn't mind."

"But I do mind."

"No you don't. I wanted to be alone with you. To speak more . . . frankly." She bit her lip. "Do you mind if I speak frankly?"

Nick didn't want to answer directly. "Can you tell me why you and your husband split up?"

"Is it important?"

"Perhaps."

"So perhaps not?"

"Perhaps not," Nick agreed reluctantly. He decided to move the conversation on to less contentious matters. "Tell me, Mrs. Turner, what sort of poetry did he write?"

"Modern stuff. You know, no rhymes, no meaning, no sales."

"So you were short of money?"

"Will trained as a graphic artist. Designing logos for microwave meals and other socially useful things. Then his father died—that was a few years ago—the family was well off, and Will was left some money."

"Some?"

"Two million pounds. That was his downfall, really. He dropped out of the rat race and we lived off the inheritance while he painted and wrote. Tried to sell his canvases to the trendy galleries in Notting Hill with no success. I suppose there's only so much incomprehensible art even the bourgeoisie can digest."

Nick perceived a scornful tone in the woman's voice.

"So when Will failed as a painter," she continued, "he attempted his magnum opus, a *Waste Land* for the nineties."

"*The Waste Land*? As in T. S. Eliot?"

"As in a long poem that no one understands and everyone says they like." She lowered her voice and gazed out at the river. "You should read it sometime, Mr. Downes. Now, may I know why you want to know all these . . . personal details about me?"

"We're trying to help your husband and we need to know what we're dealing with."

"That's easy. You're dealing with a man who left his wife."

"A man who is suffering from delusions."

"Will always was a bit of a dreamer."

"These are not dreams. They're—"

"Nightmares?" the woman asked. "You don't have to tell me about Will's nightmares, Mr. Downes. I lived with him for five years."

The conference was not going as Nick expected. He imagined that he would be encountering a distraught wife, and had even popped out to the newsagent's on the Strand to buy some man's-size tissues and herbal tea.

He looked down over the dull green lawns of the Middle Temple. From his rooms, he had a good view of most of the chambers of his Inn of Court. Hundreds and hundreds of barristers, all hungry mouths to fill, all competing for a slice of the ever diminishing criminal cake. In that sense, this was a good case, a good earner. But he didn't want it. His guts told him that he did not want it at all.

The Thames was just visible through the barren branches of the line of trees that bordered the main road. Before the Victoria Embankment was built in the nineteenth century, the river must have come right up to the bottom of the buildings, Nick thought. But now there was just a car park and a growing army of tramps who waited in dutiful line to be fed by the mobile soup kitchen.

"I didn't realize just how pretty it was here," the woman said. "A bit like an Oxford college, all cloistered and archaic. On my way here through the Temple, there was a church door open. A choir was singing. Madrigals, I think. It was so beautiful. You're very lucky to work here."

"Mrs. Turner," Nick said.

"Please call me Liz."

Nick ignored her. "Mrs. Turner, your husband is in serious trouble."

She stirred her cold cup of tea. "So you've said. But what has it really got to do with me? We were practically separated, after all."

"You were about his only family."

"Except for his brother."

"Who he has very probably murdered," Nick said.

It had been after the reconstruction of the corpse's face had been publicized that the woman had come forward. Initially, thought Nick, she must have believed it to be her husband.

"Murdered? What about the presumption of innocence and all that legal stuff?" she said.

"We're not in court now."

He felt tired. He didn't want to give her a crash course in the legal process. He really did not want to think about the case or, for that matter, about any case. In the preceding twelve months he had defended in twenty-seven trials. And each time he felt that it was he who was in the dock.

In that period, he had been convicted sixteen times, acquitted ten times, and on one unremarkable occasion the jury in St. Albans could not decide on his guilt and was hung. He had received a total of forty-eight years in prison sentences, had been placed upon three probation orders, had been deported to Nigeria and to the United States, had received three thousand pounds in fines, and had been ordered to pay compensation to a pensioner he had mugged.

And to cap it all, the previous month Nick had been sectioned under the Mental Health Act as being a schizophrenic who sniffed women's lingerie. When he thought about it, he had every right to feel knackered. It had been his *annus horribilis* of crime.

"Tell me about his brother, Charles," he said eventually.

"What is there to say? He was a professional man. Respected in his field. When the father died, Charles got the family business and Will got the money."

"What was the business?"

"You mean you don't know?"

"I'm only the defense. No one tells me anything."

"By the time it all happened last year, I'd known Charles for eight years. Five years ago, I even worked as his receptionist. That's how I met Will."

"Were they close?"

"In terms of age, yes. Will was one year older. I suppose Will must be thirty-nine now—about ten years older than me."

"I really meant," Nick said, "were they similar?"

"In looks only. In terms of personality, they were as different as Jekyll and Hyde. Charles was suave, sophisticated, highly intelligent. But Will—well, Will had a certain . . . charm. An innocence, I suppose. A naïveté."

"Were they jealous of each other, Mrs. Turner?"

She hesitated and looked at him. "I'm not going to bad-mouth a dead man, if that's what you think."

"To be honest, Mrs. Turner, I don't know what to think about this case," he said. "At all."

"Let's not argue," Liz said, smiling again, her full lips suddenly parting. "I want to be friends. Can we be friends, Mr. Downes?"

He watched her as she walked around the room, as if in some sense she owned it, looking at the briefs, fingering the leaves on his plants. The black skirt clung to her body, tracing the gentle swell of her hips, precisely defining the soft flesh of her buttocks.

She picked up a photograph from his desk.

"Who are these people?" she asked.

"My family."

"Three brothers."

"And three sisters," Nick added.

"You all look so happy."

"We are."

"That's what I've always wanted," she said.

"To be happy?"

"To have a family." There was a doleful edge to her voice, but it disappeared when she smiled again. "And do they have their own children?"

"All of them," Nick said. "Except me."

"And does Miss Fielding approve of that situation?" she asked, absolutely neutrally.

Nick was stunned. How on earth had his client's wife found out about Sally?

"Are you shocked that I know about Sally Fielding?" she asked. She tossed her hair again; it tumbled over her shoulders and Nick felt himself assailed, intoxicated with her musky fragrance.

Chapter Nine

The conversation had come to a temporary halt,
much as the discussion with Jackie had ended the previous
week. Only on that occasion Nick had got the distinct impression that when Jackie had stopped speaking she was frightened
of something. She had not wanted to talk further about the
man with the hammer, and Nick had not wanted to do anything else. It had all been rather a fiasco.

But Jackie had told him about the girl, the Chinese girl who
took him to the parlor. An addict, paranoid, alone. Ran away
from a court-sanctioned rehabilitation center. On the streets, on
the game, in demand with the professional type of punter who
liked, as Jackie put it, fucking with a girl's mind as well as
with her body.

"When I came up," Liz explained, "I asked your clerks if Mr.
Downes's wife would approve of him receiving a single woman
alone in his room."

Nick gazed silently at her.

"The senior clerk replied that Miss Fielding was used to it by
now. It was a joke, Nick."

It was the first time she had called him Nick.

"How did you know her name was Sally?" he asked.

"On the table, in your reception room, there were these brochures."

"Chambers brochures," Nick said. "Publicity. To make ourselves more attractive to solicitors."

"Well, you seem to have succeeded."

"Why?"

She did not answer. Finally, she said, "On the middle two pages, there were entries for you and Sally Fielding—and your photos. You on the left-hand side and Sally on the right-hand side. It's quite sweet, really. Like a love locket."

"We were supposed to be discussing your husband. What I need to know—"

She broke in on his words with her husky voice. "So tell me, then, is Will mad?"

"Do you mean is he insane?"

"Is there a difference?"

"Well, under the McNaghten Rules—"

"You mustn't blind me with science, Mr. Downes."

"The rules cover criminal insanity. They're named after the case of David McNaghten in 1843."

"What did he do?"

"Tried to kill the Prime Minister."

"Isn't there the defense of justification for that sort of thing?"

"You're thinking of libel. Anyway, McNaghten was suffering from paranoid delusions. The psychiatrists think your husband may be suffering from the same thing."

"So?"

"So we would like your consent. And I have to advise you on the legal implications. That's why the solicitors have arranged this conference. That's why they should be here."

She shuffled uneasily in her seat. "You want my consent? To do what exactly?"

"To have your husband . . . well, hypnotized." He didn't look at her when he said it. On the Thames, a heavily laden barge that was scarcely above the waterline hooted twice.

"Isn't that an unusual step?"

"Very," Nick said.

"Could it be dangerous?"

"We're . . . not sure." Ann Barnes, whose idea it was, had not really explained the risks to him between puffs on her cigarette.

Liz got up and walked to the far side of the room, as far away from Nick as it was possible to get. Her hair swept down past her shoulders in gentle waves on each side of her cleavage. And when she walked, the loose strands swayed, touching her breasts, left then right, to and from, in time, almost mesmerically, driving Nick bananas.

She stopped at the lone print on the wall. It was of a fragile knight swooning in the hair of a mysterious woman on horseback. Sally had bought it for him to cheer the place up a bit, as she had put it.

"*La belle dame?*" she said, reading the little title plaque on the picture frame.

"*Sans merci,*" Nick replied. "You mustn't forget the *sans merci.*"

"Does it mean—"

"The beautiful, merciless woman," he said.

"Are you fond of poetry, Mr. Downes?"

In fact, he knew only one poem. The Shakespeare sonnet. When he had tried to recite it to Sally on Waterloo Bridge he got all embarrassed and confused when some young lads pulled faces and jeered. "Stick your tongue in, mate." That was a long time ago, he remembered, when Sally and he were happy.

"What do you hope to achieve by hypnosis?" Liz asked, rousing him from these thoughts.

"What we haven't been able to achieve by any other method."

"Which is?"

"Which is the truth of what happened. Why your husband led the police to a decaying corpse by the motorway. More tea?"

She sat down again. She pretended to brush some fluff from her sleeves. "Hasn't Will given you any indication of what did take place?"

"He seems to be on some sort of religious trip. Was he particularly religious?"

"Certainly not. He was Church of England."

"And you?"

"Catholic," Liz said. "As are you." She looked at him playfully.

"How did you—"

"I think I understand you, Mr. Downes."

"How?"

"Like minds," Liz said. "Kindred spirits."

"You don't know what you're talking about. How can you be sure?"

She pointed to his bookshelf. "Anyone who has books called *Confessions* and *The Imitation of Christ* is bound to be either raving bonkers or a Catholic. I'll give you the benefit of the doubt—at this stage."

"Do you still love your husband, Mrs. Turner?" Nick asked. He decided that it was time to turn the screw.

"The police asked me that."

"Well, I'm asking you now."

"He left me."

"It *is* possible to love someone who has left you." He thought of Sally and how he had lain very still in bed and listened to her dismantling the flat.

"What do you want me to say?"

It was Nick's turn to stir his cold cup of tea. "How about the truth?"

"You're very clever, aren't you, Mr. Downes? What shall I tell you, then? That my life was ruined? Well, it wasn't. I just carried on where I left off. What else do you want to know about me?"

"Whether—"

"Whether I have a lover?"

"I'm not interested in—"

"Sex? Yes, you are." She crossed her legs, the silk of the stockings stretching transparently over the firm flesh. "I don't have a lover. I still watch television. I still read books. My favorite color is vermilion. I'm a Capricorn and a size fourteen, though I pretend to be a twelve. I go to my masseur on Tuesdays. I shop on Saturdays. I go to church on Sundays. And—"

"And when do you go to confession?" Nick asked.

"One only needs to confess if one has sinned, Mr. Downes. So I don't suppose a good Catholic boy like you ever has to go to confession."

"Oh, I pretty much have a season ticket, Mrs. Turner. Came with my screwed-up adolescence in Beckenham." He stood in front of the print and noticed how the reflected sun skimming off the Thames lit up the hair of Keats's lady in the meads. "Will you give your consent for your husband to undergo hypnosis?"

Liz Turner got to her feet and with her languid steps reached the door almost silently. "You're the lawyer. What do you advise?"

"I advise that you do the right thing by your husband."

"Which is?"

"Only you can really know that, Mrs. Turner."

She gave no answer. At least, no verbal answer. There was a swish of her hair, and she disappeared from the room without saying good-bye. He realized that she had not told him the nature of the Turner family business.

He moved to the window. The winter's sun was dropping lower and lower across the river, and the breeze on the water was getting up. He wondered where Sally was and then told himself that he did not care. Then he bit his lip and told himself that he was a stupid liar.

He opened the window for some air. The marriage of true minds, he repeated, though no one could possibly have heard it above the din of the London traffic. Before he knew it, more of the verse had come back to him. *Love alters not with his brief hours and weeks, but bears it out ev'n to the edge of doom.*

But Nick didn't particularly appreciate the delicate cadences of William Shakespeare. He was thinking about Sally. It was almost a week since he had seen her.

Suddenly, the phone rang. It was Ann Barnes.

"Can you come to the prison first thing tomorrow?" she asked.

"What's up?"

"It's urgent we hypnotize Will Turner immediately."

"Why, Ann?"

"He's disintegrating. His personality is splitting up."

Chapter Ten

On Thursday morning, Nick went to HMP Wormwood Heath as he had agreed.

"It was named after an Austrian, Franz Mesmer," Ann Barnes
said, brushing past two opaque plastic sheets that hung vertically from the ceiling.

"What was named after him?" Nick asked.

"Mesmerizing. Mesmer appeared in purple silk and put
everyone under his spell. Of course, today forensic hypnotism is
nothing like that." She pointed to the long corridor at the end
of which Will Turner was held. "No, hypnotism nowadays isn't
all 'You are under my power; drop your pants and kiss my
feet.'"

"What is it about you and feet, Ann?" he asked.

She stopped outside the cell and looked in. When he caught
up, Will Turner was standing. It was the first time Nick could
remember him being on two legs.

"God, I desperately need a fag," Ann gasped. She reached
into the long pockets of her white coat and pulled out an as-
sortment of notes and pens and a pair of scissors, and finally
found a packet of cigarettes. "So you persuaded the wife to consent?" she asked Nick.

"I don't think it had anything to do with me. I thought I'd rather frightened her off, actually. Look, Ann. This hypnotism thing, it's not going to be dangerous?"

"Well, how on earth am I supposed to know? I'm only the shrink." She looked up at the large NO SMOKING sign and blew some sharp-smelling smoke in Nick's direction.

"Why is he obsessed with the story of the whore and the child?" he asked.

"It's obviously symbolic," she replied.

"Of what?"

She paused. "Of a whore . . . and a child."

Nick gazed at the prisoner and felt a pang of concern. "I'm a bit nervous about what we might do to him."

"Why?"

"Because no one should mess with other people's minds—except, of course, parents and priests."

"Look, don't be such a coward, Nick. Nothing else has worked. No pain, no gain." She ran her fingers over the wire mesh that reinforced the glass. "Laughing Boy there is suffering from repressive amnesia. It's not uncommon to have a blank about what happened before and after a traumatic incident. Hypnotism is just a passkey into the locked-away parts of his subconscious—or some metaphorical bullshit like that. Besides which, it's great fun."

Nick waited until she had stubbed out her cigarette on the stone floor. Then he said, "So you really think we can unlock his memory of the incident?"

"I told you, people don't have one memory, but several. And each one is like a separate room. We just have to keep looking until we find the right door."

He wondered whether he could ever find a door big enough to seal away the profusion of memories he had about Sally. He had decided that the best way to get on with his life was to pretend that none of it had happened. They had never been together, they had never split up, it had all happened to other people. Except he kept thinking of Max Baptiste and his muscled body moving slowly over Sally's soft flesh.

"What about the voices he hears?" he asked.

"He only hears one voice, remember?" She looked into the cell again. "When the reason fragments, the mind distorts things. It's like seeing the world in a broken mirror. Very ordinary things become grotesque, sinister, frightening. Hearing voices, auditory hallucinations, is very common."

Her answer triggered a memory in Nick's mind. He remembered one of his bedside books. "Didn't the Yorkshire Ripper hear—"

"The voice of an evil God," Ann said. "Or something like that. People frequently hear both male and female voices, young and old, different nationalities, talking in tongues even. But having the same voice over and over again, that's—"

"Unusual?"

"Interesting," she said.

"So given all that, can he be hypnotized?" Nick asked.

"Probably," she replied. "Ninety-five percent of the population can be hypnotized—give or take the odd timid psychopath."

"But does he want to be hypnotized?"

"He better had. You can't really hypnotize someone against their will. You need someone who is compliant, cooperative, and just a little fucked up. In fact, you'd be ideal, Nick. You ought to let me try it on you one day."

"From what we already know," Nick said, trying to change the subject, "do you think you'll find a psychiatric explanation for the crime?"

"I've found one already."

"Which is?"

"Brotherhood. You see, there's a popular misconception that rivalry between brothers is quite common. Well, it's not."

"Isn't it?"

"No. It's universal," Ann said. "That's why invariably a child's first reaction is to try to kill its newborn sibling. And it makes sense. One minute there you are, lord of all you can survey from your deluxe pottyette, when suddenly a ravenous wretch has attached itself to the teats of your favorite feeding place."

"The mother?" Nick asked, trying to catch up.

"You see, Nick, our instinct toward murder is inextricably linked to our instinct to survive. It's all about living space. What Adolf Hitler called *Lebensraum*."

"Where on earth did you study biology, Ann? Nuremberg?"

"Tunbridge Wells, actually. But I accept that it's not always easy to tell the difference. Come on," she said. "We've got a trance to induce in your murderer."

As Nick reached the cell, he saw the accused man. With his back to the door, the man was reading from the Bible. Nick strained his eyes and just managed to see that he was reading from the Old Testament.

The prisoner read aloud, "What has thou done? The voice of thy brother's blood cries out from the ground."

Nick knew the passage from the Book of Genesis. The story of Cain and Abel. But there was something more.

As the man read the passage, Nick was convinced that he was reading it in two different voices.

Chapter Eleven

Ann insisted that they did not disturb the man's Bible reading. A prison officer had done precisely that two days previously and had been attacked.

"I kind of knew his brother," she had said as they waited outside the cell.

"How?"

"Charles Turner did some research in the States while I was over there. He was famous—or infamous—for a while in this field."

"Forensic hypnotism?" Nick asked.

"No. Meddling with the mind. When he returned here under a cloud, he had to work for his father—no one else would have him."

"So," Nick said, finally understanding, "they were both—"

"Psychoanalysts. You know, people who aren't medically qualified who get paid an obscene amount of money for asking you about your hopes, fears, and memories of potty training."

"And you?"

"I tend to concentrate on the potty training. But these people were in private practice. There's stacks of money to be made from the psychotic mind. Never underestimate the money in madness."

"So why was Charles Turner notorious?"

"His father was originally American. Old family, East Coast, very conservative. Came here and made a fortune pandering to the neuroses of bored society wives—eased them through the Harrods sale, prepared them for the monstrous hats at Ascot. But when his father died, Charles turned the practice upside down. Made it a City practice. You know, executive cocaine heads with more money than nasal membrane."

"What's wrong with that?" Nick asked.

"He also experimented."

"So do you."

"Yes, but this guy did more experiments than Dr. Frankenstein. Only the monsters that Charles Turner was supposed to have created were not quite as lovable."

"Supposed?"

"The Institute of Analysts was about to strike him off last summer when . . . he disappeared. Case notes, tapes, documents, and all. Still, the prosecution have probably told you all this."

"Actually, Sally hasn't—"

"It was rumored he was using some twisted form of regression therapy."

"Which is?"

"Which is one way to abuse your patients, have sex with them, and make them take the guilt."

Nick glanced into the cell and the man closed the Bible, paused, and then opened it again and continued to read.

"Could the hypnosis go wrong?" Nick asked.

"Unlikely."

"Only I . . . I sort of heard something about this other side to him. A darker side." He didn't want to mention the prostitute to Ann, so kept it vague. "I was just thinking, couldn't we be releasing that part of him?"

"Conjuring up the dark side? Come on down, Mr. Hyde? Look, the only way to deal with it—if it exists—is to confront it."

"But that's precisely what I mean. Isn't it dangerous? Haven't there been cases where things have gone wrong?"

Ann paused. "I only know directly of one. When I was in the States. Shrink hypnotized this woman, something went wrong. She jumped at him and bit off his ear."

"What was he treating her for?"

"An eating disorder." She half smiled. "Well, that's how the story goes."

"What happened to the shrink?"

"Put it this way: He didn't need to buy Nicam stereo." She looked into the cell. "Bible study over. Come on."

Nick followed behind her with great reluctance. "I hope they've fed him," he said.

Ann Barnes took the prisoner's wrist and felt for his pulse. She looked him full in the eyes and smiled. Her forehead, Nick noticed, could have been no more than fifteen inches away from the patient's. She gently put the back of her hand on Will Turner's temple.

"What are you doing?" Nick whispered.

"Checking his temperature."

"Why use your hand?"

"Well, it was that or shove a thermometer up his bottom. And I wanted to spare your blushes, Nick, notwithstanding your expertise with your beloved rhythm method."

"Why not put the thermometer—"

"In his mouth? He might bite the end off and poison himself with mercury." She turned to the patient. "You're a little excited," she said. "I really want you to try to relax."

Nick did not see any response on the man's face.

"It's all right, Will. We're here to help you," Ann said. "You mustn't be frightened. All we want is to help you to remember what really happened. Is that okay?"

Again, Nick discerned no response. Before they had come in, he had asked Ann how she was going to induce the trance. She had told him that she really didn't need to. Will Turner had been walking around in a trance ever since he had reappeared.

"All right, Will. Everything is fine," she said. "We're going to try something a bit different now." She took the other hand as well and put the two of them in her lap. "I want you to open your eyes and look at this light," she said.

She took out what looked to Nick like a ballpoint pen with a soft beam in the end of it. Nick looked at it as Ann continued to talk in her gentlest tones, and only looked away when he began to feel drowsy himself.

"Concentrate on the light, Will," she said. "Concentrate on the light. There is no need to blink. In a while, your eyelids will begin to feel a little bit heavy. Take your time. There's no hurry at all. Your eyelids will begin to feel heavier and heavier. Then you might like to close them—only if that's what you want. Heavier and heavier, until they shut."

Will Turner's head began to move slowly from side to side and his pupils started to disappear. Then his head slumped forward, and his mouth fell open. A little saliva began to dribble from the corner. With a pulse of alarm, Nick saw the man's teeth. He couldn't forget Ann's story about the one-eared shrink.

"There is nothing to listen to but my voice, Will. Can you concentrate on it? Can you do that for me? That's good. You're doing fine, Will."

As she continued to speak, the man's limbs suddenly became rigid.

"What's happened?" Nick whispered.

"*Flexibilitas cerea,*" Ann replied.

"What on earth—"

"First level of hypnosis. Complete rigidity. A hard-on for the whole body. I've been out with several men who suffer from that." She turned her attention to the patient. "Let your breathing become deeper, Will. Feel the air filling your lungs. And then let it out slowly. In and out very slowly."

Then the man slumped forward. His body was suddenly flaccid. He seemed to be unconscious.

As Nick looked on fascinated, Ann's voice filled the room with gentle words and pleasant thoughts. But Nick was on edge; images of the mutilated corpse crowded into his brain.

The man began to sit up straighter. He pushed his shoulders back a little and closed his mouth.

"He's moved out of the flaccid level," Ann said. "Thank God. A flaccid man's about as useful as a bucket with a hole in it. Next stop the subconscious."

Nick whispered, "Can't he hear us?"

"Only when I speak directly to him," she replied. "He's on a trip, Nick. He's no longer here anymore. He's wandering off somewhere through his mind. Heaven knows where he is."

"What level are we on now?"

"The third. This is where the fun really starts." She winked at him and then turned back to the man. "Can you tell us where you are, Will?"

"I'm on a hill."

"And where is the hill?"

"I don't know. But it's very high and it's all white."

"Don't worry. It doesn't matter. What is the weather like?"

"Hot. It's summer."

"And are you alone?"

"Yes, I think—no, wait."

Ann leaned forward. "Who's there, Will?"

The man ignored her question and said, "Don't you know what's been going on?" He said this in a second voice. A cooler one, more precise, more clinical.

"What does the person look like?" Ann asked.

The man didn't appear to hear. "But I still love her . . . do it, then. Do it, I don't care, do it. We're too near the . . . we're going to—"

He let out a piercing yell that seemed to fill the room with something more than noise. Something worse, something horrific.

And though Will Turner had not moved a single inch, it had sounded to Nick as though the wretched man had been falling, an enormous distance, falling at great speed without reaching the bottom. But falling from where? And why?

Chapter Twelve

Being late for court was the professional nightmare that Nick dreamed about most. And on the Friday of that week, on the day he was supposed to make the second bail application on behalf of Will Turner, he ran down the Old Bailey corridors breathless. Mr. Justice Cromwell would be furious. He was fifteen minutes late.

The previous night, he had not been able to sleep owing to the session with Ann Barnes and his client, which had left him with a nagging sense of doubt. What if everyone had made an awful mistake? The assumption was that the deranged defendant had murdered his brother. What if that was wrong?

Will Turner's bail application was scheduled for 10:15 A.M. As Nick scurried out of the robing room, the bleep on his plastic watch sounded half past the hour. He ran faster, once dropping his papers and twice catching his gown on door handles.

When he finally reached the corridor Cromwell's court was situated in, he had a moment of intense panic.

"Where on earth is my wig?" he said, loud enough for anyone in the vicinity to hear. He frantically thought back through his movements, trying to remember where he could possibly have left it. "Where *is* the wretched thing?"

"On your head." The voice was smooth, the assured voice of a woman who always catches the waiter's eye, who can always hail a cab. "Just calm down," she said. "It's on your head."

Nick reached feverishly for his hair, again dropping the copy of the notice of application for bail. When he was satisfied that his head was indeed crowned with thick horsehair, he looked at the woman.

She was dressed in an expensive suit that was obviously made by a fancy designer like Chanel. It was Liz Turner.

"Hadn't you better hurry?" she said. "Won't the judge be waiting?"

"What on earth are you doing here?"

"I came to see you . . . perform, Nick."

"You can't go into court. Bail applications are private sessions."

"Actually, I came to see you, Nick."

He surveyed her face, the smile, the moist lips accentuated by lipstick, the slightly affected breathlessness of her speech.

"What's going on here?" he asked.

"I suppose I am allowed to stand surety for my husband, am I, Mr. Downes? Even if the unworthy wretch did leave me?"

Nick did not answer. He fought with the contradictory emotions racing through his body. In truth, he *was* secretly pleased to see Liz. What was happening to him?

"Shall we try to get my husband out of the clink?"

She started to walk toward the wooden doors of the court. She reached the sign hung across the handles: NO ENTRY—JUDGE IN CHAMBERS.

She blinked very slowly so that for a moment her eyelashes seemed to mesh. "You'll have to tear yourself away from me, Mr. Downes. You're meant to be trying to free my husband. Remember?"

Inside, the court was already in session. Sally was on her feet and addressing the judge. Nick did not look at her, nor did he look at Cromwell. He dumped his papers and stood up.

"I must apologize to you, M'Lord, for—"

"Don't interrupt," the judge snarled. "Miss Fielding and I were just speculating on what possible excuse you could have. We came to the conclusion that there could be none. Is that right, Mr. Downes?"

Nick did not know what he could say. What would the judge have made of the truth? I haven't been able to sleep, M'Lord, as I think that there might have been a dreadful mistake. I think that my client might be innocent. Do you remember innocence, M'Lord? It's that thing we're born with. It's what we read about in legal textbooks but are never supposed to meet in practice.

"Do you have any excuse, Mr. Downes?" the judge asked again.

Nick opened his mouth, thought again about lying, but desisted when he saw Sally. He said, "No, M'Lord. I do apologize."

"You should also apologize to Miss Fielding. She's been inconvenienced, too."

Sally looked well. The bags under her eyes had gone and even her hair seemed to shine. Life away from Nick obviously suited her. Yes, he thought, I should apologize to Miss Fielding for walking out of my life. I should really apologize to her for moving in with my best friend.

"These things happen, M'Lord," Sally said, sitting down.

"Are you reapplying for bail, Mr. Downes?" The blood was starting to drain from the veins on Cromwell's scalp.

"Yes," said Nick. "There has been a change of circumstances."

Sally shot to her feet. "Yes, there have been several important changes recently. The *situation* has changed radically."

"May I have a moment with m'learned friend, M'Lord?" Nick asked. The judge nodded. Then Nick moved right up to Sally's earlobe. He could smell perfume. But it was no longer the one he had bought her. This fragrance was new, more expensive. Probably a present from Max. "Just cut out the innuendos, will you?" he said.

"What do you mean, Nick?"

"All this 'recent changes' stuff. You left me, but I'm a big boy. I can cope with that—but not with the lies. Are you sleeping with Max?"

"What does he say?"

"He won't confirm or deny it."

"Well, I'm not sleeping with him."

"Not yet?" Nick asked.

"Not yet."

"Can we get on?" demanded Cromwell.

Nick shuffled his papers once more. "M'Lord, we now know who the defendant is."

"And your best point *was* that there was no connection between him and the victim? Is that still the position?"

"Not quite," said Nick.

"So what is the connection?"

"Umbilical," Nick said. "They're brothers."

The judge threw down his pencil. "Perhaps I've missed something. But how does that improve your position?"

"It doesn't," Nick said.

"Then why mention it?"

"Because it's the truth."

"The *what?*"

"The truth, M'Lord. I suppose my main point is that the defendant's wife is outside the court."

Cromwell picked up the pencil again, standing it on its end ready for its next launch. "So you're going to tell me that your client has a home to go to?"

"No," said Nick. "They're separated."

"Mr. Downes, is this a serious application?"

"Deadly serious."

"On what basis?"

"On the basis that my client is very probably innocent. You remember innocence, M'Lord?" Nick muttered sotto voce.

The judicial veins throbbed, the official pencil teetered on the launchpad, but before a syllable could emerge from the open mouth, Nick spoke again. "You see, Mr. Turner has relived the incident."

"Relived?"

"Under hypnosis."

"Oh, yes," said the judge. "That well-known and reliable technique."

"No," said Nick, not rising to the sarcasm. "It's not reliable at all. In fact, it's very unreliable and—"

"Dangerous?"

"Yes, and very dangerous. In fact, forensic hypnosis is in its infancy."

"Infancy, Mr. Downes? It hasn't yet emerged from the forensic womb," the judge said. "It hasn't even been conceived. It's still a glint in the psychiatrist's eye."

"Yes, M'Lord. But we've had the defendant produced from the prison. He's downstairs in the cells. Dr. Barnes is going to hypnotize him again as soon as Your Lordship rises. Unless, that is, Your Lordship grants him bail."

The judge was speechless and gawped at Nick in the way that Native Indians must have looked at the first Europeans as they strutted into the Americas with piles of glass beads and a multitude of fatal diseases.

Sally cleared her throat. "The Crown still objects to bail, M'Lord."

"On what basis, Miss Fielding?" The judge's words were barely audible.

"The bones found with the corpse are *genus rodentia.*"

"What did you say they were?"

Sally pulled her gown around her shoulders. "I didn't, not exactly. They're from the suborder *Myomorpha,* we think."

"Of course they are," Cromwell replied.

"Well, forty percent of all mammals are rodents, so it's not been an easy job."

The judge put his chin in his hands. "Have you ever felt that you've chosen the wrong profession, Miss Fielding?"

Sally looked at her feet. Nick noticed that she licked her lips repeatedly and they were beginning to chafe. This was like the old days. Perhaps she wasn't doing as well as she had tried to make out? He enjoyed seeing her sore lips.

Cromwell asked, "What possible significance can a pile of rat remains have?"

Sally's tongue undertook a quick tour of her mouth. Nick saw her jaw drop open, but just as she was about to speak the doors of the court were flung open.

"The court is in private session," bellowed the judge at the figure that ran into the court toward Nick. "The public is not admitted."

The woman tugged at Nick's gown and pleaded with him. "You've got to come. You've got to come."

"Who is this woman?" demanded Cromwell.

"Oh, this is the defendant's wife," Nick said in his politest tone, as Liz Turner dragged him from the court.

Chapter Thirteen

By the time Nick had been let into the cell area, the prison officers had stopped trying to remove the ligature by hand.

"Someone's gone for a knife," the supervising officer told him.

Will Turner looked strangely at peace as he hung from a latch on the outside of the cell door. At least, his expression from the neck up was peaceful. Nick even imagined that he had a faint grin on his face.

But it was different beneath the laceration in his neck. Beneath the . . . what was it exactly? Nick wondered. A piece of cord? A tie? It was difficult to tell with the blood. From the neck down, the man's body struggled for air. The chest heaved, the arms flailed about. It was as if there were two men trapped inside, Nick thought, just as Ann Barnes had said. One wanting to live and the other . . . smiling, waiting quietly for death.

"Don't know how it could have happened," the officer said. "None of my men have ever left the door open before. We stick to the Home Office guidelines."

Nick looked at Will's feet and how, given the tightness of the ligature, they barely touched the ground.

"I don't know what that thing is," the officer said. He was clearly distressed and pointed to the knot over Will's neck.

But Nick knew. He looked at the scars on the man's wrists where the bandages had once been and wondered whether he had cut his veins with just this in mind.

He also wondered if Will would die, and then he felt sad as he was beginning to look forward to the trial. He was beginning to think that he could save Will, if only he would live.

Then there was the unmistakable odor of cigarettes and the tap-tap of heels.

"Get out of my way, you idiots." Ann Barnes pushed the group of prison staff aside. "Anyone would think you hadn't seen a suicide attempt before."

The senior officer shook his head foolishly. Ann thrust her briefcase into his midriff and, while he held it, she rummaged around and pulled out her scissors.

"Hold his feet," she shouted at Nick.

As he obeyed, she began to cut at the ligature with the scissors, the blades gnawing away at the bandage like the incisors of a small animal. Nick didn't dare look at the blood. He felt the weight of the body in his hands; the bottom of the trousers for some reason felt damp. Then he opened his eyes.

"Panic over," Ann said.

Nick placed the body on the floor and was confronted with Will Turner's face. His tongue was blue and protruded through the gaps in his teeth. The smile had gone.

"I think he'll live," Ann said. "Anyone got a fag?"

There will be a trial after all, Nick thought. And then it will be up to me to save him.

When Nick finally reached the public area of the Old Bailey, he spotted Liz Turner going into a conference room.

Even before he followed her in, Nick could hear her suppressed sobs. There was a dim light in the room, casting half-shadows. He shut the heavy door behind him so that no one could see in.

"I'm not crying," she said without looking up.

"It's all right to cry," he replied. "They're taking him to hospital. He's going to live."

"He must hate me."

"You don't know that."

"Everyone hates me." Again she sobbed.

"No, they don't." He looked at the beautiful, distressed face, saw the convulsing soft body. "I . . . I don't hate you," he said.

"You're just saying that to shut me up. You can go, you know. You're my husband's barrister. You're paid to look after him, not me."

Before he quite knew what he was doing, he took her hands. "Liz, look at me. I don't hate you."

"You've never called me Liz before," she said, trying to smile, but sniffing at the same time.

She slipped her arms around his neck. She appeared to him to be helpless and vulnerable and sad.

She kissed him once on the cheek.

"Liz," he protested.

"I like it when you call me Liz."

He could feel her firm breasts pressed against his chest. The flesh moved a little as she breathed. Her crotch was pressed into his, and he could feel the warmth building between them, increasing as he hardened.

"Promise to call me Liz," she whispered, her warm breath on his neck, making his head roll backward with anticipation.

His hands slid down her smooth back. He traced the swell of her hips, and she pressed into him more firmly.

He ran his hands down the outside of her thighs, and she let out a slight moan. When he reached the bottom of her skirt, he slid his fingers underneath and felt the top of her stockings. Her skin was so smooth and warm that Nick could barely contain himself.

"Should we be doing this?" she asked.

"No."

"Good."

"Liz—"

"You know," she said. "Ever since I saw your photo in that chambers brochure, I *knew* . . ."

Then she kissed him, her tongue reaching deeply into his mouth, ravenous, frantic, and he didn't care. So Sally was going to sleep with Max? Well, here he was with Liz.

She quickly dropped her hands to his trousers and ran her fingers over the hardness, sometimes barely touching his penis, driving him crazy.

He couldn't last any longer and felt he was sure to come. But suddenly she took her fingers away, making Nick ache desperately.

"You don't want me to stop, do you, Nick?" she whispered.

He shook his head.

"You don't want me to stop at all."

PART II
APRIL

I am the self-consumer of my woes—
They rise and vanish . . . like shadows

John Clare

Chapter One

On an overcast Monday in April when the trial began, Nick arrived at the Old Bailey early. He was worried sick about Will Turner's case. What possible defense could he put up? And if he could find one, who would possibly believe it?

He turned past Ludgate Circus and strolled slowly along Old Bailey. He paused when he came to the austere gray walls of the Central Criminal Court. He knew that he would find Will Turner in there, and the witnesses and a jury, but he had serious doubts as to whether he would also find the truth about why the body had been buried in a shallow grave.

In the intervening three months, he had arranged to see Liz Turner twice, and on both occasions she had stood him up. He did not know what to make of it. Perhaps he was not supposed to—and perhaps that was part of Liz's attraction, the cycle of drawing him close and then moving away, the rhythm of it, the anticipation.

As he reached the glass security doors, he bumped into Sally. She was still down to prosecute.

"How are you?" he asked. He knew that she was still living with Max.

"Is that meant to be sarcastic, Nick?"

"No," he replied. He put his wig-tin through the X-ray machine, a conveyor belt with a metal housing and a VDU, then placed his keys in a bowl on top of the device and stepped through the arch of the metal detector. It reminded him that Ann Barnes had said that it was easier to get on a flight to Israel with a suitcase full of Semtex and Saddam Hussein's autobiography than to get into the Old Bailey.

"I just don't know how you could be so insensitive, Nick," Sally whispered. One of the security guards rummaged through her handbag even though it had not set off the machine.

"Insensitive? In what sort of way?" he asked.

"Oh, I don't know. In having Max as your junior on the case sort of way."

"What's wrong with that?"

"Why have Max?"

"Thought we should keep it in the family, Sals."

"You're impossible."

"And Max is family, isn't he?" Nick paused. He saw that Sally was clearly upset and in a perverse way he took solace from the fact that he could still affect her emotions.

He continued, "Actually, it was the solicitor's choice, not mine. I had no say in the matter. If I had, I would probably have gone for someone who wasn't sleeping with my girlfriend. But I don't know—perhaps I'm just being touchy."

Sally snatched her bag from the intrigued guard. "Had a good look? Haven't you seen a tampon before? What is it with men and women's handbags?"

"Where is Max, by the way?" Nick asked.

"Still in bed."

"Your bed?"

"The one I share with him, Nick. There. Are you satisfied? Do you want to make me feel like a tart or something?"

"No." So it had finally happened. They had finally formed the beast with two backs in the dacha in Dulwich.

"Then what did you want?" Sally asked.

"To talk to you."

"Why?"

"I miss you."

"And why is that?"

"Things are different without you."

"What's different?"

"Everything. Life. Me."

"Are you having a nervous breakdown, Nick?"

He did not reply. Sally headed for the Bar Mess at the top of the building. Nick headed for the cells at the very bottom. He went to see Will Turner.

Nick was admitted to the cells below the Old Bailey by the new head jailer, a man known as Jo, who had replaced the unfortunate officer who had allowed Will Turner to attempt suicide.

It was said that Jo had once been in the Rhodesian Colonial Prison Service, having been rejected by the South African Police on the grounds that he was too violent.

"You the brief for that nutter?" he asked as Nick was signed in.

Nick nodded.

"Well, you better tell your fellah. No one hangs themselves in my nick. Not without my permission. Understand?"

"I'll try to remember," Nick said. "He has to ask your permission."

The man grunted some kind of a reply.

As the jailer led him to one of the visiting rooms, Nick turned and inspected the thick-set man. His hair was so closely cropped that it revealed the rolls of fat on the back of his neck, and his uniform was bursting at the seams.

"I was just wondering," Nick said. "Why does anyone join the Prison Service? I mean, it couldn't be for the uniforms."

"Me? I like locking people up," Jo said. He screamed to his staff down the corridor, "Bring down that nutter, if he hasn't hung himself again."

While they waited for Will, the jailer asked, "You sure you want to be in that room with him?"

"Why not?" Nick replied.

"He's Cat. A, isn't he? A major loon. Premier-league psycho stuff."

"He's presumed innocent," Nick insisted.

"There's something you better know, then."

The jailer paused, and Nick could not decide if the hesitation was motivated by a cheap sense of melodrama or an impending breach of confidence.

"Last few weeks in the Heath," Jo continued, "he's been doing things."

"Such as?"

"Attacking people. Prison staff."

"I'm his barrister."

"Well, make sure he remembers that. Just as well he's got nothing against you, isn't it?"

Nick instantly thought about Liz Turner. What would Will do if he knew? But what was there to know? He hadn't actually slept with the woman.

The visiting room Nick waited in was a little oblong space with a glass door and a tawdry carpet. At about 9:30, Will Turner came in.

"How are you feeling?" Nick asked. He scanned his client's eyes for any trace of hostility.

The man did not answer. He sat down at the table, which was covered in graffiti. "We need to talk, Mr. Downes."

"About what?"

"About what's really going on."

Nick tensed. "I can explain."

Suddenly Will grabbed his arm. "About the murder charge I face."

"Oh, that. Is there a problem?" Relief rushed through his body like a blast of oxygen. "I thought we'd discussed all the risks."

There had been two further conferences at Wormwood Heath, and it was on each of those occasions that he had arranged to see Liz Turner afterward.

"Why should I bother fighting this case?" Will asked.

"Because you're innocent," Nick said. "I know this sounds strange coming from a lawyer, but innocence does count for something."

"For what?"

"For what is right. If you say that the truth is you didn't murder your brother, then you must plead not guilty."

The man went to the glass door. Outside, Jo was studying the fantasy football game in one of the tabloids.

Will turned to face him. "Have you seen my wife?"

"Seen?"

"Yes, have you seen her?"

"Well, I was meant to see her a couple of times." Then he added swiftly, "But she didn't show up."

"She's always been unreliable," Will said. "But do you like her?" Before Nick could reply, he continued, "I'm glad, Mr. Downes. I knew that you two would get on." He looked carefully at Nick. "You do get on, don't you?"

"Yes," said Nick. "We do get on."

"I'm pleased," he said. "You two are my tower of strength. With you two on my side, I might just be able to cope. A lot of women would have turned their backs, abandoned me. But Liz isn't that type. She's only ever rejected me once, you know."

"When was that?"

"When I first proposed. I don't think she'll reject me again."

This made Nick uneasy. Should he tell Will what had happened between them? That would be the honest thing to do. But what had actually happened? Perhaps he had misconstrued things. He was good at misconstruing things; a failed relationship with Sally had taught him that.

And perhaps Liz's actions had been the understandable response of an hysterical spouse after a suicide attempt? He would have to ask Ann Barnes. He had seen a lot of Ann while she had been compiling her psychiatric report on Will Turner.

"What happened when you met my wife?" Will asked. "I bet you've been putting your heads together."

It was Nick's turn not to reply.

"You know," said Will, "comparing notes about my defense. I can't thank you enough."

Suddenly Nick felt an awful lot worse. He had to try to disguise his guilt, to mask his embarrassment. So he adopted the only strategy his profession had taught him: He asked questions.

"Don't answer this if you can't, Mr. Turner," he said. "But why did you have problems with your wife?"

"Liz and I wanted kids. But we couldn't seem to—it was my fault. Liz's very . . . Catholic. No birth control and all that. I was so ashamed, it was all my fault."

"Didn't you ever get yourself medically tested?"

"Liz did. And there was nothing wrong with her. I was the problem. I was infertile."

Nick wondered: If this was the source of the problem between them, why had Liz been so reluctant to say so?

Jo came in at ten o'clock. He said that he would have to take Will up to court. But Nick needed more time. He sensed that Will wanted to say something. When the jailer had closed the glass door, he sat down at the table.

"You know, murder trials aren't as bad as people believe them to be. Basically, a murder is an assault that goes wrong. People make an awful fuss about it because someone has died. But very often the victim means nothing to the jury and . . . sometimes little more to the accused."

"The victim was my brother."

"Well, yes. There is that in your case. But the jury won't have any idea of what your brother was like."

"All they need do is look at me."

"What I meant was, they won't know whether he was a good man or—"

"He was my brother, Mr. Downes."

"Yes, but they might think . . . I don't know, that he, well, that he—"

"Deserved to die?"

"That's not what I said."

"But it's what you meant."

"It's just about the oldest defense to murder, Will. Good riddance to bad rubbish. He won't be here to defend himself. You can say what you like about him."

"But I loved him."

Nick thought of Sally. At that moment, he imagined, she

would be upstairs putting on her robes. For an instant, he could smell her perfume, and then he realized that she was now wearing a different fragrance. The one that Max had given her.

Then he said, "The people you love can sometimes hurt you, Will. Any jury will understand that."

The defendant got up from the table. He turned sharply and began to pace to the back of the room.

"Charles never hurt me," he said.

"Not that you can remember?"

"He never hurt me."

"But how do you know?"

"I just do. I might have lost parts of my memory. I might even have lost my mind. But I haven't lost my sense of decency."

"Meaning?"

"Meaning that I shouldn't slander a dead man."

"How did he get on with your wife?"

"Well, he introduced her to me. He kept going on about this fantastic new receptionist he wanted to make his PA. I insisted on meeting her immediately."

"But surely he'd known her before he employed her?" Nick asked.

"No. As soon as he got Liz, I met her."

"And this was—"

"Just over five years before . . . it happened."

"Are you sure it wasn't *eight* years?" Nick was pretty certain that was the figure Liz had given him.

"It's my wife we're talking about, Mr. Downes. I think I should know."

"But how do you actually know all this?"

"Some of it I vaguely remember."

"And the rest?"

"My wife told me."

Nick stood up. "Well, do you also know that your brother was about to be disciplined? For professional misconduct?"

"So?"

"So we can use it to discredit him—if we need to."

"I forbid you to do that," the defendant said. "Under *any* circumstances."

Outside, Nick could hear the main door to the cell area opening and closing as lawyers left their clients and went up to court.

Looking around the visiting room, he recognized a scene he had watched in many films. Brilliant young lawyer and wrongly accused client deciding how to establish the defendant's innocence. In films, it was always so easy.

But Nick was not brilliant. And he was no longer young. And he only went to trial if he couldn't persuade his client to plead guilty. The reason was simple. Trying cases was simply that: trying. It drained Nick in a hundred different ways. And this case, he knew, would be worse. But he wanted to fight it. He wanted to fight Sal—if only Will Turner would agree.

"If you pleaded guilty, where would that leave us?" he asked Will.

"You without a trial and me with a life sentence."

"Is that what you want?"

"That's what is right."

"But how do you know, Will? How can we ever possibly know what is right? You remember so little about the actual incident, and . . ."

He stopped when he saw Will Turner sitting motionless, as if assessing the past, weighing his crimes and the punishments that should follow.

"Look," Nick said. "At least make the prosecution prove your guilt."

"I won't say I'm innocent."

"You won't have to. The law presumes you're innocent."

"Even if I don't?"

"Even if you don't."

"It's a little odd," Will Turner said.

"It's called justice," Nick replied. "Come on. The judge will be waiting."

Chapter Two

"Members of the jury," Sally began, "I appear for the Crown to prosecute this case. The defendant, Mr. Turner, is represented by m'learned friend Mr. Downes. His junior, Mr. Baptiste, is not at present with us."

Well, he was in bed with you, Nick thought. What have you done with him? Behind Sally was a young pupil barrister. She was sitting in to take a note while Sally's junior in the case, Joshua Smith, was appearing before the Court of Appeal.

Sally continued, "This, ladies and gentlemen, is a most extraordinary case. It is about a murder. But it is more than that. It is about a murder as old as the Bible itself. It is brother killing brother, what is sometimes called fratricide.

"When one person murders another, a stranger, it is an awful thing. But when a father kills a child or a brother kills a brother, we are struck with horror, for it violates the most natural of bonds, that which we hold sacred."

Nick looked around Court 8. It was in the new part of the building. The Bailey, with its numerous courts, was the great megastore of criminal justice. And the new courtrooms with their stripped wood and spongy seats were very similar to the sitting rooms of the show houses in the dockland developments just along the river.

"But this is not a simple matter of who killed who," Sally said. "In this case, even if you decide that the man in the dock did indeed kill the deceased, Charles Turner, you must decide another matter. What you have to resolve is, at the time of the killing, was the defendant in full control of his faculties, or was his responsibility impaired?"

Just then Max sauntered into court. He sat in the row behind Nick.

"Sorry I'm late," he whispered.

Nick did not respond. There was a smell he recognized on Max's breath. It was Sally.

Standing to Nick's right, looking straight at the jury and seemingly oblivious to the two men at her side, Sally continued.

She said, "Any matters of law you will take from the learned judge." She tilted her head toward the figure on the Bench at the front of the court. Cromwell sat in his red gown with his beetroot face and blunt pencil. "The law we will be considering," Sally said, "is the law of diminished responsibility. Whether the defendant's judgment was impaired. But I don't want you to be put off by all the technicalities."

Nick had just served a faxed copy of Ann Barnes's psychiatric assessment of the defendant on the prosecution. It was very late, and Sally could object, but it provided the vestiges of a defense.

However, Nick was thinking of other things. His imagination was rioting. Could he really smell Sally all over Max, or was he dreaming it? Since she had left him, all his senses seemed to have been working overtime. It was as if every part of his body felt the loss and was protesting. And it was getting worse.

"In essence," said Sally, "this case is about what was going on in this man's mind. Did he merely make errors of judgment? Or was there a motive? Did he act with malice? Is he a murderer?"

After Sally had been speaking for twenty minutes, she took a sip of water. Nick knew that she was reaching the nub of her opening speech.

"If the defendant was wholly in control," she said, "then he is no more and no less than a cold-blooded murderer. But if he was ill, then you will only find him guilty of manslaughter by way of diminished responsibility."

"Why were you late?" Nick whispered to Max.

"I overslept, so I drove in after Sally left. But the car broke down."

"You don't have a car."

"It was Sally's."

"No, Max. It was mine."

"Sorry, I forgot."

"You might have had the decency to lie," Nick said. "You could have said the tube was delayed or something."

"Is lying suddenly decent, Nick?"

"Is sleeping with Sally?" Nick was by now angry, and his voice had risen. "I only lent it to her for a few days, to move. I want it back."

Sally had heard the rumblings to her side. She used one of the old hack barrister's ploys. "I think m'learned friend wishes to object to some part of my speech," she said as she sat down.

"Is this right, Mr. Downes?" Cromwell bellowed.

Nick scrambled to his feet. "No, M'Lord," he replied.

"Well, I could hear you muttering something from up here."

"I was discussing a matter of law—and ethics—with m'learned junior," Nick said.

"Well then, your rudeness is matched only by your bad timing."

"Yes, M'Lord," Nick said, and sat down.

"May I just have a moment to speak to m'friends?" Sally asked the judge. She moved a pace to her left, and the two of them leaned to their right, away from the jury. "Can't you two stop bickering? You're not barristers, you're just pathetic little boys," she said. "Save it for the break, will you?"

She adjusted her wig and continued. "So what is the evidence against the defendant?" she said. "There is a confession, a body, and a brothel. But not necessarily in that order."

The jury sat riveted to her gentle tones. Nick looked up be-

hind him. The public gallery, high above the court, was only
half full. And that was fitting, he thought. This was only half a
trial. He looked at the dock. There was Will Turner, head in
hand, scar tissue where the bandages had once been. Little
memory, little hope, little more than half a man.

"The defendant first confessed to killing someone when he
was in a brothel in Queensway," Sally said. "The prosecution
will call the lady, a complete stranger, to whom the defendant
had paid money to have sex. But, as importantly, found on the
defendant was a claw hammer. The dimensions of the head of
the hammer matched some of the wounds to the body."

Cromwell tapped his pencil on the Bench. "You haven't really
explained the body, Miss Fielding."

"Your Lordship is absolutely correct. I'm skipping ahead.
The crucial piece of evidence, members of the jury, is that the
defendant spoke of where they could find a body. It was buried
in a chalk quarry in Kent. But here was the extraordinary
thing. The body had been covered in lime. Normally the effect
of this is to dissolve the human frame. But the wrong type of
quicklime had been chosen."

"Or perhaps," Nick whispered to Max, "the right type."

"What do you mean?" Max asked.

Sally again glanced at the two of them. "The effect of the
lime in this case was to preserve the body tolerably well."

"Thirty-nine Hilldrop Crescent," Nick said quietly.

"I thought it was found at a quarry," Max replied.

"No, Hilldrop Crescent was where the remains were found."

"In this case?"

"No. In Doctor Crippen—"

"You're never playing Monsters," Max said. "Not *now*."

"The remains of Crippen's wife were discovered because he
used the wrong lime."

"What's your point?"

"My point is, Max, perhaps someone wanted Charles Turner's
body to be found. Perhaps someone was preserving it."

Chapter Three

On the evening of the first day, Nick and Max went to Devlin's to talk tactics. There was much they had to discuss. They sat in their usual position in the wine bar, but there was no Armagnac, just a cheap South African Riesling that Max had bought. When half the bottle was consumed, Max began to speak.

"I'm sorry about the car, Nick."

Nick continued to drink the slate-colored wine with its petrol-like finish. He felt sure that Max had chosen this grape on purpose.

"Nick, I said that I'm sorry about . . . well, about all of this. I don't want you to take it personally. It's just one of—"

"Let's confine ourselves to the conduct of the case, shall we?"

"Why?"

"Because our personal conduct so rarely bears scrutiny, Max. Pass the Pretoria plonk."

More of the wine was consumed. It seemed to Nick to taste even cheaper. The bar was crowded as it always was during a week when the legal term was in full swing. Barristers in dark suits boasted to other barristers in suits of a similar darkness. The haircuts were even the same. Clean hair, clean nails—it was only the consciences, Nick thought, that weren't always so clean.

"Better look the other way," Max said suddenly.

"What do you mean?"

"The opposition."

Sally had walked into Devlin's.

Max made a face that was halfway between a grin and a wince. "Wouldn't do to be seen liaising with the opposition, Nick."

"But sleeping with her is fine?"

"We can't talk to each other anymore."

"Oh, we can talk all right. It's just not very pleasant."

"You know, I can see why Sally left you, Nick."

"And why is that?"

"Because you're a self-pitying son of a bitch."

"If we don't pity ourselves, Max, I don't think there will be anyone else to do it for us."

Sally came over with an empty glass. "Found a defense yet, boys?"

"We're talking tactics, Sally," Max said. "You'd better go."

"No," Nick said. "There are one or two things we all have to thrash out. Take a seat, Sals. Help yourself to some petrol."

Sally sat down, sandwiching Max between herself and Nick.

"I thought Cromwell was a little harsh with you," she said.

"That's the nobility for you," Nick replied.

"Nobility?"

"Mr. Justice Cromwell. Sir John. Not so much the noble savage as the savage nobleman. It's a little like evolution in reverse. What do you call that?"

"Devolution?" Max suggested.

"No," said Nick. "Decay."

"It's very easy to knock the authorities, Nick." Max seemed annoyed. "Cromwell is a member of the Knights of the Realm. You, on the other hand, are a member of Queens Park Rangers supporters' club."

"Since when did you support the colonial powers, Max?"

"Since the Brits left and the military took over my country, actually."

Nick looked at the empty bottle. "Another bottle of Rhodesian Riesling?"

"It's South African," Max said.

Nick went to the bar alone. A few minutes later, as he was returning, he noticed Max and Sally in heated argument. It made him feel good to know that he was not alone in being able to provoke Sally.

He sat down and said, "I was a little surprised that you didn't ask for an adjournment, Sally."

"Why should we do that?"

"Well, don't you want to instruct your own expert to deal with Turner's psychiatric state?"

"Why should we?"

"No real reason," Nick said, "except that it's the only issue in the case."

"The facts speak for themselves. And I was hardly taken by surprise by your expert evidence."

"We did serve it very late. I'm astonished you didn't object to Ann Barnes's report."

"There's always time," Sally said. "It's never too late to object to Ann Barnes."

The crowd in Devlin's swelled, and so did the tales of forensic brilliance. It was a typical evening in the wine bar.

Nick could sense that Max and Sally wanted to leave.

"You can leave together, you know," he said. "I can handle it."

"Where's the car parked, Max?" Sally asked.

"In some police pound."

"What?"

"Well, it sort of broke down on the way in from Dulwich."

"So where exactly is it?" she asked.

"In Lewisham police station. We'll have to go there on the way home."

"I hate to intrude on this domestic bliss," Nick said. "But can I make a suggestion?"

"What is it?" Sally snapped.

"Accept a plea of guilty to manslaughter by way of diminished responsibility."

"I thought you had something useful to say, Nick."

"It is useful. Well, to my client. It's on the table now. Manslaughter, and I'll give you the money for a taxi to South London."

Sally stood up and looked at Max, who also stood up immediately. "Look, Nick," she said. "We've got the whore and we've got the hammer. Turner's confessed in a very clinical way. He's not mad, Nick. He's evil. He's a dangerous man and he's going to go to prison for the rest of his life."

"Is that a no?" Nick asked.

Sally started to leave. Then she turned around and hissed, "Are you coming, Max?"

Max left with her.

Through the window, Nick could see them hailing a cab to rescue his car from Lewisham police station. He poured himself another glass of the Riesling, which seemed to smell even more strongly of petrol.

While he drank, he pondered Will Turner's loyalty to his dead brother. Why would he not allow Nick to blacken Charles Turner's name with the professional misconduct? He thought about the decaying corpse and the difference between premeditated murder and reckless manslaughter. It was put into some sort of perspective by the quotation on the table mat in front of him.

It makes no great difference to the person slain whether
he fell by one kind of homicide or another—
the classification is for the advantage of the lawyers.

When Nick arrived at Bayswater tube station, he popped into a late-night drugstore along Queensway. He bought himself a packet of cheese and onion crisps and a secondhand tape of Tammy Wynette's greatest hits. Then he inspected the noticeboard.

He had worked his way up the waiting list of brothels and
bric-à-brac stores that wanted to advertise. He looked again at
his card appealing for information about the cat. No one had
yet contacted him. He had been living alone now for about
three months. It did not seem to get any better. Each evening
he would return to an empty house, and he did not want to get
used to that.

The streets were comparatively quiet. Monday must be a bad
night for the vice business, he thought, just as it is for restaurants. One or two young girls stood in the shop doorways, but
they were silent. Cars occasionally slowed down, had a look,
and then accelerated away. No one seemed to have their heart in
it.

When he reached the crossroads that led to his block, he
heard a voice.

"Thought I might see you here," the woman said.

Nick looked round. "I can't speak to you."

It was Jackie, the prostitute.

"But I can speak to you," she replied.

"No, you can't. You're a witness in the case."

"Witness? To what?"

"The man told you where the body was to be found."

"Listen, honey. In my job, I know where lots of skeletons are
buried."

"But the prosecution are going to call you tomorrow," Nick
insisted.

"They can call all they like. That doesn't mean I'm going to
come."

"Don't be foolish. They can have you arrested."

"I've been arrested before. Goes with the territory."

"They'll send the police."

"What? A few boys in uniforms with handcuffs? I think I'll
be able to handle it. Anyway, you representing the mystery
man?"

"It's no mystery anymore." Nick offered the woman his last
crisp. She declined. Then he said, "You know, we could get into
all sorts of trouble if anyone were to see us."

"Oh, try to live a little dangerously for once, honey."

"I could be done for perverting."

"Perverting a prostitute? That's a laugh."

"No. Perverting the course of justice."

"And how is the . . . the course of justice or whatever?"

"Well, it never seems to run smooth. My man is in terrible trouble."

"Aren't we all? But I could see it on his face the moment he came in that time. He had *that* look."

"And what look is that?"

Jackie glanced up and down the street. "The same one you have. Come on, I'll walk you home. It's a dangerous area."

As the two of them started to walk along Queensway, Nick asked, "Is that a good look or a bad one?"

"Well, it ain't much fucking good."

"I see," he said.

"I don't think you do." The woman hitched up her right stocking and licked her lips. "You see, Mr. Nobody was asking for it as soon as he came in."

"What do you mean?"

"I think he wanted to be punished."

"But why?"

"Well, don't ask me. I'm just the woman in the blond wig, remember?"

"I never thought that. I've got nothing against—"

"Like hell. If you respected me, you would never have come to my place that time. If men really respected women, they would never go to those places any of the time. But they come all right. All night and all day they come."

"What did you mean, he wanted to be punished?"

"You've basically got two types of punter who go to a domina."

"To a what?"

"To a strict mistress for correction. Watch the dogshit."

"Thanks," Nick said as he skirted the obstacle. "Two types?"

The woman tightened the belt around her waist. The studs

scraped as the buckle moved over them. "Them who enjoys the pain and them who enjoys it when it stops."

"Aren't they much the same thing?" Nick asked.

"Want me to show you?"

"Perhaps not."

"But I just knew that your man wanted to be punished. It was as if he had so much pain in his head he thought it would burst."

"And the punishment?"

"Would make it go away, I suppose. Or block it out."

Nick turned and put the empty packet in a Keep Britain Tidy bin. As he dropped it he saw two rats feeding off a partially eaten hamburger in the bottom of the bin.

When he turned back, he thought he saw the reflection of the woman in a shopfront. But it was just a dummy. The woman had gone.

He strolled the fifty yards to his mansion block. The street door was open. Kenny, the porter, was not at his station, and Nick was delighted. Sitting just inside the entrance, looking frightened and hungry, was the tabby cat.

On the seventh floor, there was a note stuck to Nick's door. Putting the cat in the kitchen, he returned to read it.

Dear Nick,
I need to see you. Desperately.
Meet me in the Old Bailey canteen. Don't let me down.
Love, Liz.
(I miss you)

He was puzzled, not only by the contents of the note, but by its very existence. For he had never given Liz his address.

Chapter Four

"The decay of the human body is not an exact science, Miss Fielding," the pathologist said.

There were more people in the public gallery on day two of the trial. It was as if news was spreading that this case was out of the ordinary.

"Decay is not an exact science?" Sally echoed. "You mean, to put it delicately, some people rot more quickly than others?"

"Some people have a head start."

"Perhaps we'd better go back to the beginning," Sally said.

Nick sat in the front row and transferred his gaze intermittently between the prosecuting counsel and the witness. Ahead of him, Dr. David Symes preened himself and lapped up the attention.

Symes was a chief forensic examiner. He had good looks, perfect teeth, and the most appalling halitosis. Some said it was because he breathed the stench from dead bodies on a daily basis. But Nick suspected that there was something slightly off, deeper down.

Sally's eyes moved from the jury to the judge to the witness. "What I am really interested in," she said, "is whether you can pinpoint the time of death with any degree of accuracy."

"Well," said Symes, "I can't really say whether it was before or after lunch, if that's what you mean."

The witness smiled, but no one else in the court joined him. Whatever the case, whichever party had summonsed him to testify, the doctor was only ever on one side: his own.

"The body had been dead for several months," he continued. "Putrefaction had started to take place."

"What is that?"

"The process whereby the body tissues liquefy. But it's slowed down by our temperate climate and by the autumn and winter months. You see, there are a number of variables."

"Let us go back to basics," Sally said, slightly exasperated. "Where was the body buried?"

"I don't know."

"You don't?" she said, astonished by his answer to the most simple of questions.

"I was called to the scene of a suspected homicide by Her Majesty's Coroner. From my observations, it is my professional opinion that the body had not been moved for about six months. But I cannot state that as a fact."

"I see," Sally said.

"I hope I'm not being too sophisticated, Miss Fielding."

"That's not something that I ever would accuse you of, Doctor."

And so battle was joined. Nick had seen it in so many cases in which Symes had testified. It was always the same. A jousting of wits and egos before Symes would concede that a decapitated body was in fact rather dead, in his expert opinion, and that the cause of death was, on balance, likely to have been acute absence of head.

Nick had very little dispute with Symes's findings in this case. He had insisted that the doctor give evidence only to cause the maximum inconvenience to the prosecution. To Sally.

"Can we look at the injuries?" Sally said.

"Which injuries?" Symes replied.

"The injuries to the deceased, of course."

"I'm afraid you are going to have to be a little more specific."

"Did the corpse have a crack in its skull?"

"Yes."

"I hope that was specific enough," Sally said.

"It was."

"Good." Sally nodded toward the usher, who brought over a large plastic bag. She tore it apart and extracted a smaller plastic bag. In it was a hammer. "Do you see this claw hammer?" She then turned to Cromwell. "M'Lord, exhibit one."

Cromwell nodded.

The usher took the implement over to the witness box. Symes took a pair of steel-rimmed glasses from one of his jacket pockets. He inspected the hammer.

"Yes, I've seen this before," he said.

"In what context?"

"In the context of it being given to me."

"For what purpose?"

"So that I could determine whether there was any correlation between the dimensions of the hammer and the indentations to the skull." He took his glasses off.

"Well?"

"Well, there is," he said.

"In your opinion?"

"In my *expert* opinion. Based on twenty years of examining skull injuries."

Nick could hear Sally let out a little sigh of relief. She had achieved her first objective. He wondered how far she would attempt to push her luck. There were further matters contained in Symes's report, blood tests conducted on the corpse and Will Turner. But blood tests were often of dubious value. And in a case with so much evidence, Nick thought, the prosecution did not need to complicate matters still further.

Cromwell looked at the jury. "Perhaps we should rise for five minutes before Mr. Downes embarks upon his cross-examination."

Sally leaned over toward Nick. "Should give you enough time to plead guilty to murder," she said.

*   *   *

Nick spent the break looking over the photographs that had been taken of the corpse. Then he went to the dock and glanced at the defendant. While the jury had been away, he noticed, Symes had covertly squirted himself with breath freshener.

"What was the cause of death, Doctor?" he asked.

"What? Apart from the smashed cranium?"

Not the most auspicious start, Nick thought. The question was too imprecise. He would have to try again. "Can you say for certain that death was caused by the damage to the head?"

"I don't know, Mr. Downes. Perhaps he died of a broken heart and then someone pounded his skull with a claw hammer."

"Did the hammer that Miss Fielding handed you cause the injuries to the skull of the corpse?"

"Possibly," the doctor replied.

"Can you say it did for a fact?" Nick asked.

"No."

"So any other hammer with broadly similar dimensions could have caused the injuries?"

"Well, that's obvious. It's just common sense."

"Which isn't very common," Cromwell interjected.

Nick tried to ignore him. "So any such hammer could be the offending weapon?"

"Yes."

"Only you didn't say before, Doctor."

"I wasn't asked."

Nick paused and waited until the jury looked at him. Then he glanced at Sally. "No, you weren't asked, were you?" He held up the photographs and tried to gaze significantly at them. "And any similar implement other than a hammer could have caused the damage if it impacted upon the skull?"

"Yes."

"Or if the skull impacted upon it?"

"Yes . . . er . . . what I mean is—"

"Oh, there is no need to explain, Doctor. Your answer was not too sophisticated for us mere laymen."

Cromwell put down his pencil sharpener and interrupted. "What precisely are you suggesting, Mr. Downes?"

"Perhaps I should put it to the witness, M'Lord."

"Perhaps you should," the judge replied.

Nick paused and took a sip of water.

"Trying to build up the suspense?" Max whispered.

"Just thirsty," Nick said. Again he remembered how Will Turner had screamed during the final session with Ann Barnes before he had attempted suicide. "Doctor, could severe damage to the skull be caused by a *fall* from a considerable height?"

"Severe damage could. Whether this particular damage would be—"

"That's not what I asked."

Nick knew that he would get no further on this point, but he had put the suggestion into the minds of the jury. He considered what Will Turner had said under hypnosis. About the field. About the hill. About coming too close to the edge. Perhaps some of it was true?

"Let me ask you something on a related topic, Doctor. After all this time, can you be sure whether any particular blow to the skull was caused before or after death?"

"No."

"Say the body had accidentally *fallen* into the quarry."

"Yes."

"And death was caused by that impact."

"Well, I don't—"

"Isn't it possible that any particular damage to the head was inflicted only after death?"

"The scenario you are suggesting is so preposterous that—"

"But it is possible?"

There was no answer as the doctor inspected his nails and ran his hands through his greased-back hair. Finally he said, "It is possible. But all things are possible."

"Yes, even innocence," Nick said.

Sally sprang to her feet, but Cromwell had anticipated her. "There is no need to object, Miss Fielding. I shall direct the jury to disregard that disgraceful comment."

"Don't push your luck, Nick," Max whispered.

"Why not?" Nick replied. "You did." He turned back to the witness, but as images of Sally and Max's tryst flashed across his mind, he was thrown off balance. "There are a number of areas of doubt about this corpse, aren't there?" When there was no answer, he continued, "I mean, you can't even say whether the body was buried dead or alive."

"Why do you say that? If this man was buried alive, I would expect most of the fingernails to be ripped off. They weren't. You see, Mr. Downes, people try to claw their way out."

It was a careless question and Nick knew it. He was rapidly losing the attention of the jury. He had wanted to keep the cross-examination short, to end on a positive note. But there was one other matter to deal with.

"Tell us, Doctor," he said. "What else was found with the corpse?"

"Well, there was a large amount of soil."

"That's obvious. It's just common sense, isn't it? Which, as His Lordship observes, isn't all that common. But you still haven't told us everything, Doctor."

"What are you talking about?"

"I'm talking about rats," Nick said.

"Rats?" the judge asked.

"Yes, M'Lord. Little furry things with sharp teeth. Tell us about the rats, Doctor."

"I can't."

"Why not?"

"I'm not an expert in that field."

"Oh dear. We finally seem to have exhausted your expertise, Doctor."

"Yes, finally."

"But you can confirm that in the bowels of the body the remains of a rat were found?"

"So I understand."

Nick had spotted this information in an appendix to an addendum of a further report that was buried in the Unused Material. "What sort of rat was it?" he asked.

"Probably a brown rat. Black ones are, I understand, normally confined to ports and docklands."

"And does your understanding stretch to an explanation of this rodent?"

"No, it doesn't."

"Or to why the rat's skeleton was virtually picked clean of flesh?" He paused when there was no answer from the witness box. "So there are some questions in this case that remain unanswered?"

"Only one or two."

"But you see, that might be one or two too many." He sensed a sharpened judicial nib pointed in the direction of his Adam's apple. "But that will be a matter for the jury, Doctor."

It was lunchtime, and Nick knew that he had to meet Liz Turner.

Chapter Five

During the lunch adjournment, Nick went to the public canteen instead of the Bar Mess. He knew that Max and Sally would be dining together with the rest of the Bar upstairs. He bought himself a ham sandwich and a packet of cheese and onion crisps and sat at a table in the corner.

The morning had not been a success. It was certainly not a disaster, but he felt that he was doing no more than gnawing away at the edges of the case. The core of the evidence, the confession and the hammer, was unimpeachable. Will Turner would have to go into the witness box and do some explaining.

"Why haven't you been returning my calls?"

It was Ann Barnes.

"You're not still pining over Sally, are you, Nick?"

"I don't know if pining is the right word."

"Then what is?"

"I don't know, Ann. You're the psychiatrist."

"No, the head is my province. I'm afraid the heart is a bit of a mystery. You know, they say the human brain is the most powerful computer in the world?"

"Yes."

"Crap. The brain is no more and no less than a glorified lump of jelly suspended in a liquid."

"So it's no better than the body?"

"What do you mean?"

"Well, according to all those pathologists, the body is just a larder of proteins, enzymes, and fatty acids for insects to devour once we're buried."

"Speak for yourself. I'm not going to be a banquet for bugs. I'm going to be cremated and have my ashes scattered over the geraniums in the sex offenders' wing."

She sat down, placing a file of official-looking papers beside her. She looked older, Nick thought. Or perhaps it was just the lack of a layer or two of makeup. He could see the lines on her face, the first hints of aging, of decay, and he remembered what he had read about the Buddhists and the bodies in the river.

It was said that Buddhist philosophers used to go down to the Ganges just to look at the floating corpses as a way of banishing earthly vanities, of bringing home the fragile nature of life. That was all very well, Nick thought, but he was not a philosopher, nor was he a Buddhist—he was from Beckenham. However, the circumstances of the Turner case, the killing, the decomposed body, had begun to have a similar effect upon him.

"You know they moved me," Ann said.

"Who?"

"The prison authorities. From Wormwood Heath to the Psychiatric Research Center. Government funding and all that."

"What are you doing there?"

"State secret, Nick," she said, smiling.

"Why move you? Something to do with Will Turner's suicide attempt?"

"No. They said my IQ was too high. But really it was because my cleavage was too low. Bloody men. Why should my career be dictated by their hormones?"

"Well, that's what dictates their careers. Why should you be any different?"

"I suppose that technically it's supposed to be a better job. I have more responsibilities."

"But fewer admirers? So it wasn't down to our little experiment in hypnosis?"

"No. By the way, has that stuff about Charles Turner being struck off come out?"

"It can't."

"Why not?"

"Will Turner has forbidden it. I'm not sure why, Ann. But he has forbidden my mentioning it at all."

The surrounding tables were beginning to fill up with the families of other defendants, dressed in their Sunday best clothes, with young policemen reading their pocket notebooks, and with solicitors' clerks. Every now and then a message crackled over the tannoy—the public address system, summoning someone important to the front reception desk. Smoke filled the air and rain fell gently against the windows fifty feet above the London pavements.

"Why are you here, Ann?" Nick asked.

"Diagnosing some sodomite in Court Eleven."

"And the diagnosis?"

"Anal fixation."

"The defendant?"

"The barrister," Ann said. "I've brought the signed original of my report on Will Turner." She handed Nick three sides of foolscap that were unevenly typed and stapled at the top left-hand corner.

Before he could examine the contents, he felt the light touch of lips on the side of his cheek.

"Now I know why you didn't answer my calls, Nick," Ann said. "Hello, Mrs. Turner. And how is your husband?"

Liz Turner wore a discreet, simple black dress. She sat down silently between Ann and Nick and lit a cigarette. It was the first time Nick had seen her since the kiss, and she was even more beautiful than he remembered.

"I'm grateful," she said finally, "for everything you've done for my husband, Miss Barnes."

"It's Dr. Barnes, actually," Ann replied. "And really, it was nothing."

"Nothing? Well, if you say so." Liz offered the psychiatrist a cigarette, which she declined.

"I'm sure we're all as anxious as you, Mrs. Turner, to see the prompt release of your husband," Ann said.

"Your concern," Liz replied, placing her hand on Nick's wrist, "is touching. But what I really wanted to do was to borrow Mr. Downes from you for a few minutes. Can you survive without him?"

"Well, I've managed for thirty years. Anyway," Ann said, "I can't hang around passive smoking. I have psychotic people to see. It's been a real pleasure, Mrs. Turner. I'll ring you tonight, Nick."

The two of them sat in silence as they watched the psychiatrist walk to the glass doors at the end of the cafeteria.

"Friend of yours?" Liz asked him.

"Friend of Sally's, actually. Look," he said, "where did you get my address?"

"The phone book," she said calmly.

Nick had completely overlooked this. He suddenly felt excessively stupid. Just what did he think he was accusing Liz of? He tried another tack. "Why did you stand me up those two times?"

"Guilt."

"About what?"

"About seeing my husband's barrister while he was in prison. About my marriage vows."

"You're not serious."

"I promised to love, honor, cherish, and obey."

"Marriage vows?" Nick said. "They're just rules, aren't they? Didn't you say rules were made to be broken?"

"I said *some* rules, Nick."

Suddenly, she appeared to hold the moral high ground. Nick tried another line. "Why didn't you tell me about Charles Turner being disciplined for those experiments?"

"Are we getting everything off our chests, then? All right. I didn't know the full details. And anyway, I thought it was supposed to be Will on trial, not Charles." She stubbed out the remains of her cigarette. "So what's she like? This present prosecutor and previous girlfriend of yours?"

"Sally? She's very bright. Took a double first in law."

"And you, Nick?" she asked, staring deep into his eyes. "What did you take?"

"I sort of pinched a third-class degree from a second-class university and ran off before the examiners could change their minds and fail me. Shall we get another sandwich?"

"In a moment."

"All right, then. Liz, I wanted to ask you: Why did you become Charles Turner's secretary?"

"Because I was a secretary, Nick. Secretarial work is what secretaries do. Does that answer your question?"

He was struck by the hardness of tone, the same as he had encountered when, in his chambers, he had tried to explore the causes of the marriage breakup.

"Are you going to ask me again why we split?" she demanded.

"No. I was just wondering . . . being a secretary, well, it seems a little—"

"Beneath me? Don't be deceived by appearances. There's nothing that's beneath us if we're desperate enough. I've just had tons of part-time jobs. But I was filling in."

"For what?"

She stared at him. "For Mr. Right to come along. Only I soon discovered that Mr. Right doubled for Mr. Right Bastard and had a wife and some unbearable sprogs. And then I met Will Turner. He fitted . . . the bill."

"When did his parents die?"

"Oh, a few years back."

"And when did he actually receive his inheritance?"

"A few years back."

"How many years?" Nick asked.

"About five."

"And how many years ago did you marry?"

"Oh, about five," she said. She gazed coldly at him. "I know what you're thinking."

"I'm not thinking anything at all."

He looked away from her and tried to make sense of the disparate fragments of information he had been given. But the more he thought, the more confused he became.

There were more tannoys, and nervous people smoked more cigarettes. The windows began to steam over, and, as the luncheon adjournment progressed, London slowly disappeared from view. Nick saw Dr. David Symes at the check-out with an onion salad and a packet of extra-strong mints. But the two did not acknowledge each other. When he returned to Liz's table, there were a dozen further questions about her frantic note he wanted to ask, but she began to speak first.

"The police have been constantly harassing me."

"Then we can make a complaint, Liz."

"I don't think so. They do it in a most courteous way."

"But what do they want?"

"They want me to testify."

"Testify?"

"Against my husband. Can they do something like that, Nick?"

"Well, in law, a wife is competent but not compellable."

"What on earth does that mean?"

Nick stopped chomping on the sliver of processed pork. "You can give evidence against your husband if you wish. But—"

"Yes?"

"But they can't make you. I still don't understand, though. What on earth can you give evidence of?"

"Of my husband's confession," she said.

"*What?*"

"He confessed to me that he knew where the body was."

"But how do the police know what goes on between the two of you?"

"They came round. They told me it was off the record, so I

spoke to them. They asked for a statement, and I refused. When they went they asked me to sign something."

"Their notebooks?"

"I just wanted them to go. So I signed something or other. I'm not very good with small print."

"Small print? Liz, this could put your husband away for life. Why didn't you tell me about it?"

"Well, I just haven't got around to telling you," she said. "Anyway, I'm surprised you didn't know about it. Don't the prosecution have to give you all the evidence? Disclose it, or whatever the technical term is?"

"Not if the witness is a potential defense witness," Nick said. "But they should have told us about the document's *existence* at the preliminary hearing."

"So why don't you know?"

"I didn't do the prelim hearing."

"Then who did?"

"He did," Nick said, pointing to Max Baptiste, who had just entered the room with Sally. They walked purposefully toward their table. "Besides," Nick continued, loud enough for Sally to hear, "we're the defense. No one tells us anything. The police tell the Crown Prosecution Service, the CPS tell the prosecutors, but no one tells us *anything.*"

Sally drew up beside him, and he saw that she had bitten her nails badly. She was clearly upset about something. She ignored Liz Turner and said, "There's been a development."

"In what?" he asked.

"In the case, of course." She continued, keeping her eyes on Nick, "It needn't trouble your . . . friend."

"There's no need for Mrs. Turner to leave, Sally. She's not going to testify against her husband. And we're not going to call her for the defense."

"She may not like it," Sally said.

"Well," said Liz, "perhaps I should be the judge of that."

Sally sat down opposite Nick. Max remained standing rather awkwardly. Nick noticed how he would not look directly at him.

He scrunched up his sandwich wrapper. "Well, this is fun," he said. "Now what glad tidings have you got to impart?"

"The police have got the girl," Sally said.

"What girl?"

"Mary Magdalene."

"Who?"

"Oh, sorry," she said. "I'm afraid it's a bit of a Vice Squad joke, calling the prostitute Mary. You know, Mary as in the one he first appeared in front of."

"He?" Nick asked.

Sally pointed upward.

He noticed again how deeply Sally's nails had been bitten. Perhaps it wasn't all South African Riesling and domestic bliss in Dulwich.

"He as in, 'And nothing but the truth so help me God.'"

"I still don't understand," Nick said.

"You of all people must know the Bible story. After the Resurrection, after he came back from the dead, he first appeared to a prostitute. Mary Magdalene. Well, it was the same with Will Turner. After six months, he suddenly appears in a . . ." Her voice trailed off as she looked at Liz Turner.

"Yes, my husband turned up in a brothel," Liz said. "It happens. Show me a man who says he hasn't thought about seeing a prostitute, and I'll show you a liar."

"Well," said Sally, looking pointedly at Nick, "we've got the—"

"Prostitute?" Liz asked. "There really is no need to be bashful in my presence, Miss Fielding. I don't judge my husband, you know."

"But you don't seem to love him much, either," Sally said.

"What makes you say that?"

"A statement you signed that makes him guilty as sin."

"But you can't force me to testify," Liz said. "Nick told me so." She lightly touched Nick's arm with her long, varnished nails.

"I don't imagine anyone can force you to do anything at all," Sally said. "Come on, Max."

When they had left the cafeteria, Liz said, "Does she always bite her nails that badly?"

"Only when she's upset," he replied. But he did not want to speak to Liz Turner about Sally.

"Did you get my note?" she asked. Nick nodded. "I really need to see you," she said. "Tonight?"

"Why?"

"It's personal . . . and complicated." She looked around suspiciously at the crowded public canteen. "Someone might overhear. I don't want to risk it."

"What, Liz?"

"It's started again, Nick. I just don't know what to do. It's all started again with Will."

Chapter Six

Nick had a few minutes before the jury were due to be brought back from lunch. Seeing Sally on one side of him in counsel's row and Max on the other, he decided to speak to the defendant. The public gallery high above Court 8 was beginning to fill up as the audience strolled in for the matinée.

When he arrived at the dock, he saw that Will Turner was again lost in thought. He gestured to the prison officer, who let him into the dock.

"I just wanted to see how you are," he said. "I'm afraid it's going to be a harrowing afternoon. The prosecution are going to call the prostitute."

"Have you seen my wife, Mr. Downes?"

"I think I might have seen her in the public canteen."

"Oh, good. You see, they don't often allow domestic visits downstairs. Can you pass on a message for me?"

"Certainly," Nick said.

"Can you tell her . . ." Will Turner paused, as though he had to struggle to spit out the words. "Can you tell her that I love her?"

"Shouldn't you do that?" Nick asked. "I mean, something so intimate."

"I trust you, Mr. Downes. And you're sincere. It'll sound better from your lips than ever it did from mine."

"All right. If you're sure that's what you want."

"You're so good to me. It must be an awful inconvenience having Mrs. Turner troubling you all the time."

"I don't mind. Really."

"You're so good to me," the defendant repeated.

"Listen, Mr. Turner," Nick said. "I wish you'd stop saying that." He felt uncomfortable. It was not just the aftershocks of the processed pork and the smoke-filled cafeteria at lunch. It was the helpless eyes of his client which gazed at him with a naïve admiration.

"There's no need to be modest," Will said. "I bet other barristers wouldn't do as much as you are doing."

"Oh, you'd be surprised," Nick said.

"That Max Baptiste, for example. I know he's your friend—"

"My colleague."

"But I wouldn't trust him, Mr. Downes. You see, I'm rather good at judging people, and I know you won't let me down. You're my only hope, Mr. Downes. Please remember. Tell my wife that I love her."

Nick asked the usher if he could keep the judge from coming in for five minutes. He walked to the toilets at the end of the corridor, where he was sick.

"What is your name?" Sally asked the female witness.

"What's it to you?"

"To me, madam, it is a matter of staggering indifference. But I need to know for the court record."

"Well, it's Jackie, then."

"Is that all?"

"That's all you're going to get."

"Your age?"

"Over twenty-one."

"Your age?"

"Thirty."

She looked older, Nick thought. When he had seen her in

that place, she had seemed older. Perhaps every year on the street was worth two ordinary years. Perhaps it aged you twice as fast.

He tried to concentrate on the courtroom. All eyes were focused on the woman in the witness box.

Sally picked up a piece of paper. "What is your profession?"

"I don't have one."

"What do you do?"

"For a hobby?"

"For a living."

The witness did not reply.

"Look, do you work the streets?"

"No."

"No?" the prosecutor repeated.

"I have my own place."

"I see. You have your own establishment."

"No. I have my own place."

"So you're a prostitute?"

"I prefer sex worker, honey. Or masseuse. I've a certificate. From the London School of Reflex Massage."

"Can't we get on?" snapped the judge.

"Do you recall a time when the police raided your . . . place?" Sally asked.

"I can't remember a time when the police didn't raid my place. Vice just won't leave us alone. I keep telling my solicitor to do something. But them solicitors are as bad as the police."

"Was there an occasion when someone was taken by the police?"

"No."

Nick saw Sally throw down the sheet of paper she was holding.

"Madam, I have to remind you that you are required by law to answer. It is your duty."

"Listen, honey. What do you want me to do? Grass up a punter? Well, I ain't doing it. I ain't no grass. It just ain't right."

"Fascinated as I'm sure we all are by your discourse on moral philosophy, you still have not answered the question."

"Perhaps you'd like to retire for five minutes, members of the jury," the judge said.

The jury seemed reluctant to depart, Nick observed. They had to be ushered out. The judge would continue only when the large wooden door was shut.

"Refusing to answer questions is a matter of the utmost gravity," he told the witness.

She did not reply.

"Silence can be a contempt," he continued.

Nick saw her mouth open for a moment, as though she were about to say something, but then it closed again.

"I can order your detention."

"Think I'm scared of you?" the woman said.

The judge did not look at the woman as he ordered her to be taken down to the cells.

The final witness of the day was the second forensic scientist. A series of computer terminals had been arranged around the court for the demonstration. As the jury was brought back in, Nick flicked through the report the scientist had provided.

The witness, Dr. Norman White, was sworn. Then Sally asked him to begin the forensic video simulation. Despite being a prosecution witness, he too answered every question in the most arcane fashion possible.

"What are your qualifications?" Sally asked.

"I have been appointed Artist in Medicine and Life Science at the Central London Royal Infirmary."

"Which is where?"

"Balham High Street."

"And what is your task?"

"As Medical Artist, I undertake facial reconstruction from skeletal remains."

"For what purpose?"

"For the purpose of identification."

"And how did you perform this task in the instant case?" Sally asked.

There was a suspicious-looking bulge in the leather case that the doctor had hauled into court.

"I was allowed access to the exhumed corpse by the police. Then I took a cast of the skull. After that, it is necessary to put flesh on the bones, as it were."

"Not literally, I hope," Sally said.

"No, with clay and toothpicks. I seem to get through rather a lot of toothpicks. Most of the flesh has been eaten away what with one thing and another, but I suppose someone else has told you about all that."

"Yes," Sally replied. "Perhaps you can skip the more gruesome details and get to your conclusions."

"My task was complicated by the fact that insects, what we technically call invaders, had laid their eggs at the usual sites. Facial orifices, eyes, lips."

"Yes, but what was your conclusion?" Sally asked impatiently.

"You have to understand, Miss Fielding, that it is precisely these features that give an individuality to a face. The same underlying bone structure could produce two *slightly* different faces. But ultimately it was possible to re-create a three-dimensional model from the computer simulation."

"Of what?" Sally asked with relief.

"Of this."

With that, the scientist pressed a button and on the screen, line by line, a face appeared and then rotated through 360 degrees.

To Nick, it was space-age technology, like something from the new series of *Star Trek*. But, he reflected, this was not the final frontier; it was the first floor of the Old Bailey. And this was not a futuristic crime, but an almost biblical one.

Yet this was the cutting edge of forensic investigation. In future, criminals would not be caught by detectives, but by databases and digital technology. Guilt would be computed deep in the memories of vast machines. Computers like HOLMES, the

Home Office Large Major Enquiry System, set up after the York-shire Ripper fiasco, when the killer had been questioned on nine different occasions by the police before he was finally charged.

Eventually, Dr. White reached into his bag and pulled some-thing out. Nick could not see exactly what it was. But the judge seemed excited.

"Do you wish the exhibit to be passed around the jury box, Miss Fielding?"

"In just a moment," Sally said. "I think my learned friend should see it first."

"Have you not seen it before, Mr. Downes?" the judge asked.

Nick had seen photographs of the various reconstructions of the skull but not the actual model. Before he could say this, the usher had brought the skull over.

"Mr. Downes?" the judge repeated. "I asked you whether you had—"

"Seen it?" Nick replied. He looked slowly toward the dock. "Yes, I've seen it."

The model was passed around the jury box. It reminded Nick of one of those dummy's heads that can be seen in the windows of chic boutiques. It seemed unreal, except for the eyes. They were sad and pleading. But more than that, they were the eyes of Will Turner.

Then the usher came up to Nick. She whispered in his ear that the defendant wanted to have a word.

As he went to the back of the court, the model of the skull was still being passed around the jury box. Will Turner leaned over the edge of the dock.

"What is it?" Nick asked.

"I want you to tell the jury something," the defendant said.

"What?"

Will Turner shook his head vigorously as though he was try-ing to shake the words out.

"What do you want me to tell them?" Nick asked.

"That I killed my brother," he said in a tone that was almost fractured, a different voice coming through. "I want you to tell them it was me."

"Will, are you sure? Think about what you're doing."

"*Tell* them," the defendant said. "Or I will."

"What?"

"I'll tell the court that I killed my brother, that I wanted to admit it but that my lawyer refused to let me."

"And you've made up your—"

"Mind? I suppose you think I'm crazy, out of my mind? But why is it lunacy to tell the truth?"

Nick had no answer. He slowly walked back to counsel's row at the front of the court, thinking about the subtle change in the tone of Will's voice, about the corresponding change in behavior.

"There's been a development," he said to the judge.

"Yes?"

"My client wishes to plead guilty to manslaughter."

"And that's final?"

"Definitely."

The judge mumbled something to the clerk, who stood up holding the indictment.

The charge was put again.

"Stand up, Will Turner. On the first count, you are charged with the murder of Charles Turner. How do you plead? Guilty or not guilty?"

"Not guilty to murder. But I am guilty of manslaughter."

"You may sit down," the clerk said.

"I killed him," Will said, sotto voce. "I killed him."

Chapter Seven

On the evening of the second day of the trial, Nick went to Soho. There he waited for Liz Turner outside a public house just south of Shaftesbury Avenue. But she was late. So he flicked through a copy of T. S. Eliot's *The Waste Land* he had bought in the Charing Cross Road. He hoped to impress Liz with a quotation.

After the court had risen that afternoon, he had had enough time to go home, feed the cat, and then douse himself with aftershave. He had dabbed it behind his ears, on his wrists, and even under his armpits. In fact, he had put on so much that the cat would not come anywhere near him.

As he stood by the pub doorway, with an endless stream of youngish Mediterranean boys going in and coming out, he felt terribly guilty when he conjured up the memory of Will Turner. It was not so much the words that the defendant had finally uttered, words that had brought the trial to a shuddering halt. It was the eyes. Again they were the innocent, desperate eyes of a man with little hope. A man who had placed his trust in Nick. And how had that trust been rewarded?

"One of the best pickup joints in the West End."

He immediately recognized the rounded tones of Liz Turner.

She was bright and energetic and did not apologize for her tardiness.

"Of course," she said, pointing at the pub entrance, "I wouldn't recommend it. More crabs in there than in a seafood restaurant. Do you know why it's called Soho?" She didn't wait for him to answer. "This area was a royal park in the sixteenth century. 'So-ho' was the hunting cry of the forest. Of course, it's more of a jungle now."

"You look lovely, Liz," he said. "You're a constant surprise."

"And why is that?"

"You seem so cheerful. Especially after——"

"After what?"

"After all that happened today."

She did not answer at first. She gently took his elbow and began to guide him through the pretheater crowds lining the pavements. Neon lights of every conceivable color flashed above their heads. The smell of roasting Peking ducks filled the air, and the subterranean peep shows were just beginning to open.

"What am I supposed to do?" she said. "I've tried to play the supportive wife, Nick. But now, *this*. So he admits manslaughter? He says he killed his brother?"

"He says he still loves you."

"But I never loved him. And anyway, he left me, remember? And before he . . . disappeared, we were as good as separated."

"That's not his recollection," Nick said.

"Oh, of course, your client's memory is perfect, and he's completely sane." She stopped and looked at him gravely. "Will used to come crawling back every now and then."

"Why were there problems?"

"Kids," she said. "Or lack thereof. I wanted children. Will was infertile."

"So you separated?"

"Separation isn't just a physical thing. It's a state of mind. We had been separated for years, only we didn't know it."

They reached another corner, and she directed him through a huge ornamental arch. They were entering Chinatown.

"This used to be a fashionable place to live in the eighteenth century," she said. "Then in 1854 there was a serious outbreak of cholera. Nobs moved out, and the prostitutes moved in. Of course, the aristocracy still returns every now and then when they're feeling a bit horny."

In a third-floor window, high above the throng, Nick saw a young Chinese girl glancing through the dirty curtains. There was a sign scrawled in an uneven hand on the open street door. It said MODEL AND SHOW-GIRL. He was sure that Liz, too, had seen her, and the conversation died.

He finally asked, "So you split up with your husband because of children?"

"Ostensibly. Why was it you and Sally split?" She asked the question without looking at him, engrossed in a menu in the window of a restaurant on the other side of the street.

"Sally and I just wanted different things in life."

"Such as?"

"I wanted her. She wanted Max. We had a difference of opinion, that's all."

"Oh, really? You never got to the stage where her habits used to fill you with disgust? When her very voice would want to make you scream? The way she chewed her food, the way she brushed her teeth, all completely revolting. Her jokes were unfunny, her conversation dull, and—"

"It was never like that."

"Then perhaps you should still be together. But I forgot. She's with your best friend. Do you like lobster?"

"I don't like anything with claws, Liz."

"So chicken's feet are out of the question as well?"

"Sounds disgusting."

"Of course it's disgusting. It's a delicacy. First requirement of any delicacy is that it should make you want to throw up."

"So what do you like?"

"Seafood. Clams, mussels, oysters—but nothing with claws."

When he looked at her, her eyes gazed at him with such earnestness that for a moment he said nothing. "You want to know every intimate detail about me," she said. "But you won't tell me anything about yourself. Do you think that's fair?"

"All right. Sally and I disagreed about children. She wanted to put her career first, that's all. It's something anyone can under—"

"Don't you see the irony?" she broke in. "You're looking for your child's mother and I'm looking for my child's father. It's perfect."

"Perfect for what?"

"For us."

He was taken aback by her enthusiasm and the novelty of her idea. But he did not comment.

There were many people in the pedestrian precinct, only a few of them Chinese. Expensive restaurants stood next to bargain stores with stacked bookcases out front. Herbal chemists shared entrances with acupuncture centers. Coachloads of young European tourists ate hamburgers and made faces at diners. Police cars drove by without stopping.

Nick reached up to the top shelf of one of the bookcases and picked out a book on yoga for cats.

"What *is* that horrid smell?" Liz asked.

He realized that he had exposed his perfumed armpits to the air. "Must be the acupuncture center," he said.

"Perfectly vile. Listen, I have an idea." She gazed at a fly sheet on the wall of a boarded-up building. "But it's a little . . . well, out of the ordinary."

"It's been anything but an ordinary day," Nick said.

The smell of Peking duck began to fade as they crossed Shaftesbury Avenue and headed northward. Nick kept his arms firmly by his sides so that he could no longer smell his aftershave, and he tried to forget about Will Turner languishing in prison.

They had to go down a flight of metal steps to get into the club. A man on the door with two gold teeth looked them up and down and then let them enter. He took his time in particular over Nick, constantly looking at his tie. Nick feared for a moment that he would have to hold up his arms and be frisked,

but the man merely grunted something unintelligible and ushered them forward.

"What was the problem?" he asked Liz.

"Your tie, I think."

"I don't see why."

"It was obviously chosen by a deeply disturbed person."

"Sally bought it for me. In Paris."

The club was dark. About twenty square tables were
arranged around a semicircular stage. Each table had a small
lamp that gave off a pinkish glare.

"Thought you might like this," Liz said, sitting down. "The
food is terrible."

"Terrible?"

"Well, nonexistent really. But the floor show is good." She
looked at his tie. "You still love Sally, don't you?"

"It's not as easy as that. Not when you've been with someone
for twelve years."

"What do you love most about her?" She stroked the back of
his hand. "The truth."

"Her eyes. When she smiles, they're sort of tinged with this
miraculous cornflower blue. I know it sounds stupid, but—"

"Why are you here, Nick?"

"Here?"

"With me."

"I like you."

"That's not enough."

"I like you a lot, Liz."

"Better."

"To be honest, you intrigue me. There's something about
you, somewhere beneath the beauty and wit, something . . .
hurt. Something that makes me want to—"

"Yes?"

"Look after you."

"Father me?"

"Not quite," he said. "I'll leave that to your biological father."

She smiled, but it was a sad smile, a smile of affection recol-
lected, not one of humor. "He's dead."

"Your father?"

"When I was fifteen. My mother committed suicide. Daddy
died . . . of a broken heart, the same year."

"We don't have to talk about it," Nick said, seeing the tears
welling in her eyes.

"It's all right. I'm a big girl now."

Nick kissed her forehead. "No you're not."

Liz's head tilted forward and her hair framed her face on both
sides, making her appear suddenly ten years younger.

"What did your father do?" Nick asked.

"He was a lawyer, Nick. Hadn't we better order a drink?"

"Bloody Mary?"

"Perfect."

Chapter Eight

The MC had announced that the main attraction of the evening would be onstage at any moment.

"Despite everything, you always seem so cheerful," Nick said to Liz as they sipped their drinks.

"I believe there's a finite amount of happiness in the world," she said. "You've got to grab it while you can."

"Hang on," he said as a round of applause rose around them. "If happiness is finite, limited, other people's happiness means less for you."

"Less for us," Liz said. "Let's grab it while we can, Nick." She broke off. A man and a woman came onto the stage. The man was white and the woman was black. They were naked.

"I hope you're not going to pretend to be shocked, Nick?"

"It's more surprise than shock." He picked up his glass and took a sip.

"What are you surprised about?"

"Well, when you said you knew somewhere other than that Chinese restaurant, I imagined you meant a steakhouse."

"This is a steakhouse of sorts. More of a meat market, I suppose."

The man had kneeled down and the black woman was behind him.

"Now what were you saying about the case, Nick?" she
asked.

"I was saying that we can argue diminished, er, responsibility and . . . what on earth is she strapping onto herself?"

"Well, let me give you a clue, Nick. It's soft, strong, and
very long."

It was also black, Nick observed.

The lights in the room started to palpitate in time to the
rhythms on the stage. There was a hush at the tables, relieved
only by moody, sensual music, a song called "Black Magic
Woman."

"Do you like it?" Liz asked.

"Who's the band?"

"Santana."

"I think we should go, Liz."

"Oh, relax, for heaven's sake."

"I don't think heaven really comes into it. Hell, perhaps."

"What's the matter?"

"Sally is the only woman I've ever seen naked."

"That woman's not naked. She's nude. This is art, Nick—"

"It's hardly Piero della Francesca, is it?"

"Who?"

"Never mind." Sally would have known, he thought. But
Sally would never have taken him to such a place. "Look, why
is she chewing all the time?"

"It's performance art," Liz said.

The two people got onto a bed that had been rolled onto the
stage by a youth in an AC/DC T-shirt. The black woman was
still on top, the man facedown. She pulled him onto all fours
and rode him, pulling back his hair, making his back arch, his
mouth fall open.

"Performance art?" Nick said. "It's a very one-sided performance. The one on the bottom, he appears so . . . I don't know
what the word is."

"Submissive?" Liz suggested.

"On the receiving end."

"He doesn't seem to be complaining."

"I suppose submissions of law are not the only type of submission. But it doesn't seem natural. Like trying to get a square peg into a round hole."

"You call *that* a square?"

"Geometry isn't my strong point. Look, it just doesn't seem right, Liz."

"My God, you are a prude. I thought lawyers were meant to be highly sexed."

"No profession thinks about it more and does it less. I'm surprised we ever manage it after a day in court. Besides, sodomy is illegal."

"This isn't real."

"Sodomy became punishable in 1530," Nick persisted. "The king passed a statute."

"Which king?"

"Henry the Eighth."

"Oh, that paragon of sexual virtue."

The show suddenly ended, and there was a muted round of applause, the kind of halfhearted appreciation that string quartets get in the tearooms of grand hotels after a ropy bit of Beethoven. In the background, the same record kept playing.

"Doesn't he feel ashamed?" Nick said.

"Why should he?"

"I mean, the public humiliation."

"You're telling me you've never wanted to be humiliated?"

"Why should I? I've got my mother for that."

He took another sip of his drink. "Liz, I've been meaning to ask you something."

"What?"

"What did you mean when you said, it's all starting again?"

She swiveled the glass round and round and looked at the empty stage.

"You said you'd tell me," he insisted.

"It's Will."

"What about him?"

"He's becoming morbidly jealous again. He suspects I'm see-ing someone."

Nick paused to consider his next question. This was a con-versation, he sensed, that was fraught with dangers and things better left unsaid. On an ordinary day, he would have said nothing. But as he looked at the naked buttocks retreating to the rear of the stage, he told himself yet again that this was far from an ordinary day.

He finished the drink, licked his lips, and said, "Aren't you seeing someone?"

"Oh, Will means someone *serious*," Liz said.

"So you don't want something serious?"

"I didn't say that."

"You didn't need to, Liz."

He did not know whether he felt hurt or insulted. The breakup had made him hypersensitive, and he had never been in a relationship that was *not* serious. But it had been so long since he had been out there dating women, he was no longer sure whether he really understood all the signals. Perhaps he had totally misread the situation with Liz.

"Do you want another drink?" she asked finally.

"You know, I was beginning to wonder whether it wasn't a little unfair us seeing each other like this when your husband was inside."

"Did you say unfair?"

"Yes."

"How strange and innocent you are, Nick. There is no jus-tice in a bedroom."

"What bedroom?"

"Mine. Later tonight. If that's what you want. Well? Is that what you want?"

"All things being equal," he said, "it's what I want."

"But all things are never equal, Nick."

"Quite."

"So you won't?"

"I can't."

"Why can't you?"

"I've got to . . . well, feed my cat," he said.

The next act came onstage. It was another man and woman. Only she was hardly a woman, Nick thought. She was barely more than a young girl.

Liz suddenly stood up. "I want to go," she said.

Nick took out his wallet, but she threw a couple of notes onto the table. The girl kneeled down in front of the man and momentarily raised her head.

"There's something you should know," Liz said.

Nick was fixed on the spectacle.

"Getting a taste for it, are you?" she asked.

He did not answer. Although all his instincts told him that what he was watching was sinful, he had to admit that it excited him. But despite his racing thoughts, when he looked at the performers there was something more. Momentarily, the music became louder.

"Nick, I'd better tell you," Liz said. "I've decided to give evidence."

He barely heard the words and certainly did not take on board their significance. He was fascinated by the young girl on the stage, a Chinese girl. He suspected that he had seen her before—that she was the Chinese girl from Queensway.

Chapter Nine

On the third day of the trial, Nick arrived at the Old Bailey early. He had received a message on his answerphone from Ann Barnes asking him to meet her in the public canteen as soon as the court opened its doors.

He had parted company with Liz immediately outside the club in Soho. She had hailed a cab and disappeared. Left alone, he had meandered up to Tottenham Court Road and caught the tube to Queensway. He pondered the fact that on the one hand he had been offered sex, and on the other she had departed without even saying good-bye to him. Images of the club circled in his thoughts when he got home, and the world suddenly appeared rather different.

But when he arrived at the doors of the Old Bailey, on Wednesday morning, nothing had changed. The security guard was still rummaging through the handbags of young women with a thoroughness beyond the call of duty. The daily lists were still posted on the noticeboard. The tannoys were as unintelligible as ever.

Out of a sense of duty, Nick made a quick detour to the cells. He sat in the empty visiting room waiting for the guards to bring the defendant from the holding area.

"You look tired, Mr. Downes," Will said. "Late night?"

"Just couldn't sleep, really."

"What you need is a good woman to hold on to in the night. I always used to sleep better when I shared a bed with Liz. Did you give her my message?"

"Yes."

"You are so good to me, Mr. Downes. You know, I look at you not just as my lawyer but almost as my—"

"I told you. Don't go on about it. I'm just doing a job. And I'm not doing it very well." He walked to the end of the cell and gazed out of the glass window so that Will Turner could not see his face.

"What did my wife say?"

"Say?"

"When you gave her my message."

Should Nick tell him that she never loved him? Should he know of her description of how the two of them had been separated for years though they did not know it? Nick looked at the accused man, his eyes again bright with hope, his lips slightly parted.

"So what did she say?" he asked again.

"What do you think?" Nick replied.

Will Turner jumped up from his seat. He seemed to be in raptures. "Oh, I knew it would be all right. She is very forgiving, you know. I think it's because she's a Catholic. Did you know that?"

"No," Nick said, lying. He wondered why he had lied. Was he trying to distance himself from Liz? Through guilt or fear of the defendant—or both?

"You know, Mr. Downes, I think it's all going to be all right. What do you think?"

"Do you still want to admit the killing?"

"Yes."

"And plead guilty to manslaughter?"

"It's the right thing to do, isn't it? I suppose this is going to sound a bit silly, but I've learned that from you. I've got to be honest. I've got to do the right thing. I've been reading the Book of Revelations like you told me to and although it sometimes sets my mind spinning—"

"I didn't tell you to. I just knew that the story in your dream came from there. The whore and the child." He saw the jailer outside the door. "Did your wife say anything to you about giving evidence for the defense?"

"No. But I know she will help me if you ask. I think she respects you a lot. Why do you ask?"

"No reason."

"Please tell me again. My wife does love me, then, Mr. Downes?"

Nick just gave him a half-smile as he left him in the cell.

As he reached the public canteen on the second floor, he saw Sally.

"What *is* that funny smell?" she asked.

He had showered twice, but still could not eliminate the odor of the aftershave. And his cat, who, for want of a better name, he had called Catt, would not come near him. "Sally, I can't talk," he said. "I've got to meet Ann Barnes."

"Oh, I get it. You've anointed yourself with essence of Pagan Man to titillate Ann?"

"Did you have something to say to me about the case?"

She moved away from the staircase where there might have been stray jurors. "I just want to know why you didn't get this jury discharged when your punter decided to plead guilty."

"He insisted on continuing with the same jury," Nick said. "He thinks they may give him some credit for pleading guilty in front of them."

"But they're not going to find his responsibility diminished because of something like that. It smacks of great responsibility to accept he was the killer. That's what I'm going to tell the jury. I'm warning you now. It smacks of the calculating mind of a cold-blooded murderer, which is, of course, precisely what he is."

"Just say what you like, Sally. You always do."

He noticed that Ann Barnes was already inside the cafeteria and was beginning to approach the two of them.

"Are you going to call Ann to testify today?" Sally asked.

"Yes," he whispered. "Actually, I'm a little surprised."

"By what?"

"Well, we served Ann's psychiatric report so late, I'm surprised you didn't object."

"I object to Ann Barnes, not to her report," Sally said.

The door opened.

"Sally, *darling,*" Ann called. She kissed the air on either side of Sally's cheeks in a perfunctory way. Ann's lips barely landed but her sarcasm did.

"Look," said Sally, recoiling slightly, "I can't talk to you, Ann. You're the enemy. Well, just for today."

"You always were a stickler for etiquette," Ann said. "Never consort with the defense when you're prosecuting, eh?"

"Got it in one."

"Where is Max, by the way?" Ann asked.

For the first time that morning, a little color came to Sally Fielding's cheeks. Nick noticed that her nails were even more raw than they had been the previous day.

She coughed. "I think Max was in bed the last time I saw him."

"My goodness, Sally," Ann said. "You are wearing that boy out. Whatever are you doing to him?"

Sally did not reply.

"Well, I hope you're going to be gentler with me than you are with him," Ann said. "You haven't been sharpening your talons for me, have you?" Then she looked with great deliberation at Sally's fingers. "I forgot. You've got none left."

Sally walked up the stairs toward the Bar Mess on the fifth floor.

"Old friends," Ann said to him. "With the emphasis on old."

Nick led her into the canteen. He found a couple of fifty-

pence coins and bought two cups of steaming liquid that
were as bitter as the drink in the Soho club.

"I don't know why you two bother," he said.

"Then where would we get our fun, Nick?" She sipped the
drink slowly, trying not to ruin her lipstick. "How does it
feel to have all these women fighting over you?"

"Come on, Ann. You're not fighting over me."

"Aren't we?"

"No. I'm just a convenient arena. Like Waterloo."

"The bridge?"

"The place in Belgium." He thought about how Liz Turner
had hurriedly left him alone in Soho. He thought about the
carnage in the flat on the night Sally told him that she was
leaving him. "No, Ann," he said, "I'm just like a Belgian bog
that people can have a good scrap on."

"I called you last night. Where were you?"

Nick thought about the kneeling man and the woman
towering behind him in the club. "Seeing some art."

"Really? How sophisticated. I've always wanted to take up
art," she said. "I've always thought I'd be rather good at it."

"Yes," he said. "I think you would."

Nick had asked Cromwell for leave to call Ann Barnes's evidence out of turn. Ann was to testify on behalf of a foot
fetishist in Manchester and then attend a conference on Sexual Deviance and Religion in Dublin. Wednesday was the
only day she would be available for a fortnight. Sally did not
raise an objection.

Cromwell explained the significance of the recent developments to the jury.

"Ladies and gentlemen," he began, "this case has taken an
unusual turn. Mr. Turner has now pleaded guilty to manslaughter before you. What he is in fact saying is, 'Yes, I
killed my brother. But I deny murder. At the time of the
death, I was suffering from diminished responsibility.' Now,
do you want to open your case again, Miss Fielding?"

"No, thank you, M'Lord," Sally said. "The case of the prosecution remains the same. The man in the dock is a murderer. We say he is not mad but bad. He did not suffer from a lack of responsibility, but from a lack of respect for human life. He has tried to pull the wool over the eyes of the jury with one dishonest defense. Now he is trying another. Nothing has changed. Nothing. Mr. Downes's client is still guilty of murder."

Nick then called out Ann Barnes's name. He didn't dare look at the jury after Sally's lethal onslaught.

Chapter Ten

Ann Barnes preferred to affirm rather than to swear an oath on the Bible. Nick knew that some jurors would hold that against her. She was wearing a very tight suit, he observed, with many buttons. At the front it defined her chest a little more than was strictly necessary. But she was her confident self as he took her through the formalities of her qualifications and experience. Then he came to Will Turner.

"How many times have you seen the defendant, Dr. Barnes?" he asked.

"Almost on a daily basis while he was in Wormwood Heath."

"And did you work with him and examine him for the purpose of a psychiatric assessment?"

"Yes."

"And your conclusions?"

"In my opinion, Mr. Turner is suffering from paranoiac schizophrenia."

Nick would normally have wanted to have asked about the psychiatrist's methods of assessment at this stage. But he knew that some of Ann's practices were unconventional. He made a decision to leave it, and hoped that Sally would concentrate on disputing the conclusions.

"What does schizophrenia mean in lay terms?" he asked.

"It's not just split personalities like people imagine. Though in this case there could be an element of dual personality."

"I *object*," Sally snapped, rising to her feet. " 'Could' be is mere speculation. Useless and improper in a court of law."

"But in Mr. Turner's case," Ann continued, "it is also much simpler than that. He is not a man in control of his own mind. He cannot tell right from wrong. He cannot help his actions. So, in my opinion, he is not responsible for his actions."

"And did this mental state apply six months ago at the time of the . . . killing?" Nick asked.

"I have no reason to believe otherwise."

"Why do you say that?"

"He is suffering from a deep-seated illness. It goes to the core of who he thinks he is. I do not think that his schizophrenia is a recent development."

"And his memory loss?"

"It could be accounted for in part by, for example, a fall."

"How?" Nick asked, remembering his conversation with Ann about glorified human jelly and the decay of the body.

"The brain is suspended in the cranium. When someone falls or receives a blow to the brain, it can bounce around inside. This causes bruising and sometimes amnesia. But—"

"But what?"

"But typically a patient would lose memory of the traumatic incident and a short period before and after. It would depend on the extent of the injury."

"For example?"

"Perhaps a few days either way. But this man," Ann said, glancing at the dock, "has lost memory of most of his life. That is a psychiatric condition. In my opinion."

"Yes, thank you, Miss Barnes. Please wait there. I'm sure there will be some more questions."

He sat down. He noticed that Sally had not got to her feet. When he sneaked a glance to his right, he saw that she was still looking through Ann's report.

"Are you going to cross-examine?" Cromwell asked.

"M'Lord, yes," Sally said, half getting to her feet with the report in her hand.

"At *any* stage today, Miss Fielding?"

Nick noticed that the judge's sarcasm at Sally's expense had produced one or two sycophantic sniggers from the jury. He should have been pleased, but he discovered that despite everything he still felt for Sally.

"I'm afraid I only got this report recently, and I haven't fully absorbed it," she said.

"Well, would you like some time?"

"No, M'Lord. Having skimmed through it again, I don't think that will be necessary."

It was an excellent recovery, Nick knew. She'd shown that the report was a last-minute thing and that she was not afraid of it.

Sally turned to face Ann Barnes. Nick held his breath.

"Miss Barnes . . ." She spoke with exaggerated courtesy and an irony lost to all but the protagonists and Nick himself. Ann did not bother to correct her and tell her that she was a doctor.

"Are you aware," Sally continued, "that the psychiatric evidence given in the Yorkshire Ripper trial in Court One of this building lasted all of six days?"

"Yes."

"And your testimony on behalf of this . . . man has lasted all of six *minutes?*"

"Yes. But Peter Sutcliffe killed more people than this defendant."

"No, Sutcliffe *murdered* more people. Let's keep that distinction firmly in mind, shall we?"

Ann did not reply. Sally had scored again.

"I want to ask you about your report," she said.

"Yes."

"But not just yet."

She pretended to inspect the final page of the report. Only Nick could see that it was, in fact, a blank sheet that had been photocopied by mistake.

She continued, "You examined the accused in Wormwood Heath?"

"Yes."

"While you were there and while he was there?"

"Yes."

"But you are no longer at that prison, are you?"

"No."

"Why not, Miss Barnes?"

Nick got up to protest. "M'Lord, how can this conceivably be relevant to any issue before the jury?"

Before Cromwell could say a word, Sally said, "I'll let the doctor answer that. Did you jump or were you pushed?"

"I moved," Ann said. "I now work for a Government Psychiatric Research Center."

"Was it considered that your . . . talents were not best suited to a male prison?" Sally asked. When Ann did not answer, she added, "Am I barking up the wrong tree?"

"You're yapping in the wrong part of the woods altogether."

"Well, let's see about that. Do you agree that the prisoners used to fantasize about you?"

"I should hope so," said Ann.

One or two of the male jurors smiled, Nick noticed. A good sign. He had initially feared that Ann would blow up in the face of Sally's provocation. But she seemed to be regaining her poise.

"You see," said Sally, "isn't it possible that this man fantasized about you?"

Ann looked vaguely in Nick's direction. "Which man?"

"The defendant," Sally said.

"Yes, he might have fantasized about me."

"And told you what you wanted to hear?"

"I didn't want to hear anything but the truth."

"Could he have duped you into thinking that he was suffering from a mental illness?"

"Yes. That is always possible."

"And could he have lied to you?"

"On occasions. Everyone lies. Even—"

"And," asked Sally, "could you always determine when he was lying?"

"Not necessarily. But I have many years'—"

"Just answer the questions, Doctor. I'll finish with you a lot quicker if you do."

Nick turned his head to the left and surveyed the jury box. The jurors were clearly enjoying the battle of wills between the two formidable women in court. But what did they make of it all?

Sally again rustled the pages of the report portentously. It was a trick Nick had once taught her. She finally let the paper float down to the bench and then continued.

"Is it correct that you used hypnosis in your treatment?"

"Yes."

"And psychodrama?"

"Yes."

"And are these well-established psychiatric techniques?"

"Psychodrama is still in its experimental stage."

"So for whose benefit was this experimentation, Miss Barnes? Yours or the defendant's?"

"I regard that as an impertinent question," Ann said.

"Well, I don't," Cromwell said, pointing a sharpened nib toward Ann. "Please continue, Miss Fielding."

Sally's voice was rising now, and Nick sensed that she was nearing the end of her cross-examination.

"Is the defendant mad or bad?" she asked.

"Neither," Ann said. "He suffers from an abnormality of mind."

"I noticed that you did not swear an oath on the Bible," Sally said.

"No."

"Does that mean that you do not recognize the concept of evil?"

"Like the sins of the father and the seven horses of the apocalypse?"

"There were only four horses of the apocalypse," Sally said.

"Well, that's inflation for you." Ann beamed. "Evil is not a recognized psychiatric concept."

"So what was the Yorkshire Ripper, then? Suffering from a neglected childhood?"

"That's not what I said," Ann protested.

"What about Jeffrey Dahmer? What about Myra Hindley? Are you saying that they should not have been punished for their crimes?"

"They all needed treatment."

"So these people are not suffering from too much evil but from too little psychiatry?"

Ann inspected her painted nails. Nick could see a red flush rising in her cheeks, and he feared a final explosion.

"Isn't it right," Sally continued, "that in America eight people once pretended to be schizophrenic?"

"Yes. I know of such an experiment."

"And they were perfectly normal. As sane as, say . . . Mr. Downes here."

"I wouldn't like to speculate about that."

"They pretended to hear voices and imitated other classic symptoms of schizophrenia that they had been made specifically aware of?"

"Yes," Ann said.

"They fooled several doctors?"

"Yes."

"How many?"

"Half a dozen. More or less."

"More, Dr. Barnes. Many more, wasn't it?"

"Yes."

Cromwell tossed down his pencil. "You know," he said, "I wonder whether it shouldn't sometimes be the psychiatrists who are committed. Present company excluded, of course."

"Isn't it right," said Sally, "that the only people who spotted them as fakes were other mental patients?"

"So I understand."

"And all they needed to achieve this fraud on the psychiatric profession was a little inside knowledge of mental illness?"

"Yes," Ann said.

"My final question is this," Sally said. She paused and looked at the jury. "Please tell the jury, what was the profession of the defendant's brother?"

"He was a psychoanalyst," Ann said.

Nick did not bother to try to rehabilitate Ann's testimony. When she was released from the witness box, he did not look up but heard Ann's heels stepping quickly across the floor as she left the court.

"Are we back to the prosecution case?" Cromwell asked.

"Yes," Sally said.

"And do you have any further witnesses, Miss Fielding?"

"Yes, M'Lord," Sally said. "The prosecution wishes to call Elizabeth Turner."

Chapter Eleven

Liz Turner came into court without glancing at Nick. She looked completely different from the woman who had talked about lobsters and chicken's feet the night before. Her hair was up and was tightly tied back. She had a certain serenity and looked like a slightly faded maths teacher who had spent the best years of her life cogitating on the mysteries of logarithms.

As she reached the witness box, Sally handed Nick a few pieces of paper.

"What's this?" he whispered.

"Her statement," Sally said.

"Bit late to serve that, isn't it?"

"We served last night."

"Nonsense."

"Ask Max," she said.

Nick looked round at his junior, who sat with his pen poised over a blue counsel's notebook.

"I thought I gave you a copy," Max said, his lazy left eye twitching nervously.

Before Nick could say anything, the judge tapped his pencil

on the Bench at the front of the court. "Did you anticipate this . . . development, Mr. Downes?" he asked.

I should have, Nick thought. What was it that Liz had said as they were leaving the nightclub? She had agreed to give evidence. But she did not say *for whom,* and he had never suspected she would give evidence for the prosecution, for the other side. But this was a case where there were no clear boundaries of loyalties, for the lawyers or the laymen.

"Mr. Downes?" Cromwell said. "I asked you a question."

"Yes, you did," Nick said.

"Well, are you going to share the answer with the court?"

"I've just received the statement," Nick said, imitating Sally's behavior when she had been asked about Ann Barnes's report. He made a point of flicking through the statement noisily. "But I think I can manage without an adjournment for the moment. I might need to consult my client at some stage."

"Let's see how far we can proceed, shall we?" Cromwell said.

In truth, Nick wanted to hear exactly what Liz was going to say before he spoke again to Will Turner.

The usher approached Liz and asked her what religion she was. Liz said Catholic. Then she swore an oath to Almighty God to tell the whole truth. Nick was riveted.

Sally coughed once, and turned to Liz. "Are you willing to give evidence, Mrs. Turner?"

"I'm prepared to, if that's what you mean."

Cromwell interrupted. "I have to tell you, madam, that as the wife of the accused, you cannot be compelled to give evidence against him."

"But I can if I wish?" she asked.

"Yes," the judge said. "If you wish, then in law you are competent."

Sally coughed again, and the judge stopped speaking. She said, "So you are prepared to give evidence for the prosecution voluntarily?"

"Something like that."

Cromwell rapped his pencil loudly. "Now, what does that mean?"

"It means, M'Lord," Liz said, "that I've been told by the police that if I give evidence for the defense in this case, then the prosecution will pry into my past."

She glanced momentarily at Nick. What did that glance mean, he wondered. Hadn't she already begun to reveal part of her past to him?

"I've been told that if I testify for the Crown and change my story, then I will be treated as a hostile witness. And I've been told that if I agree to testify and then say nothing then I might be in contempt of court. Apart from that," she said, "I'm the most willing witness in the world."

"If you wish," Cromwell said, "you can walk straight out of that door now and no one will say a thing."

"And then the jury will not know the truth of what happened."

"Well, Miss Fielding," the judge said, "I am satisfied that this lady is perfectly aware of her rights and the risks that she runs."

Nick did not know what to do. He should have been taking notes. He should have been glancing through the statement that Liz had given to the police. But it was as if he were frozen. He sat in court and saw Sally on her feet beside him and Liz speaking in quiet tones in the witness box to the front.

Sally coughed loudly once more. "Now, Mrs. Turner. I wanted to ask you about the man your husband killed."

Sally had established that at the time of the killing Liz Turner was still married to the defendant.

"And were you still living together?" she asked.

"Sometimes."

"So sometimes you weren't?"

"Obviously."

"But it wasn't going well all the time?" Sally asked.

"I don't know about you, Miss Fielding, but I find that relationships never go well all the time."

"But then isn't it kinder to end them?" Nick felt sure that Sally glanced at him momentarily. "The point is," she continued, "your husband left you for good and disappeared at the time of the killing."

"Yes."

"Now why would he do that?"

Nick decided to get up and intervene. "M'Lord. I cannot see how this witness can give evidence of what was in the mind of another person."

Cromwell looked at Nick sternly. "Then perhaps you should read the statement that Miss Fielding has served upon you."

While Nick sat down, embarrassed, and tried to skim through the pages, Sally continued.

"What did he tell you when you went to visit him in prison?" she asked Liz.

"He told me that he was jealous."

Nick stopped reading. He had heard Liz speak of this before.

"Who was he jealous of?" Sally asked.

"His brother."

"For what reason?"

"I had known his brother longer than I'd known him."

"For how long had you known Charles Turner?"

"Eight years, more or less."

Why was it, Nick wondered, that Will had insisted that it was *five* years? Who was telling the truth? Liz or Will? Was it five years or eight? And what possible motive could there be for lying?

"What did the defendant suspect?" Sally asked.

"That I was having an affair with his brother."

"And were you?"

"I cannot see how this is relevant," Liz said.

Sally paused. Nick noticed how she rapidly licked her lips.

Cromwell stood his pencil on end and cupped his right hand around it. "Miss Fielding, perhaps the only relevance of this line of questioning is the state of mind of the defendant. What is relevant is whether he *perceived* that there was a . . . liaison between his wife and the deceased. Whether or not such a relationship did exist in fact is neither here nor there."

"This is a question of motive," Sally said.

"Isn't that what I just intimated?" Cromwell replied.

"If the affair was real as opposed to imaginary, it might provide a stronger motive."

"But there is no evidence that the defendant *knew* of the affair, even if it was real. I imagine that will be the objection of Mr. Downes."

Nick said nothing.

Sally continued, "M'Lord, it also pertains to the defendant's mental health. A man who has been betrayed by someone he trusts might have a legitimate axe to grind."

Nick again became aware of Max behind him, but when he looked around Max was continuing to take a note regardless of any relevance Sally's comment might have had to him.

"Someone obsessed by morbid jealousy," Sally said, "is a very different animal."

Cromwell was clearly losing his patience. His voice was growing louder, and his forehead was developing a complex of lines. "Whether or not the defendant knew of any actual affair is sheer *speculation.* That's the objection to asking Mrs. Turner whether there was in fact such a liaison. That's your objection, isn't it, Mr. Downes?"

"No," Nick said.

"So you don't object to Miss Fielding asking Mrs. Turner whether she had an affair with the defendant's brother?" Cromwell asked.

"No."

Nick wanted to hear the answer. And he wondered again how it was that Liz had known Charles Turner for three years longer than Will realized.

Chapter Twelve

Liz Turner stood very still as Sally and the judge thrashed out the point of law. Liz even affected to appear mildly interested—a raise of the eyebrows, a purse of the lips. The one thing she did not do, Nick observed, was to look at him.

Sally shuffled her feet to Nick's right. She tilted her head toward the witness and said, "I'm going to ask you again. Did you have an affair with the deceased?"

"No," Liz said.

"Then why all the fuss?"

"Then why all the questions, Miss Fielding?"

By now, Cromwell seemed to have lost track of the proceedings. "There, you have your answer. Can I ask why on earth you have bothered to call Mrs. Turner for the Crown?"

Sally ignored the judge and once more fixed her gaze on the witness. "Was there any discussion with the defendant about the body?"

"Yes," Liz said.

"What was the gist of the discussion?"

"On one of my visits to the prison, Will said that he knew where the body was buried."

"Did you tell the police this?"

"I didn't see the point. They already knew, didn't they? Will had already told the prostitute where the body was to be found."

Cromwell tapped his pencil. "Where is all this going?"

Again Sally ignored him. "How would you describe your husband's demeanor when he told you this fact?"

"What do you want me to say?"

"How about the truth? How was your husband *behaving?*"

Nick got to his feet. It was time to object before Liz Turner said something that might totally scupper the vestiges of his defense.

"This witness," Nick said, "is not an expert on human *behavior.*" He stressed the word in the way that Sally had. "This witness is not a psychiatrist. This witness is a wife."

The judge glowered at Nick. "Are you saying that a wife cannot say what is going on in her husband's head?"

"Not usually," Nick replied. "Or the divorce rate would double."

There were nods of recognition from both male and female members of the jury. For a moment the judge was silent, and Sally used the opportunity to approach Nick.

"Nice point," she said, smiling. But just as he was basking in her smile and proximity, she pulled back. "Of course, I never knew what was going on in your head."

"You weren't my wife."

"Who said I would have accepted if you proposed?"

"Who said I ever proposed?"

They both recoiled, and Nick felt thoroughly miserable.

"How did you describe your husband to the police?" Sally asked Liz.

"I described Will as being . . . well, not completely irrational."

Sally looked carefully at the statement. "So he was rational?"

"No."

"Well, Mrs. Turner, are you saying there is a state between rational and irrational?"

"Yes."

"What?"

"Being in love," Liz said. For the first time she looked at the jury. "My husband loved me. That's the real crime that he has committed."

"So he killed out of . . . love?"

"He killed his brother because his brother tried to—"

She stopped and, although no tears fell, she seemed shaken. Nick had never seen her like this before.

"What do you want to say, Mrs. Turner?" Sally said.

"I don't want to say anything."

"Well, you must answer."

"Why? Because I'm on oath?"

"Because it's the right thing to do," Sally said.

Liz turned in the direction of the jury, but Nick got a fleeting impression that every now and then her pupils darted toward him.

"Charles said he wanted to talk to me," she said. "He said it was important. He said it was about Will."

"When was this?" Sally asked.

"Last summer. About a week before . . . it happened. We arranged to meet."

"Where?"

"In the West End."

"Where in the West End?"

"In Soho. It was Charles's idea. He wanted to speak to me— about borrowing some money. Or I should say, some more money. He was always in debt. His practice was not doing well."

"Why did Charles Turner ask you about these matters?"

"My husband and I had a joint account. But he was useless with money. Charles knew that I was the one who really controlled the purse strings. It was me he had to win over."

"Can we return to that evening," Sally said. "Where in Soho did he take you?"

Liz looked at Nick and then at the jury. "We went to a club."

"What sort of club?"

"That sort of club," she said.

Nick did not know what he felt. He wanted to stand up and shout. He wanted to run out of court. He wanted to grab Liz by the shoulders and shake the truth out of her. But instead he sat in the front row very quietly.

"I was, I suppose, shocked by what I saw. Or perhaps not so much shocked as surprised," Liz said, echoing Nick's words. "Charles called me a prude. You see, Miss Fielding, I have had a rather strict Catholic upbringing."

"Please get to the point," Cromwell said.

"Charles suggested that we go back to his office between the City and Docklands. He ran his practice from there. He treated addictions."

"Addictions?"

"To drugs. For burned-out City types. Occasionally he got referrals from rehabilitation centers."

"Continue."

"When we arrived, he told me that he feared that Will was having a nervous breakdown. That he was mentally ill. And then it happened."

"What happened?"

"He asked me to do what we had seen in the club. I wouldn't."

"So?"

"Do I have to say?"

"Yes."

"So he raped me."

She said it in the same tone as the rest of her evidence. In the same way she had sworn to tell the truth, had said she was a Catholic.

Nick realized that Sally had gone beyond what was in the statement, that she was at times cross-examining her own witness. That it was improper. But the old proprieties were beginning to fade in his mind. He continued to sit and listen.

"Did you mention this to the police, Mrs. Turner?" Sally asked.

"No."

"Aren't you just inventing this story to save your husband?

You see, it's very easy to say anything about a dead man. He can't answer back."

"I don't want to save my husband."

"Really? Doesn't he still love you?"

"But I don't love him." Again she looked at Nick. "I never have. Besides, I'm seeing someone else."

"Does your husband know?"

"He suspects. He always suspects. He's morbidly jealous."

"But you never divorced him?"

"Sometimes we pity those who love us. I wonder whether you can understand that, Miss Fielding?"

Nick saw Sally lick her lips and play with her fingers behind her back. Had she pitied him, when he had begged her to stay?

"Will must have just lost his head with Charles," Liz said. "I didn't want him to do that kind of thing. I suppose it was very wrong. He should have let the police handle it. I guess he just lost his head."

"The truth is," Sally said, "you want him freed."

"No, I want him punished."

"Punished?"

"Crime and punishment, sin and penance. For a Catholic, they're pretty much the same thing, Miss Fielding. It's all I know. I only lost my dignity. But Charles lost his life."

Sally was silent.

"Yes," said Cromwell. "Do you have any questions, Mr. Downes?"

Nick did not get up from his seat as, somewhat flustered, Sally closed the case for the prosecution.

Should Will Turner give evidence? It was a difficult question and Nick did not know the answer.

The court had risen for lunch. As he walked to the lifts, he knew that he needed to talk to Max and that he needed to talk to the defendant. But most of all, he knew that he wanted to be alone.

Cell visits were not allowed between one o'clock and half past. So Nick dumped his wig and gown in the robing room and left the building. The sun had come out, and there were puddles on the wet pavements. The clouds that moved rapidly over the rooftops of the city appeared every now and then in the small pools of water.

As he walked, he tried to decipher Liz's motives. Was she trying to save or to sink her husband? The rape allegation might well make the jury hostile toward the dead man.

But in Nick's experience, there was a far more compelling consideration. Charles raping Will's wife provided Will with all the *motive* in the world for murdering his brother.

If Liz had calculated this, why would she want her husband to be convicted? He did not believe it would be for the money. There had to be something more.

When he reached Blackfriars Bridge, he walked halfway across. The river was flowing very fast, and to the west he could see the trees and gardens of the Temple. Beyond that was Waterloo Bridge where he had recited the Shakespeare sonnet for Sally. And now he had lost her, and his life was a mess.

Max and Nick waited in the cell for Will Turner to be produced. There was only one chair in the dimly lit room.

"You have the chair," Max said.

"Feeling guilty?" Nick said.

"Should I?"

"Depends how much of your sense of decency is left, Max."

Max slumped into the chair. "You know, Nick, ever since it happened—"

"Since what happened?"

"You know."

"You can't say it, can you, Max?"

"All right, since Sally and I got together. Ever since then you've been on such a damn high horse, you could enter the Grand National."

The door opened. Will Turner stood at the entrance and looked at the two lawyers.

"Discussing my defense?" he asked.

"Something like that," Nick said.

Max got up, and Will sat down.

Nick continued, "We need to know—"

"Whether I'm going to give evidence?" He gazed at Max. "What do you suggest, Mr. Baptiste? You've been very quiet during the course of the trial. Do you think that I should expose myself to Miss Fielding?"

"That is something I would never recommend," Nick interjected. "But if you're going to testify, we need to know what you're going to say."

"The jury will want to hear from me, won't they? See whether I'm a monster or not."

"They might already have their doubts about murder because of your wife's evidence," Nick said, not mentioning the other side of the equation. The very dangerous question of motive.

"They might?"

"Yes."

"Which means they might not?"

"Yes, Will. That's precisely what it means."

"She said she doesn't love me."

"People say these things," Nick said.

"My wife said she was seeing someone else." Again he looked at Nick. "Can that be true, Mr. Downes? Please find out for me."

Max shuffled his feet. "I think you should ask her yourself, Mr. Turner."

"Why?"

"No one should interfere between a man and his wife." Max shuffled some more, moving further away from Nick's anger. "I mean, *marriage* is special. It's sacred—"

"A sacrament," Nick said.

"I want to know who it is," Will Turner said.

"Why?"

"Because I feel like killing him."

"Can I suggest that you do not give evidence, Mr. Turner," Nick said.

"If I'm going to go to prison for the rest of my life," the defendant said, "I want to tell my story."

"But that's just the point," Nick replied. "What is your story?"

"The truth."

Nick winced. "Mr. Turner, this is a courtroom, not a confessional."

"I want to tell the truth."

"Which is?"

Will Turner took his head out of his hands. "Which is the truth," he said, his voice deeper, more gravelly.

The jailer came to the door to summon them for the afternoon session. But Will Turner exploded.

"Just *fucking* leave us alone," he screamed, banging his hands against the glass.

The jailer was shocked.

"Fuck off or I'll *kill* you," Turner shouted.

Nick instinctively shied away, stunned by the outburst.

"You've got two more minutes," the jailer called.

Turner smiled. "Thank you." He looked at Nick. "I want to tell the truth," he repeated. "Isn't that enough?"

Chapter Thirteen

The jury was already in its box when Nick and Max returned to Court 8 after lunch. Sally Fielding sat in her position in counsel's row scribbling notes for her closing speech.

Clearly, Nick thought, she does not expect us to call Will Turner to the stand. And Nick would not have called him if he had the choice. But when a man faced a life sentence, it did not seem right to try to dissuade him too vigorously. It would just have been nice to have some idea of what he was going to say.

Nick stood up. He looked once at the dock for a sign, for any sign that the defendant had had a change of heart. But the accused man was already at the door of the wooden dock.

Will Turner was led forward by two dock officers with handcuffs. They stood on either side of the witness box as Turner swore the oath. One of them yawned as Nick began to speak.

"What is your full name?"

"Will Turner."

"Not William . . . as in the artist?"

"Just Will."

"And what is your address?" Nick asked. No sooner had he said it than he realized that it was obviously an unfortunate question. "In fact, don't bother to—"

"I'm currently in Wormwood Heath prison, Mr. Downes. I'm not ashamed of that." He stared straight at Nick, not daring, it seemed, to look at the jury.

"Did you kill your brother, Charles Turner?"

"Yes."

"Did you intend to kill him? I mean, to murder him?"

"I loved my brother. I still love him. I cannot imagine any circumstances in which—"

"Even those your wife has told us about?"

"I cannot believe that Charles would have done that," Turner said. "He introduced her to me."

Suddenly, Nick felt that the little loophole Liz Turner had manufactured had vanished. And as the defendant spoke, he sensed that the loop had turned into a noose. Was this precisely what Liz had wanted? He was now in the invidious position of having to attempt to undermine the evidence of his own client. Or there would be only one verdict: murder.

"I must ask you," he said. "Do you remember the incident in question?"

"No."

"Then how do you know it was you who killed him?"

"I just do. I knew where the body was buried."

"And how did you know that, Mr. Turner?"

"I'm sorry, I don't really . . . look, it must have been me. My brother is dead, and I know it must have been me who was responsible."

"Can you tell us anything else about what happened?" Nick asked.

"No. I'm sorry."

"Please don't apologize. Just wait there. Miss Fielding may have some more questions."

When Nick sat down, he felt again as he had on Blackfriars Bridge. There he was, looking on rather uselessly as events flowed past. The trial was effectively over; the verdict was practically sealed. All that remained were the final rituals of Sally's demolition of the accused and the closing speeches.

Sally gazed at Will Turner intensely before she asked her first question. There was the hounded man on the ropes. What would it take to finish him off, Nick wondered. Uppercut? Hook? Right cross?

Sally coughed quietly and said in an understated voice, "Are you mad, Mr. Turner?"

It was the old haymaker below the belt, Nick decided. A blow that Sally had refined on him.

"Am I mad?" Will asked.

"Yes, mad," Sally said. "You know, as in not very sane."

"No, I'm not mad."

"And you say you loved your brother?"

"Yes."

"But you killed him?"

"Yes."

"So you are capable of both love and violence?"

"Isn't everybody?" the witness replied.

To Nick, Will Turner's comment did seem a genuine question. As if the poor man wanted very badly to be told the answer without having any idea what it was.

Sally did not reply. She licked her lips and shifted her wig further down her forehead. "Do you still love your wife?"

"Yes."

"Even though she doesn't love you?"

"I don't want to believe—"

"Even though she never has?"

"I simply can't believe that."

"So she might have said it just to try to get you acquitted?"

"That's all I can think," Will Turner said, his face miserable, his voice depressed.

"She says she was raped by your brother."

"Charles would have never done that."

"Did she ever tell you that she had been sexually assaulted in any way by your brother?"

"Not that I can remember."

"So as far as you know, you had no excuse whatsoever to use any violence toward him?"

"No."

"Let alone to cause multiple fractures to his cranium?"

"To cause . . . I'm sorry—"

"To smash his skull, Mr. Turner." Sally held up the police photograph of the corpse with the top of the skull caved in.

"No, I had no excuse to smash his skull."

"But you did?"

"I think so, Miss Fielding," the witness said.

Sally paused to take a sip of water and to look at the jury. "You only think you did it?"

"Yes."

"So why plead guilty to manslaughter?"

"Because I must be punished."

"Who says?"

Nick saw Turner's face flush with color, only it was a color he had never seen before. It was as if his face were filling up with blood, but this blood was not good. It was unhealthy, unclean.

Sally repeated her question. "Who says you must be punished, Mr. Turner?"

"It's . . . in here."

"Where?"

Turner's hand touched his temple briefly and then fell to his side again limply. "Here. In my head."

"Yes," said Sally. "It's called a brain. Some men are known to have one."

"No. It's more like—"

"Yes?"

"Well, it's more like . . ." He paused. "It's more like a voice," he said, and with that he broke down.

"Are you happy to continue, Mr. Turner?" the judge asked after a ten-minute break.

"I'm fit to continue, M'Lord. May I just have a glass of water?"

"Of course you may, Mr. Turner."

The judge indicated to the usher, and a white plastic cup was placed in Will's left hand. Defendants and dangerous witnesses were not given anything made of glass—in case they cracked them and did damage to themselves or others.

"Are you prepared to tell us the truth?" Sally asked.

"What would you like to know, Miss Fielding?"

"How did your brother die?"

"I pushed him."

"How?"

Nick sat and listened but he was extremely concerned. Was he the only one? Perhaps he had been influenced by what Ann Barnes had said about split personalities. But he felt that Turner's voice was now different—only marginally, but clearly different. It was the voice with which he had screamed at the jailer in the cells.

Will continued, "We had gone for a walk on the Downs. Charles was in Kent for some reason. My memory is vague on that. Perhaps it's not important. Then he told me that he always wanted Liz—"

"Your wife?"

"Yes. He told me that she might claim he tried to rape her, but that it was just a lie. We started to argue as we got to the top of the chalk quarry."

"And what form did that argument take?"

"Just pushing each other around."

"So how did it develop?"

"I think . . . I think Charles slipped and hit his head on a rock."

"Was he injured?"

Turner paused and appeared to scan his memory. "I think he was badly shaken and furious. He said that he had had sex with my wife. She had begged him for it. He said she was no better than a whore. The things she had asked him to do to her . . . I don't want to say. I don't want to say."

He seemed on the verge of tears, but Nick wondered whether they would be genuine.

"Take your time, Mr. Turner," the judge said.

"I charged at him," Will said. "I wanted to hurt him."

"Why?" Sally asked.

Again he paused, as if struggling for the right emotion. "I wanted him to feel the pain I felt. But—"

"But what?" Sally asked.

"But I didn't mean to kill him. I did kill my brother, Miss Fielding. But I didn't mean to murder him. He fell right into the quarry."

"What did you do?"

"I must have run down; I can't remember. His head was bleeding, and he had no pulse. He was dead. But I was still furious. There was a workman's shed. For some reason, some old tools had been discarded behind it. I found the hammer."

"The exhibit?" the judge asked.

"Yes, M'Lord. I hit his head again and again with the hammer. I don't know why. But he was already dead. I panicked. At first, I hid the body in the woods. A couple of days later, I returned and it was covered with flies. So I buried the body nearby. And then I disappeared."

"Until you were arrested?" Sally asked.

"Yes."

"What did you do?"

"I'm not sure. It's all a bit of a blur. Stayed in the area. Lived rough."

"So why did you not tell us all this before?"

Turner glanced at Nick and spoke softly. But there was, to Nick, a clinical edge to his voice.

"My barrister told me not to tell the court the whole truth. He said something about there being only so much truth that it was safe to tell. My barrister told me to rely on the psychiatric evidence. It was a better bet than the truth—"

Sally began to speak again. "Aren't you telling a pack of lies to save yourself?"

"How can I be saved, Miss Fielding? I've killed my brother. I've admitted manslaughter and I've lost my wife. I have no life."

His head rotated toward the jury box.

"If you think I'm lying, convict me of murder. But I'm telling the truth."

"But murder is different to manslaughter," Sally protested.

"Do you think it really makes a difference to my brother? Or—"

"Or?"

"Or to God."

All around Nick were stunned faces. In court there was complete silence. But Nick could faintly hear quiet laughter, seemingly coming from the witness box, muffled, like something emanating from the very core of Will Turner, something meant solely for Nick. Something only Nick could hear.

Finally, the judge spoke. "What have you got to say, Mr. Downes?"

"Nothing, M'Lord," Nick replied. "Except that I feel compelled to withdraw from the case."

Chapter Fourteen

The fourth day of the trial was a Thursday. It was the first in which Nick was to play no part. Having no other work to do, he slept heavily and only went into his chambers after lunch in "civvies," a pair of jeans and a jumper.

It was another bright morning, but by the afternoon storm clouds had gathered in such numbers that he had to put on both the lights in his third-floor room. Outside, the Temple was deserted. The odd tramp begged for the price of a cup of tea, but there was no one else to be seen. Coaches on the Victoria Embankment had their headlights full on. Then, as the sun broke through onto the river, a heavy sheet of hail began to fall.

It was King Lear–type weather, Nick thought. It was a shame that across the Thames the National Theatre's neon sign was advertising *The Merry Wives of Windsor.* Somehow, that ruined the effect.

He stood motionless, watching this scene until the green lawns of the Temple were covered in a white crust. He had told himself that he was going to catch up on an unhealthily large backlog of paperwork. But his thoughts were elsewhere. He had hoped that withdrawing from the case would leave him with a sense of relief. Instead, he just felt in limbo.

The phone rang.

"Nick, it's me."

He recognized the voice immediately. "I can't speak to you, Liz."

"Why not?"

"You're involved with the case."

"But you're not. Didn't Will sack you?"

"I withdrew."

"Is there a difference?"

Nick knew that in reality there was not. Outside his window, the wind got up. "Where are you, Liz?" he asked.

"Downstairs."

"What?"

"In reception."

He told himself that he should have realized. Liz had been able to phone through directly, bypassing his clerks. He should have known that she was in the building.

"Can I come up?" she asked, her voice a little hesitant.

"Why?"

"To look at the splendid view. To see you, of course. Please, Nick. I think we should talk. We have to—"

"Come up."

While he waited for her, he scrambled around his room attempting to tidy up. He kicked a fraud brief under the desk and tossed a gross indecency into the bin.

Suddenly there was a knock on the door, but before he could reach it, the handle turned.

When she came in, Nick did not know what to say. There were an awkward few moments while she paced around the room in silence, barely looking at him. And he noticed her clothes. She looked chic, sophisticated, sexy.

She handed him a small spray of flowers. "These are for you, Nick."

They were cornflowers.

"What are you working on?" she asked, before he could respond.

"My first capital case."

"How exciting. Is it one of those appeals against hanging from the Commonwealth?"

"No. It's from Bromley."

"But we don't have the death sentence in this country."

"They do in Bromley. Especially for Tricksy the pit bull terrier. Would you like to sit down?"

She sat on the edge of his desk.

"Yes," he continued, "Tricksy is devoted to his family, has big brown eyes, and a passion for biting little girls."

"I've known several men very similar to that," she said.

"We've offered them castration. But the court ordered death. They're quite tough in Bromley."

"Obviously."

"And Tricksy had even complied with government regulations. He was on a lead, registered, and implanted with a microchip."

She crossed her legs and let down her hair. She shook it, sending gusts of her perfume toward Nick.

"Did you try to get Will convicted?" he asked.

"What? For the two million?"

"Some would say it's two million reasons. But I can't believe it was just that."

"Can you believe that I was raped?" Her eyes stared at him, pleaded with him, demanded that he answer truthfully.

"All men are capable of rape, I suppose," he said.

"But if he is convicted, it leaves the way clear for . . . us."

"I didn't know there was an 'us.' "

"You didn't know you were going to kiss me that first time, but you did." Again she picked up the photo of his family and smiled. "How's your cat?" she asked.

"Cute."

"What's its name?"

"Catt."

"Isn't that rather boring?"

"It's a cat with two *t*s. And it suits him."

"I always wanted a cat, you know, when I was a kid. But I was never allowed. Funny. I often think about it. If only I had

something that was completely mine, that would love me totally, that would need me. Perhaps that's why I want children.
Dumb, isn't it?"

"There's nothing dumb about that at all."

Liz went over to the door, opened it, moved the sign to EN-
GAGED, and then closed it again. "It's very quiet up here," she
said. "Where is everyone?"

"In court. Earning money. Doing what barristers do."

"Have you got the floor to yourself?"

"There's only Donald Spicer in the room next door, but he's
out of London for six months defending two accountants from
Wolverhampton who ran a pedophile ring in their lunch hour. I
understand that's the most tax-efficient way to do it." He
kneeled down and pushed stray papers from the fraud brief
right under the desk.

"Well, Mr. Downes," she said, looking down at him. "You
could get up to all sorts of mischief up here." She picked up a
long measure of red legal ribbon, the type used for tying up
briefs.

"I suppose I could," he replied. "I hadn't really thought
about it like that."

"Well, start."

She stroked his hair gently while he was on his knees.

"You look mighty big up there," he said, trying to get up.

"Don't move," she told him, and just slightly parted her
legs.

"Why not?"

"It's much safer to submit than control."

"What?"

She nodded toward his books. "Thomas à Kempis. The *Imitation of Christ*. I looked it up."

"Oh, I don't read him. I just use the book to keep my wing
collars pressed. Can I get up? I don't like it on my knees. Re-
minds me of confession."

"But I bet your priest never did this to you."

Liz, too, slid to her knees. She put her hands around the
small of his back and began to run her fingers over his jeans.

"You obviously never met Father O'Flanaghan," he said.

"Shut up."

"What are you doing, Liz?"

"Finishing what we should have done ages ago."

She kissed him roughly on the lips. Her mouth was very wet, and a little saliva ran down his chin. Then he sensed her hands moving to the front of his trousers.

"Come out, come out, wherever you are," she said as she rummaged around. "Where are you hiding, Nick?"

"There's nothing to hide."

"Why is it that the only time men are modest is when their flies are undone?"

He put his hand on her fingers as they began to move back and forth and his penis became more erect. Strange sensations ran from his fingertips up his arms and into a guilty part of his mind.

"It's all right," she said. "I want to see you play with yourself."

Although his hand still followed its to and fro course, Liz's fingers had moved away.

"I want you to do it for me, Nick. It will really turn me on."

The humiliation Nick felt was tinged with the thrill of a forbidden pleasure.

"There's so much I want you to do for me," she said. "So much, Nick." She kissed him again, and he then felt her lips on his neck. "You see, you like it. You want to do it for me."

Nick was getting too excited. He was about to lose control.

"Faster," she said. "Let me watch you."

He felt as if he were about to burst.

Then the phone rang, and he stopped. He got to his feet and picked up the receiver.

"Hi, Nick. It's Max. I'm not interrupting, am I?" When there was no answer, he continued. "The court's assembling in fifteen minutes. There's a verdict. What do I say if he is convicted? Nick? Nick, are you there?"

"I'm here, Max."

"What do I say if it's murder?"

"Nothing, Max. You just say nothing."

When he had put down the phone, Liz stroked his hair. "That was a shame," she said. "Bad timing."

"Bad month."

Nick and Liz Turner reached the public gallery high above Court 8 at the Old Bailey just as the jury came back into court.

The clerk at the front of the court held up a piece of paper and read, "Members of the jury, have you reached a verdict upon which you are all agreed?"

"Yes," said the foreman.

"And do you find the defendant, Will Turner, guilty or not guilty of murder?"

Nick felt Liz take his hand in hers. Her nails cut into his skin.

"Guilty or not guilty?" the clerk repeated.

"Not guilty."

"And is that the verdict of you all?"

"Yes."

There was a pause while the judge wrote something before he began to speak.

"Mr. Turner, I understand you do not wish your counsel to address the court to mitigate your offense. For my part, that is the best mitigation you can have. You have pleaded guilty to the offense of manslaughter, and now I must sentence you. During the course of this case I have formed the view that you have been punished in ways that stretch far beyond the sanctions of this court. You will have to live with the knowledge that you are your brother's killer for as long as you live."

He paused and looked up at the public gallery, at Nick casually dressed and at Liz Turner beside him.

"It seems that you have also lost your wife, and, I imagine, you will find it difficult to pick up the pieces of your life. I take into account your previous impeccable character when deciding that this was a temporary deviation into crime. One that will not be repeated. There is not a defense of *crime passionnel* in this country. But the court can take such matters into account.

"In a case such as this," he continued, "there are victims and there are casualties. And you, Mr. Turner, are a casualty. In the, I have to say, tragic circumstances, I am prepared to take an unusually lenient course. I shall sentence you to a suspended sentence of imprisonment for two years."

Will Turner stood speechless and motionless.

"That means," said the judge, "that you are free to go, Mr. Turner. But I also advise that you get psychiatric treatment for the same period. I see that Dr. Barnes is in court. Perhaps she could . . ."

The dock officers tried to usher Will out. But his legs began to work only when he spied Nick in the public gallery with Liz. The case was over. Will Turner was out. And now, Nick suspected, things would get worse.

Sally, far below in the well of the court, looked up at him. What did she feel for him? he wondered. Contempt? She fingered the single string of pearls that Nick had bought her as a present when she first moved in with him.

"Forget everyone else," Liz whispered. "I'll look after you, Nick. I'll stand by you and I'll *never* leave you."

Sally stared and stared and only stopped when Liz Turner very ostentatiously kissed him.

PART III
MAY

And yet I am, and live—like vapours tost
. . . Into the living sea of waking dreams

John Clare

Chapter One

The week after Will Turner was released, Nick went to the National Gallery. It was the first Monday in May, and the trip was not his idea. As he stood on the steps and looked at the lunchtime traffic in Trafalgar Square, he reflected on the fact that he had agreed to the meeting with a mixture of reluctance and irrational hope.

He spoke when he saw her reach the top of the stone steps. "You're late."

"You're early," Sally replied.

"We said one o'clock."

"We said one-fifteen."

They were silent for a moment until Sally continued, "It was always going to take me fifteen minutes to get here from the Bailey and . . . Nick, do we have to argue?"

"Yes, I think we do," he said, stepping over a particularly disgusting pile of pigeon droppings. "I don't know why we had to meet here, Sally."

"Our little assignations used to start here when we were first together."

"Precisely."

A bedraggled pigeon landed momentarily on Nick's shoulder, causing him to hesitate before he continued.

"Damn flying rats," he said. "Why couldn't we have met at the Bailey? You were there this morning, and I've got a hearing there at three."

"At three? What is it?"

"The contempt hearing for—"

"Nick, you're never representing that Jackie woman?"

"She insisted, apparently. Of course, Cromwell went mad, but he had to accept that even a prostitute is entitled to a lawyer of her own choice. Even if she refused to testify in a murder trial. Shall we go in?"

A crowd of students with backpacks, money pouches, and very short haircuts began to invade the entrance. He pushed Sally through the glass security doors. When the two of them reached the gift shop, they finally managed to escape the teenage tide.

She turned to him. "I wanted to see you alone."

"So you chose the busiest gallery in England."

"I'm worried about you, Nick. You seem to be . . . well, kind of destroying yourself, and I wanted to help—"

"Destroy me?"

"Stop you from doing it. Well, if I could. And we couldn't speak at the Bailey. People would have seen us and it would get back to Max."

"We mustn't upset Max, must we?"

"Look, we had to meet here. You know what the Bar is like. One great big supergrass network. Nothing is private. Everyone informs on everyone else. Want to see a painting?"

"Why?"

"It's an art gallery, Nick. It's what people do in here."

They stood in front of a large plan of the gallery which was covered in glass and bore a myriad of grubby fingerprints.

"Right," Sally said. "Ancient or modern?"

"Religious," Nick replied.

"It's the Sainsbury Wing, then."

They walked along a corridor filled with American couples in matching plastic macs and Japanese tourists who were immaculately dressed. As they passed the statue of a naked man with an athletic body, a discus, and a penis the size of a small radish, Sally touched his hand.

"Don't worry about Max," she said. "It's just a thing. A passing thing. He's nothing at all, really."

"Nothing? He *is* your lover and he *was* my best friend. I wouldn't call that nothing."

Then they were silent until they stopped in front of a painting of a woman, two children, and the most beautiful angel ever painted.

"This was the first picture you ever took me to see," Sally said.

"How can you possibly remember that?"

"It was after the first time we had sex on that Friday night. You know, after that bop at Bar School. We came here on a wet Saturday morning. It made me feel guilty."

"Why?"

"Well, it's called the *Virgin of the Rocks,* isn't it? I thought you were making a point. I felt cheap, Nick. I ran to the loos and—"

"Threw up in the sink," he said.

They sat down a little way away from Leonardo's painting. Although there were a number of other works of art in the room, the two of them concentrated upon only one. People came and went, passing in front of Nick. But he did not really see them. He was aware only of the Virgin and Sally. They sat very close together, but they did not dare touch each other. He gazed at the landscape in the background of the painting. The grotto containing the holy group led onto an emerald and azure sea with strange rock formations and a hazy light.

"You never did tell me," she said.

"What?"

"How you lost your religion."

"Well, it rather lost me," he replied.

"When?"

"When I was taught that Christians went to heaven and everyone else got sent down. It seemed a little unfair. Especially if you met the sanctimonious prats in my confirmation class. Eternity with them just seemed—"

"Yes?"

"Like hell. I mean, one of them, Dominic Scully, was even learning to play the harp. You know, to get a head start. So I became a Marxist instead. Fancy a mint?"

"You weren't a Marxist at Bar School," she said.

"No. It was when I was at university, really. But I found it was the same thing as the Church. Except that one type of Glorious Day was substituted for another. We went around rolling cigarettes. We supported the workers but would never drink in the same pubs as them. They scared the hell out of us."

"So what did you do?"

"I stopped believing in anything—"

"And?"

"I was finally happy."

"When was that, Nick?"

"When I met you, Sally. Let's see some Hieronymus Bosch."

At two o'clock they entered a room of paintings from the fifteenth century. It was deserted apart from a warder who sat on a chair in the corner and whose supervision of Flemish portraiture amounted to the odd snore and dribbling onto his uniform.

They stopped in front of a painting of a man and a woman holding hands. There was a window on the left side of the painting and a mirror on the wall in the background. At the couple's feet was a dog.

"Bet you don't know what it's called," Sally said.

"The dog?"

"The painting."

"The *Arnolfini Marriage* by Van Eyck," he said.

"Now there's a subject we could discuss."

"Flemish art in the fifteenth century?"

"No, Nick. Marriage."

"Oh, that."

"Yes, that." She glanced at the warder, who continued to

snore. She moved very close to the canvas. *"Hate* Mrs. Arnolfini's dress. Dotty P seconds or what?"

"Well, I think the point is—"

"Why did you never ask me to marry you, Nick?"

"You never wanted children."

"You *know* what happened. I'm not going to discuss *it.*"

She had mentioned the big unmentionable: that which must be forgotten. That which cannot speak its name. Only referred to as "it."

"Marriage without kids is pointless," Nick said, staring intently at the painting. "I quite like the dog. You can almost see its tail wagging, the little scamp. What do you suppose it symbolizes?"

"A dog." Then she added reluctantly, "Dogs historically have symbolized fidelity, devotion, undying love."

They both sat down again, this time on an austere wooden bench and farther apart. They had nothing to say, and the only sound in the room was the grumbling drone emerging from the hairy nostrils of the warder.

Finally, she asked, "What do you suppose the dog is called?"

"Tricksy."

"Tricksy? That doesn't sound very Flemish. Nor very medieval, for that matter."

"It's not," he said.

"So who the hell is Tricksy?"

"A client of mine on Death Row. Well, in Death Kennel, really. They want to inject cyanide into his bottom."

"What an outrage."

"I'm sure Tricksy feels the same." He hesitated. "So what do you think happened to them, then?"

"Apparently they were a perfect match."

"Like us—"

"But they had no children, and things got really nasty when he was taken to court by his mistress."

He suddenly wished he had not made the comparison. "What did happen to us, Sals?"

"We were just trundling along on parallel tracks," she said.

"You were on one side and I was on the other. We went along in tandem, but we could never get any closer."

"Nor, then, could we grow apart."

"It was an illusion, Nick. When you look at rails, they seem to converge. The further you go, the closer they seem to get. But they never do. Not by a millimeter."

"So?"

"So the whole sodding show was going to come off the tracks, Nick. It was going to be a catastrophe and we both knew it but . . ."

"What?"

"But I was the only one with the guts to pull the emergency cord. I had to bring it to a halt, Nick. Before it ruined us both."

He did not answer. He stood up and inspected the canvas very carefully. Perhaps he should have felt angry, but she had only told him what he already knew and had been too ashamed to admit.

"I hear on the grapevine that Cromwell is thinking of reporting you," she said.

"He can't believe what Will Turner said about me."

"Can't he?"

"Well, do you believe it?"

"That's not the point, Nick."

"Yes, it is, Sally. It's the whole point. Are you saying you really think that I'm capable—"

"Who knows what we're capable of, Nick. Any of us."

"So you think I—"

"Nick, I'm worried about you. You've been behaving very strangely. You've been mixing with some very odd people. Murderers, prostitutes—Ann Barnes. It's all bound to have an effect."

"On what?"

"On you. I hear you've been seeing that woman."

"Which woman?"

"Look, if you're going to treat me like an idiot, then we're both wasting our time."

"So now you're going to bad-mouth Elizabeth?"

"Since when did you call that poisonous woman Elizabeth?"

"Since you shacked up with Max, actually."

"Nick, the officers in the case were telling me all sorts of things about . . . your precious Elizabeth."

"Of course, the police always tell the truth."

"God, she really has you eating out of the palm of her hand."

"What did the police say?"

"That she came on to them while they were interviewing her."

"Sheer fantasy."

"Theirs or yours, Nick? Just think. What do you really know about her?"

"What do you mean?"

"Who is she, Nick? Where does she come from? I mean, why is she interested in *you*?"

"Thanks."

"No, I just meant—"

"I know exactly what you meant, Sally. I've got to go."

"Nick, please—"

"Sorry. I've got a prostitute to defend."

"Nick, I wanted to talk—about us."

"Why bother?"

She looked at him, squarely, evenly. "Did it mean *nothing* to you?"

"It?"

"Us. Did it mean nothing?"

"Nothing at all," he replied, knowing instantly that it was the biggest lie he had ever told.

Chapter Two

After a detour to Waterloo Bridge, Nick arrived at the Old Bailey at half past two. He went straight to the robing room and put on a freshly pressed wing collar that he had rescued from the Thomas à Kempis chapter on the purity of the soul and union with God. He had to look his best. He was about to enter a cell with Jackie the prostitute.

The aftershocks of the argument with Sally were still working their way through his body. He was upset, certainly. But there was something more.

Since Sally had left him, he had done his best to deaden the effect, to dull his senses. To some extent he had succeeded. But their meeting had awoken the old emotions. It was the ability to affect his life which had first made him love her. She had taught him how to love. She had made him grow up. And then she had left him for Max.

When he got to the cell area of the Old Bailey, Jackie was already in one of the visiting rooms.

"So we meet in a dungeon for a second time, honey," she said.

"Please don't call me that."

As he sat down at the table, he saw that the woman was wearing a Lycra bodysuit and the blond wig he had seen before.

"Why did you want me to represent you?" he asked.

"I knew you more . . . intimately than any other barrister. It seemed the most sensible thing to do. I hope you agree."

"You realize the judge could send you to prison for this?"

"So?"

"So it's serious."

"I'm not frightened," she said.

"I never said you were."

"But you're frightened, aren't you, Mr. Downes? You're shaking like a little leaf. Just like when you came to see me in a T-shirt that time."

"Don't worry about me. I'll do my job. I'm a professional."

"Yeah, I heard about your professional standards during Will Turner's trial. You seem to be getting yourself into as much trouble as me."

"Look. Why do you want me to represent you? There are five thousand other barristers who could have the privilege."

"Well," she said, "I know you're not violent. I know you've got no real perversions other than the normal ones—and how many of your colleagues could we say that about?"

"Now listen—"

"But really I've asked for you because—you're *involved.*"

"What did you say?"

She did not reply.

"Involved in what?" he asked, his voice now lower in case Jo was at the cell door.

"Don't we have to go upstairs?"

"I'm involved in what? You haven't answered my question."

"You still don't understand what's going on, do you, honey?" she replied.

"Well, are you going to tell me?"

"Perhaps."

"When?"

"When you get me out of here."

The jailer came to the door. "Judge is waiting. Hurry up. He wants you."

Jackie stood up and swiveled round. "Wait for me outside the court after they release me," she said to him.

"What makes you think Cromwell will let you off?"

"Oh, he looks like a big teddy bear, really. I bet his bark is worse than his bite."

Mr. Justice Cromwell was already in court when Nick skulked in holding a copy of *Archbold,* the criminal lawyer's Bible.

"Bring in the defendant," he said.

When she appeared in the dock, the clerk to the court stood up and said, "What is your name?"

"Jackie."

"Yes, but Jackie what?"

"Jackie . . . Downes."

The judge was furious. "Are you being facetious, madam?"

"I don't know."

"Well, tell us your name."

"Jackie . . . Kennedy."

The judge fixed her with a particularly sharp pencil and said, "Madam, you are already in considerable trouble. I advise you not to make it worse." Then he turned to Nick. "Now, are you ready to proceed, Mr. Downes?"

"Yes, M'Lord."

"What do you say the appropriate procedure is?"

"Well, this is a hearing of summary jurisdiction, which means—"

"I invent it as I go along?" Cromwell said.

"Something like that."

"Your client refused to testify in a trial of the most serious nature. I suppose she should be asked whether she accepts that fact." He gazed over Nick's head and addressed the woman in the dock. "Do you agree that you were not willing to give evidence before the court last week?"

Jackie sat inspecting a small tear in her Lycra bodysuit in the region of her naval.

"Stand up when I am speaking to you," barked the judge. "Now do you accept—"

"I done nothing," she said.

"That's the point, madam. You refused to give evidence."

"If you say so, honey."

"Do not address me in that fashion. You are just adding insult to injury."

"That's sort of my speciality," she said.

"It seems as if the facts are not in dispute," the judge finally decided.

Nick got to his feet. "But the vital issue remains, M'Lord. Does that in itself constitute a contempt of court?"

"Well, I think it does."

"You haven't heard any submissions from me."

Cromwell folded his arms and put down his pencil. "Very well, Mr. Downes. But remember that I know all the facts. Make it brief."

Nick looked up at the public gallery. It was empty. All the court staff including the clerk had now left court. There was only Nick, the accused, and the judge.

"Shouldn't we have a shorthand typist?" Nick asked. "For the record."

"The tape machine is recording every syllable of your eloquent oratory for your memoirs, Mr. Downes. Now get on with it."

Nick felt decidedly uneasy. Behind him he could hear his client chewing away incessantly and every now and then twanging her Lycra shoulder straps. The judge was affecting his most miserable face, and Nick did not really have anything to say. It was another day at the office.

"The question is whether there was a serious interference with the administration of justice," he began. "Perhaps she should be allowed to go into the witness box to explain why—"

"Don't you mean, the issue is whether her refusal to testify materially affected the verdict, Mr. Downes?"

"Yes, I think—"

"And I suppose you will say that the fact that Mr. Turner

pleaded guilty to manslaughter in any event leads any sane person to the inexorable conclusion that her refusal had no effect whatsoever?"

"I wouldn't have quite phrased it like that, but—"

"And you would no doubt further say that it was not vital to know this lady's answers as the accused had confessed the same details to his wife?"

"I would, if you would just let me—"

"Of course, your best point is that she should be given an opportunity to apologize and, if she does, the normal course would be for the judge, however irascible, to take no further action at all. Especially as she had spent the best part of a week in custody. Am I right, Mr. Downes?"

"Yes, M'Lord."

"Very well. Stand up, madam. Your apology is accepted." Cromwell still had his arms folded as his voice boomed over Nick's wig. "I am persuaded by your, if I may say so, most eloquent counsel to take an unusually lenient course. I find that the contempt in this instance was not of the most dire degree. In view of the time you have already spent in custody, I am prepared to adopt the sensible suggestions of your counsel. I shall take no further action in this case. You are free to go."

"Thank you, M'Lord," Nick said.

"No, thank you, Mr. Downes."

"But I did nothing."

"Rarely in the course of British history, Mr. Downes, has one man achieved so much by doing so little."

Before Nick knew it, the judge had left court and Jackie was standing at his side. The two of them walked through the door of Court 8. Suddenly London was visible through the large windows in the opposite wall. Dirty clouds, the odd rooftop, vertical office blocks. A pigeon came to rest on the ledge of the nearest window.

Nick said, "Now I've got you free, you said you'd tell me what you meant by me being involved."

The woman behind him said nothing. But there was another voice. It belonged to a man.

"You are under arrest."

Nick's heart stopped. He turned around rapidly. He saw a man in uniform holding on to the woman's arm.

"Leave me alone," she said.

"You're under arrest on suspicion of keeping a disorderly house, abducting a minor, procuring women into prostitution, and—"

"What?" the woman asked.

"And anything else I can think of," the officer said. He was young, arrogant, and had an unusually advanced tan for May.

He led her away, and Jackie did not resist. She looked round once at an astonished Nick. He was about to call out again, What did you mean, I'm involved? But he thought better of it. He could not help remembering what Sally had said: Who are these people?

As Jackie neared the end of the corridor, she turned toward him and shouted, "Find the Chinese girl—the one who brought you to my place."

Before he could ask why, she added, "Turner's looking for her. You've got to find her."

"What's her name?"

"China White."

Chapter Three

"When I said I liked Swedish movies, what I meant was Ingmar Bergman, not—"

"Shut up, Nick," Liz said later that evening. "Just watch. You might learn something."

"I thought . . ." Nick paused as a pair of breasts twelve feet wide moved slowly across the screen. "I thought we might see one of Bergman's classics like *The Seventh Seal,* or *Fanny and Alexander.*"

"This is like *Fanny and Alexander,*" Liz said. "Only without the Alexander."

"What's it called again?"

"*Muffy Malone Gets Shafted.*"

"It's not even Swedish."

"Well, it's sort of Scandinavian, I suppose—after a fashion."

"There are no subtitles," Nick said.

"That's because there's no dialogue, Nick."

"Why did you bring me here?"

"Because I'm trying to educate you, Mr. Downes."

On the screen, the extreme close-up had faded into a soft-focus shot of two naked bodies moving with some violence to electric organ music from the seventies. The grunts from the film were echoed by the disparate audience of men. Nick noticed that he and Liz were the only couple.

"It smells in here," he said. "And my seat is lumpy." He sensed that Liz's breathing was now discernible and regular. "Liz, I said—"

"Nick," she whispered.

"Do you want me to explain the storyline?"

"Nick," she repeated, grasping his hand and guiding it toward her groin. "Can't you feel me?"

"Liz, you've forgotten to wear any panties."

"Can't you feel how . . . wet I am?"

"Yes," he said, rummaging around, a little surprised. "But what happened to your panties?"

"They're crotchless."

"In what sense?"

"In the sense they haven't got a crotch, you idiot. No, don't take your hand away."

On the screen, Miss Malone and her partner suddenly found themselves in an oriental harem. She was scantily attired in revolting pink lace. The man sat cross-legged and had a turban on his head which looked like the mess of bandages Will Turner had once worn. There was a disgusting groan from someone two rows behind Nick.

"Do they sell Maltesers?" he asked.

"What?" Liz gasped.

"Well, not necessarily Maltesers. Any sort of chocolate confectionery will do. I didn't get any lunch, you see."

"Why not?"

He had been with Sally. But for the first time that he could remember, he felt guilty about seeing Sally Fielding. It was as if he were sneaking around behind Liz's back. This is ridiculous, he thought. Liz and I haven't even had sex yet. Admittedly, my hand is in the vicinity of her crotchless panties in a porn cinema in Soho, but does that give her a proprietary interest?

"Why no lunch?" Liz repeated. "Oh, yes, carry on doing that with your fingers, Nick. Yes, just there."

Masturbation was Nick's best defense against having to reveal the truth to Liz. He did not want to lie, but suddenly the truth was uncomfortable. The heroine on the screen stood in front of the man, whose arms were still folded. Slowly he began to rip off the layers of lace and silk. She shuddered and tossed her head back as more and more of her flesh was exposed. Soon she was almost naked. The man started to run his fingers up and down her flat stomach, her legs parted, and then, to Nick's astonishment, a camel popped its head round the corner of the tent.

He felt Liz's muscles tensing and relaxing in a series of small waves. His fingers were by now very slippery, and he desperately wanted to wipe them on the seat. But he felt sure that Liz would be offended.

She turned her head toward him, her breath warm. "That was amazing."

"The camel? I suppose it symbolized—"

"Shut up," she said.

Muffy Malone was now riding off into the sunset. She was alone, apart from the camel.

"I thought she would end up with Mr. Turban," Nick said. "I suppose that was the moral of the piece: Great sex is no guarantee of true love. What would you like to do now, Liz?"

"Corrupt you," she said.

They took a cab to Notting Hill. But during the journey, Liz became increasingly anxious, as if there was something dreadful at home.

Finally, they reached the street door to a swish mansion block. Once Nick had paid the driver, he found his way blocked by Liz. She was in tears.

"We don't have to do this," he tried to reassure her.

"I want to."

"Then why the tears?"

"He's been following me."

"Who?" he asked, then, realizing it could only be one person, added, "We can get an injunction against Will."

"He's still my husband."

"We can get a nonmolestation order."

"He hasn't been molesting me." She looked around nervously. When she was satisfied that it was safe, she continued, "The only person who has been molesting me is you. In the cinema. And it was *great*."

Nick smiled. "Can we go in?"

She took his hand.

The fourth-floor flat was on the correct—that is, more expensive—side of Notting Hill Gate. An open-plan lounge ended with a balcony affording a view of the communal gardens, which were immaculately kept. On the terrace were several window boxes containing plants that had run to seed.

"You need to do a bit of gardening," Nick said.

"Can't," Liz called from the kitchen. "I'm sure it's become a place of Special Scientific Interest by now. Probably a breeding ground for newts or something."

Nick thought he heard a cat in the hawthorn bushes four floors below. It reminded him of his Catt with two *t*s. But most of all it reminded him of the night Sally had said she was going to leave him. The whining stopped, and so did Nick's guilt about seeing Liz.

"Drink these." She poured out two Bloody Marys.

"What, both of them?"

"Yes, both of them."

"Why?"

"I want to get you drunk and then I want to make love to you," she said. "Take your trousers off."

"What, here?"

"No, Nick. On the balcony so the neighbors can see your bottom."

"What about your marriage vows?" he asked. "Some rules aren't meant—"

"Fuck them," she said.

Tentatively, Nick undid his zipper.

"Now undo your belt," she commanded.

"What about your husband?"

"I no longer have a husband. Take off your pants."

He complied with the order. "Now you," he said, reaching for her clothes.

"No. Just watch," she said, beginning to undress. "You don't mind watching, do you?"

She had a body that was full, yet well nurtured. She had clearly, Nick thought, paid more attention to it than she had to the pot plants that stood drooping around the lounge, looking sorry for themselves. Finally, she kneeled in front of him, completely naked apart from a single string of pearls around her neck. Like the one Nick had once bought Sally.

"I'd better put this on," he said, reaching for his trousers.

"What is it?"

"Liz."

"Ah."

Nick had known that this moment would come, and he was determined to be prepared. However, it was the first time that he had used a condom.

Liz took him into her bedroom, a room full of mirrors of every conceivable shape and color.

She lay on the huge brass bed. She opened her legs slightly and pulled him onto her. He slid in. Her breasts were flattened by the position, but the nipples stood out. He slid his lips over one and then the other. Liz moaned a little as he moved his mouth away from them altogether. She reached out with her mouth for his body, her lips apart, her tongue snaking out, straining to touch his bare flesh.

He kissed her neck. All the time the rhythm of his thrusts was increasing. Even through the condom, he could feel her warmth. She ran her hands over the small of his back, guiding him, pushing him deeper into her. She bit his ear softly, his neck harder. His bare flesh rubbed against hers. Her cheeks flushed; small beads of sweat ran along her cleavage. She moved her thighs, her hands pushing him in deeper.

"I want to look after you," she whispered.

He did not reply.

"I want to own you, Nick."

She started to jerk toward Nick, lifting all but her shoulders off the bed.

Suddenly, she spun him around, and now she was on top. She grabbed one of his wrists and then the other and lifted them above his head, toward the brass bedstead.

She lifted herself off him, and for a moment his erection was free, but he did not want it to be; he needed to be inside her again.

She gently lowered herself onto him, giving him what he wanted, and he moaned with the thrills of pleasure that shot through his body.

She leaned over his face, her breasts hanging, tantalizingly, just out of the reach of his mouth. And then she reached further forward and her left breast touched his lips. He licked all around the nipple. He felt his right hand, somewhere above his head, being tied.

Then her right breast stroked his chin, his cheeks. He reached out with his tongue, then felt his other hand being tied.

Liz started to raise and lower herself. Now he was very hard, and she seemed to pivot on his erection, spreading her legs wide, voraciously, to take all of him.

When he finally glanced up, he saw that his hands were tied with red legal ribbon. He was captive, helpless, loving it.

She lowered her head, her hair falling wildly over Nick's face. She whispered, barely audibly, next to his ear, "What would you do? Will could come in any minute. What would you do, Nick?"

Nick struggled against the bonds, but as the ribbon cut into his wrists he knew it was useless.

"Will could come in," she said, breathless. "He could see us fucking."

She was kissing his neck, running her tongue over his throat, gently biting it. He closed his eyes, savoring the pleasure of it all, feeling drops of sweat from her falling, splashing onto his face, his lips.

She pulled his hair, forcing his eyes open. And in twenty different mirrors, from all angles, the one reflected in the other, he saw the naked flesh, the man tied to the bed, the woman's breasts inches from his face, their bodies joined invisibly.

He could feel her muscles tightening. She lifted her knees and he felt as if he would reach her womb. But when she came, she made no noise. She let the waves move through her body in silence, only shuddering audibly when Nick came as well.

They lay there looking at each other but not speaking. He fought an urge to close his eyes and sleep, to forget everything that had happened that day. But eventually he slid out of her and she untied his wrists. He turned onto his front.

"Are you all right?" she asked.

"Fine and dandy."

"Why do you always have to mess about, Nick?"

"Is that what I do?"

"Yes, that's precisely what you do."

She moved her hand toward Nick's groin and started with horror. "Nick, where's it gone?"

"The erection?"

"The condom."

He glanced down at his bare penis, which had returned to normal proportions. When he looked on the bed and saw nothing, he realized that there was only one place the condom could still be.

"I'll sort it out," she said. "You go to sleep."

Hours later, Nick was awoken by a faint sobbing next to him. The central London half-darkness was reflected in all the mirrors, and he could just make out Liz curled up to his side.

"I want you to leave," she said.

"Why?"

"In your sleep. You kept doing it."

"What?"

"Calling out a name."

"A name?" Nick asked.

"Sally."

Chapter Four

The next day, Nick and Ann Barnes sat at a glass table drinking coffee. The chic café was opposite the Soho Catholic church, which urged penitents to SAVE OUR SPIRE SO WE CAN SAVE YOUR SOULS.

Inside, the café was full of young men using their mobile phones and older men in casual clothes going through the contact ads in *Time Out*.

"I'm surprised you agreed to meet me in Soho," Ann said, sipping the jet-black coffee.

"I had nothing else to do," Nick replied.

"Liar."

"I wanted to meet you." He played uneasily with his cup. "Besides," he said, "I have to find someone."

"Who?"

"A girl."

"You?" she asked with incredulity. "A *girl?* Where did you meet a girl?"

He could see no good reason to conceal the truth. "I met her outside a brothel, Ann. Someone's asked me to find her."

"What's it got to do with you?"

"Nothing. I never actually did anything with her," he said. "She just took me inside the salon and——"

"Hold it right there," she interrupted. "Don't say another word."

"But, Ann. All I paid for was——"

"Look, Nick, I'm going to give you the psychiatrist's caution."

"The what?"

"One more perverted admission and I'm obliged to call the men in white coats."

He picked up a teaspoon, added more sugar to his cup, and pretended to be interested in the church opposite.

"Does Sally know about the . . . salon?" Ann asked. When he did not reply, she added, "Don't tell her. Don't tell anyone. Ever."

"I'm not ashamed."

"I don't imagine you're very proud, either. Men do these things, Nick. It's natural. It's not your fault, it's all down to the lumps of testosterone floating around your body."

He listened to the bleeps of mobile phones being turned on and off. Above him, huge brass fans circled slowly, conveying the smoke and noise around the room.

"I'm still waiting," she said.

"For what?"

"For a lump or two to float in my direction. But you seem obsessed with those other women."

He looked into her alert eyes. As hard as he tried, he could see only a friend.

"I mean," she continued, "I know I don't have Sally's beauty and I certainly don't have Liz Turner's . . . sexy weirdo appeal. I know I've been around the block a few times." She looked away from his gaze. "All right, I've been around the block more times than a New York cabbie, but I'm a safer bet than the others. If you're not careful, Nick, one day soon you're going to end up doing it doggie-doggie with Liz Turner. Those childbearing hips, that man-eating figure, an irresistible mixture of mother and mistress. You don't stand a chance unless . . ."

He hurriedly drained the dregs in his cup. "Fancy another?"

"Oh my God," she said. "You *have* done it with her, haven't you?"

He did not reply.

"Nick," she said with astonishment, "you have—"

"Yes," he said. "Well, when I say yes, I mean that I have, but not doggie-doggie. It was more of a reverse missionary with a disappearing condom thrown in."

"When?"

"Last night."

"Where?"

"Her place."

"But why?"

"I . . . actually, Ann, I don't know. I've been behaving a little strangely lately. Ever since—ever since Sally left me. I can't explain it."

"Well, don't," she said.

"But I thought it's supposed to be better to talk things through."

"Bollocks. Propaganda disseminated for the sole purpose of keeping therapists and social workers in business."

He glanced up at one of the fans above him. His eyes began to feel heavy, as they had when Ann Barnes had hypnotized Will Turner. He had been thinking all morning about how Liz had cried herself to sleep as he silently left the flat at 4 A.M.

"I sort of did something wrong to Liz Turner," he told Ann. "How should I make it up?"

"Say it with flowers. In her case, a Venus flytrap."

"She's not as bad as everyone thinks."

"Is that your brain talking or an equally wobbly part of your anatomy? Look, Nick, I don't mean to intrude—actually, I do—but do you know what you're getting yourself into with Mr. and Mrs. Psycho?"

"I can handle it."

"That's the problem. You seem to be handling too much of it."

"What do you suppose will happen to your favorite patient?" he asked.

"Actually, I'm a bit worried. If the therapy doesn't work, he could—"

"What?"

"Well, go off. At any time. His anger is a time bomb, and anything could trigger it."

"Why didn't you say this in court?" he asked.

"No one asked me."

"Jesus, Ann. What do you suppose he could do?"

"Kill again. Another espresso?"

Five minutes later, Ann returned with two steaming cups.

"So why are you in Soho?" he asked as she sat down again.

"Work."

"What have you been up to, then?"

"Oh, the usual cavalcade of perverts and paranoids. Except I've got quite an interesting one coming up at the Bailey. Chinese bloke. That's why I'm in Soho."

"What's he up for?"

"Apparently he's been deliberately slipping cockroaches and rats' droppings into the sweet and sour pork."

"So what?"

"I know. If he had bunged the roaches on an earthenware dish with a bit of puréed yeast he could have called it nouvelle cuisine and charged a hundred nicker a head in Knightsbridge. But sadly for Laughing Boy, it was in Soho. And one of the Vice Squad ate it and was poisoned. Some mysterious tropical disease."

"What's your chef being done for?" Nick asked. "Administering a noxious substance?"

"Well, that or an obnoxious cockroach," she said. "Anyway, my job is to say whether he's bonkers or not."

"And is he?"

"Well, in my book, anyone who tries to poison a member of the Porn Squad can't be completely mad. The person who was really certifiable is this expert they are going to call to deal with the rats' droppings."

"Who?"

"Some zoologist. A sort of Doctor of Forensic Feces. A real

loony from the hospital, you know, the tropical diseases place in
Soho. I mean, the most exotic thing you can get in Soho is the
clap. Ridiculous, isn't it?"

"What's wrong with the doctor?"

"Nick, this man spends his entire professional life sniffing
little rat turds. It makes the law seem like an acceptable occupation."

He wobbled back and forth on his chair as she took a cigarette from the packet in her handbag. "What do you know
about rodents, Nick?"

"Nothing."

She lit the cigarette and, after inhaling deeply, said, "Well, I
was quite an expert on rats—even before I read the report of
Dr. Droppings."

"How come?"

"I've been out with quite a few. First thing you should know
about a rat is that he'll never tell you he's married. Second
thing you should know is that he'll do anything for a blow
job—"

"Ann, what did the doctor actually write?"

"He said that rats are opportunistic, nocturnal, and breed all
year round. Rather like barristers, if you ask me."

Nick did not reply.

"Did you know," she continued, "wherever you are in central
London, you're only thirty feet away from a rat? Of course, go
into Devlin's and that distance is reduced to a glass of Frascati
and a groping free hand."

"Where are all these rodents, then?"

"Everywhere," she said. "There are rats in the restaurants and
down the tube. In the basement and crawling up your toilet
bowl. In fact, about the only place they don't want to be these
days is in the sewers."

"Why not?"

"They're upwardly mobile, you see. Taking over London.
There's a real fuss, you know. They think there might be black
rats in that Chinese restaurant."

"So?"

"Black rats were the medieval plague carriers. But fortunately they're quite rare now. Originally came from Southeast Asia. Possibly China itself. But they're only meant to be found in docklands nowadays."

"In London?"

"Mainly. That's why there's the fuss. They might be spreading. Apparently they're very commensal."

"They're *what?*"

"Commensal. According to the report, it means living in close proximity to man."

"Like in his digestive tract?" Nick said, thinking of the corpse and the scavenged skeleton of the rat. "I wonder what your expert would say about that."

"I'll see if I can find out, if you like," she replied. "Still, you've got to feel sorry for the Vice Squad bobbie."

"Why?"

"Well, one day PC Plod is booking prostitutes in Soho, and the next he's got bubonic plague. It's a bit of a tragedy." She looked at her watch. "Look, I'm running late. I've got to dash."

"How sure are you about Will Turner going off?" he said as he walked with Ann to the door. But she did not answer.

On a wall beside the arcade opposite, he saw a council poster. DON'T FEED THE RATS. AVOID DISPOSING OF LIQUID WASTE.

Suddenly his espresso appeared much less appetizing. He tried to think of something to do to while away the time until the clubs opened. Could he work out the connection between black rats and the bowels of the murdered man?

"Look," Ann said, "I shouldn't really do this, but . . . can you come to the psych center tomorrow?"

He didn't need to think twice. "I can. But why?"

"Something has come up in Will Turner's sessions, Nick. Something I've never seen before."

Chapter Five

After Ann left him, Nick wandered around Leicester Square until he could not bear to hear another evangelist. He browsed in the bookshops of Charing Cross Road until he could not look at another critique of T. S. Eliot's poetry. And he drank enough tea to cause permanent damage to his bladder. He was waiting for one thing. For the club to open.

He managed to string out a cup of Lapsang souchong for almost an hour in a Lebanese café with newspapers in Arabic. He took out his copy of *The Waste Land* and flicked through the pages.

But he could think of nothing except the debacle of the night before. When they discovered that the condom was still inside Liz, Nick was terrified. Images of antenatal classes, nappies, and the Child Support Agency whirled around in his head. Liz, for her part, had simply fished the offending object out.

Nick did not fully understand his emotions: Did he not want children? Of course he did, but not right now, not unexpectedly, not with Liz.

At 8 P.M. he left the café and walked through Chinatown to the club. It was a warm evening, but the city did not yet have its summer stench.

At the entrance to the club, the doorman who had frisked him before was on duty. His tuxedo was as neat as ever, his demeanor just as coarse.

"Bit keen, aren't you?" he said to Nick, all the time eyeing him with suspicion.

"Aren't you open yet?"

"Oh, we're open all right, but the acts don't really start until later."

"I don't really want to see the acts."

"What do you want? A drink?"

"I want to find one of the girls."

"One of our artistes?" the man said, wiping his nose on his clean suit sleeve, leaving a shiny streak. "Not allowed."

"Why not?"

"Rule of the house. No perverts or punters backstage."

"But I'm neither," Nick protested.

"Ain't you?" The man laughed but did not give the impression that he was particularly amused. "Anyway, which girl was it?"

"China White."

"Sure you don't want a boy? No offense, but you look the type." The doorman looked up and down the street. He came a little closer to Nick. "You want China? She was here."

"So can I come in?"

"No," the man said.

"Why not?"

" 'Cause she's scarpered."

"Run off?" Nick asked.

"Isn't that what I just said?"

"Yes, I suppose it was. Where has she gone?"

"I don't bleeding know, do I? Tarts don't leave a forwarding address when they scarper."

"Why did she leave?"

"You plod?" the man asked. "Only you got that crap sort of dress sense. Look, I don't want no trouble from Vice."

"I'm not the police."

"Who are you, then?"

"A friend," Nick said.

"Sure. And I'm Saddam Hussein's auntie. You see, people might get the wrong idea. What with you asking all them questions. They might think what you really want is a good hiding. No one asks nothing round here. Understand?"

Nick decided that he had better go. The trail had gone cold, and he was getting into trouble. But in his mind, he still heard Jackie's voice saying: Find the Chinese girl. You've got to find the girl. China White.

Nick hailed a cab and resolved to visit Liz Turner. He wanted to apologize both for his squeamish behavior and for his nocturnal mumblings about Sally. When the taxi stopped in Notting Hill, he went into a late-night drugstore. There he attempted to buy some flowers. But the blooms that remained were all shriveled.

In the corner of the shop, next to the cheap greeting cards and girlie magazines, was a collection of small china animals. One stood out. The moment Nick saw it, he knew he had to buy it for Liz. He remembered again what she had said about her childhood. He bought her a china cat.

Leaving the shop, he felt as if he were rescuing the poor thing from the sleaze and tack around it. Liz had always wanted a cat; now he would give her one.

He reached Liz's mansion block. As he was about to sound the buzzer, someone came through the door. Nick slipped inside. He rapidly climbed the four flights of steps and was breathless by the time he arrived on Liz's landing. He was about to knock on the door when he realized that it was on the latch.

Pushing it ajar, he saw Liz. She was naked on the floor. Above her was a man. When he looked more closely, he saw who it was and dropped the china cat. It was Will Turner.

And as Will Turner moved above her, arching his body, thrusting slowly in and out, Liz stared at Nick. He was sure that she smiled.

Chapter Six

The next day, Nick went to the Bloomsbury address that Ann had given him. He arrived shortly before midday, intending to accompany Ann to the West Kensington Magistrates' Court, where they both had commitments.

The research center was in a crescent of white stucco buildings near Regent's Park and the zoo, but it was creatures of a very different nature which came under Ann Barnes's forensic eye.

She met him at reception and led him through labyrinthine corridors.

"Officially it's called PRIC," she said. "The Psychiatric Research and Investigation Center. But hardly anyone uses the acronym."

"Is it well paid?"

"As much as any government wage slave job ever is. Great pension if you haven't slashed your wrists from boredom beforehand."

They finally reached an office that had Ann's name on the door. Once inside, Nick saw that the room was as chaotic as some of Ann's conversations: piles of papers, plastic reconstructions of brains, fashion magazines.

When he had sat down in front of her desk, he asked, "What is it you're actually doing, Ann? I know it's sensitive and all—"

"It's secret. An Official Secret."

"Never mind."

"I'm helping to develop a new polygraph. All this James Bond subterfuge rubbish—I thought the Cold War was over."

"A polygraph?" he asked. "A lie detector?"

"Yep. Every home should have one."

"But they aren't admissible as evidence in court."

"The world does go on outside the Old Bailey, Nick. HMG uses them to screen candidates for the secret services and to debrief defectors—though God knows where anyone can defect from anymore."

He looked at a large television screen in one corner of the room. "What's all this to do with Will Turner?"

"He's going through therapy, and since I did my Flo Nightingale act and saved his life he'll have no one else but me. A psycho of impeccable taste, really." She smiled, revealing a multitude of fine lines around her eyes. "So I've come out of retirement—I'm still an approved shrink under the Mental Health Act."

"How's he responding to treatment?"

"You'll see in a mo. I've sort of killed two birds with one stone—using Turner's therapy to monitor the progress of the prototype polygraph."

"Does he know?"

"Nick, he hardly knows who he is."

"How do you mean?"

"Let's watch a video."

She stood up and rummaged in a box full of tapes with strange names on them, beginning to panic when she couldn't find the right one. "It's here somewhere," she said.

Nick moved across to help just as she fished out the video she wanted with a triumphant shout. "This is it."

"But it says *Lanzer*," he said.

"You'll see why in a tick," she told him, sliding the tape into the video machine beneath the television.

The screen was a fuzzy mess of electronic lines, and nothing concrete appeared for what seemed to Nick like ages.

"Don't say I've wiped it," she groaned. Suddenly the picture cleared and there was a clear image of an interview room, very similar to those in a police station.

Nick could just make out the back of Ann's head and shoulders in the bottom right-hand side of the screen. Sitting opposite her in a chair, with wires attached to various parts of his anatomy, was Will Turner.

Then the soundtrack came to life.

Ann's voice came through the speakers. "The time is one thousand hours. My name is Dr. Ann Barnes. Are you comfortable?"

The man nodded.

"Please speak all your answers for the machine," she encouraged him softly.

"Yes, I'm comfortable," he replied.

Nick saw a jagged red line shoot along the bottom of the screen. "What's that?" he asked.

"Polygraph reading. They're computerized and visualized."

"What does it mean?"

"That he's lying. He's not comfortable at all. Just watch."

On the screen, Ann asked another question. "You're not *really* comfortable, are you?"

"No," the man said.

The line at the bottom of the screen became flat and even.

Ann turned to Nick. "Now he's telling the truth."

"That's incredible," he replied.

"I know. Imagine if we could develop a pocket polygraphette. Women could take it on every date. Are you married? Are you sleeping with other women? Do you really fancy little boys? The potential uses are endless." She looked at the screen. "This is the bit."

"Could you tell us your name?" she asked the man.

"Is it important?"

"For the record."

"My name is Will Turner," he said quietly.

Nick was amazed—for the line at the bottom of the screen went crazy.

"That," Ann said, "is what I wanted you to see."

"He's *lying?*"

"According to the machine."

"But why have you labeled the tape Lanzer?"

"Later in the therapy session, he starts talking to this other voice."

"The other voice? The one from the prison?"

"Yes," Ann said. "And he keeps calling it Lanzer."

Chapter Seven

Later that afternoon, Nick found himself in the West Kensington Magistrates' Court listening to Ann Barnes giving evidence. The court was part of the Civic Center complex, which included the Registry Office and the Divorce Court.

A one-step laboratory of human relationships, Ann had once called it. Registry Office, Criminal Court, Divorce Court: marriage, acrimony, divorce—throw in an undertaker's, Ann had said, and you had the complete service.

Nick was due to represent Jackie again. It was all very odd. Although he could have refused the brief, he was curious to find out more about the prostitute's strange request to him about the girl China White.

Jackie's case was in the Thursday afternoon list after Ann's. Ann was still, much to her annoyance, catching up with her caseload from before her move to the Psychiatry Center.

"The defendant," said Ann from the witness box, "took out his dentures and . . . how can I put this?"

The stipendiary magistrate, Peter Canning, intervened. "Please don't pull any punches with me, Dr. Barnes."

"Very well, sir. The defendant took out his false teeth and offered to . . . do things for other men on the tube for twenty pence."

"And you regard this as psychiatrically abnormal behavior, Dr. Barnes?"

"Even for the Northern line, sir."

Nick glanced from counsel's row to the man in the dock. He appeared to Nick to be far from miserable and even gave him a toothless grin when their eyes met.

"Dr. Barnes," Canning continued, "did the defendant ever tell you why he did it?"

"Why he did what?"

"Why he traveled from Chalk Farm to Golders Green charging twenty pence a go?"

"He said he didn't think people would pay him more than twenty pence. But he did have sixty-seven pence on him, which is a bit of a conundrum."

Nick did not really listen as Ann went into the psychiatric niceties of why the man should be sectioned off into some mental institution or other. To him, the defendant just seemed to have demonstrated a little entrepreneurial spirit, and his only mistake was to have undersold himself quite drastically.

The magistrates' court was typical of a busy London center of summary justice. It was cramped and full of dark wood and wrought iron. The dock was so near to counsel's row that a mischievous defendant could easily have leaned over and prodded his lawyer with a pencil. Strange smells emanated from the cell area below the court. Even stranger decisions emanated from the Bench.

"Yes, I am convinced," said Canning, "that the accused represents significant danger to commuters using the Northern line. When it's actually running, that is. And having also considered a written psychiatric assessment, I grant the Hospital Order. The court will adjourn for five minutes."

"All rise," bellowed a policeman with a clipboard whose job it was to call the list.

The defendant reached over the dock and grabbed at Nick's suit. "Does that mean I'm free?" he asked him.

Nick looked at his vacant eyes. "Something like that," he replied, as the confused old man was led into the cells.

By the time he had disappeared, Ann Barnes was at Nick's side. "Seems like you've made a friend," she said, grinning and displaying a perfect set of teeth marred only by the nicotine stains.

Nick, however, was upset. "Was it really necessary to lock him up, Ann? I mean, what harm was he doing?"

"Didn't you hear his form being read out? Indecent assault, indecent exposure." She paused as an incoherent scream came from the cells below. "Indecent life, basically. I know what you're going to say: We all lead indecent lives—except you, of course, Nick. You're so prim and proper that butter wouldn't melt. But this man is dangerous, Nick. He's got more diseases than Don Giovanni's dick. Come outside. I need a fag."

As they left the court, there was another yell, only softer, and then another. By the time Nick reached the court door, all he could hear was the man's sobbing from the cells below.

Ann stubbed her cigarette into the tiled floor with the Metropolitan Police logo. "So you're defending the prostitute again?"

"Yes."

"Nick, why are you getting involved with these people?"

"They're sort of getting involved with me, Ann."

The court foyer was full of policemen reading notebooks and defendants shouting at their children.

"How dangerous do you suppose Will Turner might be?" he asked above the din.

"He could be perfectly harmless—"

"Could he be faking?"

"Possibly. It has happened before. A serial killer in America pretended he had multiple personalities and fooled all the shrinks till the police found psychiatry books in his cellar."

"Ken Bianchi," Nick said. "The Hillside Strangler."

"How did you—"

"Monsters," he replied. "A sort of hobby of mine. Kenneth Bianchi. Supposed alter ego, Steve. Six women murdered. Los

Angeles, late seventies. At least two prostitutes. Murdered his victims in private and then dumped them on the hillsides of L.A."

"God, you know your psychopaths."

"But I don't really understand them. You see, Ann, if Turner is not schizoid and he's not faking, then what is he?"

"Evil," she said.

"I thought you didn't recognize the concept."

"Jesus, Nick. I could be wrong. Can't we change the subject?"

He waited for a couple of Territorial Support Group police officers to pass. "How long has Canning been a stipendiary magistrate?" he asked.

"Why ask me?" She looked somewhat annoyed.

"Weren't you amorously connected with Canning when he was still at the Bar?"

"Who told you that?"

"Sally."

"Oh," she said, "then it must be true. Is this the same Sally who moved in with your best friend? You know, the truthful, reliable one?"

Nick did not answer. Sally had hurt him. But if anyone was going to criticize her, it was going to be Nick. He thought again of their trip to the National Gallery and how for a moment, just a moment, they were almost happy again.

"All right," said Ann. "I did see Canning once."

"What was he like?" Nick asked. "Isn't he a member of Mensa or something?"

"Sure. IQ one-fifty-one, penis size three. He has a tiny bladder and all the tackle to match. That's why he's always rising from the Bench. Can't hold his water." She reached into her handbag and produced an unopened packet of cigarettes. "So tell me what Miss Whiplash is up for."

"Keeping a disorderly house."

"Is that a crime? Christ, if the police ever saw the state of my flat—"

"And for procuring young girls into prostitution."

"And what about the men who the girls are procured for? What happens to them?"

"Nothing."

"Bloody typical." She was suddenly quiet. "Oh, shit," she said eventually. "Promise me you won't do anything stupid."

"Why?"

"I want to warn you about something."

"What?"

"She's in there."

"Who?"

"I just saw her."

"Who, Ann?"

"Max's girlfriend."

"Sally?"

"Isn't that what I said? Look, why don't you give me a ring sometime? Live dangerously for once."

"They're calling my case," Nick said, and he walked toward the court.

"I'm seeing Will Turner for the second time later on," Ann said. "I'll contact you if anything comes up."

Sally was already on her feet as Nick joined her in counsel's row.

"May it please you, sir," she said to Canning, "I appear on behalf of Her Majesty's Customs and Excise. The defendants are, I understood, unrepresented."

Nick looked at the dock where three Chinese men stood.

"This case is about drugs importation," Sally said. "These men were arrested last night. Can I call the Drugs Squad officer in the case? He is liaising with Customs."

"Of course, Miss Fielding," he said.

As the suited officer came to the witness box and was sworn, Nick moved closer to Sally.

"Hi, Sals," he whispered affectionately.

"Go and talk to your girlfriend," she replied.

The words were barely audible but they cut into Nick deeply.

"Sally," he said, "don't be like that."

"It's so nice to see you . . . again," she said with an exaggerated smile to the young, good-looking officer. "Can you tell the court what was found when the premises of these defendants were raided?"

"On searching their restaurants in Notting Hill, we found large quantities of Turkish Brown and special Thai."

Canning wrote the information down.

"Was anything else found?" Sally asked.

"Yes," the officer replied.

"What?"

"There were two frightened girls living in the basement. We assume they were the couriers. They have been physically abused and we are liaising with the DVU at Notting Hill Gate station on this."

"DVU?" Sally asked.

"Domestic Violence Unit."

"Anything else found?"

"China White," the officer said casually.

The words startled Nick. He shot to his feet. "What is China White?" he asked.

Canning was furious. "Are you in this case, Mr. . . . . Mr.—"

"Downes," Sally said. "Nicholas Downes of counsel. And no, sir, Mr. Downes is not instructed in this case."

Nick looked at Canning, who was doing the best impression of a miffed bullock that Nick had ever seen. "I apologize, sir," he said.

Canning pointedly ignored him. He turned to the officer and said, "Please tell the court—for Mr. Downes's benefit—what China White is."

"It's heroin, sir. Very high-grade heroin."

But Nick was already heading for the cells where he knew the prostitute Jackie would be.

Chapter Eight

"She's called China White and it's something to do with heroin," Nick said to Jackie.

Jackie was behind bars, but these were not the individual cells Nick had come to expect. Instead, there were two large holding areas, one for men and one for women. It looked to Nick rather like a jail in a Western movie, with miserable prisoners clutching at bars that ran from floor to ceiling.

"What's it got to do with you what she's called?" she replied. Her ski pants were even more frayed, and the toothless entrepreneur from the Northern line gawped at her unrelentingly. "What are you staring at, Granddad?" she shouted.

"He can't help it," Nick said.

"That's what all men say." She tried to pull the edges of the Lycra closer together, in the process making the tear worse. "So have you found her?"

"No," Nick said. "Will you tell me why I should?"

"I might. Listen, I'll do a deal with you."

He moved right up to the bars. "I hardly think you are in a position to bargain."

"Tit for tat. You scratch my back, and I'll—"

"Tell me everything about the girl," he said.

227

She smiled. "Well, we are getting frisky, aren't we, honey?"

"Do you want bail or not?"

"Dunno. I've grown quite attached to all these handcuffs and chains. You see, Mr. Barrister, you have your chambers and I have mine. Only my chambers are for punishment and pain."

"So are mine, actually," Nick said.

The policeman with the clipboard peered down the stairs that led up to the court. "You're next but one, luv," he said to Jackie. "Unless you're lining up some business."

Jackie was furious. "Stick it up your—"

"I'll see you upstairs," Nick said.

When Nick left the cell area, he went through the foyer again. Ann Barnes had gone. But Sally blocked his way.

"Nicholas," she said sarcastically, "you remembered."

"Pardon?"

"And I thought you'd forget."

"What?"

"Oh, surely May the tenth means something to you?"

Nick rummaged through the rather dilapidated establishment that was supposed to be his memory bank. It was shut.

"May the tenth," Sally repeated.

"Sinking of the *Belgrano?*"

"You *pig,*" she shouted, causing a pair of officers to stare at them.

"Sally, what are you on about?" he asked.

"You know, Nick, your capacity for tactlessness never ceases to amaze me. You remember how many years one of your lags got for bonking in the bogs, but you don't remember my birthday."

"Is it today?" he asked, knowing the answer perfectly well.

"Yes."

"Ask Max to take you out to celebrate, then." He was about to engage in some further vitriol when he looked into her eyes. He felt sure there were tears, though she would not let them fall.

She took a firm hold of his elbow and steered him to the entrance steps.

It was a warm afternoon, and there was a crowd outside the far corner of the civic complex, by the entrance to the Registry Office.

"Look at them," she said, glumly, pointing to the couple in the center of the group.

"What are they doing?" he asked.

"They're getting married, Nick. What do you—"

"But what *are* they doing?" And then he realized. The couple were deaf and were signing to each other, using their fingers, making shapes, lightly touching their faces.

I *love* you.

I love you.

I love *you*.

"They can't even speak," Sally whispered, as if intruding, "and still they can tell each other how they feel. And here we are: two supposedly articulate professionals, and we can't say—"

"Perhaps that's why," Nick replied.

"So why do we always have to fight?" she said, blowing her nose.

"Because we, well . . . you know, each other."

Her eyes brightened. "What did you say?"

"You heard me."

"So do you, still . . . Nick?"

"I never stopped," he said.

The list officer called from the doors of the court. "You going to represent that lady, or what?"

Nick moved past Sally, brushing her hand slightly, their fingers intertwining just for a moment. "I'll never stop, Sals," he said.

Joshua Smith sat in counsel's row, looking very serious. "Ah, Downes," he said. "You in this porn affair?"

Joshua was the stepson of Mr. Justice Sullivan Smith, a judge of the High Court, and a great chum of Cromwell. He had in-

evitably grown up, it seemed to Nick, with a wig on his head.
It also seemed inevitable that he would go prematurely bald
and would have a penchant for hanging. It was all ordained.

The magistrate had risen yet again, and Nick wondered
whether it really was in his best interests to have so many
carafes of water on the Bench in front of him.

"I'm for the lady defendant, if that's what you mean," Nick
said to the prosecutor.

"That's exactly what I meant," Smith said in a sneering tone.

Nick did not like it. "I'm surprised to see you down here,
Smith."

"How do you mean?"

"You know, the son of a High Court judge down among the
dead men in the magistrates' court."

"Firstly, he's only my stepfather. And secondly, it's good experience for me. See how the other half lives and all that. Why
are you here?"

"Oh, I'm the other half."

Canning came back into court suddenly.

As the two barristers got to their feet, Smith whispered,
"False modesty is the worst form of conceit, Downes."

"No," Nick replied. "Conceit is the worst form of conceit. Or
didn't Stepdaddy tell you?"

"I hear you had some fun in the Turner trial," Joshua said,
mockingly. "Such a shame I missed it. But you know how it is
when the Court of Appeal calls."

"Are you actually in this one, Mr. Downes?" Canning asked.
"Or are you putting in another guest appearance?"

Nick did not bother to answer. He smiled shallowly and
poured himself a large beaker of water as noisily as he could.
Canning looked distinctly uneasy.

Smith began, "This is the first appearance of this defendant
in respect of the new vice charges that you will find, sir, on
your register. They include a range of serious sexual offenses
and are quite complicated in nature. That is why I, as counsel,
have been instructed at this early stage rather than leaving it to
the good offices of the Crown Prosecution Service."

The magistrate waited patiently until the tide of verbosity subsided. "Can't we shorten matters?" he asked. "Presumably there is no application for bail with charges of this gravity?"

"I fear there is," Smith said, looking at Nick.

"As you know, sir," Nick said. "There is a right to bail—"

"Unless I find grounds to the contrary," he snapped. "Yes, thank you, Mr. Downes, for the lesson, but I did learn something about the basic principles of jurisprudence in my seventeen years at the Bar."

Then why don't you ever apply them? Nick wondered. But he said nothing. He looked toward the dock, and Jackie winked at him, which made him blush.

"I think your client wishes to give you some instructions, Mr. Downes," he said.

Nick went to the side of the dock as far away from the prosecutor as it was possible to get in so cramped a space.

"What is it?" he asked.

"Get them to call the officer, honey."

"Why?"

"He's the most bent copper in Vice."

"I don't see how that will help your application for bail."

Somewhere toward the front of the court, Smith was again on his feet. "Perhaps it would assist all parties if I called the officer in the case," he said.

"Tear his head off," Jackie whispered as Nick returned to counsel's row.

As the policeman took the oath, Nick tried to assess what he was dealing with. The man was tall and had a deep tan. It was the officer who had arrested Jackie at the Bailey. He wore a gray suit with a handkerchief in his pocket as if he were going to a wedding. If he had been, it looked as if he would have gone on to arrest all the bridesmaids and handcuff the vicar.

"I object to bail, sir, on behalf of the Soho Vice Squad. We have good reason to believe that the accused is part of an international ring that imports young girls to sell into prostitution. We have obtained statements from some of the victims and will shortly interview the rest."

Joshua Smith sat down.

"Do you have any questions, Mr. Downes?" Canning asked.

"Just a few," Nick replied. He looked at the officer and tried to think where to strike first. "Help us with this, Officer. Where are you stationed?"

"Near Piccadilly."

"So where did you get your tan? I mean, you couldn't have got it sunbathing in Leicester Square in April?"

The prosecutor shot to his feet. "Firstly, I cannot see how this is possibly relevant. And secondly——"

"I got it in the Far East," the witness replied over him.

"Were you there recently?" Nick asked.

"Yes."

"So you, yourself, have no *direct* knowledge of anything illegal done by this defendant?"

"No, but——"

"Just answer yes or no," Nick said. He glanced at Jackie, who smiled. It was the only point Nick could think to raise, but he could not just sit down. That would have looked stupid. "And what were you doing in the Far East, Officer?"

"We've traced the ring from Thailand to mainland China to Hong Kong. Some girls are from once-respectable Hong Kong families whose businesses have collapsed now that the territory is due to be returned to China."

"And what happens to the girls?"

"They're brought in illegally and sold as concubines."

"As what?" the magistrate asked.

"As sex slaves," the officer replied.

"And how are they paid?" Nick said.

"In drugs."

"Which drugs?" Nick asked, although he suspected that he already knew the answer.

"Speed, heroin, cannabis. But mainly heroin. It's——"

"More addictive?" Nick said.

"Precisely."

Canning was again becoming irritable. "This is all very interesting, but where is it all leading, Mr. Downes?"

Just then Jackie hissed from the dock. Nick got the permission of the court to speak to her again.

"Look," she said, "forget about bail. I'm safer inside."

"Safer?"

"Never mind. Just remember what I told you. You've got to find China."

"Tell me *why*," Nick insisted.

"She's in danger. I should have told you before but I was too frightened. I'd seen him before. He'll kill us. He'll kill all of us."

"Who? Turner?"

"When he came for girls, he always used a different name. Luther or Lanzer or something. But it was China White he wanted. He always asked for her. You've *got* to find her."

"Did you say *Lanzer?*" Nick asked, remembering the video.

"You heard me."

"How do you know he wants to kill you?"

"I phoned my place yesterday."

"From prison?"

"We're allowed one personal call. They said he came to the parlor. And he had a hammer."

"But where should I look for the girl?"

"Just find her," Jackie whispered, standing up in the dock. She faced the Bench and shouted, "What's the use? Can't get no justice in a gaff like this. I want to go down."

"Take her to the cells," Canning said.

As the jailer took hold of her, she started to struggle.

"But where should I look?" Nick whispered. "Bayswater?"

"No." Jackie broke free from the jailer's grip, in doing so ripping the identification badge from his tie. She rushed to the bars of the dock. "You of all people should know," she said. "Start at the beginning. Right at the beginning—where the body was buried."

Before she could explain further, the jailer dragged her into the cells, and all Nick could hear was another scream from Ann Barnes's psychotic commuter.

Chapter Nine

When Nick returned to his flat after court, he was lost in thought. If his former client had been calling himself Lanzer, what was his purpose? The man had been to the Bayswater brothel looking for China White. But what was the role of the girl? Lanzer seemed to be the identity of the second voice in Will's head. But who—or what—was Lanzer?

Thinking about these things, he almost bumped into the person waiting outside the street door to his block. It was Liz.

She smiled at him uneasily, but Nick could see dried tear tracks on each of her cheeks.

"What are you doing here?" he asked.

"Dinner," she said, pointing to a brown bag of groceries propped against the glass door. "My treat. Seafood. Clams, mussels, oysters. No claws. You see, I remembered."

"How did you know I'd be here?"

"I spoke to your clerk—he remembered me. He said you'd go straight home after court."

"What if I've already eaten?"

"Have you?"

"No."

"Well, then. Can I come in?" She glanced up and down the street anxiously.

"Why have you been crying?"

"I'm ashamed—of what I did yesterday evening. With Will. I did it to . . . make you jealous."

"Why?"

"I want you to want me, Nick. To need me. To be with me." She took his hand and raised it to her lips, kissing it gently. "Forgive me."

"Come on, Liz."

"Please."

Before he could answer, there was a raucous shout from across the road. He looked up but could not see where the noise was coming from. Then, again, an incoherent shout, searing, almost primal.

Liz grabbed him. "It's him."

"Will?"

"He's been following me."

Nick heard heavy thudding, the approaching steps of a man accelerating.

"Come on," Liz shouted. "Let us in."

He fumbled with the keys, feeling her pressing against him, his palm sweating. He looked up and saw the crazed face of his former client charging down the road, fifty yards away. Again he tried the key.

"Come on," Liz shouted.

The key turned. Liz almost pushed him through the opening door and he stumbled over the bag of shopping. She leaped over him, and he climbed to his feet and shut the door.

"Get away from the glass," she shouted.

As soon as she said it, he saw, almost in slow motion, a brick spinning through the air, and heard a desperate yell from the man outside. He covered his eyes and felt shards of glass showering against his body.

He stayed as he was until he heard Liz speak.

"He's leaving," she said.

"Are you all right?"

"Forget about me," she replied. "It's all my fault. I should have guessed he'd follow me here. He follows me everywhere." A tear welled in her eye. "Nick, I don't know how much more of this I can take."

He took her left hand in both of his. But something was wrong. When he inspected her fingers, the nails had all been bitten away and were raw.

"You see," she said, trying to smile through the tears that were now falling, "no claws."

Nick knew of only one other person who bit her nails so badly—Sally.

When he edged slowly past the broken door, he could see Turner running up Queensway, past the row of telephone kiosks, toward Hyde Park. Startled shoppers looked at the fleeing man, but no one tried to stop him.

Nick checked himself. He didn't seem to be cut. But Liz was crying.

"Let's go up," he said.

Catt ran to the flat door when Nick opened it, but for some reason he was very apprehensive of Liz.

"I've never got on with cats," Liz said.

"But you always wanted one?"

"I was going to get one, when I was fifteen. But my step-mother never let me. Said she was allergic to them. I was allergic to her."

"Stepmother?" He couldn't remember her mentioning one before.

"Oh, she was only on the scene a short while. An awful woman. Used to lock me in cupboards, all that Victorian kind of stuff."

"You've really been through the wars," he said. He pointed outside. "What are we going to do about Will?"

"I should have divorced him when it started."

"What?"

"His infidelity."

"With whom?"

She paused and picked some tiny glass fragments from her clothes. "With that girl. The Chinese one."

"China White?"

"Will used her for a model—after Charles had finished with her."

"Charles?"

"She was one of Charles's patients. Passed on from brother to brother like she was a piece of property."

Nick looked at her, the full figure, the fantastic mounds of hair, the opal eyes sparkling with tears. He joined her on the sofa.

"Have you ever heard the name Lanzer?"

She bit her lip and shook her head.

"Does it mean anything to you at all, Liz?"

"Should it?"

"I don't know. It's something to do with your husband. It's a pseudonym he's using or . . ."

He couldn't explain the "or" to her. What could he sensibly say? Or it's another part of his persona struggling for control of his soul? Too melodramatic, too Catholic.

"I'll try to find out about it if you like," she said.

"So what do we do now?"

"Salvage the seafood?" she suggested.

"Shouldn't we call the police?" he asked.

"This isn't about the police, Nick."

He knew she was right.

She leaned closer to him. He smelled her hair, saw the smooth skin of her chest appearing above her low-cut top.

"Friends?" she asked.

"Friends."

"We've got a bit of an up-and-down relationship," she said.

"That's what makes it so good."

She kissed him, slowly at first, and he felt again how soft and wet her lips were. Her tongue explored his mouth gently, tenderly, and she stroked his cheek with the back of her hand. He glanced down and saw how her cleavage was accentuated. He could feel her nipples growing hard against his chest.

She stopped only when the phone rang.

"Ignore it," he said. "The answerphone is on."

He started kissing her again, but both of them had their eyes open and the phone kept ringing and the magic had gone.

She slumped back against the cushions. "I suppose you'd better answer it."

He got up from the sofa and snatched up the receiver, shouting, "Yes?"

There was no answer.

Liz looked on quizzically.

"Who *is* it?" he asked.

There was a rhythmic intake of breath at the other end.

"What's going on?" Liz asked.

He put his hand over the mouthpiece. "Dirty phone call, I think."

"I thought only women got them."

"Only women and me, it seems." He removed his hand and said, "Now look. I'll call the police and they'll trace—"

"She's *there,* isn't she?" The voice was low, dark, troubled.

Nick knew instantly who it was: Turner.

"She's there with you now, isn't she? What is she doing? Crying on your shoulder?"

"Why don't you just leave her *alone?*" Nick shouted.

"What are you doing with my wife? Fucking her? Yes, I bet that's it. I bet you're fucking her. She's got her legs spread wide open and she's waiting for you. Enjoy. Enjoy it while it lasts. She'll fuck you up so badly you'll never be able to put the pieces back together."

"You're mad," Nick said.

There was a click at the other end and a dialing tone.

Liz's face was pale and frightened.

Nick tried to smile, to reassure her. "I'll put the answerphone on. Next time he calls, I'll tape it."

"Why?"

"Evidence."

"For what?"

"For anything that might happen."

Liz stood up and paced across the lounge. "That's *it*. I've had enough. Call the police."

"I can handle it."

"No, call the—"

"I *want* to handle it, Liz. I'll sort it out. I'll look after you. Trust me."

Relief washed across her face. "You mean it, don't you? You really mean it."

"Yes."

"Oh God, Nick."

"Let's salvage the seafood."

Chapter Ten

The tomato and basil sauce bubbled away gently on the oven, filling the kitchen with warm, sweet fragrances. It sizzled slightly when Nick added a good measure of Chianti Classico, and he began to feel light-headed when he drank a whole glass himself.

"Chef's privilege," he said to Liz as she sat cross-legged in the corner.

"Meany." She smiled. "I was going to do the cooking."

"But I want to do it for you."

"So what can I do?"

"Put something on the stereo."

"What?"

"Something good, and you get a slurp of wine."

She shot out of the room like an excited child in search of hidden presents.

Nick looked back to the sauce, which was almost done. Time to put in the seafood. As he worked in the clams and mussels, he could hear strains of smoochy Latin music wafting in from the lounge, reminding him of beaches and palm trees.

He reflected on the fact that Will Turner had not called

again. But he was beginning to understand Turner's obsession. It could be reduced to one word: Liz.

She embodied a magical balance between vulnerability and sensuality. If she were sadder, she would be pitiable; if she were sexier, she would be cheap, off-putting. But she had it right; something had made her right. She provoked in him lust and the desire to look after her in almost perfect proportion.

"What's the music?" he called, not recognizing the CD as one of his.

"Radio." She came back into the kitchen and put her arms around his waist. "Sorry, but I'm not into country-and-western music."

"Not *yet*. Stick with me, kid, and you'll see Tammy Wynette as the creative genius she really is."

"Promise?"

"Promise." He smiled back at her. "So who is this band?"

"Santana, I think. Sweet salsa for the soul, the DJ said."

She dipped her finger into the sauce. "Guest's privilege," she said sheepishly, as if she had done something naughty.

He looked into her eyes. There was a change of hue—the shadow of another emotion had washed over her. "What's the matter?" he asked. "Too much basil?"

"It's perfect."

"Then why the Quasimodo face?"

"Thanks."

"Oh, I didn't mean it in an ugly sort of way. Just in an 'in some sort of pain' kind of way."

"I was thinking about something from my childhood."

"What about it?"

"It's nothing, really. I was just being stupid. That's the thing about you. I feel safe. I can let my shield down, but I don't always like what I see."

"So what were you thinking—about your childhood?"

"That I was about as miserable as I can imagine anyone ever being."

"Can you talk about it?"

"Don't get me started, 'cause by the time I finish, you'll have about a teaspoonful of sauce left."

"Then I'll make some more."

"You would, wouldn't you?"

"Yes, Liz."

"You're a good man, Nick. I don't deserve someone like—"

"You're always putting yourself down."

"I've been well trained."

"By whom?"

She paused and at first appeared distracted, but then she spoke, as if the needle had found the groove. "The first weekend my stepmother moved in, she cooked a big dinner. It was, you know, a getting-to-know-you meal for all of us. I didn't know what to make of her, and Dad said he loved her, so I thought; why not make an effort? Give her a chance, at least. Dad was out, and I went into the kitchen and there was this big pot of sauce on the oven, *ragu* or *bolognaise,* and I just dipped my finger in. I looked at her and said it was good—actually, it needed more salt—I said it was great, but Dad liked more tomatoes, something like that. She grabbed my hand and shoved it deep into the pan and held it there. She turned up the heat and held it there, saying, 'Like it now? You stupid little bitch.' "

Nick looked into the pan on the stove and saw the surface bubbling like the pools of a scorching hot natural spring. He shuddered when he imagined a young girl's fingers being held under the surface. "What did your father say?"

"When he came home, I said nothing."

"Whyever not?"

"She said she'd get me put in a home, that my mother had once been in a home and she would see to it that I'd end up in one also. No one would believe me, everyone would believe her, she'd say it ran in the family, that I had tried to attack her or something. I was very frightened and only young. What could I do?"

Nick gave her a glass of the deep ruby wine, and she drank most of it silently. She looked at him but did not speak.

"I'm really very sorry, Liz. I know that sounds hopelessly in-adequate, but—"

"No, it doesn't. I've never told anyone before, I don't think I could have told anyone else before. Not before you, Nick."

Suddenly the concoction in the pan seemed decidedly unappetizing to him. "Want to go out and grab a Chinese or whatever?"

"I'm fine. And it smells great. It's just that there are certain things in my past—all our pasts maybe, I don't know—unhappy things, you never think about them, well, not often, and then suddenly they're triggered, and boom. Am I completely off my . . . or can you see what I'm saying?"

Nick knew that there was one thing he had never discussed, had sworn he never would discuss with anyone except Sally, an unhappy thing, one that was triggered increasingly often.

"I know what you're saying, Liz."

"Then share something with me." She gazed at him intensely, her eyes moving over the contours of his face, her eyelashes seeming to open and shut in slow motion as if she didn't want to miss a moment, the slightest nuance. "Let me know you, Nick. Just a little. Let me in."

"I find it so hard to talk about it."

"Let me help you try, then."

"Come on, Liz. Some other time, perhaps." But he had not known of any better time in the last five years, and the memory of the pain, of the effort he had expended just to control it, had weakened his resolve.

"Let me do the work," she said. She took his hands, and he could discern the warm stickiness where her finger had been dipped in the pan. "If I asked you a question, would you tell me the truth?"

"I've never lied to you."

"I don't suppose you've ever lied to anyone, Nick." She took a sip of Chianti. "Does it concern Sally?"

"Yes," he said hesitantly.

"What a wild stab in the dark," she said.

"I suppose you don't need to be a brain surgeon to work that one out."

"Did it concern marriage?"

"No."

"Children."

He paused, but she added quickly, "Why did you and Sally never have children?"

"She had her career and—"

"No, *really*. You were well off, in love, healthy, perfect mating material. So why didn't you?"

He took a deep breath. The kitchen windows were largely steamed up with the cooking, but there remained an oval of glass through which he could see the neighboring rooftops and the low gray clouds that moved between them, promising, threatening, rain. "Something happened," he said.

"What?"

"Five years ago. No one knows. I keep trying to forget it myself."

She looked deep into his eyes. "What happened? Nick, you're frightening me."

He hesitated. Was "it" too intimate? He had wanted to tell someone every month of every year since it had happened. Now, finally, he wanted to tell Liz.

"Tell me, Nick."

"Liz—"

"She had an affair and got preg—"

"No."

"A miscarriage?"

"*No.*"

She paused. "Oh my God. She had an abortion, didn't she?"

He did not reply.

"Nick, she had an abortion. I'm right, aren't I?"

"Yes."

There. He had admitted the great unmentionable. He had admitted "it."

"Oh God," Liz said. "My poor baby."

"Know what's worst? I keep thinking about what it would have looked like. Thinking of names. I always see it as a little boy."

There were tears in Liz's eyes.

He continued, "You know, there's all that weird stuff, like they talk about on *Oprah,* but it happens. I sometimes see him in my dreams and I try to talk to him but he never answers. And I keep saying, Please forgive me. Please just forgive me."

"Oh, Nick," she said, hugging him tightly.

"But he never speaks to me, Liz. Never."

"I would never do that, Nick. If I ever got pregnant, I would never, *ever,* do that."

When they kissed, Nick suddenly felt a huge sense of release. Why on earth had he not mentioned it to anyone before? Perhaps it was just Liz who had made it possible?

"I forgot to thank you," she said finally.

"For what?"

"For my cat. It's the first time in my life anyone's ever got me a cat." She stroked his face. "Know what? I think this might just work."

"What?"

"Us." She smiled. "Don't you see? We've been on an inevitable path to each other all along. But we never knew it. Other people, other relationships, they were just stepping-stones to this, to us, to now. They were paths we had to follow. The things that have happened, even all the terrible things, I'm convinced they were somehow ordained, planned, fated."

Nick tried to catch up.

"What do you think?" she asked.

"Well . . ." he said, teasing her. "Well, I really think—"

There was a loud crash at the window.

They both looked around, startled, fearful. For a moment, Nick wondered how Turner could have reached the seventh floor, and then he smiled.

"What's funny?" she asked.

"It's just a bird, flew into the window. Sometimes happens. Don't worry. It's nothing."

She laughed too. "Got you off the hook," she said. "Now I seem to remember asking you a rather important question."

But before he could answer, the phone rang.

And after the previous call, it sent shivers through his body.

"Do you want me to answer it?" she asked.

"No, we'll record it."

The two of them walked to the lounge.

There was a high-pitched tone, then a voice coming through the machine.

Sally's.

"Why are you never in these days?" she said. "God, Nick, I really need to speak to you."

He noticed the distressed undertone in her words.

"Nick, I need to speak to you before it's too late," she continued.

Liz approached the machine with a mixture of curiosity and hatred.

"Nick," Sally added. "I loved our little chat at court. Whatever happens, I just wanted to say how much I have always really—"

Liz tore at the cable. The phone clattered to the floor, cracking the plastic casing.

"*Liz,*" Nick shouted, "what the hell are you doing?"

"Leaving," she said.

"Come on, Liz."

"You still love her, don't you?"

"Liz."

"Well, go and have a child with her. Ask her to have your baby, ask her not to . . . kill it this time. But leave me alone. You're just leading me on. You don't really want me. I bet you never did. I don't want to be second best again, Nick. I was second best to Daddy when *she* came on the scene. I was second best to China White and I'm *not* going to be second best to Sally Fielding."

She started toward the front door. When she turned back toward him, there was a single tear track on her left cheek. "And your fucking sauce needed salt," she said.

Chapter Eleven

Nick had spent a restless night.

He could not sleep after the frantic Liz left him. So when he finally got out of his sweaty sheets at seven o'clock, he phoned his clerk. He told him that he was ill, and, inconvenient as it was, the course of justice would have to cope without his assistance for one day.

He gazed out of the window. He noticed again that the London sky was never quite blue, as if it was diffracted through a prism of toxins and gases and pollutants. The sunset the evening before had been purple, and the dawn was nearly pink. Below, in Queensway, the tramps who slept in the shop doorways woke and pottered into the subterranean lavatories, and in the distance he could just hear the growing hum of the traffic racing along Bayswater Road.

Again he pondered the prostitute's ominous words over his bratwurst and eggs. But he could not eat. Start at the beginning, she had said. With the corpse. But why with the corpse?

An hour later, the Friday traffic on the motorway was hell. In fact, it was worse than that. It was hell at a standstill with country-and-western music coming through the speakers. Eventually, the traffic crawled eastward from Surrey, and Nick

cheered up when he finally saw the sign that marked the border between that country and Kent. He knew he was nearing
the scene of Charles Turner's burial.

Immediately past the sign, he took the slip-road off the M25
and drove along a track parallel to the motorway. He had to
double back westward toward Surrey before he reached the
quarry.

He parked the car, pulled on his new white trainers, and
took a deep breath of country air. Then he coughed violently
on the exhaust fumes from the M25 at the bottom of the hill.

He had brought the bundle of photographs from the trial.
There were various prints of the scene taken by the Kent Con-
stabulary. Using these, he tried to orient himself.

Beyond the lower edge of the chalk quarry he found some
fields. They were very near to a bend in the motorway. He
spun around on his Reeboks, trying to find the exact location
of the grave, but without success. He was certain of where the
wasteland should be. But the spot was a burgeoning field.

At the entrance to the field were the remains of a bird, possibly a wood pigeon. Here and there the bones were exposed
and were being picked clean by an army of insects crawling
silently over the carcass.

He recalled the reports about Charles Turner. The flesh had
become a repository for a variety of insects: flies and beetles,
devil's coach-horses and spiders. The face had been partially
eaten by maggots, and it was because of this fact that it was so
difficult to identify the body, to reconstruct the face with any
degree of precision, to be sure that the corpse did in fact once
belong to Charles Turner.

"It's rape," came a ferocious shout from behind him.

He looked round hurriedly.

"You can't go in there. It's rape."

"What is?" he asked the scruffy man who was walking
through the yellow crop waving an ominously large spade.

"That field's planted with rape seed, and this is private
property."

"I only wanted—"

"Listen. The strange thing about private property is that it's private. So piss off before you get shot."

"Look," said Nick. "All I want to know is where the grave was."

The man paused and looked at him. "You come about the body?" He nodded. "The grave was down by the road," the man said over the roar of the traffic.

This confused Nick even more. He saw an unbroken stream of vehicles clinging to the six tarmac lanes as they wound their way over the gentle hills that were the Kentish Downs.

He asked the man, "How could no one have seen anything?" He thought again about the Hillside Strangler and how he murdered his victims in private and then dumped them on the hillsides of Los Angeles.

"Look how they drive," the man replied. "They don't see the car in front of them, so how are they going to see anything else?"

Of course, Nick thought, the body could have been buried at night. The trip to Kent seemed to have ended in a dead end. When he looked at his trainers, they were covered in a black sludge.

The man laughed. "That's the crap what washes down from the motorway," he said. "Looks like you need a new pair, mate."

With that he started shoveling a large pile of granular substance that Nick vaguely recognized.

"What's that?" he asked.

"Lime."

"Quicklime?"

"Same thing."

"What are you doing with it? I mean, isn't lime some sort of bleach?"

"Not this stuff," the man said. "This lime is fertilizer. I was dead pissed off about that madman using my fertilizer to bury the body."

Nick walked slowly back to the car considering the possibilities. Perhaps Will Turner had accidentally buried the body in the wrong type of lime—to preserve it for some reason?

Again he conjured up the images of the corpse, of a form that was once human and had been abandoned. He felt miserable, for the victim and for himself. More than anything else, he wanted to see Sally.

An hour later, Nick found an old red-painted phone box and rang his answerphone for messages. Although Liz had cracked the casing, the mechanism still worked. Sally had not called; Ann Barnes had. She had left a message so long that it had used up the remains of Nick's tape. Eventually, she got to the point.

"I've done some more snooping into rats and rodents. Brown rats, it seems, are far more common in the countryside than the black ones. And they burrow underground. Maybe that's how they came across the Turner corpse? Give me a ring. I'm going to leave the video of the latest therapy session with Mr. Psycho for you. See what you make of *this*. Remember the Hillside Strangler. *Ciao*."

When he returned to his car, he put on Radio 4, hearing the presenter announce a gale warning for the Channel. The gale was moving quickly toward the southern coastline.

His car was parked on a track that ran between the quarry and the crest of the hill, perhaps a quarter of a mile above. Trees grew intermittently on either side of the track, thin trees, tired-looking, exposed to the winds at the top of the hill, their roots barely managing to cling to the soil.

While he listened to the shipping forecast on the radio, a group of people walked slowly over the brow of the hill and between the trees.

They were a disparate group of about twenty, a combination of young and old, sporting a mixture of anoraks and leather jackets. They appeared to walk in silence, absorbed in themselves, indifferent to Nick. The younger ones were frail, barely more nourished than the trees that surrounded them.

The group passed Nick without saying a word, though one

or two of the younger members coughed loudly and painfully. They all continued strolling down the path toward the quarry except for one. A young girl who was Chinese in appearance. Nick got out of the car.

"He's been here," she said, standing in front of a dead tree trunk.

It was China White.

"Who's been here?" he asked her. "Lanzer?" The girl did not reply. "Are you all right?" he continued.

"I wasn't here when he came."

"When was that?"

"Yesterday morning."

"I need to talk to you," he told her.

The girl wrapped her thin arms around her chest. Nick noticed how the veins were black and stuck out through her flesh like tree roots.

"I'm burning up," she said.

"Fever?"

"Fires. In here," she added, touching to her head. "Anyway, that's what you said before."

"What was?"

"That you wanted to talk—to our Jackie."

"I was confused."

"That's something I can understand." The girl rubbed her forearms, and one or two of the veins stood out proudly. She winced in pain.

"Why are you here?" Nick asked.

The girl indicated toward the crest of the hill where the treeline eventually stopped. The two of them walked together until they reached the brow. From there, stretching westward, was an undulating landscape of green relieved only by a building that was being renovated.

"Your home?" Nick asked.

"My sanctuary. It's a rehabilitation center," she said finally.

"I didn't know there were any rehabs in Kent."

"There aren't."

"But I thought you said—"

"You know," the girl interrupted, "I've never seen the sea. I'd like to, some day. I'd like to buy a house by the sea. Right by the water."

"So those people, were they also patients?"

"And staff. They make us go for a walk every day for fresh air."

"Next to the M25?" But the girl did not reply. Nick looked at the building. It was a modern prefabricated structure. The walls were covered in scaffolding, and there were workmen all over the roof.

He looked into the girl's eyes, square on. He had been too ashamed to gaze at her in this way in the street outside the massage parlor. "I hope you don't mind," he said. "But can I ask you about the—"

"Drugs?"

"Are you better? I mean, weren't you Charles Turner's patient?"

The girl laughed, but the humor seemed incapable of reaching her eyes, which remained fixed and distant. "Put it this way," she said. "It can only get better."

"How do you mean?"

"Well, I've been chasing the dragon so long—"

"Taking heroin?"

She nodded. "You see, there comes a time when if you chase the dragon enough, it turns and then . . . it chases you," she said.

"Jackie says you're in danger."

The girl laughed again, although the pupils remained lifeless.

Nick took her left arm, his fingers wrapping themselves around it as though it were a thin piece of bamboo. "Did you hear what I—"

"He doesn't just want me," she said, scratching her veins.

"Then who?"

"All of us. All of us who know."

"Know what?"

"What he really is."

"Who is Lanzer?" Nick asked.

"Lanzer is the name he used."

"Who used?"

"Charles Turner."

"Why did he use a false name?"

"He used it when he was picking up prostitutes."

The girl paused before she walked toward the rehabilitation center, saying, "I'm burning up."

Chapter Twelve

By the time Nick reached London, the Friday evening rush hour traffic was easing, and he had listened twice to his tape of Tammy Wynette's greatest hits.

After he had met the girl, he had driven aimlessly around the Kentish countryside, trying to make some sense of what he had been told. How could his former client be Charles Turner?

The storm he had heard about on the radio seemed to have followed him around the M25 from Kent. Clouds, full to bursting, tracked across the six lanes of the orbital, but the rain started to fall only when he reached the river.

As he crossed Hammersmith Bridge, his spirits revived when he thought of his encounter with Sally in the magistrates' court the previous day. Amid the bustle and sleaze of the court lobby, they had exchanged a moment of affection. It provided him with a scintilla of hope.

By the time he had opened the door to his flat and his cat with two *t*s had scampered onto his lap, he had almost forgotten his strange meeting with the Chinese girl in the woods. Ann Barnes had left a parcel which had been delivered to his door. He knew it was the video of the second therapy session with his former client.

Then the phone rang. It was Sally.

"Nick," she said. "Where have you been? I've been ringing you all day."

"I've been out, Sals," he gushed, hardly able to contain his excitement at the sound of her voice. "I've been . . . well, you wouldn't believe what I've been up to. First, I tried to find the grave."

"Nick," she interjected, "I want to speak to you."

"And I really want to speak to you, Sals."

"No, Nick." She paused, as if she were trying to find the right words. "What I mean is, I . . ."

"What?"

"Well, what I mean is, I *need* to speak to you."

He continued to play with Catt, who was curled up on his lap, rubbing his white beard against Nick's fingers.

He swallowed. "What do you want to speak to me about?"

"I've been meaning to tell you for a little while."

"Tell me what?"

"Only, whenever we see each other we're always fighting or—"

"What?"

"Or you're so cute that it just breaks my heart."

He stopped stroking his kitten. "I think you should just tell me, Sally."

"Oh God. Now you've gone all serious and are calling me Sally."

"It is your name. I think you should just come out with it. We'll both feel better."

"I'm not so sure."

"Sally—"

"All right, then." She took a large breath. "Max has asked whether I want to get engaged."

Nick was confused. "Engaged to whom?"

"To him, of course. Now please don't go mad, Nick. Nothing's settled, no date for the wedding has been set or anything."

"*Wedding?* One minute you're holding my hand in the magistrates' court and the next you're ordering a wedding dress."

"I shouldn't have told you," she said.

"Don't be ridiculous. You had to. You couldn't keep it a secret from me."

"Why not?"

"Do you think I'm that naïve, Sally? I would have found out. You can't keep a secret at the Bar, you know."

"Oh, Nick," she said, a painful lilt in her voice. "Everyone else knows already. I'm sorry."

He dropped the receiver. He was stunned. It was not so much that his old life had come to an end as a scary feeling that a new one was about to start.

Nick was still dazed when he slid the videocassette into the recorder. Before he knew it, the fuzzy images on the screen had been replaced by the clear picture of the interview room at the Psychiatric Center.

Again Ann had her back to the camera, and the same man was connected to the polygraph with fine wires.

"How are you today?" Ann asked.

The man sat morosely.

"Will you speak to me today?" she persisted.

He did not look up.

"There was some confusion about your name," she said.

"I don't care."

He noticed that the electronic line stayed calm. This was the truth.

"Is your name . . ." Ann's voice trailed off. Then, after a deep breath, she asked, "Is your name Charles Turner?"

The man looked up.

"Is your name Charles Turner?" she repeated.

With that, the man jumped to his feet, in the process tearing the wires from the machine. He pushed the polygraph over, smashing it, and advancing toward the camera as Ann Barnes retreated.

"You know who I *really* am," he shouted.

Chapter Thirteen

Nick did not know how long he had been sitting on the sofa watching the blank screen. Finally, he noticed Catt scratching at the door, making a strange sound.

"Are you ill?" he said. "You can't go out. It's not safe out there. For either of us."

He told himself that he never wanted to see Sally again. But he knew it was a lie, and that made him feel even more miserable.

There was a knock on the door but he did not answer. Then the knocking became a banging. He put on his new pair of slippers and answered. It was Kenny. Before he could do anything, the Chinese porter had forced his way into the flat.

"What is it, Kenny?" he asked, glancing around furtively, hoping that his cat, who was there illegally, would not give himself away.

"A lady come round," the porter said. "She leave a message for you."

"Well," said Nick, trying to stand in front of him, "can I have it then?"

"Not written down," Kenny said. "The management committee not raise my salary this year."

Nick reached into his pocket and produced a pound coin.

"How I'm supposed to get new wife?" Kenny said. "Not on pittance they pay."

"How is the hunt going?"

Kenny sucked in air deeply. "These modern girls," he replied. "They all fucked up. Once they only want children. Now they want rights. Huh."

Nick realized that he had lost the porter's attention. Kenny had seen the cat. He leaped over and grabbed it by the scruff of its furry neck.

"Must have climbed in the window," he said, holding it at arm's length.

"Must have," Nick replied.

"You want me to drop it to ground? Smash its head. Make a nice mess." The porter held the helpless cat near the glass panes, as its little legs scrabbled about in the air.

"Put it down immediately," Nick shouted.

"Why?"

"He's mine."

"But you—"

"I know," Nick said. "I'm not supposed to have him. But I have, all right? What are you going to do about it?"

As Kenny held the cat, its body started convulsing, as if it were regurgitating something. And as the porter shook it, Catt opened his mouth and vomited something onto the carpet. It was the head of a small animal. When Nick looked more closely, he saw that it was the head of a rat.

The porter dropped the cat, which ran into a corner behind Nick.

"I report you," Kenny said. "Then you lose the cat."

"Do you serve any purpose in life, Kenny, apart from making people want to kill you?"

"I don't under—"

"It doesn't matter. Just tell me the message and then go."

The porter eyed the cat. "Woman ask you to go to see her tonight."

"Which woman?"

"Say her name is—"

"Barnes?"

"Turner," Kenny said. "Mrs. Turner. She say she know something about . . . Lanzer."

When Nick had slammed the door on the porter, he stroked Catt before starting to clean up the mess. He listened again and again to Tammy Wynette singing "Stand by Your Man." More than at any time he could remember, he really wanted to cry.

He decided to walk the mile or so between his flat and Liz Turner's. The rain was unrelenting, and although he had an umbrella, the gusts of wind along the Bayswater Road lashed the water horizontally onto his clothing and the frame of the umbrella was blown inside out.

When he pressed the intercom, Liz buzzed the street door open without saying a word. She stood at the door to her flat as he arrived on her floor, and in the half-light she looked different.

"It's gone all limp," she tried to joke, indicating the battered umbrella in his hand. He gazed at her, not knowing if he could speak, not knowing even if he wanted to.

"You're absolutely soaked," she said.

He did not reply but stayed in the hallway dripping a large puddle onto the floor.

"You look like a drowned rat," she added. "Whatever is the matter?"

Tears welled in his eyes, but he did not say a word.

"Sally?" she asked.

He nodded, and it was then, when he looked properly at her, that he realized what was different. Her hair had been cut. Cut into a style more like Sally's.

She led him into the lounge, and there, next to the telephone, was the china cat he had bought her.

His shirt was damp and clung to his body in the same way his court shirts did after a difficult cross-examination.

He felt himself approaching that state of being known in law as automatism and in life as despair. His life appeared empty and senseless, without reason, without hope, without Sally. She would marry Max, and Nick would lose her forever.

He felt numb. It was as if it was all happening to someone else. Then Liz began to ease the damp clothing away from his body. It was only when she started to undo his trouser belt that he spoke.

"I got your message," he said.

She nodded.

"About Lanzer," he continued.

"Later."

"You've kept the cat."

"I love the cat."

"Why?"

"Because it's the most thoughtful thing anyone has ever bought for me." She moved away from him, unsure of what to do next.

"Have you given it a name?"

"Given *her* a name. And it's Lizzie, because I figured she's a little like me when I was young, you know—she was all alone, only she was in a shop, but we were both surrounded by grotesque things. Both brittle, china, easily broken." She took a deep breath before she said, "I'm sorry for what I said about Sally and the abor . . . I didn't really mean it."

"Yes you did."

She looked down at the floor and whispered, more to herself, "Yes, I did."

When she glanced up, she had a distant look in her eyes again, as if she was there in the present but was also trying to reel in the past, or that part of it that mattered.

"God, does that make me a wicked, bad . . . I don't know . . . evil person, Nick? I just want you. I don't want to share you, any part of you, because that's what I want to give you in return: all of me, everything that I am, that I feel."

She slowly raised her left hand and stroked the top of her right breast with the back of it, half closing her eyes, her head falling backward an inch, her lips almost parting, a thin film of saliva between them. "I feel so much for you, Nick. And I want you to have all of me. Does that frighten you?"

"No," he said.

As she stood with her legs slightly apart, he could see the gentle swell of her *mons pubis* beneath her tight trousers. Her left hand slid down over the soft flesh of her stomach and rested on her hip before it traced part of the length of her upper thigh.

She approached him again and moved the side of her head past his right shoulder and next to his ear, whispering, "Fuck me, Nick. Here, now. Fuck me."

He could feel her breasts against his chest, moving over him, suddenly touching his arm, and then her hand dropped and stroked between his legs, making him strain painfully against his trousers. She undid his zipper.

"But I'm soaking wet," he protested.

"And I'm not?"

"I need a shower first."

"After," she said.

"I'm dirty."

"It's the only way."

He looked at her—at the pearls, at the bitten nails, at the styled hair—and he was utterly confused.

"Love her," she continued. "Love *her,* love Sally, but *make* love to me." She placed his hands on her breasts and moved them over the soft flesh, making the nipples hard. Then, using his fingers, she started to tear the sheer material of the blouse.

He closed his eyes to avoid seeing the hair that reminded him so painfully of Sally, to avoid seeing his photograph looking out at two people entwined.

Then again he felt his hair being pulled roughly, as she had pulled it when they had first made love, when he had enjoyed, despite himself, despite everything, the loss of control and her soft, bittersweet, disturbing power over him.

His head was forced back, increasing the tension in his body which he knew only sex would release. He saw in his mind the spinning images of her bedroom, the mirrors, her naked body, the full curves, the breasts above his face, inches from his mouth, her flesh against his, and he tried to lose himself in them, to forget—Oh God, he thought to himself, to forget *Sally.*

His hair was yanked again, and with the thought, the realization, the pain of losing Sally forcing his eyes open, he saw the man.

It was his former client.

The man strode over and hit Liz Turner viciously around the face, causing her lip to burst.

Nick stood where he was as she crawled against the wall, crying, "It was him. It was him. Look. He's torn my shirt. He made me do it."

"I don't believe you, you *bitch,*" he said.

She cowered in the corner, blood from her lip dripping onto her chin and neck.

Then the man removed something from his jacket. For a moment, Nick could not see what it was, but when Turner raised his hands above his head, it was obvious. A claw hammer.

Liz crawled along the wall to the telephone, all the time being stalked by the man.

"*Bitch,*" he shouted again.

He smashed the hammer downward, to Liz's right, shattering the china cat.

"*Bitch,*" he repeated, smashing a vase to her left, powdering her hair with fragments. The claws got caught in the telephone wires.

Nick knew it was his chance. He rushed at Turner and struggled with him for the hammer.

Turner was much stronger, crazed, manic. In the background, Nick could hear Liz crying out: "Oh, God. Oh, God."

The claws scraped against Nick's arm. A bolt of pain shot into his brain.

But suddenly the handle was in his hands and he ripped with all his strength.

Turner fell to the floor next to the bleeding Liz.

"Go away," she cried. "Go *away.*"

The two men looked at her.

"Go *away,* Nick. I *hate* you. Just leave me. Just leave me alone."

Turner got slowly to his feet. "You're a dead man," he said.

Nick raised the hammer in front of his face so that he could see Turner's head in line with the claws. "I didn't do what she said."

"You're *dead,*" he repeated, approaching Nick.

Nick smashed the hammer as hard as he could onto a glass coffee table to his left. Shards flew in all directions. "I'll use the hammer on you, Turner. I swear I will."

The man stopped.

"So what are you going to do about it now, Turner?"

The man was silent, his eyes bulging, showing no fear of the hammer in Nick's hands.

"So what are you going to do, Turner?" Nick said. "Or is it *Lanzer?*"

There was no reply.

"What are you going to do?" he repeated.

"I'm going to call the police," was the man's only response.

PART IV
SEPTEMBER

Even the dearest that I love the best
Are strange—nay, rather, stranger than the rest

John Clare

Chapter One

After discovering Nick and Liz together, Will Turner had indeed called the police. The police had called the Crown Prosecution Service, and the CPS had called it Grievous Bodily Harm, Attempted Rape, and Indecent Assault. For his part, Nick had called Sally to defend him. And Sally had called Nick all sorts of names before she agreed. She had finally given in and called it an act of pity. However, he secretly hoped that deep down one could really have called it something approaching, if not actually, love.

The legal conveyor belt had trundled into action. The system seemed to be falling over itself to get Nick in court, in the dock, and in prison.

In the interim, he had ceased taking briefs and had spent most of his time in his apartment with his cat or wandering the streets of Bayswater. He had observed more carefully than ever the street life of the area, he had read books about the law of sexual offenses; in short, he had become an expert in the many manifestations of vice: brothels, buggery, incest; indecent assault, indecent exposure, indecent photographs; prostitution, public decency, public morals; attempted and actual rape. In three months, he had digested a potted history of human virtue

269

and had tried to forget about Sally's impending marriage to Max.

"What if I don't recognize the jurisdiction of the court?" he asked.

"No use," Sally replied. "The court will recognize you."

They were sitting in one of the conference rooms at the Old Bailey. It was the type of room that seemed to be specifically designed to exclude all fresh air and to retain the pungent odor of last year's urine. It was a Monday morning, and it was the first day of Nick's trial.

It wasn't the conference room in which Liz Turner had first kissed him, but it might as well have been. All he could think about was that first kiss and whether, if he had been stronger and had resisted, things would have been different now.

"What if I pretended to be . . . what's the term? Mute of malice?" he continued. "You know, like I was struck dumb?"

"The Forrest Gump defense? That would be plain stupid," Sally said. "Besides, who would notice the difference?"

"Thanks for those words of reassurance, Sals. Who's our judge?"

"*Your* judge," she said. "Not mine. You're the criminal, remember, not me?"

"Well, who is it?"

"I'm afraid there is good news and bad news." She got up from the rickety table and moved toward the wall of the conference room.

"So who have I drawn in the judicial lottery?"

"That's the bad news, Nick. It's the bully-in-chief."

"Cromwell?"

"None other."

"So what's the good news?" he asked. "He's not suddenly died, has he?"

"No. The good news is, I've been to see the list officer to see if we can get the case moved to another court."

"Excellent, Sals."

"And the very bad news is—"

"You didn't mention any very bad news."

"The very bad news is," she continued, "that you're stuck with Cromwell. I suppose that technically you could insist on a judge who has had no professional contact with you, but everyone knows about it. Besides, I can handle Cromwell, and better the devil you know and all that."

"Perhaps you're right," he said. "But the fates seem to be conspiring against me."

"Only in the way that they conspired against Julius Caesar. Cheer up, Nick, for heaven's sake. Things could be worse, you know."

"How?"

"Well, we could have a decent prosecutor against us."

She picked her brief up from the table and started to tie the pink ribbon. Nick knew that this was a sign that she wanted to bring the conference to an end. It was what he used to do when his clients began to bore him or he had grown tired of their lies. And there on the back sheet of the brief was his name. Not in the place he had seen it so many times before, under the word *Counsel*. The case was *Regina* versus *Nicholas Downes*. So there was Nick arraigned against the Queen, against the Crown, and, above all, against Mr. Justice Cromwell. It was hardly a fair contest.

"Don't you want to know who your persecutor is?" she asked.

"No."

"It's Joshua. Isn't that fantastic?" She beamed.

"Joshua Smith? But he knows me."

"And we know him. The case was returned to him at the last minute. No one wants to touch it."

"But can't we object to him?"

"Are you mad? He is perfect. Can't cross-examine his way out of a wet paper bag. And he's agreed to drop the Attempted Rape."

"I don't care. I didn't do any of it. Sally, I want to object." He thought again about the case of the Edwardian gambler Robert Siever, and how his barrister had become his judge. But with Smith as prosecuting counsel, he felt that things were becoming a little too claustrophobic.

"Nick, it's the one thing in our favor. Well, that and your legendary charm with the opposite sex."

"Let's hope we have a lot of women on the jury," he said.

"I *was* joking," she snapped.

"How's Max?" he asked.

They were still together. Three months later, and Sally and Max were still together. When Nick had used his one phone call from the police station, he had got their answerphone in Dulwich. He had heard Max's voice as all around in the police station people screamed and cell doors slammed. He had wanted to speak to Sally, and all he had got was Max's recorded voice, saying, "Sally and I are busy right now."

"You know, Max is a little peeved that I've taken the case," she said eventually. "But he's just going to have to put up with it."

"So why did you agree to defend me, Sally?"

"The truth?"

"The truth," he said.

She sat down once more and bit her bottom lip before she began to speak. "I agreed to defend you, Nick, because no one else wanted to do it. Well, no one any good, I mean. You see that press pack outside?"

He nodded.

"This is a national story. It will make the headlines. And the word around the Bar is that it is a *loser*, Nick. It's the sort of case that ruins reputations."

"So I've been abandoned?"

"When the Bar turns on one of its own, it's not satisfied with mere daggers like Brutus and his chums. No, when the Bar moves, it murders and assassinates and annihilates. Don't underestimate the politics of the situation."

"Politics?"

"The Bar has to compete. That means it has to be squeaky clean. That means it has to get rid of its dirt."

"Like me?"

"Like you," she said. "Well, allegedly. You see, if the Bar is seen to be ruthless in punishing one of its own, then it implies that the rest of us are clean. That's the theory. Look, cheer up. I've never lost a case defending at the Bailey."

"You never lose anything, Sally."

"I lost you. Well, almost—"

"*Almost?*" Nick said.

There was a loud crackle, and the tannoy summoned all parties in the case of Nicholas Downes to Court 8. Sally stood up hurriedly and opened the door.

"Almost?" he repeated as he passed her. "Sally, you said almost."

"It's *almost* time to go to court," she replied. "That's all. I see you're wearing my Paris tie again," she added, changing the subject.

"It's my lucky tie," he replied.

"Let's hope it works."

He was about to enter the dock, about to be prosecuted by the son of a High Court judge, but, Nick hoped, he might have at least one reason to be happy.

"Oh, and Nick. Tonight, when you leave court, don't give the media maggots any photo opportunities. Be discreet."

At about 12:30, Smith sat in the empty court reading his brief. "Pleading?" he said as Nick and Sally walked in.

"Yes, we're pleading," Sally said.

"That's good. Some common sense at last."

"We're pleading not guilty, Joshua," she snapped. "So you're going to have to do some honest work to earn your money for once."

"Oh God," the prosecutor said, yawning. "How excruciatingly boring."

The two of them spoke in front of Nick as if he was not there.

"Look, if your punter pleads to the violent assault," Joshua continued, "I might be persuaded to drop the groping. I've already abandoned the rape charge. The old slapper probably asked for it, anyway. Why don't you take some instructions, old thing?"

Sally was furious and did not reply.

Suddenly there was the cry of "All rise," and Mr. Justice Cromwell marched into court, his gowns of office draped around him.

"The prisoner should be in the dock," he said.

"That means you, Downes," the prosecutor said with a sneer.

"Look, just trot off into the playpen," Sally whispered to Nick.

The gate to the dock was opened, Nick's clothes were patted down by an officer to check for weapons, Semtex, and cigarettes, and before he really appreciated what was happening, he was staring at the back of Sally's wig and gown and was about to have the charges put to him.

This was the moment he had thought about the most. This was the beginning. Many times during the intervening months, he had wondered if he should just plead guilty. Then there would be no trial. Then it would all be over. Maybe, like Will Turner, he could get away with a suspended sentence. His career at the Bar was over anyway, and that he did not particularly regret. But it was the shame of it all. That was the worst aspect. The public humiliation. Everyone watching, everyone talking, everyone knowing. That was definitely the worst.

The clerk to the court was on her feet. She picked up the indictment and cleared her throat. Now, thought Nick, why don't I just end it now? Plead guilty and get it over with.

But as the clerk began to read, Nick looked up. Sally had turned around and smiled at him. This was an old smile, a pre-Max, pre-everything smile. And Nick knew that there was only one thing he could do.

"Is your name Nicholas Downes?" the clerk asked.

"Yes."

"And is your address . . ."

Nick had forgotten that one of the indignities of being an accused is that your name is announced at the beginning of a trial. It was almost always mentioned by the press.

When the clerk had finished reciting Nick's place of residence correctly, the next question, the vital one, was asked. "Nicholas Downes, on the first count, you are charged with—"

"Stop," blasted Cromwell. "Stand *up* when the learned clerk addresses you," he said to Nick.

Nick had been sitting down. For years he had sat down when the charges were put to his clients. It was always the poor buggers in the dock who had to stand up and be counted. Suddenly, the legal process was somewhat alien to him. Things were the wrong way round—he was at the back of the court, not the front; he had to stand up and face the charges while the barristers sat in their seats.

Nick remembered what Ann Barnes had said about the diseased mind, how it distorts, how the most ordinary things suddenly appear to be grotesque, sinister, and frightening. And he wondered how much of a grip he was going to be able to keep.

"Continue," the judge said, when Nick had got to his feet.

"Nicholas Downes, you are charged with Indecent Assault, contrary to the Sexual Offenses Act 1956," the clerk read. "And the particulars of the offense are that you indecently assaulted Elizabeth Turner. How do you plead? Are you guilty or—"

"I'm not guilty," Nick spluttered.

"Wait until the learned clerk has finished the whole question," Cromwell shouted. "Can't you control your client, Miss Fielding?"

"I do apologize, M'Lord," Sally said. Then she turned around and stared at Nick. The smile had definitely vanished.

The clerk coughed loudly. "Nicholas Downes, on the second count you are charged with Grievous Bodily Harm contrary to Section Twenty of the—"

Yes, I know, Nick thought to himself. The old Offenses Against the Person Act of 1800-and-whatever-it-was. But it wasn't against *the* Person. It was against Liz Turner. And it wasn't an offense—at least, not by Nick.

"Is your client still with us, Miss Fielding?" Cromwell asked.

"I think so, M'Lord," Sally replied.

"Well, find out why he hasn't entered a plea to the second charge."

"Yes, M'Lord." Sally moved quickly to the back of the court and stared up at Nick.

"Hi, Sals," he whispered.

"What on earth are you doing?" she asked.

"Thinking about justice."

"Well, you've come to the wrong place. This is a court of law, remember? And justice is no longer on the menu. Now just say not guilty to the second charge and we can eat our sandwiches and you can have your cheese and onion crisps."

When she had returned to her position in counsel's row, the clerk again asked the question.

"On the count of causing Grievous Bodily Harm to Elizabeth Turner, are you guilty or not guilty?"

Nick looked around the court as they all waited for his answer. Why are you always asked first whether you are guilty, he wondered. In all his years at the Bar, it wasn't something he had ever considered before.

"Are you *guilty* or not guilty?" she repeated.

"Not guilty," Nick said finally.

"So, we have a trial," the judge concluded. "We'll swear a jury at two o'clock."

"May Mr. Downes have bail within the precincts of the court building?" Sally asked as a matter of routine.

"I have no objection." Joshua yawned.

"Well, I do," the judge bellowed.

Nick saw Sally shooting to her feet again at the front of the court. "M'Lord, as you well know, Mr. Downes is a man of previous good character and—"

"I know nothing, Miss Fielding. In this court, justice is blind. It is my practice to remand defendants in custody over the luncheon adjournment. As *you* well know, Miss Fielding."

"But, M'Lord, surely this is an exceptional case?"

"Actually, you're quite right, Miss Fielding. This is an exceptional case. An exceptionally serious case. No bail. Take him down, Officer."

As the judge strutted out of court, his gowns billowing behind him, Sally just managed to dash to the dock as Nick was being taken away.

"God, I'm sorry, Nick."

"Don't worry," he said. "I suppose Her Majesty's Prison Service will have to cough up for my cheese and onion crisps."

"At least it will be better than the Bar Mess."

"I'll just look at it as a judicial luncheon voucher. Still, things can only get better, can't they?"

Sally opened her mouth, but, Nick noticed, she did not actually answer. Finally, she said, "We can try the High Court if Cromwell refuses bail overnight."

"Room 101?"

"Yes."

"A cage of rats," he said as he was ushered to the cells, remembering again the torture scene from Orwell's *1984*.

Chapter Two

Nick had been in his holding cell for half an hour. His curled-up sandwich remained on the bench next to him; his mug of heavily sugared tea in its soft plastic beaker was untouched. He sat and stared at the locked door.

I've been in prison cells before, he thought. I should be able to cope with this. But he had never been in a cell alone. He had always had a client, a client who depended upon him. He told himself that a prison cell was just another room. But so was a gas chamber, a mortuary, so was the condemned man's dungeon.

He stared at the door and remembered how Will Turner had looked as he had tried to hang himself from the hatch, from the wicket gate. He remembered the weight of the body, the dampness in the trousers and, above all, he remembered the smile. One part of Will Turner's face was smiling, while the other was racked with pain.

And now, he thought, it's him on the outside and me on the inside. Their lives had crossed, their paths linked and twisted, a tangle that Nick was helpless to unravel.

He got up and moved to the wicket, running his fingers along the cool metal edges. How easy it would be to end it, he thought. The guards had even forgotten to take his tie away. His fingers moved quickly and the knot in his tie was simply undone. But as he wrapped the silken material again and again around his hands and thought about ligatures, the cell door opened.

"You got a visitor, Downes," Jo said, deliberately clanking his keys of office. He had cropped his hair still further.

"Who is it?" Nick asked.

"A lady. Well, sort of."

Jo got hold of the tie in Nick's hand and wrenched it away. "I told you," he said, "no one hangs themselves. Not without my permission."

He was led past the reception desk and into one of the visiting rooms. Sitting there was Ann Barnes.

"Just popped in for a quick chin-wag," she said. "How the devil are you doing?"

Nick slumped onto one of the plastic chairs.

"Well, we are in a talkative mood, aren't we?" Ann continued.

"What . . . what are you doing here, Ann?"

"I work here, remember? Well, almost. I look at the Bailey as my field office. A sort of archaeological dig for the mind. I'm always here. How's the trial going?"

"It hasn't started, actually."

"And you're already banged up? Sally must be doing a splendid job. How is she, by the way?"

"Still with Max."

"Don't worry. It's the old story. Boy meets girl. Boy loses girl. But doesn't it normally end with boy winning girl back?"

"Not in my case," he said, dolefully. "It's more like girl runs off with boy's best friend. Boy hangs himself."

"Another postmodernist love story," Ann said. "How boring." She opened her handbag and took out a new pack of cigarettes. She unwrapped the cellophane, took out a cigarette, and lit it. After she had taken a long draw, slowly releasing the smoke through her excessively parted lips, she offered the packet to Nick.

"I don't smoke, Ann."

"Take it anyway."

"Why?"

"You might need it."

"For what?"

"For prison," Ann said.

"*Prison?*"

"You remember prison, Nick. Look, snout is the best currency in the slammer. You can use it to bribe some twenty-stone armed robber not to bugger you senseless." When he did not reply, she added swiftly, "I'm only joking, Nick."

"I'll get bail tonight."

"Of course you will. Has the judge said?"

"Actually, he hasn't." As he spoke, he grabbed the packet of extra-high-nicotine cigarettes emblazoned with the warning SMOKING KILLS.

"That's the idea," Ann said.

"Either they leave me alone or I'll give them lung cancer," he said.

She blew a cloud of vaporized toxins toward his nostrils. "Anyway, let's talk of less tasteful things. Who's prosecuting you?"

"Joshua Smith."

"Not that little runt?" she said.

"How well do you know him?"

She stared a little too knowingly at him.

"Jesus, Ann. You haven't . . ."

"So I was going through my attracted-to-little-runts phase. It's no big deal. What if I'm a little on the rampant side? It's not a crime."

"Is there anyone you *haven't* slept with?"

She paused and then stubbed out her cigarette quite violently. "You," she said.

"Don't be silly," Nick said. "We can't."

"Why not?"

"I think of you like my sister."

"Even better."

"Isn't there a psychiatric term for that sort of thing?" he asked.

"Yes," she said. "Fucking amazing."

Just then, the door to the visiting room was opened, and Jo came in.

"Your presence is required upstairs, sir," he said sarcastically to Nick.

As he was led along the corridor, Ann came to his side and whispered mockingly, "If I can be of any help, Nick. Fags, condoms, drugs."

"Drugs?"

"Well, if you want the drugs, you'd have to kiss me first." She smiled. "Isn't that how drugs are smuggled across in prison visits? Mouth to mouth? Give them a French kiss and some Colombian cocaine at the same time?"

"Ann," he said, not really listening to her dissertation on dental drug dealing, "there's a rehab somewhere in West Kent. By the motorway. Find out what you can about it."

"Sure. But why?"

"I know someone who went there," he said.

"Who?"

"That Chinese girl I told you about. From the brothel."

Smith stood up and turned very deliberately to face the jury. "Members of the jury," he said. "I appear to prosecute this case, and m'learned friend, Miss Fielding, appears for the defense. The first thing you will want to know is what the case is all about. I can answer that very easily. It is about two things: firstly, sex. Secondly, violence."

Nick glanced at the jury. Two of them, both Asian women, looked back at him. They must think I'm a rapist with a chain saw, he thought. He had to look away.

"The accused," he said, "is Nicholas Downes. He is a barrister, but I know you will not hold that against him."

The prosecutor waited for a chuckle from the jury box, but none was forthcoming. Nick saw that Sally was now sitting facing the jury, and he could see the left-hand side of her face. She gazed at the jurors intensely. Her eyes were cool and beautiful and blue.

"In May of this year, the defendant went to the address of the complainant in this case, Elizabeth Turner. She and Downes had been having an affair even though the lady was still . . . well, married."

Again, two of the women on the jury looked toward Nick and scowled. He turned to Sally for reassurance, but the glower she gave him was even worse. What did she find so distasteful? he wondered. The fact of the Turner marriage or the affair? Or both?

"Mrs. Turner had ended the liaison with Downes. She had seen the error of her ways and wanted to effect a reconciliation with her husband. But Downes could not accept it. Driven by sexual desire and, I have to say, by jealousy, Downes forced his way into the flat in Notting Hill. Once inside, he ripped off the victim's clothes."

At this, the jailer sitting at Nick's side glanced up from page three of the *Sun* and began to pay real attention.

"Downes stripped her and ordered her to have sex with him. When she refused, he struck her viciously about the face. This caused cuts and bruising. These injuries were photographed at the Domestic Violence Unit at Notting Hill Gate police station. This is the subject matter of the second count of the indictment." He paused to allow the jury to catch up. "But still Downes was not satisfied."

Sally glanced again at the dock. By now, Nick was so ashamed that he could not bear to look her in the eyes.

"The accused forced the helpless victim to the ground and tried to . . . insinuate himself into her. He only failed because he was unable to get . . . well, an erection."

Nick noticed that a couple of the court reporters sniggered to each other and jotted down the juicy tidbits. He could imagine the headlines already: LIMP LAWYER LATEST.

"Fortunately for the poor lady," the prosecutor continued, "her husband returned and stopped the assault."

HARDLY A HARD-ON, M'LUD.

"Mr. Turner was able to call the police as the accused man fled. Later that day, Nicholas Downes was arrested in his home in Queensway before he could escape any further."

Nick sat alone in the dock and wondered how it could have all come so far. Some of what the prosecutor had said was partially true. He had torn off parts of Liz's clothing. But hadn't she asked him to do it? Or had he imagined it?

"Of course," he concluded, "I should remind you that the accused is *technically* presumed innocent, and the prosecution have to prove the case beyond reasonable doubt."

This concession was of little comfort to Nick. It was rather like standing a man in front of a firing squad and then saying "Of course, we could all miss."

The prosecutor took a deep breath and pulled his gown tightly around his shoulders. "But don't get bogged down in legal technicalities, members of the jury. This case is not about presumptions. It's about people. And when you have heard all the evidence, you will have no doubts at all that the man in the dock is guilty as charged."

No one in the court looked at Nick except for Smith. The prosecutor smiled briefly at him as he finished his speech and asked for leave to call the first witness. It was to be Liz Turner.

Chapter Three

The judge clearly wanted a break from Smith's oratory before he allowed the complainant to testify. So as the jury trudged out for their midafternoon mug of PG Tips, Nick was taken into the holding area behind Court 8. Sally joined him.

"How are you enjoying the show so far?" she asked, sitting down next to him on the bench.

"Usual tedious prosecution drivel," he said. "But—"

"What?"

"But it's different when they're speaking about me, Sals. I can't explain it, but I already feel guilty."

Her eyes moved over his face with great deliberation. "And are you?"

"What?"

"Guilty."

"*What?*"

"You heard me. Are you guilty, Nick?"

"You have to ask me that?"

"I don't have to, but I want to. I mean, are you denying everything they're saying?"

He stood up and edged against the wall opposite them. With his back to Sally, he said, "I wouldn't put it exactly like that."

"Then how would you put it?" When he did not respond, she repeated in a louder voice, "Nick, just how would you put it, *exactly*?"

"Do we have to row?"

"No. We don't have to. But why break the habit of a lifetime just because you're in the dock for groping a woman?"

"And for assaulting her," he added. "Don't forget to throw that in, too."

"Look, sooner or later, Nick, we're going to have to tell the truth."

"We never did before, Sals."

"Oh, do shut up."

"What happened to 'The customer is always right'? You're meant to take your instructions from me, aren't you? Wasn't that the first thing we learned in Bar School?"

"No, the first thing we learned was that everyone is innocent until proven guilty. And you know what, Nick? It's a lie. It's a dirty, disgusting lie. If there's one thing I do know, it's that our clients will cheat and scheme and lie to squirm their way out of trouble."

"Well, that's your problem, Sally. You see the courts as a place where an unrelenting tide of human detritus flushes through the system."

"It is."

"And am I . . . part of that tide?"

"God, Nick. You're so naïve. Don't you see that as a lawyer you immediately start at a disadvantage?"

"Why?"

"Because people think lawyers are a bunch of dishonest, deceiving, greedy crooks. I think that, and I'm your barrister. You're a man and a lawyer and you're presumed guilty; lawyers are dishonest; men abuse women. You've already been convicted by history. Sex cases are notoriously difficult. It's one-on-one, behind closed doors, there are no witnesses—and, in your case, the complainant has serious injuries. But the worst part—"

"There's *worse*?"

"You're really too old to be making a debut in the dock. You ask the questions that no one wants to answer. And that makes everyone suspicious of you. And if they're suspicious, they may just find you guilty."

"I'll take my chances."

"In what?"

"In the system working."

Sally laughed.

"I mean, can't we just let justice take its course?" he asked.

"Justice? Certainly not," she said.

"So what will we do?"

"We'll fight dirty, of course."

"Sals, I've been meaning to ask you. In your view, what are my chances?"

"Oh, pretty average—"

"Good."

"For a hopeless case, that is," she added.

"Look, Sals, I want you to know I've done nothing you'd be ashamed of."

"Oh, well, that's a *great* relief, Nick."

"It might look bad, but I'm really—"

"Don't try to convince me, Nick. Save it for the jury."

The door that separated the holding area from the courtroom suddenly opened, and the jailer slipped his head into the room.

"The judge will be coming back in a minute," he said.

Sally got up and forced Nick to sit on the bench below her. "I'm afraid it might get a little rough in there," she said.

Nick looked up at her, at the chafed lips and at the features that for so long he had taken for granted.

"But always remember," she said, "I'm on your side, Nick. Never forget that."

"Thanks."

"Look, things may get a little desperate. I mean, if she comes across well. We may have to resort to desperate measures. Don't let it all get you down."

"Down? I'm almost at the bottom anyway. To sink any lower, I think I'd need scuba diving equipment and a pair of flippers."

They both smiled, and then he added, "What did you mean by desperate measures?"

"I might have to cross-examine your beloved Mrs. Turner about her previous sexual history."

Nick realized that because one of the allegations concerned a sexual offense, it was possible that Liz might be dragged through the dirt. It was a practice he had always profoundly disagreed with.

"I don't want you to do that, Sals," he said.

"Why not?"

"It's so unfair."

"Tell me, is what she's doing to you particularly fair, Nick?"

"That's not the point. Pillorying a woman about her private life is so sexist."

"In a war, Nick, you don't worry about what Germaine Greer would have done."

"But if we put in Liz's sexual history, can't she put in mine?"

"You haven't got one. Apart from me, that is. And I threw up in the sink after the first time we—"

"I miss you, Sals."

"I know you do," she said, putting her hands on his shoulders. "Look, I may be living with Max. But believe me, I'm alone too, Nick. Just like you."

The door was pulled wide open. It seemed to Nick like the drawing back of a stage curtain. And there was the set before him, the props and the cue cards and the cast. But as he sat in the dock and watched the proceedings, he couldn't decide whether he was one of the actors or merely part of the audience.

Liz Turner came into the court with deliberate strides. She walked very slowly, as if she was appearing only with the greatest degree of regret. Everything about her was understated and quiet and bland. Her hair had grown out and was back to its more usual style.

It was as if the stuffing had been knocked out of her. The lumps of her body had been somehow rearranged so that she no longer looked sexual and curvy but rounded and comforting.

She looked for all the world as if she had been hauled out of a Bible class in Basingstoke where she had been singing alleluias to the eternal joys of the Christian marriage. To Nick, she might as well have been a different person.

By now she had reached the witness box. The usher stood in front of her and asked, "What is your religion?"

"Christian," she replied.

A Bible was then thrust into her hands like a parking ticket. The usher was one Nick knew well. Doreen was a woman of about fifty who had spent twenty-five years in the Central Criminal Courts swearing in witnesses and reading cooking recipes from the color supplements.

"I'm very sorry," Liz whispered to the judge. "I suppose I should have said. I'm a Catholic. A practicing Catholic. Does that matter?"

Cromwell inspected her sheepish eyes and seemed delighted. "Please don't concern yourself with that, madam. This is an ecumenical court. All beliefs are welcome. It's just refreshing to see someone who still holds some."

Nick watched with amazement as the woman who had taken him to a sex show featuring a particularly large rubber implement swore to tell the truth, the whole truth, and nothing but that.

"What is your name?" the prosecutor asked.

"Elizabeth . . ." Her voice trailed off as she reached her surname.

"I'm afraid you will have to do better than that," he said. "I know it must be a rather intimidating experience, but you must speak clearly."

"Perhaps you would like to sit down?" the judge asked.

"No, thank you. I'll . . . try to stand. I'd prefer to."

"Can you repeat your name?" the prosecutor asked.

"Elizabeth Turner."

"And are you married?"

"Yes."

"To whom?"

"To Will Turner."

"I don't want to pry unnecessarily into your private life, but did there come a time, for whatever reason, when you and your husband lived apart?"

Nick wanted to get to his feet and shout out. But that was Sally's job. He had to trust her. He looked at her, saw her back, her wig, saw that she was clearly going to do nothing, and told himself again that he had to trust her.

"Our marriage had certain . . . difficulties," Liz said. "Which we have now resolved."

"Did there come a time when you met the accused, Nicholas Downes?"

"Yes, he was counsel who was instructed to defend my husband."

"And did your contact with him remain on a professional lawyer-client level?"

"For my part, yes. But then he suggested that we should go out."

"Together?"

"Yes."

"And where was your husband?"

"He was in custody on the charges he was facing."

There was a murmur around the court which seemed to Nick to well from every quarter and then converge upon him in the dock.

"So," Smith continued, "while your husband was in prison, this . . . barrister propositioned you?"

Sally got to her feet. It was a leading question. But Liz cut her short.

"I want to be fair to . . . Nick. He didn't proposition me. Well, not then. He merely said that he wanted to discuss some sensitive aspects of the case. It's the only reason I agreed. I wanted to do anything to help my husband."

"And did he eventually proposition you?"

"Yes."

"And did you eventually get involved with him sexually?"

Nick noticed that she looked down. At the same time, Sally glanced at him, and he could feel his face on fire.

"Yes, we became intimate," Liz whispered.

"And did you want that intimacy to continue?"

"No. When Will was acquitted and released, I came to my senses. But Mr. Downes would not accept that it was over."

"Can we now move to the night in May? I think it will be agreed that the accused came to your flat. What happened?"

"Nick was furious about my decision to end it. He said that he loved me. He said that he had never loved anyone else. He said—"

Sally had got to her feet. "M'Lord, I object," she said, her voice faltering somewhat.

"And what is the basis of your objection?" the judge asked.

"This . . . conversation is not contained in any statement. If the Crown wishes to rely upon new evidence, it should be served upon the defense in written form."

"You can hardly be prejudiced," the judge snapped. "I'm sure that your . . . client has told you everything that happened according to him."

Sally did not reply.

"But I suppose that if you insist that all the *technicalities* be complied with," the judge continued, "I can send the jury out after Mrs. Turner has given evidence so you can consult. If it is really necessary."

"Please continue," the prosecutor said.

"Nick started ripping off my clothes. Slowly at first. And then more violently. I was too terrified to do anything. He told me we had to . . . do it. Those were his words. Do it there on the floor like animals. But I refused."

"And?"

"And he started to hit me around the face."

"Where did he hit you?"

"I'm not sure. It was so many times and my whole face hurt."

"M'Lord," he said, "there will be photographs of the injuries for the jury tomorrow. Please continue, Mrs. Turner."

"Then he climbed on top of me and tried to—"

"What?"

"Force himself inside me."

"And could he?"

"No."

"Why not?"

"Because my husband came home and pulled him off. I was in shock and I'm afraid I don't really remember any more."

The prosecutor surveyed the stunned faces in the jury box. His job done, he sat down with a flourish of his gown.

The judge looked at the clock on the court wall. "Miss Fielding," he said. "It is getting rather late in the day for you to be able to complete your cross-examination."

"Yes, M'Lord. But I'd like to begin."

Chapter Four

Nick knew Sally's tactic well. Always try to fire the odd salvo before close of play. Don't leave the jury with an untarnished witness overnight. Try to claw back a little ground before the jurors return to their families and fish fingers. But he wanted to speak to her first, before she fell headfirst into more of Liz Turner's lies.

"Don't you want to consult with the defendant before you begin?" the judge asked.

"I'll do that when the court rises," Sally said, ignoring Nick's gestures. And then, before the judge could respond, she continued, "Now, Mrs. Turner." She surveyed the witness in silence, and the tension continued to build in court until she shouted, "You've told the court a pack of *lies*, haven't you?"

"Certainly not."

"Tomorrow, I shall explore them in detail. But tonight—"

"Why should I lie?" Liz interrupted. "It's hard enough standing here and telling the truth." In desperation Sally tried to cut her off, but Liz continued to speak. "Can you imagine the humiliation, Miss Fielding? Being swabbed down there when I was at the Domestic Violence Unit. Having to give a urine sample, having to answer all those intimate questions. No, I don't think that I'm lying."

Sally paused and seemed to Nick to be rattled. When she finally began to speak again, it was in a faltering voice. "We'll come to all that tomorrow," she said, "but for the moment, let's just concentrate on one thing. You told us that the . . . accused—"

Why isn't she using my name? Nick thought.

"You told us that the reason that the accused did not enter you was because your husband came home."

"Yes."

"So it had nothing to do with the fact that the accused could not get an erection."

"That's not what I said."

"Isn't the truth that you've just been caught out in a lie? You see, you told the police that Mr. Downes couldn't—and I quote—get it up."

"True," Liz said.

"But you haven't told the jury anything about that."

"True."

"Well, why not?"

Liz Turner looked directly at a couple of men on the jury and said, "Because I wanted to save him from embarrassment."

"And accusing him of a serious sexual assault? Is that part of your desire to save him from embarrassment?"

"He is guilty of that."

"Oh, I see," Sally said sarcastically. "So are there any other little details you have withheld just to save Mr. Downes embarrassment?"

"Do I have to answer that question?" Liz asked the judge.

Before he could reply, Sally interjected, "Yes, you do. Unless His Lordship says otherwise. Now what else have you not mentioned?"

Liz was silent.

"What else, Mrs. Turner?"

"I haven't mentioned that—"

"Yes?"

"That I'm *pregnant*, and Mr. Downes is the father," she said.

As Sally stood speechless, the judge got to his feet. "Yes, I think we'll call it a day there, members of the jury. Your client can have bail overnight, Miss Fielding."

Everyone rose, and the judge walked out. People left court hurriedly, glancing at Nick, sneering, smiling, scolding. He sat in the dock and waited for the room to empty, until there was no one left except himself and Sally.

"We need to talk," he said to her.

She did not reply.

"Sally, I said we really need to—"

"Talk? Why bother? Everyone will be doing the talking for us. You date your client's wife, grope her, than put her in the pudding club. Congratulations, Nick. How can the Lord Chancellor possibly refuse you Silk?"

"Sally, please. You know how I feel about you. I still—"

"Go to hell, Nick. Go straight to hell."

She stormed off and left him alone. Hell? Nick felt that he was already there.

As he walked out into the corridor in a state of bewilderment, he watched Sally's gown disappear toward the robing room. Then he heard someone whisper his name from a conference room. He advanced gingerly and peered into the partial darkness. Sitting in the far corner was Liz Turner. He tried to put the light on, but it would not work.

"I need to see you, Nick," she whispered. "I don't want to do this. They're forcing me to testify. There may be a way out."

He was stunned.

"Look," she said, "meet me at that bar, the one by Blackfriars Bridge. Be there in thirty minutes. Nick, *don't* disappoint me."

Nick sneaked out the back way of the Old Bailey, the rear entrance normally used by Treasury counsel. If he was going to be front-page news, he wasn't going to give the media pictures of him cowering before the cameras outside court.

It was a five-minute walk to the bar Liz had mentioned.

The Hanging Judge was once the haunt of hard-drinking

barristers and the City of London Police. But with the eighties boom it was modernized, yuppified, and rendered completely banal.

When he entered the black plastic and chrome salon, Liz Turner was sitting in a corner with two glasses of tomato juice in front of her.

"I hope you don't mind Bloody Marys," she said.

Nick looked on aghast.

"You're looking well—considering." She tried to smile. "Nick, I said—"

"What the *hell* do you want from me?"

"To show a little commitment, Nick."

"To what?"

"To our child."

"How do you know it's mine?"

"Will's sterile."

"What about—"

"Are you calling me a tart? Do you think I'm a whore, Nick? Is that it?"

He thought about his first meeting with Will Turner, about Will's obsession with the Revelations story of the whore and the child. He thought about the arguments he had had with Sally over children.

He did not know what to say.

A record clicked onto the jukebox. Pulses of guitar and bass.

"Let me do the talking," Liz said, over the music. "I love you and you love me. No, don't protest. I know you do. We should be together. And we can."

"How?"

She sipped her drink. "Forget Sally."

"She's forgotten me."

"She's defending you."

"For old times' sake."

"Forget her. That's the price. It's not too much to pay, is it? Why would she agree to marry that other man if she really loved you? Will she really be a loss? Think of what you have to lose and what you have to gain."

"Gain?"

"Me." Then she repeated what she had said to him in the public gallery at the Old Bailey when Will Turner had been acquitted. "I'll look after you, Nick. I'll stand by you and I'll *never* leave you."

Nick tried to gauge what he was dealing with as the music filled the bar.

"So, how will you work this?" he asked finally.

"I'll say Will forced me to lie. He's a convicted killer, isn't he? Wouldn't he be in breach of his suspended sentence and put away?"

"So *did* Will force you to prosecute me?"

"I had to pretend to Will that I was unwilling. But he called the police, and it all got out of hand. I'll blame Will and retract my evidence."

"Admit perjury?"

"I'd do it for you, Nick. What would I get if I pleaded guilty to that? A year? Two years?"

"Possibly a suspended sentence, actually—if you blamed Will. Six months at the worst. Out in three."

Her eyes lit up. "You see. We could be together for the birth. I'd go to prison for you. If that's what it takes to win you, I'd do it, Nick."

"You know," he said slowly, "I always thought it was Will who was crazy. But it's you, Liz. It's you."

Her eyes blazed. "Don't force me to destroy you, Nick."

"What do you mean?"

"If I can't have you, Sally Fielding never will."

"You can't touch me. Not anymore."

"Try me."

"I'd prefer ten years in prison to ten days with you."

"I *hate* you," she hissed.

"No, Liz, you hate yourself. I don't know what happened in your past, but you hate yourself."

She picked up her glass and threw the contents at him, soaking his face, staining his face red.

"Is that the best you can do?" he said. He noticed how her grip tightened around the thin bulb of glass.

"This is your last chance," she said, squeezing the glass tighter.

"I feel sorry for you, Liz," he said.

With that she shouted, *"Bastard,"* and crushed the glass in her bare palm, slicing her flesh. A fold of skin fell loose.

Nick could see blood pouring immediately from the gash in her hand onto the floor, broken pieces of glass with Liz's blood on them falling from her grasp onto the ground.

"Bastard," she cried again. "Leave me *alone.*"

Two men rushed over from the other side of the bar.

Nick struggled with her, grabbing her hand as she tried to use a razorlike shard of glass to cut her other wrist.

"He's *attacking* me," she shouted as the men arrived.

"Leave her alone," the bigger of the men ordered.

"Go away," Nick replied. "This is private."

"Leave her," the man yelled, and yanked Nick to his feet by his jacket.

"You're sick, Liz," he said quietly.

The man pushed him against the wall. "We're police officers. Off duty, but still Old Bill. One more word from you, mate, and you're nicked." He turned to Liz. "Now what did he do, madam?"

Liz was sobbing helplessly. "He tried to grope me and when I threw the drink in his face he started to attack me. He crushed the glass in my hand and tried to drive it into my wrist."

"That's what I saw," the second, smaller man said. "I saw them struggling with the glass."

Nick was astonished. "Where did I grope her, then?" he demanded.

The second man was silent.

Nick took off his tie and gave it to the first policeman. "She's got a bad cut," he said. "You'd better wrap this around her hand. She's losing blood rapidly."

The officers were unimpressed.

"Who the fuck do you think you are?" the second sneered. "Dr. Kildare?"

"Do you want to report him, love?" the first asked Liz.

She paused.

"We could arrest him for grievous bodily harm," he added.

Nick looked from Liz to the officers and then back to Liz. Finally, she shook her head. "Lovers' tiff," she said.

"Is he your boyfriend?" the first asked.

"My fiancé," she said.

"Is that right?" he asked Nick.

Nick was silent.

"Just leave," the second man told him. "Now."

The two men began to examine the raw flesh on Liz's palm for broken glass. When they were satisfied that there was none, they began to wrap Nick's tie—Sally's tie—around the bloodied hand.

Nick walked away slowly. But Liz left the officers for a moment and came up to him.

She held out the cut hand, wrapped in the now-damp tie. "You see," she said. "You *do* care."

"Liz, I'm only going to say this once more. You're ill. Seriously ill. You need help before you really—"

"I'm going to have your child, Nick," she interrupted, her eyes on fire. "I'm going to nurse him and bring him up. And I'm going to teach him to hate you."

Chapter Five

Nick and Sally sat in the public canteen on the morning of the second day of the trial. Sally had sent a message to the judge asking him to keep the jury out for an hour or so. She needed to take further instructions.

Nick arrived back at their table and put a plastic cup down in front of her.

"Coffee?" he said.

"Thanks."

"Sugar?"

"Yes."

"Is it one lump or two? I seem to forget, Sals. Funny, that."

She threw a pile of tabloid newspapers down on the table. "I *thought* I told you not to give the press any photo shots when you left."

There was a close-up photograph of Nick on the front page of each national newspaper.

"But I went out the back way."

"Where did they get the mug shot, then?"

"Let me see that." It was only when he looked more closely that he realized. "Oh my God. It's her."

"Who?"

"Liz," he said. "Don't you see? This is the shot from the chambers brochure. Can't we prove that the press got their photo from her?"

"They'll protect their sources," she said. "But I bet she did it anonymously."

Nick saw his full name *and* address emblazoned across the national headlines. "Isn't there meant to be anonymity in sex cases?" he asked.

"Only for the victim."

"Only for Liz," he said. "So she gets protection but I don't."

"That's the law, Nick."

"And that's fair?"

"I don't make the law, Nick. Men do. Men called judges and politicians. Don't complain just because for once it favors women." She was out of breath by the end of her tirade. She paused and tried to smile. "Where's your lucky tie?" she said, obviously trying to change the subject.

"Don't ask."

"Where is it, Nick?"

"Liz Turner has it—"

"*What?*"

"I really don't want to talk about it, Sals."

A pair of uniformed police officers with glasses of orange juice passed, and Nick reflected on the absurd events of the previous evening.

"Why did you give Liz Turner my tie?" Sally asked.

"Her hand was cut. The police were going to arrest me, but she saved the day."

"What on earth were you doing seeing her?"

"There were some things we both needed to say."

"You're in breach of your bail, you idiot. Cromwell could lock you up for just that. You're not allowed to approach prosecution witnesses."

"She approached me."

"Doesn't matter." She took a sip of her coffee and shook her head. "So what were you two lovebirds talking about?"

"Changing her story."

"You mean, perverting the course of justice. That's all right, then. And I thought you might have been doing something wrong."

"It's not perverting, Sals. Just steering back onto the straight and narrow."

"Did you succeed?"

"It's hard to tell. The police were about to arrest me. I assume the answer is no." He saw the color drain from her cheeks. "Don't worry. I don't think Liz will mention it."

"Whyever not?"

"It's hard to explain. But for the first time I think I sort of won." He smiled.

Sally looked at him and was not amused. "How could you not have told me that you fertilized that woman?"

"I didn't know."

"No. Why should you know that the bride of Frankenstein has little Nick junior gestating in her *womb*?"

"Sally, don't use language like that."

"Like what? Like *womb*? Well, where else is the little darling meant to gestate? In your wig-tin? Still, it's an easy oversight, I suppose."

"Sally—"

"Look, when are you going to give me some real answers?"

"Fire away."

"Oh, don't tempt me, Nick. If I fire, I'll blow your bloody head off." She picked up her cup and then put it down immediately. "Now tell me. How do you know you're the father? What about—"

"Her husband? He's sterile."

"Why did you run off when Will Turner arrived?"

"Two reasons."

"Such as?"

"Firstly, I didn't want to exchange pleasantries with the husband from hell when my flies were undone. And secondly—"

"Yes?"

"I had to feed my cat."

"Rubbish. You haven't got a cat."

"I have now," he said. "Now I've got a cat."

Sally looked amazed.

"Well, I've got him for the moment," he said. "He's on a bit of a suspended sentence with the management committee, really."

"Do you realize, Nick, that your whole future is at stake?"

"Yes."

"Well, can you tell me why I'm asking you about how you've put the main prosecution witness in the pudding club, and you're telling me about Tiddles the cat?"

"He's not called Tiddles, actually."

"So what's he called?"

"Catt . . . with two *t*s," Nick said.

They both picked up their plastic beakers of liquid caffeine, took a sip, winced, and looked at each other.

"Why did we never have a cat?" he asked.

"I'm allergic to cats," she said.

"And what about children?"

"Well, call me a cold career woman, but I've got this strange aversion to carrying around a parasite for nine months. And then there's the pain."

"Pain?"

"It's called labor, Nick. It's how babies are born. It's in Genesis, isn't it? 'In pain shalt thou bring forth children,' and all that."

"When Eve was punished?"

"For pinching an apple. A first offense. I mean, probation perhaps. I want to know, I really want to know, why you're going to have a child with *her*?"

"How do we know she's really pregnant?"

"The cowardly cry of men down the ages, Nick. Look, if one of your spermatozoa has had the gall to attach itself to one of her ripe little eggs, at least have the guts to admit it."

He took another sip of the tepid black sludge. "I just didn't know about the child before, all right? I mean, it's hardly the most romantic way to discover you're going to be a father."

"What do you mean?"

"Darling, we're going to have a baby—*that's* the sex fiend who attacked me, M'Lord."

"What did you expect?"

"Chocolates would have been nice." But he knew that he could not conceal his fears any longer. "Oh, God, Sally. I'm in such a mess. What on earth am I going to do?"

"You're going to pull yourself together and fight back, that's what." She opened the brief in front of her by carefully untying the red ribbon, then picked up her fountain pen, and said, "Now, tell me how it happened."

"What?"

"The not particularly immaculate conception. Presumably you did practice birth control of some description?"

"That's the problem. I really didn't have enough practice at all. I mean, you were on the pill, Sals. And I'd never used one of those . . . things before."

"So it split?"

"Well, it sort of got lost."

"Lost? What, beforehand? You couldn't find the packet?"

"No," he said miserably. "Afterward. Look, I didn't do it deliberately."

"What? Make her pregnant or make love to her?"

"I think we should stop fighting and start cooperating. Let's call a truce, Sals."

"Fine by me."

"Good. It's agreed, then," he said. "You scratch my back and I'll—"

"I can't scratch your back, Nick."

"Why not?"

"I've got no nails left."

He inspected the hands that were ceremoniously thrust in front of his face. "You've bitten them all off."

She stood up and gazed at him through the tobacco smoke. "Last night my diet consisted entirely of chewed fingernails and chocolate Hob Nobs biscuits."

"But why?"

"All I could think of was our child in another woman's womb, Nick. I hope you're satisfied. You bastard."

"Did you say—"

"Yes, I did. You *bastard*."

"No. You said, 'our child.'"

"Did I? Well, I meant *your* child. Look, you know what I mean."

"No, you definitely said—"

"I'm glad you've got a cat, Nick. I'm glad you've got someone at home." She turned sharply to avoid his eyes. "You shouldn't be alone."

Leaving the beakers of coffee, they headed toward the doors of the canteen together. Nick thought about the forensic evidence in the first trial, how the pathologist had said that people tear off their nails when they are buried alive. Perhaps Sally was trying to claw her way out of something, a relationship she didn't really want with Max. Perhaps things weren't so settled; perhaps there was some hope. But his wishful thinking was interrupted when his way was blocked by Joshua Smith.

"Just thought I'd tell you," the prosecutor said. "We have a bit of a surprise witness." He laughed in an ostentatious manner. "It's not too late to plead guilty, you know."

"How can it be a *bit* of a surprise?" Sally asked.

"Let me put it this way," Smith said. "It's a surprise to me, but it shouldn't be a surprise to you."

Chapter Six

Sally told Nick to wait in the canteen until she had finished conferring with Joshua Smith. He clawed his way through the banks of tobacco smoke and indulged in some determined passive smoking. If the rest of his life was to be ruined, he didn't see why his lungs should get away scot free.

When he sat down once more at the table, he thought about what the prosecutor had said about a surprise witness. Things were piling up against him. Lost in these thoughts, he did not notice the person approaching him until her studded belt was inches away from his tonsils.

"On the run from Brixton Prison?" she said.

When he looked up, he could just see a familiar face buried beneath a couple of crusted layers of makeup.

"Ann, is that you?"

"Of course it's me. So I overdid the war paint a bit. A girl has to look her best for her big moment in court. I can't resist getting made up for my bit part in the legal drama."

"So you're actually testifying in another court today?" he asked.

"Any moment now I'm going to have to swear that the cockroach and cat food chef of Old London Town is not completely bonkers. How on earth did you get bail?"

He gestured toward the empty seat.

"The judge seemed to forget that I was a bail risk," he said.

"So how's the case going?"

"Oh, pretty much like the Guildford Four—the first time round."

"That bad?"

"There's been a bit of a development," he said.

"Such as?"

"Such as Liz Turner saying I've fathered her fetus."

"That's not a development. That's a disaster. That makes the sinking of the *Titanic* look like a bit of a bump with an iceberg."

"What am I going to do, Ann?"

"The right thing."

"Which is?"

"Run. Scarper. Hide from the paternity police."

"*Who?*"

"The Child Support Agency, of course. Look, shave your legs, change your name to Sister Mary O'Donnell, devote the rest of your life to the poor in Calcutta, and you might just get away with it."

By now Ann's voice had risen, and the astonished families of the various robbers and rapists appearing in the rest of the building looked on disapprovingly.

"Ann," Nick whispered. "Grateful as I am for the suggestion, it does seem a tad impractical."

"Perhaps," she whispered back. "Alternatively, you could play it by the book."

"How do I do that?"

"Deny everything, of course. I mean, how do you know that the uterus-usurper is yours?"

"That's what I said."

"Of course you would, Nick. You're a man. And, as history has proved, all men are bastards." She took off one of her shoes and proceeded to examine the razorlike stiletto.

"But I don't want to be a bastard," he said. "I've tried, I mean, really tried to be—"

"What? Politically correct and all that? Like a New Man? Let me tell you, there's no such thing as the New Man. All there is, is the old model with some fancy new lies. The trouble with men is that they all have the same design defect."

"Which is?"

"A man's body is not big enough for both testosterone *and* tenderness. And when men have the choice, decency always loses out to doing it doggy fashion."

"You have a very dim view of men, Ann."

"It's a recognized psychiatric phenomenon."

"Called?"

"Manhood."

Tannoys were beginning to sound as parties were summoned to court.

"I almost forgot," she said. "You know I said I think I can help?"

"Yes."

"Well, I think I can help. In two ways."

"But how?"

"You're charged with a sexual assault, aren't you? So the victim—"

"Liz Turner."

"Her evidence should really be corroborated, backed up." Her thumbnail summary of this rule of evidence produced a nod from Nick. "So," she continued, "the prosecution presumably are relying on—"

"Will Turner to corroborate her evidence," he said. "So?"

"So why don't we show that Will Turner is an unreliable witness?"

"How?"

"By calling . . . me. You know, the videos and all that."

"Ann, thanks, but—"

"Can't you call medical evidence to show a witness's unreliability?"

"Yes, but—"

"Good. Well, I can testify that Will Turner is about as reliable as Dr. Jekyll after he's downed a test tube of chemicals and said 'I think I'm coming over a bit funny.' "

Before he could answer, there was another tannoy. This time it demanded Ann's presence in court immediately. She slipped on her stiletto and used the back of the chair to balance herself as she stood up.

"At least think about it," she said, pulling down her skirt. "Don't think I look too tarty, do you?"

"You look fine." Then he remembered what she had told him. "You said that you could help me in two ways, Ann."

"It's all a bit complicated. But you remember we talked about rats?" When he nodded, she continued. "Well, do you know what they eat?" He shook his head as she said, "Normally it's cereals and seeds and stuff. You know, bloody hippie food."

"Seed? Like rape seed?"

"Well, I don't know about that. But I do know that they also scavenge. They'll eat meat and bone. *Any* meat and bone."

"Like human?"

"Most of us taste rather like chicken, I hear. You see, the dead rat in the corpse might have been feasting upon raw psychoanalyst tartare when the rat snuffed it."

"Maybe the human flesh was infiltrated with lime, and the rat was poisoned?" he said.

"I suppose that's one theory."

"Is there another?" he asked.

"Just a hunch of mine."

"Does it explain why the rat's skeleton had been picked almost clean?"

The tannoy crackled and insisted that Dr. Ann Barnes should attend court forthwith.

"Got to run, Nick."

"Ann?"

"Look, it might have something to do with Freud and phobias," she said, scuttling off on her high heels. "It's just a hunch."

Chapter Seven

When all the parties had congregated in Court 8, Sally told Nick the bad news.

"They're going to call Kenny to give evidence," she said.

"Kenny?" he replied, getting into the dock. "What on earth could he testify about?"

"Smith wouldn't tell me. They're still photocopying the statement. He just laughed in an obnoxious way and . . . Nick, you didn't grope Kenny in the—"

"Lobby?"

"Or anywhere else obscene?"

"Of course not. What makes you say that?"

"Oh, nothing really. It's just that one minute you're St. Francis of Assisi, and the next you're into snuff movies. It's a bit of a change."

There was a commotion at the front of the court as the judge stormed in. Sally crept to her place in counsel's row where, Nick observed, she was separated from him by a dock, a couple of benches, and an engagement ring from Max. Very soon, Liz Turner was back in the witness box, and Sally was on her feet to continue her cross-examination.

Liz had a clean bandage wrapped tightly around her palm.

"Are you all right to continue, Mrs. Turner?" the judge asked. "We can adjourn if—"

"Just a small accident," she said, and looked at Nick.

"Are you happy to continue?" the judge repeated.

"Perfectly."

In the area of court separating Nick and Liz, standing at the end of counsel's row, Sally glanced at a sheaf of notes, put them down, and then looked straight at the witness. "Would you say, Mrs. Turner, that your husband is a normal man?"

Even from the dock, Nick could see that Liz had been taken by surprise.

She spluttered out, "I don't see what possible relevance this could—"

"Just answer the question," Sally said. "Is he normal?"

"That very much depends on your concept of normality, Miss Fielding."

"Not on mine. On yours. My views are utterly irrelevant."

"Well," Liz said, smiling, "if you say so. Can you be more specific? Normal in what way?"

"Oh, in a killing other people and burying them in a shallow grave sort of way," Sally said in a deadpan fashion.

"He was acquitted of murder."

"But pleaded guilty to manslaughter?"

Liz did not reply.

"Correct?" Sally insisted.

"Correct."

"And help the jury with this. Manslaughter with regard to whom?"

At this, the judge intervened. His pencil orbited momentarily around his eyelids. "Please don't forget, Miss Fielding, exactly who is on trial in this case," he said.

"Yes, M'Lord."

"So what pertinence can this line of cross-examination have?"

"Perhaps I'll have the witness answer that . . . *if* Your Lordship pleases."

Nick was sweating profusely. Don't push your luck, Sally, he thought. Don't push your luck.

"Now, Mrs. Turner," Sally continued. "Who was the victim? What was the identity of the *man* who was *slaughtered?*"

"His brother, Charles Turner."

"And, turning back to your case, is your husband, Will Turner, the only other witness to this . . . *alleged* attack by Mr. Downes?"

"There is nothing alleged about it. But, yes. Will is the only other witness."

"You see, you have told the jury a pack of lies."

"Have I?"

"And the truth is that you are a thoroughly dishonest, manipulative, scheming woman—and I mean that with all due respect."

Liz did not answer.

"You say that Mr. Downes was the instigator of this . . . sexual liaison between you," Sally continued.

Liz nodded.

"Isn't the truth," Sally said, "that Nicholas Downes has all the sex drive of a wet blanket?"

"Maybe with *other* women."

The judge coughed. "Miss Fielding, men find some women more . . . provocative than others. It's just natural."

"So, M'Lord," Sally said, "is blaming your lover when the two of you are caught naked by your irate husband. That's just natural." She turned to face the witness. "And that is precisely what happened here, is it not?"

"What?"

"You were scared to death of what your husband might do to you when he burst in on you and the defendant."

"Why should I be scared of my own husband?"

"No reason. Except that he had already killed his brother with a claw hammer and buried the body by the M25." She paused momentarily. "So you blamed Mr. Downes. You said he forced himself upon you."

"Rubbish."

"And your husband caused your injuries."

"Sheer fantasy."

"No, Mrs. Turner. The only fantasies in this case are your sexual ones about Nicholas Downes."

"About *him?*"

Liz looked at the dock with complete incredulity. "It was your . . . client, Miss Fielding, who had all the perverted ideas."

"Oh, really?" Sally said in an unimpressed fashion.

Nick, however, was on edge. Don't push it, Sals, he thought. Don't push it.

"He took me to a sex club."

"What? Nick Downes?"

The judge again intervened. "Can you give the jury any other examples?"

Sally tried to protest. "M'Lord, I don't see how this can possibly be relevant."

"As I seem to remember you saying to me earlier, Miss Fielding, why don't we let the witness answer that." The judge was clearly having fun. "You opened the door, Miss Fielding. You put the defendant's sexual character at issue."

"No, I—"

"Didn't you say that he had all the sex drive of a wet paper bag?"

The prosecutor used the opportunity to get to his feet. "Actually, it was a wet blanket, M'Lord. I have a full note. Question: Isn't the truth that Nicholas Downes has all the sex drive of a wet blanket?"

"Thank you," the judge said. "Now, you were going to give us another example, Mrs. Turner."

Nick could see the court reporters with open mouths and pencils poised waiting for the next circulation-boosting detail.

"Well, once," Liz said, "he . . . well, did *things* to himself and made me watch. I was so shocked. It was so unexpected, I mean, in his chambers."

The judge was horrified. "In his *professional* chambers?"

"Yes."

"In the Temple?"

"Yes."

Nick could see Sally rummaging through her notes. But her

heart no longer seemed to be in it. She looked up only when the judge spoke to her.

"Do you have any more questions, Miss Fielding?"

"Only this," Sally said. "Isn't it right that you made the defendant rip off your clothes?"

"Is that a serious suggestion?" the judge asked.

"Certainly," Sally said. "I'll repeat the question. Isn't—"

"There's no need," Liz replied. "Why would I ruin my suit? It was *Chanel*."

Cromwell asked, "Do you have any more questions for this lady, Miss Fielding?"

"No, M'Lord."

"You're quite sure? It's your last chance. So she can be released for good?"

Sally nodded.

The court adjourned to await the arrival of Will Turner. Sally stormed off to the Bar Mess, which was off limits to Nick as a defendant. Other people involved in the trial headed off in search of a cup of tea, leaving Nick alone in court except for the dock officer.

When he looked out into the well of the court, he thought about what Sally had said about prison food and the sex offenders' wing. Perhaps he should start to reconcile himself to the fact that this was almost inevitably going to be his fate. Perhaps he should change his plea. But he did not have sufficient opportunity to consider these options, as there was a creak from the outer door of the court.

When he looked up, Liz Turner walked in.

She went up to the dock officer and said something to him that provoked the question "Are you sure?" She nodded, he shook his head in disbelief, and before Nick knew what was happening, he was led into the holding area behind the dock with Liz Turner.

He did not care. He no longer felt threatened by her.

"Thought you might be a bit lonely," she said when the officer had shut them in together.

"I can't speak to you," he said.

"But I can speak to you. The judge has released me from giving evidence."

"Look, what on earth are you up to now?"

"I wanted to return your tie." She took it out of her handbag. "You see, I've dry-cleaned it and—"

"Just *cut* the small talk, Liz."

"And I also wanted to tell you something."

"What?" he asked.

"I wasn't Charles's secretary."

"Then what were you?"

"His *patient*." Before he could say anything, she continued, "For three years before I met Will. That's why I'd known Charles eight years—not five like Will thought."

He looked at her in astonishment, but she displayed no emotion, staring at him evenly.

"Charles diagnosed me as obsessional, neurotic." Having said this, she rapped twice on the door so hard it turned her knuckles white.

"Why are you telling me all this?" he asked.

The door opened and, as the dock officer came in, she whispered in his ear, "To torture you, Nick."

"I could mention it in court."

"No one would believe you. Besides," she said, smiling in the way she had when Nick had caught her making love to Will Turner, "besides, I could be lying."

"I could check Charles Turner's records."

"Oh dear. Hasn't anyone told you? They've disappeared, Nick—when Charles disappeared. They've all gone."

Chapter Eight

That afternoon, Will Turner stood in the witness box and surveyed the court.

Nick had given Sally Ann Barnes's videos of the two therapy sessions. He felt sure that if the judge could be persuaded to admit them in evidence, Will Turner would be blown away. Ann had taken a grave risk breaching Turner's psychiatric confidence, but she was willing to do it for Nick: if *only* the videos could be admitted in court.

"Mr. Turner," said the prosecutor, "there is no dispute, I understand, between the parties that on the day in question, you were still married to the complainant, Elizabeth Turner."

Will stared back, his hands resolutely in his pockets.

"And it is also agreed that it was on that night you walked in on the defendant and your wife. Mr. Turner," the prosecutor insisted. "You do remember the night in question?

"I know this must be very distressing, Mr. Turner. But I'm afraid you must tell us about what happened. When you came through the door, where was your wife?"

Will said nothing.

"Is something the matter?" This time it was the judge. "Your mind seems to be on something else, Mr. Turner."

There was no reply.

"Do you have any other witnesses?" the judge asked the prosecutor.

Nick could not hear what Smith said.

In fact, he did not really hear anything else after that. He stared intensely at Will Turner and observed the sudden change that came over the man. It was as if something inside him had snapped.

But he had not betrayed his former barrister. And for that, at least, Nick was grateful.

But there was a problem. The videos had not been used. They couldn't be used directly as Will Turner had said nothing. Nick just had to think of a way of sneaking them in.

To his surprise, Nick felt a certain sadness when he saw Turner's performance—whether it was Will Turner or his brother.

He had toyed with the idea of telling Sally what Liz Turner had said to him about her being a patient. But what if it was all lies? When he eventually said to Sally that he wanted to speak to her about Liz, she was furious. She refused to hear any more about "that woman"; and she had already heard quite enough. Besides, she had been released as a witness.

The next witness was the forensic scientist, Dr. David Symes. After he was sworn, he testified that blood had been taken from Liz Turner's clothing and analyzed.

Smith stood as tall as he could—he barely reached five foot six—and asked, "And was there, Doctor, any other blood present on the garments apart from that of the victim?"

"Yes," Symes said, displaying his perfect teeth to the jury.

The jury likes him, Nick thought. But then they were outside halitosis range.

"And did you manage to determine the group of the blood?"

"Yes. There are four major groups in the ABO blood grouping system: A, B, O, and AB. Mrs. Turner is group O. But there is also some AB blood present."

"And is that significant?"

"Yes."

"Why?"

"AB is a relatively rare group. It is present in about only three percent of the population."

"And did you analyze the blood sample given by the accused, Nicholas Downes?"

"Yes, I did."

"And what group, Doctor, is Mr. Downes?"

"He is AB," the scientist said, grinning again.

The prosecutor sat down, casting a knowing look at the jury, and Nick saw Sally rise to cross-examine with some reluctance. As she was about to ask her first question, however, a policeman crept into court behind Smith and handed him a fax. The prosecutor examined it, and his face dropped. He tugged Sally's gown and handed it to her. But Sally cast the paper down nonchalantly and turned back to the witness box.

"Does the blood test prove that the blood on the complainant's clothing is in fact the blood of Mr. Downes?" she asked.

"No."

"I see," she said knowingly.

"But it proves it *could* be his blood. With a blood test, all you can really do is see if the suspect can be excluded. If he was one of the other three groups, then I could have said it definitely doesn't belong to Mr. Downes. But it fits. And given the rarity of the group AB—"

"But you still can't be sure?" Sally interrupted.

"No."

"And in the country, there must be about two million people with the group AB?"

"Something like that," the doctor agreed reluctantly.

"And the blood could belong to any one of those people?"

Symes did not answer.

"In theory?" Sally insisted.

"Yes, in theory," he said finally.

Sally put down her copy of the forensic report and asked the judge for his forbearance. When she arrived at the dock, she beckoned Nick forward.

"Well done," he said.

"Standard cross-examination of an expert," she replied. "Something's come up."

"What?"

"I'll tell you when we adjourn. It concerns your beloved Liz. Hold tight till then." She paused. "But we can't take it any further with Doctor Dog-Breath, can we?"

"Not really. Except," Nick said, "for one thing." With that, he handed Sally another forensic report. "Ask him about that, Sals."

By the time she had reached the front of the court, he could see that she had come to the part of the report that he had highlighted with a marker pen.

"One more thing, Doctor," she said. "Is it right that you were the forensic examiner involved in the case of Will Turner?"

"I was. I had to examine the body. But I forget all the details. I see a lot of bodies, Miss Fielding."

"Well, allow me to remind you." She gestured to the usher to take the report to the witness box. "Is that your report from the Turner murder trial?"

"It is."

"And do you stand by it?"

"I do."

"Tell the jury, then," Sally said, for the first time looking confidently at the jury, "did you examine the intimate body samples of the suspect, Will Turner?"

"I did. In order to—"

"I don't care *why* you did it," Sally snapped. "Just tell us, what is his blood group?"

Symes flicked through the pages. "I'm afraid I can't find where it—"

"The highlighted passage," Sally said.

"Yes, I have it."

"The group, Doctor?"

"Well, it appears to be—"

"Not appears," Sally said. "What *is* the group?"

"Group AB," Symes replied. "The same as the—"

"I think we've all worked that one out," Sally said. "Without the undoubted benefit of your expertise. Yes, thank you very much, Doctor. I have finished with you now."

The judge rose very soon after that and the case was adjourned for another day with the age-old formula, "All manner of persons having anything to do with my Lords of the Queen's Justices depart hence and draw nigh tomorrow at ten-thirty in the forenoon. God save the Queen and my Lords the Queen's Justices."

In the corridor outside Court 8, Sally drew Nick into a corner. "Time to talk," she said.

"What was it about Liz?" he asked.

"Nothing much . . . just her criminal past."

Chapter Nine

"Never do that to me again," Sally shouted at Nick when they were safely inside a conference room minutes later.

"You always complained that I never used to surprise you, so—"

"So now you've started? Nick, you idiot, what on earth were you playing at with the second forensic report?"

"The art of warfare is nine-tenths surprise."

"Who said that?" she asked.

"Hitler, I think."

"Now I know you've gone completely bonkers." She took off her wig and tried to suppress a smile. "Besides, you're meant to surprise the enemy, not me."

"Sorry, Sals," he said.

"I suppose I should have guessed," she replied.

"Why?"

"Well, you shared Turner's wife. I suppose it's only right that you share his blood group as well."

"What were you going to tell me about Liz?"

"In a moment," she said. "Just let me calm myself."

He looked at the small beads of sweat that sparkled on her forehead. Sweat that was the result of her efforts to defend him.

Again he was happy. And emboldened by the adrenaline in-
duced by the trial, he went further than he intended.

"I was thinking, Sals. Would you like to go for a drink?"

"I always like going for a drink."

"No, I meant with me. To Devlin's."

"Yes, Nick. I would even like to go to Devlin's with you."

He smiled and said, "That's fantastic. I'll be two secs. I just
need to see a man about a dog—"

"Except I can't, Nick."

"But I thought you said—"

"I can't. Not tonight. I'm meeting Max's parents."

"Can't you cancel?"

"No. We're drawing up battle plans. You know, for the—"

"Wedding," he said glumly. "I thought the bride's parents
did all that."

"Not if the groom's are this rich."

He remembered the awful phone call when she had first told
him. And despite everything he told himself, the pain was just
the same. Barrister and client walked in silence to the lifts at
the end of the corridor.

He tried to smile. "So where are you meeting them?"

"Le Gavroche."

"They *must* be rich."

"Stinking."

"What do they do?"

"Own a bit of property."

"What's it called?"

"West Africa," she said. "Listen, we might have to have Liz
Turner recalled."

"Why?"

"The police have found a previous conviction she had."

He was stunned. This type of information should have been
disclosed prior to the trial.

"Someone made a mistake," she said. "They didn't check her
record under her maiden name."

She handed him a faxed piece of paper with a Criminal

Record Office number at the top. It was what lawyers called the 609 or CRO. Previous convictions.

The name was Elizabeth Bridewell.

1987. Central Criminal Court. Child Abduction. Probation Order 3 years—condition of psychiatric treatment.

"Apparently, she took a child from a shopping mall in Bayswater," Sally said, getting into the lift.

He held the door open. "It's a spent conviction," he said. "The judge might not let us use it."

"We can try. But I doubt she'll reoffend."

"Why?"

"Why pinch another kid—when she's going to have yours? I'll see you tomorrow, Nick."

After Catt had been fed and had curled up on the sofa, Nick decided to go for a walk. Queensway was just beginning to become busy. He wandered around aimlessly, trying to forget about Sally and Max. After ten minutes, he sought the sanctuary of a late-night bookshop. Bookshops, he decided, were good places for loners. In a bookshop, there was nothing wrong with being on your own.

He was looking for nothing in particular, but before he knew it, he found himself in the psychology section. The bookshop was one that he had passed many times but had had no reason to enter. It was called the New Age Lifestyle Bookstore and contained everything you could wish to know on psychology, psychiatry, and piles.

There were books that expounded the intricate theorems of psychoanalysis using a series of cartoons. It somehow seemed inappropriate, he thought. It was rather like explaining God with a series of equations. He was browsing quickly from title to title when he suddenly came across a book on Freud. Hadn't Ann Barnes muttered something about Freud and phobias?

As he opened it, he tried again to forget about Sally and Max out dining. But why should I forget her? he thought. It's her problem, not mine. I can be mature and balanced about this. But nonetheless he thought about Le Gavroche, the plans, the wedding. I hope she chokes on her food, he muttered, glancing at a chapter on obsessional neurosis.

On the page in front of him was a strange drawing. There was a cutaway section of a torso with little arrows pointing to the anus, the sphincter, and the rectum, which Nick had hitherto assumed to be the same thing. At least, in school, all three words had been hurled at him as terms of abuse and were used interchangeably.

How could Sally already be making arrangements for the wedding? Hadn't she told him that it would not be for ages? Perhaps she had just wanted to save his feelings? Perhaps she was being kind? Perhaps she was a cold, lying . . . in the midst of the bowels in the drawing, Nick saw a sketch of a small creature.

It was a rat.

He was stunned. The photographs of the disinterred corpse from the first trial spun in his mind. He turned the page of the book and read on with trepidation, hardly daring to believe what he was reading.

It was one of Freud's case histories. A Viennese soldier. An obsessional neurotic. Obsessed that someone he loved might suddenly be killed. The soldier heard about a Chinese torture in which a pot of hungry rats was tied to the buttocks of the victim.

A *Chinese* torture.

According to the book, rats had curved incisors, constantly growing, with a chisellike edge. They could eat through wood, soft metal, flesh. Human flesh. Freud described how rats gnawed their way out through the anus of the victim. Nick turned back a page to the drawing. There was a rat—was it a dead rat?—in the bowels of the victim. Who could possibly know about such a thing?

An obsessed psychopath? Or an analyst, perhaps? He considered another alternative. Charles Turner? Charles Turner was an analyst. He might know. He might know about all these things.

The book went on to state that obsessional neuroses could often be traced back to sexual disorders and fixations.

But who had the disorder? He thought about how Liz had taken him to the sex club, to the cinema. He thought of the allegations made against Charles Turner to the effect that he had abused his clients. Who was unbalanced? Liz? Charles? Both?

As his thoughts raced through the various permutations, he again imagined Sally. She was holding Max's hand, talking of their marriage. There was the woman he loved planning her life with another man. And there was Nick. Alone in a late-night bookshop. Looking at a rat munching its way through the anus of an Austrian soldier.

The truth of a quite bizarre explanation bounced around inside his head. The oldest crime in the book, Sally had once said. Brother killing brother. But who had killed whom? He remembered what the facial reconstruction expert had said: The same underlying bone structure could give rise to two *slightly different* faces. Who was alive and who was dead?

He looked at the name of Freud's case history.

It was called "The Case of the Rat Man."

Chapter Ten

The next morning, Nick woke at eight.

His mind was crowded with half-formed thoughts: He imagined Will Turner's face, as he had seen it before the claws of the hammer in Liz's flat. Then he saw the head of the skeleton, half consumed by insects, and the one seemed to merge fantastically into the other.

He got up, showered, and shaved, seeing these faces fading in and out of each other. He gave Catt far too many biscuits, he put too little milk in his own tea, and he thought of the day ahead in court and the indignities still to come.

As he was about to leave the flat, a padded envelope was shoved through the letter box and thudded onto the floor mat beneath.

For a moment he hesitated, almost as if the parcel was in some way contaminated. There was a growing pile of mail on the table next to the front door, and he was tempted to add the envelope to it. Ever since the trial had begun, he had felt that his life was on hold, was in some way in limbo. He refused to acknowledge anything except the case, and the mail remained unopened.

But this parcel was different.

Printed in large, deliberately childish capital letters on the rear was the direction:

If undelivered—
Please send to Mrs. Sally Baptiste (née Fielding)
Barrister
Temple, London

He had to open it.

Slicing through the padding with a kitchen knife, he was at first confused by what he saw.

It looked very much like scrap paper. Hundreds of snippets from newspapers. And then he realized.

They were all photographs of himself.

Taken from national magazines, all cut to shreds, like the pieces of some sick jigsaw, his image mutilated, torn, defiled.

He rushed to the phone in the lounge and called Sally's number. There was no answer.

Breathless, he dialed again, tipping all the fragments onto the carpet as the phone rang, seeing his mouth, his forehead, his shoulders, all rearranged on the carpet a dozen times, distorted like a Picasso painting.

Suddenly there was a click on the line.

"Sally?" he breathed.

"Who *is* this?" Max asked.

"It's Nick."

"What do you want, Star?"

"Sally."

"Too late."

"Pardon?"

"You're too late to get her. She's already left for court. Was it important?"

He paused. Perhaps he was overreacting? And besides, what could Sally do?

"No, it's not important."

"You'd better run off to court, then," Max said. "Don't want to be late for Mr. Justice Cromwell."

He put the receiver down and gazed at the fragments on the carpet. What could he do? The envelope had to have come from Liz Turner. But how could he prove it?

He arrived just as court was about to reconvene. He didn't have time to explain the envelope to Sally.

Will Turner did not reappear to give evidence, and although the prosecution applied to have the case adjourned to make further enquiries, Mr. Justice Cromwell ordered the trial to proceed.

The final prosecution witness was Kenny, the porter.

As the man hurried into court, Nick noticed him looking lasciviously at the two young Asian girls on the jury. He was no longer wearing his portering uniform, but had dressed himself in a black sweater, rather like, Nick thought, the man who delivered the Milk Tray chocolates to unsuspecting young ladies.

"Is your name Kenneth Ng?" the prosecutor asked him.

"You pronounced it wrong," Kenny barked.

Taken aback by this onslaught from his surprise witness, Smith tried to retrieve the position. "I'm sorry, er, sir."

"That's good."

"And is your address—"

"Why you want to know my address?"

"It's just for the court record that—"

The judge intervened. "Does anything turn on the exact residence of this witness, Miss Fielding?"

Sally shook her head.

"I'm grateful to Your Lordship," the prosecutor said. "Now then, Mr. Ng. Let me ask you about an incident concerning the defendant. I understand there is no dispute that you know him."

"Who's the defendant? The man in prison?"

"Well, the man in the dock. Nicholas Downes."

"Should be in prison," the witness whispered under his breath. "For what he do to me."

Nick was appalled. Why had Sally not objected to such

gratuitous remarks? They had not spoken to each other that morning. Perhaps she's still hungover, Nick thought. Perhaps the celebration of the impending union of West Africa and West Kensington at Le Gavroche had been too good.

"Well, let's see what Mr. Downes did do to you," Joshua said. "Do you remember the night of his arrest?"

"Sure. The cops come, and I showed them where the fugitive was hiding."

"And where was that?"

"In his flat."

"And what had happened earlier that evening?"

At this point, Sally got to her feet. She pulled at her gown and said, "M'Lord, I cannot possibly see how all this is relevant."

The judge glanced at the porter's statement in front of him. "How do the prosecution put this?"

As Smith was about to answer, Nick realized that the jury was still in court. Normally, when a point of law is argued, they are sent to their room so that they do not hear anything they should not. He quickly scribbled a note to Sally about this.

But before Doreen, the usher, could tear herself away from the *News of the World* guide to erotic fast food and waddle to the back of the court, the prosecutor had replied.

"We say that it is one continuous course of conduct. It shows motive," Smith said.

"And motive is always material," the judge added.

"Quite. But more than that, it shows a hostile attitude toward Mrs. Turner. It rebuts any possible defense of accident. This sexual assault was coldly premeditated." Smith looked at the jury at whom the comment was really aimed. And then he added for the sake of decency, "Er . . . M'Lord."

Sally's objection was overruled. But more than that, the Crown had gained an opportunity to make a speech and talk up the importance of Kenny's evidence. It couldn't have been a bigger disaster, Nick thought, even if Sally had tried. Even is she had *wanted* it to be a disaster. And that thought made him shudder.

The prosecutor continued to Kenny, "Now, before we were . . . interrupted, you were going to tell what the—"

"Prisoner?"

"Defendant," Smith replied in a token way. "What the defendant had done."

"I tell him about the message."

"From whom?"

"From Mrs. Turner. He get very upset."

"And?"

"And he say he want to kill . . . her."

Nick noticed a few mutters from the jury box. It was a bad sign. He also noticed that the judge was smiling, and in the hierarchy of foul omens, that was even worse. But he knew that there was one thing Kenny hadn't mentioned, one thing Nick hoped would never come out.

Sally got to her feet to cross-examine.

"You're an utterly deceitful man," she said to the porter.

"I'm not the liar."

"Mr. Downes never said he wanted to kill Mrs. Turner."

"He did."

"Mr. Downes said he wanted to kill . . . you," Sally said in a deadpan way.

The judge's grin widened. "Do I understand that your client wanted to kill two people that night?"

"No, just one," Sally said. "And for a very good reason."

"Is there ever a good reason for murder?"

"There is sometimes a good reason to threaten it," she said.

"Leaving aside about whom the threat was made. Do you accept that shortly before the . . . incident with Mrs. Turner, your client had issued a death threat?"

"Certainly," Sally said.

Again, Nick shuddered.

Then she turned back to the witness. "Didn't you say you were going to throw his cat out of the window?"

"He not allowed to have a cat."

"But didn't you threaten to do that?"

"No." Kenny appeared indignant. "No."

"Is that an entirely truthful answer?"

"Truth is, I say I smash its head and make a nice mess." He smiled as if to say, So what?

Sally clearly thought that she had made her point. But Nick was far from convinced.

"That's not the end of the matter," she said. "At that time, weren't you looking for a wife?"

"So?"

"Relevance?" the judge asked.

"Motive," Sally replied. "As Your Lordship *may* know, motive is always material." She turned back to the witness. "How were you going to obtain a bride? Were you going to join a dating agency for lonely hearts?"

"No."

"Romantic meals with chocolates and flowers, perhaps?"

" 'Course not," Kenny said.

"How then?"

"Buy one," he said proudly.

"Weren't you annoyed that Mr. Downes and the other residents were not paying you enough to afford a young girl?"

"Can only get older one on the pittance they pay."

"And you were furious about that?"

"Yes."

"And that's why you've invented a pack of lies about Mr. Downes," Sally said, looking at the two Asian girls on the jury.

Nick was tense, hunched up, worried. Don't push it, Sals, he kept thinking. Don't push it.

Kenny did not reply at first.

"Aren't you lying?" Sally insisted.

Kenny smiled. "I saw what he have."

"I beg your pardon?"

"I saw what he got in his hand when he come back to the flats."

Nick subsided. He knew that Sally had gone too far.

"What did Mr. Downes have?" she asked, glancing at Nick.

"The hammer."

"What hammer?"

"Claw hammer."

Sally smiled graciously at the judge and said, "May I have a moment with my client, M'Lord?"

"Certainly, Miss Fielding."

Nick knew that the judge would allow the defense all the time in the world to dig itself an even bigger hole.

When she arrived at the dock, Nick sensed that she was about to explode. "Tell me Kenny is lying about this."

He was silent.

"So what do I say, Nick?"

"The police never found a hammer on me," he whispered.

"But did you have one?"

"They never found it, did they?"

"But is it true?"

"I hid it."

"You *concealed* evidence?"

"Only in the technical sense of the word. And it was evidence against Turner, really. He used it, not me. Why do you think Liz Turner didn't mention it?"

"But you accept that Kenny saw you with a hammer?"

"If he had eyes in the back of his head."

"Want me to ask him that?"

"No further questions, I think, Sals."

"Idiot."

He watched as Sally walked with commendable dignity to the front of the court and said, "Yes, that's all, M'Lord."

The judge leaned forward. "That's all? You *accept* that Mr. Downes had a claw hammer in his possession on the night in question?"

"I don't deny it, M'Lord."

Kenny smiled at the girls as he was released from the court, and Nick wondered whether the jury had believed all he had said. But even if they hadn't, he began to fear that at least *some* of the mud was beginning to stick.

During the luncheon adjournment, Nick was once more kept in the cells. He tried to decide whether or not to tell Sally about his discovery of the Rat Man case, about his increasing suspicions concerning the identity of Will Turner. He thought again about the cage of rats in Orwell's *1984* and compared it to the rats that Freud had described. Had he made a genuine discovery, or were his thought patterns becoming more and more abnormal?

His musings were interrupted by Jo, who told him that he had a visitor.

It was Ann Barnes.

When they were settled on opposite sides of a table in one of the visiting rooms, she said, "I've got some news."

"About the rehab clinics?"

"Yes. Do you want to know now?"

"No. Later, Ann. I don't want to think about the case for a few moments. Can't we just talk about something normal?"

"I'm afraid you've come to the wrong place. Abnormality is my business," she said, opening a fresh packet of cigarettes.

"Come on, Ann."

"I'm serious. Normal people don't kill people. They don't murder their spouses." She puffed a cloud of smoke in Nick's direction. "Actually, they do. They give them ulcers, heart attacks, varicose veins and, worst of all, children. Only we don't classify it as murder, we call it marital bliss. How's Sally, by the way?"

Nick looked miserably at the glowing ash at the end of the cigarette hanging from the side of her mouth.

"All right. Let's talk about the case," he said.

"What about it?"

"Well, we won't need you to testify about Will Turner."

"Mr. Frankenstein went gaga in the box, did he?"

"Something like that. But tell me a little about Freud and the Rat Man."

She ran her long nails through her coiffured bob. She paused and then said, "I contacted that expert on your behalf."

"Dr. Forensic Feces?"

"What no one seems to have appreciated is that rats can be *cannibalistic*."

"So?"

"So Rat One could have chomped its way into Turner's body and for some reason died."

"Poisoned?" Nick suggested. "With quicklime?"

"And Rat Two could then have decided that he preferred to eat his mate rather than a clapped-out psychoanalyst." She smiled triumphantly. "Hence the rat in the bowels. And the scavenged skeleton."

"But what about Freud and the Rat Man?" he asked.

"It was just a hunch, Nick."

"Why *just* a hunch?"

"Think about what you're saying," she replied. "Theory One: Ronnie the Rat burrows in his field and comes across a corpse. Being a bit peckish, he eats his way into the bowels of the body. But by now the lime-infested flesh is too toxic, and Ronnie dies. One dead rat. Next, Rat Two comes along and, being a bit of a cannibal, he eats his dead mate instead of the decaying human corpse. It's the sensible choice for the discerning rodent. Because the poison is at one stage removed, the second rat wanders off."

"It fits the facts," Nick said. "But—"

"Theory Two," Ann interrupted. "A man tortures his brother to death by having a rodent eat its way through his anus and into his bowels. On the whole, Nick, you're safer sticking to science than psychiatry. I think the rat is a red herring. That's all."

There was a rattle of keys in the corridor outside. Nick could hear whispering and a young woman's voice.

"Is it true," he asked, raising one of the points he had read in the book, "that neurotic obsessions often stem from a sexual disorder?"

"Do dogs bark? Of course it's true."

"What sort of disorders?"

"Fetishes. You know, dressing up in uniforms, preoccupation with punishment and pain. But as a criminal barrister, you should know all about that."

"What else?"

"Other so-called passive perversions, like voyeurism."

"Stealing things?" he asked.

"Possibly."

"Like children?"

"Dangerous. If there was some traumatic episode in her childhood that made her obsessed with the concept of family—then possibly."

"What if both her parents had died?"

"It depends on how the parents died," she replied.

Nick tried desperately to review what he knew. Liz's mother had committed suicide. She had not told him why. Her father had died . . . of a broken heart? Did that seem credible? And what had happened to the stepmother?

The jailer left his station behind the front desk and advanced toward them, bearing more keys than a car thief.

"Jo," Ann whispered to Nick, "used to be in the Rhodesian Colonial—"

"I know," he replied.

"From Bulawayo to the British Prison Service," she said. "Do you suppose that's going up or down in the world?"

The jailer put his arm on Nick's shoulder and looked at Ann. "So what have we got here, Dr. Barnes? Psycho or sex fiend?"

"Business thriving, Jo?" she replied.

The man did not answer. Ann whispered in Nick's ear, "Watch him."

"Why?"

"Bent. More backhanders than a Wimbledon finalist." Then she said out loud, "Got to run, Jo. Be gentle with him."

Nick was led back toward his cell. Then he remembered the purpose of Ann's visit. "What about the rehabs?" he called along the corridor.

"There are none," she said. "At least, not in Kent. You must have been dreaming it, Nick. I'll double-check. Ring me later at the psych center."

Chapter Eleven

Nick was really depressed. In twenty minutes, he would have the opportunity to give evidence in his own defense. He would have the chance to save or condemn himself in the eyes of the jury. And all he could think about was Sally.

He could hardly manage to turn his mind to what Ann Barnes had said. How was it possible that the place he had visited in Kent did not exist? But he kept returning to what Ann had said about Liz's past.

It depends on how the parents died.

The door to the cell opened again, and the robust jailer appeared. "You've got another visitor," he said.

"It's a bit like Charing Cross round here," Nick replied.

"King's Cross, more like."

"How do you mean?"

Jo merely smiled and ushered someone else into his cell. It was China White.

"Right," he said, "this . . . lady has already paid me the entrance money, so to speak. Anything else, you negotiate with her."

"But I'm due in court," Nick said.

Jo looked down his right arm, past his watch to the crisp ten-pound note in the hand. He smiled again at Nick. "Relax. You've got twenty minutes. But I reckon it'll all be over in two."

"Isn't this a bit unusual?" Nick asked.

"For Bulawayo, yes. For Britain, no."

He shut the door, and Nick was left alone with the girl from the club.

He looked at her and said, "What on earth are you doing here?"

"Just listen," she replied.

"Why are you here?"

"Jackie sent me."

"Why?"

"You must ask her that."

"Jackie was in custody in May. What happened?"

"She made a deal." The girl scratched the black veins on her arms. She was thinner and paler than Nick remembered her, almost visibly older.

"Jackie says you've been good to her. She doesn't want that woman to destroy you."

"Liz Turner? Does Jackie know Liz from somewhere?"

"From somewhere."

"Well?"

"She'll tell you."

"No, you. Now."

"Speak to Jackie."

"Please."

"Liz worked with Jackie . . . as a prostitute."

"When?" he asked.

"Meet Jackie, she'll—"

"When?"

"Jackie says that it was fourteen years back. When Liz was released from prison."

"*Prison?* What was Liz in prison for?"

"I don't know."

"What?"

"Honest."

"Do you realize the trouble I'm—"

"You *must* meet Jackie," she said, all the time keeping her eyes firmly on the floor. "She knows."

"What did Liz do?"

"Jackie says it was something terrible."

"Can't you say?"

"Jackie will tell you."

"When?"

"Tonight at nine."

"Where?"

"The church."

"Which church?"

"Soho. The one with the—"

"Steeple appeal," Nick said. "What's all this about?"

"The man."

"Will Turner?"

The girl was silent.

"Is he someone else? Is he Charles?"

"Jackie knows."

"Is he Charles?"

"I must go."

"Please tell me—"

But the girl was banging hard on the cell door. The jailer was there almost immediately and opened up.

"Christ, Downes," he said. "One minute thirty seconds. An Old Bailey record."

The girl slipped past him and ghosted up the corridor.

Nick shouted through the wicket gate after her, "Come back. Please come back."

Jo held his crisp ten-pound note up to the light to inspect the watermark. "Want seconds already, Downes? Christ, man, you're a frisky one. No wonder you molested that woman."

There were still fifteen minutes until the afternoon session began. But Nick was wondering how Liz could possibly have been in *prison* when there was nothing to that effect on her record.

*   *   *

"Religion?" Doreen, the user, asked.

"Pardon?" Nick whispered back.

Everything seemed very different from the confines of the witness box. A wooden podium at the front of the court, it reminded Nick of a pulpit. But there was no congregation, only a jury. And they were concerned not with their own sins but with those of the man in the box. He finally realized that he was no longer a spectator. Now he was the spectacle itself.

Doreen turned away from the jury and said to him very quietly, "Well, have you got religion or not?"

"I was brought up a Catholic."

"That'll do."

A Bible was thrust into his hand, and a printed card held six inches from his eyeballs.

"I swear by Almighty God," he began slowly, "that the evidence that I shall give shall be the truth, the whole truth, and nothing but the truth."

Then he said to himself, "So help me God." He glanced at the ceiling of the court. "Are you listening?" he whispered.

The holy prop was flung onto the usher's table alongside the other sacred books of the world and a cut-out recipe for ratatouille.

"What is your name?" Sally asked him.

"Nicholas Downes."

"And your occupation?"

"Criminal . . . criminal barrister, really." He felt the scowling looks of the jury and swore that he could hear the *click-click* of the knitting needles beside the guillotine. He had decided to give evidence, to put his head on the block. Now it was up to him. He had to impress the jury. "You see, I sort of specialize in crime," he said.

"I think we've got the point," Sally said. "What sort of crime?"

"Rape, robbery, riot. Burglary, buggery and fraud. Your run-of-the-mill stuff, really."

The judge coughed loudly. "So you have some experience of sex crimes?"

"Yes," Nick said. "But not as much as Your Lordship."

"That was a most impertinent reply," Cromwell fumed.

"It wasn't intended to be."

Sally tried quickly to change the subject. "Your age?"

"Thirtysomething."

"Married or single?"

"Single," Nick said, looking at Max's ring on her finger. "Single and no prospects of being married."

"And outside the Bar, what do you do?"

"Nothing, really."

"You must do something. We all do something."

"Well, I have a cat, a car, and a flat in Bayswater."

"Is that all?"

"That's all," he said.

"I want to ask you about the complainant, Elizabeth Turner. How did you meet her?"

"I was defending her husband on a charge of murder. It was a professional acquaintance."

"And did it *stay* that way?" Sally asked, with just a hint of sharpness.

"No," Nick said.

He wondered why she was making it all sound so black and white. The defense needed grayness. Juries needed grayness to acquit. Grayness meant doubt and doubt meant a not guilty verdict and a dash from the dock into the nearest public house.

Sally continued, "Did it become—"

"Intimate?" Nick asked.

"Sexual?"

"Well, sort of—"

"Come on, Mr. Downes. Did you sleep with her or not?"

"Well, yes."

"How many times?"

Nick did not reply.

"How many times?"

Smith got to his feet to protest. "M'Lord, perhaps m'learned friend for the defense shouldn't badger her own . . . witness. Firstly, it's improper. Secondly—"

"Is the rate of intercourse relevant, Miss Fielding?" the judge asked wearily.

"Very," Sally said.

But relevant to whom? Nick wondered. He instantly recalled the flavor of all the arguments they had once had about how he no longer wanted sex during the week. He remembered how he had frequently rejected Sally's advances when he came back from court. He remembered how their rate of intercourse had ended up at a grand total of zero.

"I slept with her once," he said.

"And is she having your baby?" Sally asked, her voice higher, slightly tremulous.

"I don't know."

"Do you want her to have your child?"

"No," he said. "No, I don't."

Sally paused to sip some water. He saw her chafed lips, the blood in her cheeks. What was it? Concern? Anger? Hatred? Contempt?

Up above him, the public gallery was full. People he would never know hearing all about his life, his mistakes, his failures. And enjoying it. Enjoying it for free.

"On the night in question," Sally asked, "do you accept that you went to Mrs. Turner's flat?"

"Yes."

"And you tore some of her clothes?"

"Yes."

"And you were partially naked yourself?"

"Yes."

"And you touched her breasts?"

"Yes."

"And you wanted to have sex with her?"

"Well—"

"And you *wanted* to have sex with her, Mr. Downes?"

"Yes," Nick said.

"Well, Mr. Downes, please tell the jury, what on *earth* is your defense?"

Nick was silent. He looked at Sally, and she looked away.

Then he took a shallow breath and said, "I have made many mistakes in my life. I know I have. I seem to let things run. You know, not paying attention to them until it's too late. That's how I ruined the one relationship in my life that . . . well, meant anything."

"Please, Mr. Downes," Sally said quietly. "You mustn't—"

"No. I ruined it. It was me. I took it for granted, and it died. And I killed it. It was my fault. So I suppose I was lonely and even a little confused when I met Liz Turner. I was flattered that an attractive woman like her should find a self-pitying, burned-out barrister attractive. But she did, and I was grateful for that."

"Tell me about that final night," Sally said.

Nick looked at her, and this time she did not look away.

"That night, I was in shock. I was convinced I had lost the woman I—"

"Yes?"

"Loved."

"And had you?" Sally asked.

"Perhaps."

"Probably?"

"Beyond doubt. Beyond a reasonable doubt."

"But not definitely," she said.

"That's not my decision." He looked at her for a moment before he continued. "I just couldn't be alone. Not that night. Liz had called round and left a message. So I went over."

"And then?"

"And then the rain had soaked my clothes, and she started unbuttoning them. She put my hands on her breasts. She started to tear at the material. Mr. Turner came in. He punched her about the face. He used the claw hammer. But I took it away from him. And he said he'd call the police."

"And then you left?"

"Well, I pulled my clothes on first."

No one laughed or even smiled.

"And then you left?" Sally repeated.

"I ran."

"Why?"

"Because I was frightened."

"And why were you frightened, Mr. Downes?" she asked.

"Because I knew what he was capable of."

"Anything else?"

"Because I knew who he *really* was."

"And who was that?"

"Possibly someone very different from what we all thought," he said.

"Who?"

"His brother, Charles Turner."

Sally sat down. It was the prosecutor's turn to cross-examine.

Chapter Twelve

Smith momentarily raised his wig and scratched his sweaty scalp. "You are trying to pull the wool over the jury's eyes," he said to Nick.

Nick did not answer. It was more of a statement than a question.

"I mean, all this . . . stuff," Smith continued, unable to find a better word, "all this stuff about Mr. Turner not being who he says he is. It's a complete red herring, isn't it?"

"Perhaps," Nick said. "I just thought it would explain why I—"

"Do you have any evidence that Mr. Turner is his brother?"

Nick thought about Ann Barnes's experiments. Here was his great chance to introduce Will Turner's videos. "I've seen a polygraph test and videos—"

"A *polygraph?*" the prosecutor interrupted, his voice bristling with ridicule. "Such psychiatric mumbo jumbo isn't admissible in law—as you know perfectly well."

"But they're trying to develop a more accurate one."

"Who?"

"The government."

"So why haven't we heard of this splendid scientific break-through?"

"Because it's a . . ." His voice trailed off.

"Because it's a what?" Smith asked. "Because it's an *Official Secret*, Mr. Downes?"

Nick nodded.

"So is this the position? You're relying on unlawful evidence and you've breached the Official Secrets Act—not to mention Mr. Turner's right to confidentiality?"

"I know it sounds bad, but—"

Smith pulled his gown around his shoulders and ignored Nick. "Let's examine what *really* sounds bad, shall we? Didn't you take to your heels after you committed the crime?"

"I didn't commit any crime."

"Well, fortunately for you, that's not a matter for me, but one for the jury."

Nick was stung by the onslaught. He felt he had to recover some ground immediately. He decided to play his only other card. "I have some information."

"What information?"

"About Liz Turner," he said. He paused to allow the tension to build. "She used to be a . . . prostitute."

Suddenly there was an explosion of fevered chatter around the court. The judge almost fell off his seat. "This is a matter of the utmost gravity," he snarled. "Allegations of such baseness against the character of a lady must be backed up by unassailable evidence, Mr. Downes. So *what* is your evidence?"

"I was told by—"

"I *object*," the prosecutor shouted. "Hearsay evidence."

"But I want to know," the judge insisted.

Nick realized that he was cornered. He had no option but to press on. "I was told by . . . another prostitute."

"Friend of yours?" the prosecutor smirked.

Nick did not reply.

"When were you told this?" the judge demanded.

"Today."

"Where?"

"In the court cells."

"A prostitute visited you in the court cells?" the judge asked incredulously.

"Yes."

Cromwell turned to the jury. "Please strike from your minds the outrageous slur on the character of Mrs. Turner." He looked again at Nick. "And if your allegation is not backed up with proper evidence, Mr. Downes, you will answer to me later."

Nick knew that there was only one thing for it. He *had* to meet Jackie that evening. She could testify firsthand.

"Weren't you furious that Mrs. Turner was going to get back with her husband?" counsel for the prosecution continued.

"Her husband is . . ." Nick was unsure whether or not to say it.

"What? Her husband is what?"

"Dead," Nick said. "At least, I think he is."

The judge coughed loudly again. "May I remind you, Mr. Downes, that it is you who is on trial and not Mr. Turner."

"Yes, M'Lord," Nick said.

"Whichever Mr. Turner it actually was," the judge concluded.

Nick looked at the jury. He had made another mistake. Their obvious hostility was matched only by his feeling of helplessness. He tried to collect his thoughts, but when he looked back toward counsel's row, he saw Max Baptiste glide into court and sit behind Sally. She turned round, and they put their heads together.

"Didn't you go out with Mrs. Turner while Mr. Turner was in prison?" he continued.

"Yes."

"And did you kiss her?"

"She kissed me."

"Do you accept that you kissed each other?"

"Yes," Nick said, seeing Sally's face practically touching Max's, seeing his lazy left eye practically winking at him.

"And did you take her to a sex club?" the prosecutor continued.

"She took me."

"Did you go with her to see naked bodies cavorting around onstage?"

"Yes."

"And did you take her to see a pornographic film?"

"She took—"

"Did you see a sex film together?"

"Yes," Nick said.

"And what was it called?"

"*Muffy Malone Gets* . . . something to do with the adventures of Muffy Malone. All I really remember is that it involved a camel."

Sally stood up. "I must object to this line of questioning. What on earth have the adventures of—"

"Muffy Malone," Nick said.

"What have they got to do with the issue that the jury will ultimately have to decide?"

The judge put down his pencil and rubbed his eyes wearily. "What do the Crown say about the . . . Malone material?"

"I can sum it up in one question," Smith said.

"Well, then, I wish you would," Sally retorted.

The diminutive prosecutor turned back to Nick. "Taking into account the French kissing, the Swedish movie, the sex club in Soho, do you agree that you have the sex drive of a wet blanket?"

"No," Nick said.

"So how would you describe yourself?"

"About normal."

The judge began to scribble the words down as though they constituted a fatal admission. "And we all know what *normal* men are like," he said, nodding at the women on the jury.

"Can I put it this way?" the prosecutor said. "You accept that you were caught, as it were, with your pants down with Mrs. Turner."

"Yes."

"And after the police were called you left the scene?"

"Yes."

"And you accept that Mrs. Turner was caused those injuries at that time?"

"Yes."

"So the only real question for the jury is who caused the injury?"

"Yes," Nick said.

"You, a barrister who was seeing a client's wife while he was in prison, or the husband, Will Turner, who you say is *dead?*"

Nick did not answer.

"Well, I don't imagine the jury will have too much difficulty sorting out that thorny problem," Smith said, sitting down.

Sally did not bother to reexamine him. He was led back to the dock, passing Max Baptiste, who smiled at him but said nothing. When he was again locked in the dock, Mr. Justice Cromwell asked whether the defense intended to call any further evidence.

"Possibly," Sally said. "All I can say at this stage is possibly."

Sally asked Nick to meet her in Devlin's after court. But she did not give a reason. The legal term was not yet in full swing, and when he arrived early that evening the bar was unusually quiet. He joined Sally at a table by the window, but they did not buy a drink. For a minute or so they were silent, then Nick began to speak.

"Why did you want to see me here?"

"I just did, Nick. Can't I have a conference with my client?"

"But why Devlin's?"

"The truth?" she asked. He nodded. "I'm meeting Max here later. But I still wanted, needed to see you. God, it's all such a mess."

"I understand, Sals. Sometimes . . . it's hard to be a woman."

"That's the truth."

"No, that's Tammy Wynette," Nick said. " 'Stand by Your Man.' "

He played with the mat that was sticking to the table. "I don't know anymore," he said. "All I do know is that there is no greater love than jumping into the trenches and fighting for someone's freedom."

"Please, Nick. Don't use words like that."

"Freedom?"

"Love."

There was an uneasy silence between them. More barristers came in after a long day in the Legal Aid salt mines, and Devlin's began to come alive.

"So how did I do?" Nick asked, trying to change the subject.

"Do you want an honest answer?"

"Not really."

"You were by far the worst witness I have ever seen."

"You're not all *that* optimistic, then, Sals?"

She laughed but did not reply. She took her wig from her bag and shook it vigorously. "Needs airing. It's still damp with sweat, thanks to you, Nick."

"Do you think I should plead guilty?" he asked.

"Certainly not."

"Why not?"

"Because you're innocent, Nick."

"And how do you know that?"

"Because I know you. God, I've never seen anyone give so many honest answers. Jesus, Nick. You could have lied a bit, you know." She spun her horsehair wig on her ring finger. "Look, the case may be hopeless. You may be bang to rights, up guilty creek without a paddle, and the jury may convict you, Nick. But I certainly won't."

"That's all right, then. For a moment there, Sals, I was beginning to panic." He paused and looked at her before he continued. "What's this other evidence, then?"

"I may have one last trick up my sleeve," she said. "I should find out later this evening. But assume it will come to nothing. I don't want you to be disappointed."

They sat together a little longer. Nick again felt the warmth of just being near her. For a while he basked in it. But then he wondered if this would be the last time it would happen before she became the Princess of Upper Wherever-it-was.

She looked carefully at him and rested her fingers on his arm. "Nick, the truth is I'm worried about you."

"Why?"

"You look tired and hungry. Have you been looking after yourself?"

"I cook every night."

"Cook? I don't mean shoving a chicken vindaloo ice-lolly into the microwave. I mean proper food. Not something that has to be blasted with radioactivity to be edible."

"Well, I haven't been having much proper food," he said.

"I knew it. Well, I want you to look after yourself because—"

"Because no one else will?"

"Just because," she said.

The two of them stood up and headed toward the doors. He walked slightly behind her, and every now and then she brushed against him and he could smell her perfume.

"So what are you doing tonight?" she asked.

"Meeting someone."

"Male or female?"

"Female."

"Oh, that sounds exciting." But there was anything but excitement in her voice. "So who's the lucky lassie?"

"A prostitute."

"*The* prostitute? For God's sake, Nick. What's happening to you?"

"You mean you don't know?"

"I suppose it's none of my business," she said.

"Not anymore."

"So where is this romantic rendezvous taking place?"

"Not Le Gavroche."

"Where, Nick?"

"In a church graveyard. In Soho."

"You will be careful?" she said.

"What's the point?" he replied. But by then the door had opened, and Max Baptiste had walked in.

"I hear the trial's going well, Nick," he said. "At least, as well as could be expected." He placed his arm around Sally's waist. "Come on, honey. I'm really hungry."

When they had gone, Nick slumped back down at the table. He ordered a glass of Armagnac and tried to ignore the amused whisperings around him. I'm innocent, he kept telling himself. I'm innocent.

He had a couple of hours to fill before he was due to meet Jackie at the Soho church. So, remembering Ann's suggestion in the court cells that he ring, he phoned her at the psychiatric center.

"Ann," he asked, when she answered the phone, "are there any psychiatric records at your workplace?"

"We have a database, if that's what you mean."

"Say I wanted to check up on someone's psychiatric history?"

"Judge misbehaving, is he?"

"Seriously, Ann. Could we check up on Liz Turner?"

"The database only covers notable cases of lasting psychiatric interest," she said. "And then only initials are used for reasons of confidentiality."

"It's something to work with," he said.

"It's a long shot."

"Let's try."

Chapter Thirteen

As soon as Ann had ushered Nick into the computer room of the Psychiatric Center in Bloomsbury, she told him the bad news.

"I've done a thorough search of the database. There are forty-five entries under LT and ET. I cross-referenced those with psychoses involving a female patient and her parents." She looked at him sadly. "I'm sorry. Nothing."

All around him, VDUs and gadgetry hummed.

"Can we try EB and LB?" he asked. "Her maiden name was Bridewell."

Ann swiveled on her chair and tapped the keyboard. "Cross-ref with parents?"

He nodded.

There was a single bleep.

"It's too vague," she said. "The machine wants more information."

Nick scoured his memory. Then he recalled what China White had said about Liz working as a prostitute with Jackie when she came out of prison.

"Can you check any entries fourteen years ago?"

351

"That's better," she said. Again she tapped the details into the computer.

The two of them waited.

Yet again there was a single bleep and a blank screen.

"It *was* a long shot," she said. "Still, you know you asked about Freud's case—the Rat Man?" She reached into her briefcase and brought out a hardback textbook. "You might like to have a read of—"

Nick grabbed her hand. "Can you check fifteen years ago?"

"Why?"

"Liz Turner came out of prison fourteen years ago. Perhaps the crucial incident was fifteen years ago."

With a certain resignation, Ann typed in the latest details. As the machine screamed, Nick flicked through the book on the Rat Man. He just reached the pictures of the rat in the bowels when there was a bleep from the computer.

It had found an entry.

They huddled around the screen as text appeared.

Subfile: Entry found. Example of "Borden Complex."

"What on earth is that?" he asked.

"Beats me."

"You're meant to be a psychiatrist."

"I don't know *every* dark corner of the human mind. Hang on—"

EB. 15-year-old girl, had been living with her father.

"Sound familiar?" she asked.

"Liz is about thirty now," he said. "So the age fits for fifteen years ago. But Liz said something about a stepmother."

Biological mother suffered profound psychiatric reaction to daughter's birth. No response to psychotherapy or drug treatment. Rejected baby. Confined under Mental Health Act—without child. Mother committed suicide. Father, a lawyer, remarried.

"It's her," Nick said. "I know it's Liz. But how could the real mother have been *so* mentally damaged by birth?"

"Ten percent of all women suffer some sort of postnatal illness. Every year, dozens take their own lives or that of their child."

"Ann, that's—"

"What? Terrible? Save your tears. It's men who get them pregnant in the first place, then pump them with drugs, then put them in asylums, then abandon them altogether." She paused, as though she had got something she had always wanted to say off her chest. "But what did Liz *do?*" she asked.

The cursor on the screen paused and was stationary, flashing while the next tranche of Liz's history was accessed. Ann, impatient, was about to fiddle with the keys.

"What *did* she do?" she repeated.

And then it came up.

EB murdered stepmother. Multiple fractures to cranium with claw hammer.

Nick's jaw dropped.

EB begged father to cover for her. Murdered him when he refused. Bodies buried by motorway.

"Hasn't any of this been disclosed to you?" she asked.

"It's not on the criminal records," he said. In his mind, he leafed through pages of his favorite textbooks. "I think I understand the Borden Complex."

"Well?"

"Lizzie Borden. Heard of her?"

"Vaguely."

"Massachusetts, USA, 1893. Charged with murdering her father and stepmother. She used an axe. Crushed their heads."

"I remember," Ann said. "Doesn't the poem come from that case?"

Nick nodded and said:

> "Lizzie Borden took an axe
> And gave her mother forty whacks.
> And when she saw what she had done
> She gave her father forty-one."

Groups of words flashed again on the screen. And here was the truth about Liz's guilt, buried deep within the memory of a computer.

EB convicted of both murders. Convictions quashed on appeal. Judge made "errors of judgment" during trial. EB released next year. Subsequent history unknown . . .

"It wouldn't appear on the criminal records," Nick said. "The records would have been destroyed when she won the appeal. Look, can you print this out?"

"It's confidential, Nick."

"Let Liz sue me, then," he said as Ann set the laser printer into action. "I've got to go."

"Where?"

"To Soho. To meet the prostitute."

"Look, Nick," she said. "I think it's all getting too dangerous."

"Ann, you don't realize. I've got to find the prostitute and force her to testify about Liz. It's just something I've got to do."

By the time Nick arrived in Soho, the church was completely boarded up. In the three months since he had last been there, the sign saying SAVE OUR STEEPLE SO WE CAN SAVE YOUR SOULS had fallen down. The door was locked. It was already nine o'clock, but there was no trace of Jackie.

He tried to work out what he wanted from her. Further information about Liz, certainly. But if Jackie was willing to testify on his behalf, she would provide the missing link: She could establish that the EB on the database was Liz Turner, a murderess, a psychotic. Jackie could save him, but why was she late?

He sat on the steps of the church and glanced at the book Ann had given him.

He looked at the chapter called "The Obsession of the Rat Man."

Around him as he began to read were fallen segments of the old church spire. As he turned the pages, the buzz of the London traffic receded. And he read about a sad man. A man who had lived and died decades previously.

The Rat Man was born in Vienna in 1878. By the age of

fourteen, he was devoutly religious, masturbated occasionally, and suffered from rectal worms.

The man became obsessed with a form of Chinese torture involving rats, similar to the rat torture from Imperial China as described in Orwell's *1984*.

The book stated that the Rat Man first had sex when he was twenty-six, died when he was thirty-five, and was called Ernst Lanzer.

Ernst Lanzer.

Nick tried to work through the permutations. So was that why Turner had called himself Lanzer? Was it a twisted joke? Did it confirm that the surviving brother was really Charles Turner? Perhaps the case involved more than the odd cannibalistic rat. Perhaps the rat wasn't the red herring Ann Barnes had thought?

There was a loud crash.

Startled, Nick leaped to his feet.

The sound came again, and with it a dreadful smell.

He edged around the side of the church as the wind got up, fanning the repulsive odors his way. Another crash. And then he saw it. He laughed at his paranoia when he saw the shutter of a church window banging against its metal grille in the wind.

Behind the church was some waste ground, once a cemetery, but now covered with black bin-liners, spewing rubbish.

He would simply have to wait here for Jackie, rotting refuse or not. After all, she had sent China White. Jackie *wanted* to see him. She would be along soon.

A flight of pigeons, strands of flesh hanging from their beaks, shot in Nick's direction, forcing him to duck.

There she was.

Jackie.

Lying among the rubbish, her eyes pecked out, but still wearing her blond wig, her skirt pulled right up, revealing her dark pubic hair, rats swarming over her bleeding body, fighting each other for the right to make the next incision into her flesh.

Her Lycra top was ripped open; her breasts were exposed and

bleeding. All around her was a high-pitched whining. There were rats everywhere, tails as long as their bodies, climbing onto Jackie's frame, sniffing at open wounds, licking blood.

There was a gash in her midriff. Her entrails were being devoured. A rat was feeding on the contents of her stomach.

Nick threw up.

Jackie was his hope. And here she was. Jackie might have saved him. But no one could save her.

He dared to look up finally, weak with retching. A crevice in her head, smashed with a claw hammer?

A rat leaped over another for the opening, for the blood, trying to force its way into the cranium, for what was there.

Nick could see bite marks like strange love bites on the flesh of her bare thighs, and he wanted to throw up again, but he could not. His stomach lining felt as if it was tearing.

He tried to kick the small creatures away, but there were too many of them and they had tasted blood. All that was left was the girl, China White. She was his last hope of linking Liz Turner to prostitution. And Nick knew where he must go. To the place in London where China White was most likely to be.

Chapter Fourteen

When Nick arrived in Bayswater, Queensway was still quiet. It was barely 9:30, and trade had not yet picked up. He had decided that the first place to search for China White was the massage parlor.

As he walked from the tube, the usual pitches for the working girls—the doorways, the shop entrances—were all empty. It was as if the vice trade had uniformly upped sticks and set off in search of other pastures.

But when he reached the entrance to Jackie's brothel, the answer to this puzzle presented itself immediately. Fastened on the stairs that led from the street to reception was a piece of paper.

It was a warrant. A search warrant.

Nick carefully examined the carbon paper. The Vice Squad had raided two hours previously. The security door at the top of the stairs had been smashed down with what Nick suspected to be sledgehammers. In reception, chairs had been overturned. The television was still on, however, and the satellite cartoon channel was still playing. But there was no one about.

He slowly climbed the second flight of stairs that led to the bedrooms.

From the room at the end of the corridor, he could faintly hear muffled breathing. It was from the room that Jackie had once used, he remembered.

He advanced past open doorways that gave onto bedrooms in disarray. The noise of breathing got slightly louder. The police had obviously ransacked the whole establishment, overturning the furniture, smashing the locks, arresting the occupants.

When he stood at the entrance to the final room, he saw a woman. But it was not China White. It was Liz Turner.

She was handcuffed to a chair. Something had been shoved into her mouth, and stockings had been used to gag her. As he moved toward her, she groaned again and again. Each time louder, each time more desperately. With her head she indicated to Nick. To the doorway behind him.

And it was only when he turned around that he glimpsed the flash of metal, felt the blow of the hammer, saw briefly the man who had struck him. Will Turner.

The first thing Nick saw when he came round was a leg. He looked further along the linoleum-covered floor and saw another leg. Then another. There were four in all. Spread out, but still. Like an animal standing to attention. He raised his eyes and saw that it was a horse, a vaulting horse.

In an instant, he remembered where he was. He tried to raise his head but he felt as though someone had pulled his eyes back into his cranium and spun the room around him. Then he saw blood on the floor. My blood, he thought. It must be my blood.

"What's going on?" he asked, his throat dry, his mouth barely opening.

The man towering way above him spoke very softly. "It is really quite simple," he said. "We're going to have a trial."

"A what?"

"A trial. You're a lawyer, she's a witness, and we're going to have a trial."

"But why?" Nick asked. "What do you want to find out?"

"The truth."

"About what?"

"About me."

Nick tried again to raise his head. In the opposite corner of the room, he could see Liz Turner. She was still handcuffed to the chair, but the stocking gag had been removed.

"Who do you say I am?" the man asked.

Nick realized that he was helpless. He needed time. Time to think. He would have to humor the man until he could think of a plan.

"Who do you think I am?" the man repeated.

"I think you're Charles Turner," he said.

"And who do you say I am?" the man asked Liz.

"Will," she said. "Don't be stupid, Will. Why don't you let me go—"

"*Who?*" he shouted.

"All right, all right. You're Will Turner," she whispered.

"Good," the man said. "The prosecution say one thing and the defense say the very opposite. An excellent basis for a trial. Any questions?"

"What if I . . ." Liz gasped. "What if I don't play along?"

Nick could see the man picking up something from the bed.

"Then you get this," the man said. He held a syringe containing a vile-colored liquid close to the vein in Liz's neck. "If you don't play along, then you get the syringe. It really is quite simple."

Perhaps I should shout out, Nick thought. Scream, even. Perhaps someone would come. But what if they did not? This was Bayswater. Who would pay attention to a scream from a brothel?

And anyway, how long would it take for help to arrive? He could hardly move. What could the man have done to him by then? How many blows of the hammer would it take to kill him? Perhaps he was lucky that he wasn't dead already. He would just have to wait.

"Right," the man said to Nick. "You can be the prosecution. You start."

"Can you help me sit up?" he asked.

He was helped up and propped by the side of the bed. He

was even given a wad of tissues, which he held against the gash
in the top of his head. For a moment the dizziness passed, and
he could focus on the other side of the room and Liz Turner.

"Who killed Jackie?" he asked.

"*What?*" the man demanded.

"It was you, Liz," Nick said.

"I had to kill her," Liz pleaded with the man. "The prostitute
was plotting. With this barrister. They were going to have your
suspended sentence activated—by saying that you had threatened her with a claw hammer."

"It's lies," Nick protested. "Jackie knew about Liz's past. Ask
Liz how she used to make a living."

"I was a secretary."

"You were a prostitute," Nick said, seeing the confusion
clouding the man's face. "A . . . whore. Remember the story
you were obsessed with. Revelations. The story of the whore
and the child."

She tried to interrupt, but Nick persisted.

"Charles wanted his brother's wife and the two million," he
said, inspecting the drying blood on the sodden tissues. "The
problem was that they couldn't live together. Not really. Not
while Will was alive. But there was an easy solution."

"Which was?"

"Murder Will," Nick said. "They were not twins, but there
was a great similarity in appearance. But I don't understand
this," he added. "There are no rehab centers in Kent."

"It was in Surrey," the man said. "It was just across the
county border. Didn't you see the sign on the motorway?"

Nick remembered that to get to the quarry he had doubled
back on himself once he had passed the Kent–Surrey border.
Obviously he had crossed back into Surrey.

"So what is the . . . evidence?" the man asked him. "You
know, the evidence that I am—"

"Charles? You called yourself Lanzer. Only someone interested in psychology would know about that. The rat in the
bowels of the corpse. That was taken from a Chinese torture
that Freud had heard about in Lanzer's case."

"Is that it?"

"There's more," Nick said. "You never let me tell the jury that Charles was struck off. Why would you protect Charles unless . . ."

The man let the arm holding the syringe drop. The dirty needle pointed vertically downward, and a sphere of the fetid liquid gathered at the point and dripped slowly onto the floor.

"But," Nick continued, "there is only one other person who would really know the truth of all this."

Liz Turner stared resolutely at the stockings at her feet.

Chapter Fifteen

Finally, Liz spoke. "The truth is . . . you *are* Will. You're the man I married. You're the man I live with. Charles was trying to kill you. He lured you to Kent by saying that he was going to take China White out of the rehab. You remember China White? Your model?"

There was a flicker of recognition on the man's face.

Liz paused and looked at him earnestly. "You're a good man, Will. You wanted to stop Charles corrupting China. You wanted to save her. You *must* know that."

She continued, "Charles had a gun. You and Charles fought at the chalk quarry, and Charles fell—just as you said in court. Only it was an accident. You fell, too. You damaged your head—that's why you've been having all the problems, Will."

The man glowered at Nick and picked up the claw hammer. Liz was winning him over.

Nick desperately thought it through. There had to be a flaw in her story. Then he shouted, "Why were *you* there, Liz?"

"Because . . ." she stuttered.

"Because you were part of the plot to murder Will?"

The man looked at Nick. "Why would she kill me?"

"You're sterile," Nick said. "She wanted a child—any child.

Charles could give her that. He could give her a different life. That's what she wanted, the whole deal, someone who understood her desires, someone who liked the things she liked. Bad things. Evil things. She has to get what she wants. If things go wrong, she lies. If people get in her way, she kills them."

"I *don't* believe you," the man said.

"She's desperate, *obsessed*," Nick shouted. "She's pregnant. With my child. Ask her."

"It's lies," she protested.

"Why do you think you became fixated with that story in prison, Will?" Nick said. "The whore *and* the child."

Again there was a flicker on the man's face.

"She's obsessed with children, Will. With families. Ask her how her father died."

Liz was silent.

"Did she tell you he died of a broken heart?" Nick asked.

The man nodded.

"She killed him," Nick continued. "And her stepmother. She killed them both with a claw hammer and buried them by the motorway."

"It's all *lies*," Liz cried.

"Look in my pocket," Nick said, gesturing with his head, not wanting to provoke the man by reaching for his pocket himself.

The man removed the printout and digested its contents. He showed it to Liz.

"It could be any EB," she pleaded.

The man nodded and began to undo the ties that bound her.

She rubbed the freed wrists in turn. "EB could be anyone," she said, going up to him and kissing him.

"And it's not you, Liz?"

"I love you, Will," she said.

He in turn kissed her gently on the forehead, his lips barely touching her skin, his eyes closing, as if relishing the moment.

"He's nothing," Liz continued, indicating Nick. "Oh, Will, we're going to be *so* happy together."

The man stroked her hair, making the silky strands smooth

and brilliant. They kissed passionately in front of Nick, and as they kissed they lowered themselves onto their knees, facing each other on the ground as Nick and she had done in his chambers.

It looked as if they were praying.

Liz turned her head, looked at Nick, and smiled. He knew that she had won.

"Once he's gone, Will, we'll be together. Just the two of us. Just like it was." Her eyes blazed at Nick. "Forget everyone else," she said. "I'll look after you, Will. I'll stand by you and I'll *never* leave you."

For the first time Nick could remember, Will Turner smiled.

And it was then that the claw hammer smashed into Liz's skull, crushing bone, making blood spurt from her head. And making a sickening sound.

Turner struggled to remove the hammer from the wound, and when he did, it was almost as if the metal claws in her skull were all that had been keeping her upright.

The metal crashed down again on Liz's head. Her hands momentarily came up to protect herself, and then dropped to her sides. She fell to the floor, her dark hair covering her face, the odd muscle twitching before she was finally still.

Turner examined his wife's blood on the end of the hammer and looked down at her steadily. His smile had been replaced with an expression of curiosity and horror combined.

"She lied," he said.

Nick nodded.

"Her lies must have triggered my memory. Or a part of it," he continued. "When they were about to kill me, when I begged her to help me, they taunted me with her murders. They said she had murdered before."

"Move on, Will," Nick said.

The man shook his head, standing directly above the dead body. "I remember, she brought the claw hammer. She brought it. She would have killed me with it."

"Give me the hammer, Will."

"I've lost everything: my wife, my brother—I've even lost

my mind. It's as if . . . since he died in the quarry—Charles, Lanzer—it's as if he's here, in my head."

"We can help you," Nick said. "And they can't hurt you anymore."

Will Turner advanced toward him and raised the claw hammer above his head.

"Oh, Will," Nick said, "you don't *have* to do this."

"Yes, I do."

Nick felt dizzy when he saw the metal inches from his head. He could smell the rust, he could see Liz's blood on the blunt end, strands of her hair caught in the claws.

As Turner raised the hammer in preparation for the blow, Nick tried to close his eyes, but he couldn't.

"I don't want to hurt you," Turner said.

There was a gush of air and the hammer smashed into the plaster inches from Nick's temple, spraying his face with powder.

Turner raised the hammer again. "I *don't* want to hurt you," he said, smashing the hammer on the other side of Nick's head, the bloodied metal and the claws a blur fractions of an inch from his face.

Turner stood above him, his face contorted, Nick knowing that there would be no more talking, that this would be the final blow. As the metal flashed in front of him, Nick saw one thing with perfect clarity: Sally's face.

He loved her more than his life and he would never see her again. But if there was another life after this one, if there was another chance, then—

The sharpened claws of the hammer were driven with great ferocity through Turner's eye socket. There was a thud of collapsing flesh and bone, and Nick saw blood seeping from the ruptured pupil as Will Turner fell in a tangled heap on top of his dead wife.

*　　*　　*

Nick had an overwhelming need for attention, and in the absence of anyone else who cared for him, he knew he could find it with Catt.

Very gingerly, he made his way out of the massage parlor and staggered along the street.

Outside, Queensway was hardly any busier than it had been before the hammer blows, before the bizarre trial, before Will Turner's suicide. As he passed a shop doorway by the traffic lights, he heard a voice.

"Where's Jackie?"

It was China White.

"Where's Jackie?" she repeated.

"Dead."

"And *him?*"

"Dead, too," he said.

He saw that the girl was dressed in white and was staring up at the sky with empty eyes. As the lights changed, the artificial glow colored her face red, then amber, then green.

"I was wondering," Nick said. "Where will you go now?"

She ignored him. When she finally spoke, her teeth shone brilliantly. "We stayed together for a while. After he had buried the body. Living rough, living with travelers. I looked after him. But the voice took over. Lanzer took over everything. There was some kind of evil in him."

"And some good?"

"And some good," she said. "The Will side was good."

"So what will you do?"

"Work."

"The streets?" Nick asked.

"The clubs."

"Are you sure you want to do that?"

"What choice do I have? It pays. I know it's not a good, safe job like being a barrister, but—"

"But what?" Nick asked, again feeling the wound to his head.

"But it takes some guts to be center stage and take your clothes off in public."

"I think I understand. You know, the courts and the cabaret aren't so very different."

The girl didn't seem to be listening. "I'm going to save all my money. And one day I'm going to buy a house by the sea. Right by the water." Then she hesitated, and her voice dropped. "So how did he die?" she asked.

"Suicide. The hammer."

China White nodded.

"Will you call the police?" Nick asked.

She nodded again.

Across the junction, Nick could see the upper floors of his apartment block. He stared up at the windows and tried to work out which one was his own, needing to establish how far he still had to go. Then he noticed that the lights had turned back to red. And when he looked in the doorway, he saw that the girl had gone.

Slowly, he crossed the road. And finally, he reached the street door of his mansion block. It was not a particularly cool September night, but he could not stop shivering. He looked up at the night sky, but there were no stars, just the neon glow of the city. In fact he could not remember when he had last seen the stars in London. But he didn't care. He was alive. Battered, a bit bloodied, but nonetheless alive.

As he put the key in the lock, a hand was placed on top of his. It belonged to Sally.

Chapter Sixteen

"It's a bit early to have a hangover," Sally said, looking at Nick as he held his head.

"Slight accident," he replied.

"With what?"

"With a claw hammer, the blunt end thereof."

"With *what?*"

"A claw—"

"It's Will Turner, isn't it?" she said.

"Don't ask."

"Shouldn't we call the—"

"Just don't ask, Sals."

He opened the door and let Sally into the lobby. Kenny's desk was empty. Having pressed the button for the lift, he turned to her and inspected her face for any clues as to why she had come to see him.

"You look tired," he said.

"You don't look so hot yourself. Nick, what on earth has happened?"

"I'll explain later," he said. "But what are you doing here?"

"I wanted to give you this." Slowly she took an envelope out of her handbag.

"Why didn't you post it?"

"Some letters should be hand-delivered."

"Why?"

"You'll see when you read it."

As he put his hand out, she quickly snatched back the envelope, tore the letter into small shreds, and stuffed them into her bag.

"Now I'm here, I might as well tell you myself," she said.

He looked into her eyes, but she immediately lowered them to the floor. Her cheeks were flushed, and he could see that she had covered her lips with moisturizer.

"What is it, Sals?"

"I don't know how to put this."

"Try."

"All right, but don't interrupt me until I've finished. Agreed?"

"Agreed."

She raised her eyes, and her gaze went straight through Nick. Then she said, "I don't want to marry Max. Deep breath. Stay calm, girl. I want to marry . . . you."

Nick was stunned.

"Nick? Did you hear what I just . . . I've offered to make an honest man of you. Well, that's all I was going to say. So I've finished. Now you should say something like: not on your life or silly bitch or go and jump in a—"

"The lift's arrived," he said. "Would you like to come up?"

"For fuck's sake, Nicholas Downes, I just offered you my hand in marriage and all you can say is the lift's arrived."

"But it has," he said, opening the metal grille. "Would you like to come up?"

They both got into the tiny elevator and it shuddered to life and climbed slowly upward.

"What about Max?" he asked.

"Oh, he'll be fine. Women are queuing up to be the Crown Princess of Upper Whatsit. Besides, after a few months in his Dulwich dacha, I realized he was just like all the other men in the world. Well, except for you."

"How do you mean?"

"Only interested in sex. Every night the same. He came, he snored, he conked out. And I figured there's got to be an easier way to spend one's life. Like . . . with Nick."

"Thanks, Sals. I'm touched."

The lift jerked to a halt on the seventh floor, and Nick again felt the growing lump on his head. Momentarily, his vision grew hazy, but as he reached the door of his flat he was lucid again.

"There's someone I want you to meet," he said to Sally.

"Who?"

"My best friend."

As soon as the door was open, Catt rushed toward him and rubbed against his ankles.

"Oh, she's adorable," Sally said.

"It's a he, actually."

"So this is your best friend?"

Nick nodded.

"At least," she said, "I can't run off with this one."

They walked into the lounge, where months before Sally had slowly dismantled what had remained of their lives together. It felt strange to see her back in that room. He had convinced himself that she would never be there again, that she had left for good.

He staggered against the sideboard, accidentally hitting the automatic control of the stereo. And then the walls began to advance and recede and he felt light-headed. He slumped onto the sofa, and Catt jumped onto his lap.

"Let me see your war wound," Sally said, sitting down beside him. She took a handkerchief from her handbag, licked it, and dabbed at the cut on his head. "What *is* that dreadful sound?" she asked as twanging guitars filled the room.

"Tammy Wynette's greatest hits."

"I never knew she had any."

"Several," Nick said. "She's a creative genius."

"I thought you were going to meet a—keep your head still, Nick—a prostitute."

"I was."

"So where is she?"

"Dead."

"And Will Turner?"

"Dead."

"And the Creature from the Black Lagoon?"

"Who?"

"Liz Turner."

"Dead."

"Jesus, Nick. Why can't you stay at home and watch crappy soap operas like the rest of the adult population? Still, I've got the goods on the Turner woman."

"What do you mean?"

She licked her lips but did not answer the question. "You haven't responded to my proposal, you know."

"I know."

"Well, are you going to?"

"No, Sals. No, I'm not."

"I see."

"Good."

"I suppose it's my fault, really." She looked momentarily at the blood on her handkerchief. "Nick, can I ask why not?"

"It's simple. I don't want to accept your proposal, Sals."

"I see."

"Because—"

"What?"

"I have my own reasons."

"What reasons?"

"Tomorrow."

"Why not now?"

"Because the police are coming. But you can kiss me, you know. It's been a bit of a rough day."

As they kissed, Nick could hear "Stand by Your Man" on the stereo and police sirens in the street outside. But he had other things on his mind. He still stood charged with sexual assault.

Chapter Seventeen

The next morning, Sally stood at the front of Court 8 at the Old Bailey and explained the situation to Mr. Justice Cromwell.

The court was in chambers, in closed session, just as it had been right at the very beginning, when Nick had first applied for bail, before he knew of Will Turner's identity—before he had even met Liz Turner.

But now he was in the dock.

"So what *is* the truth of all this, Miss Fielding?" the judge demanded.

Sally straightened her gown. "There was a plot to kill Will Turner forged by his brother, Charles, and his wife, Liz. Charles wanted the two million pounds that his brother had inherited; Liz wanted a child. Her husband was infertile. Once Will Turner was dead, Charles could masquerade as his brother and no one would know the difference."

"So who *was* killed at the chalk quarry?" the judge asked.

"Charles Turner," Sally replied, "only by accident. Charles Turner had a gun. Will begged his wife to intercede on his behalf, but she was a stranger to mercy and the more decent human emotions; she was herself a convicted murderess, and—"

"Why hasn't the court been told this?"

"Liz Turner murdered both her father and her stepmother. With a claw hammer. But was released on appeal. The trial judge had made severe errors of judgment."

"I suppose it *occasionally* happens," Cromwell snapped.

"At the quarry, Charles brought out his gun, but Liz Turner had brought a claw hammer," Sally continued, ignoring him. "There was a struggle, and both brothers fell into the deep pit. Charles was killed, his skull crushed. Will suffered severe brain trauma but survived. He panicked and buried the body, but amnesia had set in."

"Where did he spend the time between the death and his reappearance at the brothel last Christmas Eve?" asked Cromwell.

"A Chinese girl, someone who had modeled for him, looked after him. But Will Turner became increasingly mentally unstable. A darker side of his psyche, a side he was convinced was his dead brother, took over. He became psychotic and dangerous."

Nick saw the judge sitting on the Bench, trying to absorb the shocking details, every now and then glancing at him in the dock.

"What, then, was the role of Mr. Downes in all this?" he asked Sally.

"When, in May, Will Turner caught Mr. Downes and Liz Turner . . . in flagrante, Liz lied. At first, she lied to protect herself from her psychotic husband. But then she realized that she could use the false allegation of sexual assault against Mr. Downes to exert pressure on him."

"For what reason?"

"To have him for herself. To compel him to forget . . ." She turned slightly and her eyes met Nick's. "To forget the woman he really loved and who really loved him."

Nick wanted to cry out, to shout, to scream for joy. But the judge asked another question. "For the record"—he sneered— "who was this woman?"

"Just another woman, M'Lord," Sally said. "The court might feel that her precise identity adds nothing to the record."

"If you say so, Miss Fielding. I suppose you know best."

"M'Lord," Sally said, again glancing at Nick, "the Domestic Violence Unit at Notting Hill Gate police station took a urine sample from Mrs. Turner."

"Why?"

"It's routine when there are certain allegations of sexual assault," she replied. "Having had my doubts about her . . . veracity, I got the sample tested. The results are clear. Liz Turner was not pregnant."

The judge looked at the prosecutor. "Do you accept all this?"

Joshua Smith nodded wearily. "We have decided not to proceed any further against Mr. Downes in the light of all the developments."

"Very well, bring the jury back in," Cromwell said.

Before Nick knew it, he was standing up and facing the foreperson of the jury, one of the Asian women.

The clerk stood up at the front of the court and said, "Members of the jury, do you, on the direction of His Lordship, find the defendant, Nicholas Downes, not guilty of all charges?"

"We do," the woman said.

"And that is the verdict of you all?"

"It is."

Sally got to her feet immediately. "Might my client be discharged, M'Lord?"

"He may."

The judge then addressed the jury. He was trying to give them an anodyne account of what had happened, but Nick heard nothing. He stumbled out of the open dock and sat at the side of the court. He looked at Sally and she smiled at him, the old smile.

Minutes later, he stood in the sunshine outside the Old Bailey with Sally.

"So where do we go from here?" he asked her.

"There's only one place we can go," she said.

* * *

It took them fifteen minutes to walk to the middle of Waterloo Bridge. The tide was turning, and the river swirled beneath, now and then reflecting the clouds that scudded across the sky.

"Do you think we can still love each other?" Nick asked. "I mean, after all that has happened."

"I still love you, Nick," Sally said.

"Why?"

"Because 'love bears it out to the edge of doom,' you idiot," she said with a smile.

Nick was ecstatic. "Our sonnet. That was Shakespeare."

"And this is me," she said, taking his face in both her hands and kissing him passionately, only stopping when they were both breathless. "So why won't you accept my proposal?"

"Because I want to propose to you myself."

"What did you say?"

"Look, I'm afraid I can't get down on one knee or anything, because in the state that I'm in, I'll probably never get to my feet again."

"Nick, repeat what you just said."

"I want to propose to you myself."

"But *why*?"

"Because—"

"You're mad?"

"Because I love you, Sals. Because I've always loved you. Because I can't imagine life without you. Well, I can. And it's really shitty. Because I want to have your children—or is it the other way round? God, my head hurts. Look, in a nutshell—"

"Yes?"

"Will you marry me, Sally?"

Sally Fielding smiled simply but completely.

"Come on, hurry up," he said.

"I'm savoring the moment."

"Why?"

"A girl's got to think carefully about such things."

"Naturally."

"Right," she said. "I've thought about it."

"And?"

"I'll marry you, Nick. And I'll have your children. And I'll teach them to love you as much as I love you."

Nick looked into Sally's clear eyes and he could have sworn that they were shot with cornflower blue.